THE ULTRA LONG GOODBYE

BOOKS BY PATRICK SWENSON

THE UNION OF WORLDS
The Ultra Thin Man
The Ultra Big Sleep
The Ultra Long Goodbye
Slightly Ruby

Rain Music

BOOKS EDITED
The Best of Talebones
Imagination Fully Dilated
(with Bob Kruger)

THE
ULTRA
LONG
GOODBYE

PATRICK
SWENSON

FAIRWOOD PRESS
Bonney Lake, WA

THE ULTRA LONG GOODBYE

A Fairwood Press Book
November 2023
Copyright © 2023 Patrick Swenson
All Rights Reserved

First Edition

Fairwood Press
21528 104th Street Court East
Bonney Lake, WA 98391
www.fairwoodpress.com

Cover image © Artemis Swenson
Cover and book design by Patrick Swenson

ISBN: 978-1-958880-15-9 (Trade)
978-1-958880-10-4 (Hardcover)

THE ULTRA LONG GOODBYE

"Swenson's innovative blend of classic noir and science fiction rises to a perfect, twisty-turny crescendo to complete his trilogy."
— Beth Cato, author of *A Thousand Recipes for Revenge*

"Swenson delivers a fast-paced story full of plot twists. A fascinating read."
— Brenda Cooper, author of *Edge of Dark*

Praise for *The Ultra Thin Man*

"This splendidly lively SF debut alternates between the narrations of Alan Brindos and Dave Crowell, two irreverent gumshoes who work for the Network Intelligence Organization of the eight-world Union in the year 2113. Swenson provides Shakespearean riffs on identity as Brindos is transformed and becomes a target for the NIO . . . Pig Latin, an exotic drug, a comic strip, and a retractable penis add colorful detail to a show-down that puts love and sacrifice at the heart of the self."
—*Publishers Weekly*, starred review

"The thriller pacing carries the story along until the structure of the conspiracy becomes clear . . . All in all, an entertaining piece of storytelling."
—*Booklist*

"*The Ultra Thin Man* races like a bullet train from one adrenalin-arousing development to the next . . . Exciting, inventive, and explosive."
—Nancy Kress, author of *Yesterday's Kin*

"Swenson keeps the pages turning in this slick, clever noir novel. Wonderful world-building, a terrific read, and an auspicious debut."
—Robert J. Sawyer, author of *Flashforward*

"Patrick Swenson charts a twisty journey through a futuristic landscape of aliens, detectives, murder, political intrigue, grand space opera, and unforgettable characters. It's great fun. Turn the first page and you'll forget where you are." —Jack Skillingstead, author of *The Chaos Function*

"Swenson's [novel is] informed by a Chandlerersque sensibility, with its short, crisp sentences and snappy one-liners. It's truly a terrific read."
—John Dodds, *Adventures in Sci-Fi Publishing*

"A sprightly SF thriller . . . fans of future noir should enjoy the ride."
—*The Hamilton Spectator*

"Action, mystery, and furry aliens . . . what more could I ask for in a book? . . . I burned through *The Ultra Thin Man* at light speed and can't wait for the next installment. This SF noir thriller is storytelling at its best."
—Kristene Perron, co-author of *Warp World*

"Interstellar conspiracy, enigmatic aliens, bizarre drugs, body-morphing technology, 'Thin Men,' and the fate of the Union . . . just a few of the elements that make The Ultra Thin Man awesomeyeay. I just love this stuff."
—Patrick Heffernan, *Mysterious Galaxy*

Praise for *The Ultra Big Sleep*

"Swenson's future-noir story of alien invasion is deep, vast, and fast. Full of high stakes, unexpected twists, and a truly evil force or two, *The Ultra Big Sleep* is a great read."   —Brenda Cooper, author of *Edge of Dark*

"*The Ultra Big Sleep* combines ultra big worldbuilding with an ultra fast plot. Sleep will be the last thing on your mind. An impressive sequel."
—Ted Kosmatka, author of *The Flicker Men*

"Pick up *The Ultra Big Sleep* and hold on to your molecules; they're about to be shaken and stirred in ways you can never imagine: a light-speed, stand-alone noir follow-up to Swenson's admirable debut novel, *The Ultra Thin Man*."   —Michael Bishop, author of *Brittle Innings*

"Swenson's thrilling sequel blends future sci-fi with the grit of a noir detective tale. Lost love, fine whiskey, quantum travel, alien conspiracies—*The Ultra Big Sleep* has it all." —Beth Cato, author of *The Clockwork Dagger*

"Patrick Swenson's deft touch with complex themes of interstellar noir resonate in *The Ultra Big Sleep*. With mystery, danger, and intrigue on every shore . . . A great ride!"
—Fran Wilde, author of *Updraft*

For my family

And for Shelby, who insisted

THE
ULTRA
LONG
GOODBYE

CROWELL

1   THE CLIENT MET ME IN MY OFFICE ON WESTERN AVENUE, IN downtown Seattle, just blocks away from the pier. My partner and I had opened my business right after the first Ultra scare, and in the quiet rundown atmosphere of the decaying city, we managed to eke out a living.

The office was about the size of a small kitchen, and in one corner was a sink, small fridge, and microwave. My living quarters lurked behind a plywood wall I'd put up temporarily when I moved in.

"Dave Crowell," I said, when he sat down at my desk. I extended my hand and he shook it.

"My name's Morgan."

He was a big man, wide in the shoulders, seemingly all muscle, and taller than me by a good six inches. He had close-cropped brown hair. A hint of gray ran through it. He wore a nice suit, a three-piece, but it didn't cover up the fact that he was built like a jump slot mechanic. Seriously. You had to have some heft and power to manipulate slot beams and wheels.

He wasn't bigger than my alien partner Tem Forno, of course, who was hiding on the other side of the plywood wall. Forno was a Second Clan Helk, and I didn't like him scaring away potential customers. I had a feeling, though, that this guy wouldn't blink at the presence of a Helk. But it often worked better to keep my trump card tucked up my sleeve.

"Morgan. Is that a first name or a last name?" I asked.

"Just Morgan."

"I'll need more than that if I take on your case."

"Seriously, it's just Morgan. My legal name. You can look it up when you need to. I'll give you my residence, identification, and all that."

"Okay, Just Morgan. Go on."

He pulled at the vest of his suit, trying to get comfortable in my less-than-comfortable chair. "I need you to find someone for me," he said.

"And do what?"

"Bring him death," he said.

I stared at him, surprised. "I'm sorry?"

He shrugged. "You'll do what you *need* to do, and then I want him back here. It doesn't matter how you do it, or what condition he's in when you do."

"Use whatever means necessary, is that it?"

"That's it."

"You have a general idea about where I should look? And don't you fucking dare say 'The Union.'"

"You don't want to know who?"

"Not yet. Where?"

"Barnard's Star."

The hardest colony to get to, naturally. That is, other than the alien world of Helkuntannas, which took an arm, a leg, a special visa, and more red tape than it took to wrap up a clan of Helks to get to. My survival skill of saying "no" to jobs off world kicked into gear, and I said, "No."

"Why not?"

"I don't—"

"—do off world jobs, I know." He pointed an index finger at me. "But this one's *different*."

"No."

"Your most famous cases have been off world, Mr. Crowell."

"I find it a lot easier to stay alive when I keep myself at home."

"I will make it worth your while."

"That's what they all say."

He pointed again. "But this one's *different*."

"Will you stop saying that?" I leaned back and rubbed my eyes. "You don't even know my fees. Retainer, expenses, cost per day—"

"And off world fees."

"—cost per jump-slot station, TWT fares, VIP class. You have enough for all that?"

"Is this where your Helk partner comes in from behind the wall there and starts making me look small?"

So Morgan knew about Tem Forno. Good for him. Regardless of Morgan's size, Forno *would* make him look small. "He had a hard night bashing heads. He's taking a nap."

"I can give you information. As a means of payment."

"Not a chance."

"You're the only person for this job, and the only person who could use this information."

"Information doesn't pay the bills, Morgan."

"Then I'll cover all the costs, too."

"No, I can't—wait. You will?"

He nodded.

That made me pause. Morgan was slick, and I didn't just mean his dapper suit and imposing presence. He was pushing all the right buttons. Except for the off-world button.

"You want to know the information?" Morgan asked.

"I assume you don't mean all of it, or I wouldn't be motivated to find your missing person."

"You assume correctly."

"Spill."

"Are you in?"

"Not until I hear some of the information."

A wisp of a smile crossed Morgan's face. "Only fair." He reached into his inside suit pocket and pulled out an object.

A card. Not just any card, but a Tarot card. He placed it on my desk with a snap, as if he'd dealt the last card of an important poker hand.

It was The Fool.

I widened my eyes. "Are you trying to tell me something?"

Morgan sat back and said nothing. He crossed his arms, not an easy feat in his fancy suit.

"Really nice," I said. I opened my desk drawer and pulled out a stack of cards from the same Tarot deck. I was not as deliberate as Morgan had been and slapped the whole thing on the desk. The backs of these cards featured two hemispheres of planets top and bottom, thin stylized lines connecting them like wires, the color palette a deep purple. "I've got about thirty cards of my own. How does yours help me?"

He shrugged. "Well, for starters, you don't have this one."

"How do you know?"

"Because there's only one deck like this one, as I'm sure you and Tem Forno have figured out by now. If I have this card, you *don't*.

You've been actively looking for these, with a purpose in mind."

I had been, and his card did indeed match my own deck. How much should I tell Morgan? I could sum it up briefly and explain how my dad had gone missing when I was sixteen; that I'd found out after all these years where he was; that the means to get to him had been lost forever. Okay, not a nutshell. A complicated cornucopia of space and time, alternate universes, matter and antimatter. He'd been stuck with the Ultras—a dying breed of aliens living in an antimatter universe. The Ultras had tried to invade our own universe to extend their lives. A portal of sorts had helped them do this, but it was now destroyed, and the universes were nowhere close to one another.

Yeah, it sounded unbelievable whenever I thought about it. It didn't end there, though. It'd all started with body morphing and secret conspiracies, and ended with sleep, phases of memory, and quantum travel.

Complicated. The death of a best friend, a former partner, figured into the weariness I'd come to know.

And then there was the Tarot card in the possession of an alien client, Terree—a Memor who had undergone an intersexual assignment and morphed male—given to him by his dad, Greist Sahl-kla, who'd been involved in the whole thing. A card that had offered unknowable questions and promised impossible answers.

The Chariot.

Terree had given me the card in much the same way Morgan now offered The Fool. There was no way to get to my dad, according to known science, but thinking there might be significance to this card, I tasked Forno to find the rest of the deck. And he *did* find a whole bunch of it. *We* did. Except—there were 78 cards in this Tarot deck, and we only had twenty.

"Who are you, really?" I asked Morgan.

He leaned forward again and put both elbows on my desk. "I'm retired."

"Retired what?"

"Envoy."

"You're an *Envoy*?" That was interesting. A year ago, I'd found out my dad was a full-time Envoy before he disappeared. Terree's father Greist had also been an Envoy.

"Retired," he said. He pointed to The Fool on my desk. "You

don't need too many more cards. You only need the Major Arcana, and a couple more."

"What?"

"Major Arcana. Twenty-one picture cards, all numbered, except for The Fool, which is unnumbered."

I rolled my eyes. "Jesus, I know what they are. But I need a couple more cards . . . to do *what*?"

Once again, he leaned back. He spread his hands in a gesture that said he'd given me all he was going to give me about that.

"But I have to find this guy on Barnard's," I said.

He nodded.

"And kill him."

"Not exactly."

"How do I not exactly kill him?"

"You bring him a Tarot card."

"Which one? A poisoned one or something?"

"One you don't have yet, but you will."

"*Which one*?"

"Death."

Well, shit. That made sense. I was wavering, and he knew it. I wanted him to get rid of the smug smile on his face. "If I take this on, I'm taking Tem Forno with me. That's extra expense."

"Of course. Believe me, you'll need him."

"He's going to check you out in every way possible first. Your information, your claims—everything about your story before I commit to the job."

"Whatever he can find."

I looked at The Fool more closely. From my view, he was upside down because Morgan had set it there that way. In that position, it signified *reluctance*. The fool was dressed in bright clothes, like a harlequin, and carried a stick on his back with his possessions. A white rose was in one hand and a white dog by his side as they approached the edge of a cliff. I'd researched this card and all the others. I knew more about Tarot than I wanted to know, to be honest.

The fool's journey.

The Fool was the protagonist of the story. I guess that was me. It meant I was about to abandon every commitment I had and ignore every excuse I had made, make a leap of faith, and begin anew the search for truth, wherever it took me. A search for my dad.

I picked up the card and turned it upright. I frowned. "I bring Death to this person. But you want him back. Why?"

"I made a promise."

"Promise to whom?"

He didn't offer up a name.

"All right," I said. "I'll need to know as much as I can about this person I'm bringing back."

"There's very little known, in some respects. He's a mystery. A secret. You know more about him than *I* do. You know how to find out *more* about him, too."

"Who is he? Do I know him?"

His smile widened. "Oh, you know him."

"Have I met him?"

"That's a very interesting question with no easy answer. Yes. And no."

"Shit."

Morgan reached into a jacket pocket—an outer one this time— and withdrew a crumpled photo. You didn't see too many of those anymore, unless they were antiques, or someone was as nostalgic as I was about our lost past. He put it on my desk in the same spot The Fool had been, but he spun it around toward me.

The portrait was a little dark, but I could see perfectly that he was a Helk. My heart skipped a beat as I shot a pained look at Morgan. "What the fuck! *Are you serious*?"

He nodded.

The Helk in the photograph showed no discernable emotion, but I believed his face was mocking me. Challenging me.

The next evening, I waited for Forno out on the old ferry terminal, darkness shrouding Elliot Bay, and the few weak lights from one of the taller buildings did little to improve my mood, even if I did have an antique flask in my hand. In my other hand was Morgan's old photo of a familiar face that also didn't fill me with cheer.

Continuing the search for my dad had become a possibility. Too bad he was in a different universe traveling away from ours at cosmic speeds. The information Morgan had given me suggested I might end up figuring something out about it and lead me in his direction.

Also, shit would likely blow up in my face, maybe rip a hole in our universe, and risk the destruction of the Union of Worlds.

Well. I'd been *there* before.

Seattle, 2115, first world of the Union, now a backwater, since the seven colonies offered new thrills and chills to humans and aliens alike. This migration to the stars made it difficult to keep my detective agency afloat.

Seattle had never felt as quiet as it did during the Fourth of July in 2115. Occasionally, some cheap mortar firework sputtered in the night sky, but it wasn't anything to oooh and ahhh about. During better days, nonstop pyrotechnics would've made the city look like a war zone.

Those days were long gone.

The holiday hadn't travelled well, either. Fireworks, flags, and parades didn't follow colonists to the colony worlds, where the idea of independence was quite meaningless. Well, okay. There'd been that incident on Temonus, but I preferred not to remember those days.

A firework thumped and a thin trail snaked upward above the deserted Smith Tower. *Oh, the anticipation.* There was a light retort at the top of its trajectory and a handful of weak green and red balls appeared fitfully, floated for a few seconds, then disappeared.

"Oooh," I said.

I tipped the flask to my mouth and took a long sip of an expensive brandy I'd managed to procure thanks to friends in high places. It was pretty stupid to drink a fine brandy like that from a flask. It should be sipped from a real brandy glass, but who else besides me even knew about that in this day and age? Mention Helk ale or the blue poison, however, and folks couldn't shell out enough money for that experience.

The most important thing about a VS fine brandy from France was to enjoy it. Savor it. Even cherish it. I didn't have a fine library or a crackling fire to sit in front of in an overstuffed leather chair. There wasn't a piano bar down the street I could hang out in and misquote *Casablanca*, another relic from our past that most people would have no knowledge of. Just nostalgists like myself. "Play it again, Sam." Sip from the brandy glass. Relight my cigar. At best I might be able to power up a stupid neon holostick.

Technology was not concerned with the finer things. It wasn't concerned about nostalgia. In much the same way, the Union didn't concern itself with much of anything related to Earth. At least in Seattle, a polite infrastructure remained to make life comfortable. Well, *mostly* comfortable.

I was older now. A little less spring in my step. I mean, granted, only a year had passed after the defeat of the Ultras and the destruction of the portal between our universes, but I came back from it aged, a side effect of quantum travel. A plus to the side effect was that I could get a senior discount at Zola's.

Where was Forno?

He was supposed to check out Morgan's personal information. Because Forno was a Helk, he was good at scaring information out of people. I wanted to know if the guy was telling the truth about the job he wanted us to take on. It was a job I hadn't *wanted* to take on, because lo and behold, it would take me off planet, but he'd promised he would make it worth my while. Famous last words.

I took out the photo the client had handed me yesterday during our meeting at my office and stared at it.

"Crowell?"

I came out of my reverie on the ferry dock. The night had darkened considerably. Tem Forno had called my name and I didn't like that I hadn't heard him approach. It wasn't like a Second Clan Helk could *creep.*

"Everything checks out," Forno said. In the dark, his leathery face was as featureless as Morgan's photo. It wasn't like there were any bright fireworks displays to light up the bay. "I mean, we'll need to follow up on some things, but basically, the Morganism is legit. Retired Envoy, no black marks, long career."

"Morganism? Jesus, Forno."

"You like it? Me too. That's what I'm calling him from here on out. So do you want to do it? Shall we get this show on the highway?"

"On the road, Forno."

"Oops."

I looked at the photo in my hand, at the image of a First Clan Helk that had become famous and infamous all at the same time.

"Yeah, let's do it," I said. "Let's go find him."

Of *course* it was him:

Terl Plenko.

CROWELL

2 THIS WAS WHERE IT GOT INTERESTING.

Morgan had asked us to bring a Tarot card, which we didn't even have, to a far-away colony, to someone who'd long been thought dead, including all the copies of him. Yeah, the body morphing thing: instigated by the Ultras in a clever secret invasion to create hybrids so that the dying Ultras could live in our universe in human bodies. Didn't I already say it was complicated?

Terl Plenko had gained notoriety as the leader of the interstellar terrorist network known as the Movement. Evil terrorist Plenko turned out to be a copy of the original, however. My old partner Alan Brindos unwillingly became another Plenko and paid the ultimate price for it. But that was another story, and a painful one.

What about the *original* Plenko, though? The one who'd died in the Rock Dome on Coral Moon? Coral was destroyed, causing colony planet Ribon to become uninhabitable. That was just it. He *died*.

"Was it ever proven?" Forno asked me, scanning the DataNet on his comm card.

It was the next morning, and we were sitting in Zola's, a café a few blocks from my office that doubled as a hangout for data-heads and the like. Actually it was called Zola II, but very few patrons called it that. Louise Nichols, the new owner, was doing her best to revive it after it had shut down three years ago. Alan Brindos and I used to eat at the old Zola's, back when we worked our first detective agency, before the contract work with the Network Intelligence Organization. Before the Ultra scare. I'd even been here before that, sitting with my partner Shirley McCoy during my tenure with Seattle Authority. Not much had changed about the place, except the name, and maybe the French fries, which weren't quite as good.

"Was what proven?" I asked.

"That Plenko died."

"Hard to look into that when the whole moon is gone," I said.

"Good point."

The staff at Zola's liked Tem Forno. Sure, he stood out like a sore, well—*Helk*—but he had developed a taste for coffee. He drank a *lot* of coffee. Zola's was full service, and I didn't drink coffee. I sipped at my preferred blue poison, Temonus whiskey. It clashed with the French fries, but what did I care? I was having a drink at 10:00 in the morning.

Forno somehow looked smaller in here, another reason why he was so welcome in Zola's. We sat at a back table, and he always took the low-rider chair, and he slouched a little, his bulk somewhat hidden in his overcoat, which once belonged to Terl Plenko, and then to Alan Brindos. He smiled a lot more, too, and gave customers the idea that even Helks could be friendly.

"Did you find anything on the DataNet?" I asked.

"Not really."

I fumed inside, not happy with his nonchalance. "What about your famed underworld contacts?"

"I'm still recovering from the last time you had me use them."

Our waiter, Ian, passed by. I asked for more Ranch dressing.

Forno grimaced. "Don't you ever get tired of French fries?"

"There aren't many Earth delicacies left."

"Please don't spend all of the Morganism's expense money on French fries."

I popped a fry and gazed out toward the front of the café. Several data-heads laughed as they lost themselves in their immersion specs. I ignored them. If Louise wanted help, she'd give me a sign and I'd send Forno to scare them. With a Helk around, I didn't get the chance to show off my own muscles these days. Damn it.

"It doesn't make sense," I said. "I can understand how Morgan's pockets can be so deep, having been an Envoy—"

"And retired."

"—but that line of work, helping mediate interstellar squabbles, doesn't put him in Terl Plenko's path, real or copied."

"You are *so* wrong, I'm surprised you can live with yourself."

I tried to ignore that, but my impatience won out. "What do you mean?"

"Envoys travel the Union. They get around. Your dad? And Greist? Both Envoys, and see where that got them. Plenko. Ultras. Right in the thin of things."

"Thick of—goddamn it, why do you do your stupid-Helk act when there's no one around to appreciate it?"

"Because it upsets you." Forno straightened a little bit in his chair and came about a foot closer to the ceiling. "Look, the Morganism knows something about your dad. He has to."

"Why? Because he knows—or thinks—that Plenko is alive? Because he had a Tarot card we were missing, and mentioned another?"

"Because he said he promised someone he'd bring Plenko back."

"What does that prove?"

Forno chugged the rest of his coffee, his third cup, which had only been brought to him five minutes earlier. He used the menu inset into the table to order another one, his finger skimming across the flashpaper. "What do you remember about the Rock Dome and what happened there?" he asked.

"You're not answering my question."

"'Answer a question with a question and you'll be a wise Helk,'" Forno said, quoting a Helk aphorism. "Humor me."

Ian brought me more Ranch. I thought back two years ago, when I'd sent Brindos to Temonus to look for Plenko. It happened after seeing a holovid of an ill-fated attempt to gain information from a Movement sympathizer.

Dorie Senall. She'd fallen 100 floors to her death in the city of Venasaille rather than give the NIO any clue about Plenko. She'd done so willingly because she'd been a *copy*. The real Dorie Senall, who was still alive, had been married to the real Plenko. They had gone to Coral Moon to tour the Rock Dome.

I humored Forno with that story. "When Coral blew, Dorie escaped," I finished, "but Plenko was lost at the Rock Dome, and didn't get off that moon."

"What else did she say about that time?"

"Lost while they were there touring or some such. Left the area with a be-right-back to her, and never returned."

"You went to visit her last year after the Ultra shit went down," Forno said. "On Ribon, in one of the new reclamation domes."

I nodded, but I didn't like where this was going. Dorie and I based our friendship on the few interactions we'd had over the past few years. We were friends, but distant as colony worlds. Close enough, he guessed, if you counted the jump slot possibilities. "If anyone knows anything about Terl Plenko," I said, "it's Dorie Senall."

"Last year, you had a TWT voucher, and free passage, thanks to a gift from the Kenn. Is it any easier getting visas to Ribon these days?"

"Maybe a little." I wondered if it was Dorie who Morgan promised about finding him. The question was: if that was true, would she risk having him brought to her? He might have enemies. She'd be better off going to wherever he was hiding.

Ian brought Forno's coffee. "Here you are, Mr. Forno."

Forno beamed. "Ah, thank you, young Earthling," he said, perpetuating his benevolent alien act. Humble and appreciative of all the finer things Earth had to offer. Which wasn't much.

"Well," I said as he gulped down half the cup, "we know someone who can help."

"You mean NIO Assistant Director Jennifer Lisle."

I nodded.

"She's not still mad at you for the incident last month with the RuBy bust, is she?"

"Almost everyone is mad at me. NIO, Seattle Authority—"

"Because that was *priceless*." He paused. "The shipment that got away, I mean."

"Shut up, Forno. How was I supposed to know Jennifer had them staked out?"

"If you ask her for visas to Ribon, you'll want to get the visas for Barnard's Star, too. If, that is, you're willing to take this job."

"We promised Morgan we'd tell him later today."

"What're we telling him?"

It was insane, of course. I recalled Dorie Senall's words to me when I hinted I still had a desire to look for my dad. If alive, he was in another universe. Moving away from us. Closed to our kind amid our miniscule understanding of the truth of it. I'd given in to her practicality. An alternate universe made of antimatter? How could I possibly get there? Or my dad get back *here*? By magic?

But. Was that what these Tarot cards were for? The fact that Morgan had acknowledged the cards, however, and even gave us one of his own, suggested there was something important about them that extended beyond fortune telling. And bringing in his trump card, the once-thought-dead Terl fucking *Plenko*?

Jesus. Insanity breeds insanity, they say. At least I thought that's what was said. Sometimes I confused old sayings and well-meaning nostalgia with wishful thinking.

Forno was waiting for an answer. I ate my last French fry and wiped my hands on my own jacket. I felt my blaster tucked in there. "Do you *think* we should tell Morgan yes?" I asked.

"Yes."

"Yes, why? Because he's given new hope?"

"What kind of hope would that be?"

Once again, I fought back an angry retort. It wasn't fair of me. Forno had weathered his own storms on Helkuntannas. Lost people, too. He understood loss just as much as hope.

For a full fifteen seconds, we just stared at each other. I guessed we should accept the job. "There's an old saying, Forno. 'Hope is not a strategy.'"

"Do you believe that?"

"Not really," I said. My expectations for finding my dad weren't just a feeling. Any time I thought about my dad, I felt that those expectations could influence a positive outcome. "You get what you expect," I continued. "If you don't have hope, even the most brilliant plan is doomed from the start."

Forno seemed to find this statement true. He grinned. "So?"

"Looks like we're working for Morgan."

"The Morganism."

"I'm not calling him—"

"A retired Envoy who's been around. He breathes, functions, and has a mind of his own." He grinned. "See? Morganism."

"Shut up, Forno."

I pinged Jennifer Lisle at NIO headquarters in Chicago after we left Zola's. An automated message looped me to her answering service.

"Regarding what, sir?" a man's voice said.

"Travel visas."

"I'm sorry, Assistant Director Lisle doesn't handle that sort of thing—"

"Just tell her Dave Crowell called with an urgent message. She'll want to call me back." At least I hoped so. In my mind I saw the RuBy bust downtown near the old Authority building go down in flames when I showed myself and tipped off the sniffers. I'm *sure* she wasn't still angry about that.

Forno disappeared somewhere, and I went for a run. Forty minutes later, I entered my preferred workout "gym" near my place and spent another forty minutes lifting. It was possible Morgan's size and hefty build had prompted me to work harder.

Later that day, back at my desk, I awaited word from Jennifer. I was a little miffed she hadn't called right away. Maybe she *was* still upset. Morgan had checked in too, but I had to put him off for a while longer. I picked up The Fool, Morgan's Tarot card, and looked at it closely. Of course, I'd looked closely at *all* the cards Forno and I had found, but I couldn't place any extra significance to them, other than that they were in remarkably good shape for being as old as they were. One thing we hadn't done yet was hire someone to analyze and test them. We couldn't begin to appraise the value of the cards, since it wasn't even a complete set. I didn't want to draw any attention to them in case anyone other than me was out there looking for them.

If there was any significance to The Fool, it was the symbolic meaning: that whole reluctant journey thing. Seems I was destined to start one. That is, if Jennifer Lisle ever called me back.

I shivered, equally surprised and relieved that she'd contacted me. I'd already decided to go see Dorie, and now here she was, contacting me with an urgent matter. Dorie, the widow of Terl Plenko. There was a real possibility she wasn't a widow after all. It didn't seem *likely*, but if what Morgan had said was true, I had to believe my fool's journey had indeed begun.

My comm card beeped a few minutes after I read Dorie's message, and belief turned to certainty. NIO Assistant Director Jennifer Lisle was on the line.

Well, now. Looked like I had a good reason to go to Ribon.

"Hi, Jennifer," I said cheerfully. "Thanks for calling me back."

"The answer is no, Crowell," she said.

SENALL

3   AT THE START OF THE FIRST ULTRA SCARE, WHEN CORAL Moon had blown up and its fragments intersected with the colony world of Ribon, the planet was decimated, and very few colonists were evacuated in time. Dorie Senall involved herself in the reclamation project, and soon took over the day-to-day operations building the New Venasaille Dome. Life was near impossible outside the dome, but colonists had trickled back. A lot of things had happened since then.

Becoming governor was one of them.

Dorie Senall had no reason to believe the newest reclamation dome, simply christened West Dome, would join the New Venasaille Dome in voting the Union Party line when the colonists settled in, and the dome's infrastructure allowed for regular council meetings. But she'd been wrong before. The north dome, New Coral, favored the Separatist Party and elected past assistant governor of New Venasaille, Tom Sakson, as its new leader. It wasn't long before Tom started a lot of noise about New Coral becoming self-governing, wanting nothing to do with any other domes.

She should've seen this coming during the six months he worked for her when the reclamation project started on Ribon. He'd taken many trips to New Coral on her behalf when her job dug fingernails into her, and she couldn't leave her office in the Brindos Building. He'd taken liberties with his given agendas and met with those very men and women—as well as a few Memors and Helks—who would later help him get a toehold there. Dorie had never expected to rise much higher in Ribon politics, but those who believed in her said she was a natural at it.

But she was still learning.

She'd learned a little from Terl when he dabbled in politics before everything went to hell with the Ultras. So when she was voted in as governor of New Venasaille, and the Brindos Building became the dome's seat of power, she rarely left, except to tour the progress of the East Dome, which was still under construction. The East Dome had a long way to go before it considered colony resettlement, let alone its politics. When New Coral became operational and the number of colonists increased enough to run a provincial government, Sakson resigned from New Venasaille and took a few of his cronies with him to New Coral.

Which is why it worried her when the new assistant governor of New Venasaille, Aditya Thakur, came into her office with news from Sakson's camp in New Coral. Thakur was younger than Dorie by five years and had lived on Ribon before the crisis. He'd been one of the lucky ones to get out but returned to help rebuild the colony. He came onto her staff as an energetic but inexperienced assistant, and quickly rose in the ranks until elected assistant governor. That kind of speedy advancement happened in a rebuilding community with limited space. Limited space, fewer citizens. He turned out to be perfect for the job, however, and she relied heavily on him.

And what about me? she wondered. Perfect for the job? Or was she just someone flailing along, someone around New Venasaille at the right time, her heart in the right place? When elected governor, it surprised her. True, the voting bloc was small, but it meant a lot to her.

She hadn't had thoughts like these until recently.

Dorie stared out the office window at New Venasaille, the dome's arch showing a bright yellow sheen today. Several flitter drones left the Operations Building across the street and headed toward the far end of the settlement, no doubt to facilitate the ever-present need to inspect dome infrastructure. She recalled a recent problem with the West End recyclers—"End" being a relative term.

"Tell me, Adi," she said when Aditya Thakur cleared his throat for the second time.

"Yes, ma'am." His voice was strained, although he had a soft high voice to begin with.

"I assume it's bad if you took the time to come here instead of sending it to my card." Dorie turned toward him. The man had jet black hair, cut short to his scalp. He wasn't a big man, barely taller than her, but he had an imposing presence she liked when he was out campaigning. He looked extra sharp in his black suit and tie. "What's Tom up to?"

"He's called a special session of Congress and cites a charter mandate that allows him provincial jurisdiction."

Dorie almost wished for the days she was simply an artist's wife, although she didn't long for her RuBy-hazed days of irresponsibility. She figured, someday, Sakson would use it against her. "We know what that means," she said.

He tapped his comm card and scanned it. "He's calling for a vote to keep New Coral separate from the Ribon government. In two days. Joint assembly. To be held in New Coral's dome."

"Damn it, what's his fucking *hurry*?" she yelled. She wished Sakson was in front of her now. She'd kick him in the shins. She closed her eyes, trying to control her thoughts. "Analysis?"

"Of the possible outcome?"

"Of *anything*." She shook her head. "Sorry. Yes. Does he have the votes? He may want to be his own dome, and he has all the support he needs there, but can he carry enough councilors here?"

"He has his sympathizers."

"I know."

"Many of them will jump domes if the vote carries."

"Good for them."

"Good only if we can replace them with Union Party members. What if a vote comes up here in the future? Could we see New Venasaille turning Separatist? West Dome? East Dome? What if we all become our own governments on Ribon?"

"Would that be so bad?" She surprised herself by asking that question. Was she softening her stance?

"It doesn't make a lot of sense," he said. "Not with four domes so close together. Relatively speaking of course."

"It'll confuse the hell out of the Union government on Earth. 'What are we going to do about Ribon?'" She hadn't been too happy with President Richard Nguyen's hands-off attitude regarding the colonies. It seemed to her his concern should be on high alert, post-Ultra scares. "They've asked that question before."

"I can schedule a press conference. You can take a stand. Feeds go out to both domes. You have a few provincial councilors attached to West Dome who get to vote, too, even if they can't yet occupy their own dome."

She waved a hand. "Yes, of course. Do it. I'm sorry you must be both assistant governor and sometimes errand boy."

"And the bearer of bad news."

She sat down at her desk and tapped the DataNet terminal. "You're right. Stop doing that."

Thakur grinned. "Anything else? Coffee? Tea? Something stronger? You look tired. Distracted. Anything else going on I should know about?"

Yes, there is. "No, I'm fine. Tea, please. Have Ross do it. You have work to do. I want to be at the podium tomorrow, first thing. Invite all the media, give *The Observer* and *Dome News Daily* front row seats, and make sure Sakson doesn't block anything. It would be like him to do it and claim ignorance."

"Will do."

"Thanks, Adi."

Aditya Thakur gave a little wave and left her office. When her door closed, she looked at the door where he'd disappeared. As fast as Adi had climbed the ranks, maybe it would be better if he had her position instead. He was a quick learner and had a presence about him that made people turn their heads. Maybe she'd done enough here. Maybe she should move on.

As soon as she thought it, though, she knew she couldn't. There was so much more to do. She would feel more confident, she was sure, when the next two domes were built, and more colonists arrived. She had promised herself, and others. There was no better way for her to honor the memory of her love, Terl Plenko. He would have appreciated her commitment to bring Ribon to importance again.

Thinking about Terl also made her think of Dave Crowell. They'd been linked from the start, and in more ways than one, during both Ultra scares. Dave had seen her new life, briefly, on his visit here a year ago. *I'm doing something good here,* she'd told him. *I'm not the wild girl you first met.* Certainly, she wasn't the imposter Dorie Senall that had run with the Movement and the false Plenko.

I couldn't have wished her a better death than a 100-floor dive from a tall building.

Dave Crowell had believed in her from the start, unsurprised at her good turn here at New Venasaille. He had done more good for the Union than almost anyone, twice saving it from the Ultras. There were only so many times one man could save the Union, but if a third time came, she was sure Dave would be there. Reluctant, maybe, but in the end, he'd be drawn in, particularly if it threatened someone he cared about.

The Ultras were gone, however, as was their universe. As was his dad, the one person Dave barely remembered, but most wished he could see again. The one human he knew who was lost in that Ultra universe. The dad she'd told him he had to forget.

It's over. You can't possibly get to him.

Her secretary Ross brought her tea. Dorie sipped at it, thought about the press conference, about Sakson and New Coral, and decided she couldn't deal with any of it until she had her lunch. She left the office and sat down in the cafeteria, tea in hand. Once there, she felt better and transcribed her speech through her comm card. She would hit Sakson hard. She'd appeal to the voters to stand firm and keep Ribon united.

As she finished, a message pinged her card, surprising her. It was Warden Max Rydell asking if she could come to the Bubble as soon as possible.

The Bubble was a small dome ten miles from New Venasaille. Ironically, amid all the fuss with the Separatists and their agenda, the Bubble was self-sustaining, and Dorie was completely fine with that. No colonists lived there. In fact, only a couple dozen citizens lived there. Their jobs were to work the facility contained within the Bubble and its population of more than thirty Thin Men. It was a research center.

It was a prison.

After the second Ultra scare, Union officials decided a facility to house Thin Men on Ribon made a lot of sense. Take the most notable Thin Men and test them, prod them, and—well, who knew whatever else they did to them. That wasn't her department or, frankly, her concern. The only worry she had was the facility's proximity to New Venasaille. The idea was to further isolate these Ultra-created copies. Change the landscape. Change the control. See if that offered up any other clues about the process that made them. If, by chance, Thin Men escaped the facility, they wouldn't get far outside the Bubble. But you never knew.

"Why do you need me?" she asked Rydell, annoyed that her lunch had been interrupted. She had only now sat down with her tea and hoped to eat something. Everyone on staff, and even some from New Coral, knew she expressly refused to take calls or answer pings during her lunch hour. That included Max Rydell. The VERY URGENT label made her pick up the coded call. She read the message abstract before hitting accept.

"Someone is asking for you," the warden said.

"Your staff?"

"A subject."

In the Bubble, Thin Men were known as subjects, not inmates. Subjects as in "test subjects." That was her guess, anyway. "Who is it?"

"She asked me not to say, but hoped during her rest period you might visit."

She. "You allow that? Withholding a subject's name?"

"In this case, yes."

"What is it about?"

"She didn't say that either."

The warden didn't add anything else. It wasn't up for debate, even if the governor of the dome was on the line, everything coming from the top of intelligence circles throughout the Union. "When is her rest period?"

"It started fifteen minutes ago. There's a two-hour window."

Shit. If she agreed, she'd have to cut her own lunch short, get to the shuttles, and work her way through the Shell and the domelock. At least she could bypass Shell security checks and get to the outer skin without delay. There'd be security checks on the other end, however, and restrictions on what she could bring with her into the subject block.

"Okay," she said after a brief pause. "I'll be there. I'll want more information about the—subject—when I arrive."

"Certainly. Not like I haven't got anything else to do. At least it alleviates the boredom of this job a little."

She broke the connection and stared at her tea. Councilor Jamey Rosas passed by with his cafeteria tray full of something that smelled delicious. They nodded at each other. So much for lunch.

The short ten-minute flight from New Venasaille to the Bubble was uneventful. There wasn't much to look at but the planet's ruined lifeless surface. As expected, the wait at the Bubble's domelock took longer than at New Venasaille. Dorie passed through the security ring, and once they tagged her with the Bubble's visitor card and made sure she had nothing else with her other than what she was wearing, an attendant led her through the facility to the subject block. The Thin Man's rest period was nearly over; she wouldn't have but fifteen minutes with the subject.

Warden Rydell waited at the last security door.

"Max," she said with a forced smile.

"Governor Senall, good to see you."

He started cycling through the DNA lock on the security door. It immediately made her think of Terl, who'd been a DNA lock expert. It was one of the things that had got him in trouble in the first place. She saw Terl stamped all over the design of this door. When it was open, Rydell handed her a new card.

"What's this?"

"Ident of your Thin Man."

She glanced down but didn't open it. The dark flashpaper did nothing in inert mode when she rubbed her thumb thoughtfully over the surface.

"You wanted more information," he said. "Are you going to look at it?"

She stared at the card a little longer, then shook her head. Standing there at the door, thinking about Terl and his DNA locks, she decided not to brief herself on the subject, figuring it didn't matter who it was. It was a Thin Man. What else did she need to know at this point? She felt more comfortable shielding herself from the knowledge, creating distance between the Thin Man and her, like the buffer zone between the Bubble and New Venasaille. Close by, but hard to get to unless invited.

Rydell shrugged, then extended his arm through the door. "Off you go, then. Room 15 on the end, right-hand side."

Room, not cell.

In the few years since coming back to Ribon, she had never been in the subject area. She'd been to the Bubble's admin areas, but never here. Never wanted to examine Thin Men. Never wanted anything to do with that process. Now here she was, striding purposefully down a well-lit hallway to talk with one of them. Blinders on, staring straight down the hallway. Just get it over with.

She was surprised to find the door to Room 15 open. When she took time to scan the hallway, she saw several other doors open. They weren't locked in? The doors were not barred and had no communication system she could see for visitors wishing to converse with a subject without entering its space. She didn't see anyone inside the rooms. Still out during their rest periods, apparently.

"I'm not a prisoner," the voice in the room said.

Dorie didn't recognize it. She'd thought maybe she would. Somewhere in the deepest, most secret compartments of her heart, she'd entertained the thought that this had all been a ruse, and that the creature in the room was not a Thin Man, but a human; that this was not a copy, but an original. And if not an original, then a myth. A legend. A martyr.

Dave Crowell had found *his* martyr. He had run into the man known as Vanderberg Parr, who turned out to be a Thin Man, a copy of Crowell's deceased partner Alan Brindos. A Thin Man who was also part Ultra, who, in the end, had found a way to help Crowell and others, closing a portal at the cost of his own life. On the official end, the story was all about Vanderberg Parr. Crowell didn't tell the NIO or Kenn or any other agency about the Brindos that Parr had become.

So she didn't blame herself for thinking for a few brief hopeful moments, that it would be Terl Plenko inside that room. The voice was indeed female, however, and the bubble burst.

"Come in," the voice said. "Please. Don't be afraid. You're perfectly safe."

She raised her chin and entered the room. The light was dim in here, but she could make out the subject sitting on a single bed. At once, she felt she should recognize the subject, although even now, after all these years, she'd never been good at telling them apart from one another.

A Memor.

Her ponytail was short, just above her shoulders, orange hair with wisps of white throughout. Her face had some wrinkles and her lips were chapped. She looked tired.

"Hello," the Memor said, inclining her head. She wore a long, simple gown of blue made of a heavy fabric. "Do you know who I am?" She pointed at the ident card in Dorie's hand.

Dorie shook her head.

"My name is Lorway."

Lorway! The Memor from the Science Consortium who had helped the Ultras infiltrate the Union, and then disappeared. Presumed dead. This Lorway was a copy, a Thin Man who in the end had helped Dave Crowell quantum travel to the Ultra world known as Rook.

In the days before the Ultras, Dorie had been one of those who believed the alien Memors could play mind tricks: influence thoughts and actions and manipulate memories. If they were that powerful, then why not believe they could actually suck memories from your head? As it turned out, they *could* put you to sleep. Memors had a thing called The Memory, or shared memory, which Crowell had been subjected to so he could find out more about his dad. Most humans in the Union thought differently now, although there would always be ignorant people out there.

Still, Lorway was a Thin Man. Even after her good deed for Crowell, she had to be rounded up with the others and studied. It didn't surprise Dorie that Lorway had been transferred to this facility.

"Does my name bother you?" Lorway asked when Dorie didn't speak right away. "Frighten you?"

Dorie smiled, more to calm herself than to alleviate the Lorway's worries about her fears. "No, of course not." She didn't know what else to say at this moment.

"I'm sorry I couldn't give more information than I did in the message. Bubble officials had to handle and approve the message, of course."

Dorie looked around Lorway's room, now that her eyes had adjusted to the low light. It wasn't much smaller than a studio apartment, and it was furnished like one. Not a cell, at all.

"I'm not a prisoner," Lorway repeated. "I mean, at least not in the way you normally think of prisoners. I'm locked up in this facility, but as you can see, I have a modest, comfortable dwelling. I get to have some personal possessions, and I was allowed—on the Union's credit, of course—to purchase some other practical items. I have some mobility around the subject area, particularly during rest time."

Dorie was afraid to ask what happened when it wasn't rest time. "I understand," she said, not wanting to know more about that.

"I'm as comfortable as can be expected," Lorway said. "Don't worry about me."

"Do you have a message for me or something?" Time for all this to get to a point. The rest period would be ending soon.

"I do, and I don't."

Dorie frowned. "If you're going to answer like that, we'll get nowhere, and you'll be out of time out and back to—whatever they do to you."

Lorway lowered her head, and her green eyes bore into Dorie's. "My message is not in words."

"What's the message then?"

Lorway stood and went to a dresser that had multi-colored drawers and a mirror framed in an iridescent material. The dresser was bright, and likely the alien had picked it out on one of her Union-paid shopping sprees.

"A gift," Lorway said, opening the top drawer. "Something of value to no one except perhaps a serious collector, or maybe a lover of nostalgia. I believe your friend Dave Crowell counts. You might consider giving it to *him*."

"What—?"

Lorway turned, and she held in her hand a card slightly bigger than her comm card. She pushed it out toward Dorie. "This."

The card was just paper with images printed on it. Real paper, not flashpaper. She took it. "What is it?"

"A Tarot card."

Dorie nodded. "I've heard of them." She looked closer at the card, at the two planets, thin connecting lines, the purple color. She turned it over and she recoiled in surprise. "It says—" She glared at Lorway, suddenly suspicious. "It says Death."

"Death. Yes, a powerful card in a Tarot deck, but you don't need to worry about all that."

"What do I worry about then? What the fuck does this mean?"

"That's for you to figure out."

A knight—a skeleton in armor—rode a white horse and carried a black flag with a white blossom and the number thirteen on it. At his feet were the bodies of other humans. "What—I mean *where* did you get this?"

She only looked up at the ceiling.

They might have certain freedoms, but Max Rydell and his security personnel were watching. Maybe listening. "What do I do with it, then?"

"I already told you."

"You did?"

"Maybe it would be a nice gift for Dave Crowell. Because I think he's collecting the set."

"Dave's love for antiques and the past is fun and all, but honestly, it has nothing to do with me. You should keep it."

"It doesn't help me any, either, and I have no sentimental attachments to it. You should see him."

"I have work to do—"

"Your days at New Venasaille are numbered, Dorie Senall. You *know* that." The Memor sat on her bed again. "It has everything to do with you. It has everything to do with those you love." She stared hard at Dorie. "With those you *loved*."

Dorie felt her face redden. She wanted to say something, but the tightness in her throat made her work at it. The Tarot card was shaking in her hand. "Terl?"

"It's no secret you have enemies, Dorie," Lorway said. "I've heard the rumors. I'll probably get a reprimand from the warden for bringing it up, but think about it. How long can you put this off?"

She said, "Put *what* off?" in a whisper, but all she could think about was *Terl*.

"The inevitable," the Memor said.

"I don't know. I can't just leave—"

"You shouldn't wait too long. Spend a little time now and it will go a long way to heal the past. You'll have to work your way toward understanding. Do anything you can now to move things along."

Dorie's hand still shook, as if spasming, and she found she couldn't stay on her feet. Her legs gave way, and she sat on the floor, a coldness gathering in her core. "Call Dave," she mumbled, knowing she'd have to be careful about her rivals finding out anything about all this, but her thoughts said *Find Terl*.

Lorway put a hand on Dorie's head. "Death isn't death when it's a new beginning."

CROWELL

4 "WHAT DID JENNIFER SAY?" FORNO ASKED WHEN HE CAME back to the office. I hadn't moved from my desk since the conversation with the assistant director.

"Where did *you* go?" I asked him.

Forno poured from the pot, and the coffee had to be old and super strong by now. He plopped into his Helk-sized chair of tubes and mattresses and gave me a sour look.

"I'm trying to be a wise Helk, answering a question with a question," I said.

"Uh huh." He sipped the coffee and gave a sigh of contentment.

There was no accounting for taste. The taste of *coffee* taste, anyway. I didn't drink the stuff, so I couldn't tell a good cup from a bad cup.

"I went home," Forno said. "Got some beauty sleep."

"Keep work—"

"Don't say it, Crowell."

"Jennifer said no."

"Then what did you say?"

"Pretty please."

"She still said no?"

"Until I added a cherry on top."

"Seriously."

I had the DataNet open via the clunky terminal on my desk, and a notification pinged me. I thought it might be Jennifer, but she'd said what we needed would come to the comm card.

A message. The fact that it was there, and unregistered, instead of on my comm card, made me take notice. Shit was weird these last few days, leading me on an uncertain path, so naturally I didn't think twice before accepting it and scaffolding it through various layers of Net security. Tucked in tight to the buffer, I opened the message. It was simple. Urgent, but unspecific:

I MUST SEE YOU. COME AS SOON AS YOU CAN. —D.

"What the hell?" I whispered.

"What is it?"

I didn't answer. I thought I knew who'd sent the message, but I pulled up a locator prog and attached it to the message. The terminal whirred and clicked like the antique it was, and I waited for the origination trace. By association, I'd confirm who the sender was. A minute later, the trace came through, and I was certain of who'd sent it. The message had come from Ribon.

"It's Dorie Senall," I said.

"What?"

"It's *Dorie*. An unregistered ping, but it's her. She wants me to come to Ribon. Wanting to see me, but not saying what. Just said it was urgent."

My comm card snicked with incoming data a bit later, and I picked it up from my desk. I stretched the flashpaper and confirmed what I'd received, then sent some of it on to Forno. "Visas to Ribon," I said. "Leaving tomorrow. I just sent yours to your piece-of-shit comm card."

"She gave in to your irresistible charm, huh?" He leaned as far back in the chair as he could. He rested his head against the plywood wall.

"You should check and make sure you got the visa."

"My card's at home."

"Jesus, Forno, you shouldn't leave that thing. There's vital information in there. Private stuff. Your place isn't very secure." I added, "When you're not there."

"Forgot it."

"How about your Helk-sized blaster? Bring *that*, did you?"

He nodded. "What about Barnard's?"

"She's working on those. It's a bit more involved. She'll send them when she has them."

"Truthfully, what did you really say to Jennifer?"

"I apologized."

"There you go. Not so bad, was it?"

"Four times, at least, and a promise not to do anything rash while I'm on Ribon or Barnard's."

"Doing something rash on *Earth* count? Because you're already headed in that direction."

"It'll take a few more apologies, I'm sure."

I'd told Jennifer I was visiting Dorie, but I knew she was curious why Forno was also going. Or why we were going straight to Barnard's from there. I wondered if Jennifer had knowledge of Morgan. Probably. Probably knowledge that might be extremely useful. But I couldn't bring her in on this right now. I didn't know what she—or more accurately, the NIO—would do if they got wind of Terl Plenko being alive somewhere. I trusted her, but the rest of NIO brass still made me nervous, particularly after Ultra copies had been discovered inside the organization.

"So maybe this is all coming together," Forno said. "All related."

We stared at each other, waiting. One of us would say something, I was sure. Or maybe not. Forno made some Helky grunts in his throat, and I tapped the desk with my fingers to a little rhyme in my head. *Stickman, Stickman, coming to our house . . .*

"Dorie will have questions, undoubtedly," I said. "She'll want to know what's going on with Morgan. I don't know how much I can tell her."

"You don't know what she has to say either. Her message."

"Forno, it's *Plenko*. If he's truly alive, I honestly don't know how she'll react."

"The same way when she found out he was dead, I suppose." He leaned forward and the chair creaked. "She might already know. That could be why she pinged you."

I nodded and drummed my fingers again, this time without any specific rhythm in mind.

"Tell her what you know about Morgan," Forno said. "Everything. If he's hiring us, we can't be shy about that. He didn't say we couldn't. For all we know, Dorie knows him. Or of him."

My card snicked again. I checked it and said, "We're good for Barnard's."

"Jennifer?"

"Visas and travel vouchers. No excuse now."

"Then we go," Forno said.

"To Dorie first. We'll see what she has for us." I laid the comm card on my desk and picked up the Tarot cards. All that we had, including the Fool. Yeah. It seemed foolish, thinking these cards could mean anything at all. I hadn't started this whole process for nothing, however. They meant *something*.

The chair groaned dangerously as Forno stood. "I'll go pack."

"Check your card for the time. I'll see you at the Station. I assume you're going to get yourself there. Run over, or something."

"I'll be there with chimes on."

The next day, I stopped at the Emirates Building near the old Seattle Center. I entered the foyer with its glass and silver beams and holo windows that opaqued from time to time to reveal Union worlds and their attractions. They looked much the same as the ones I'd seen a year ago. Ted Hartman, virtual immersion star, still beamed at me and assured me I was in good hands.

The bubble-like reception area was home to the receptionist, and Jesus, it was the same guy from a year ago. They may have cleaned house of all the bad guys and Thin Men, but apparently Nick the receptionist was still in good standing. Did he ever go home? Did no one else have a shift? Nick's perfect brown hair waved freely as he greeted me.

"Worlds Away," he said. "I'm Nick. How can I—"

"Hello, Nick."

"Mr. Crowell, so nice to see you."

"I have an appointment with the director."

"That you do."

After several security checks (I hadn't even brought my blaster this time), I was allowed into the back rooms, and Nick escorted me to an office on the second floor. It disturbed me, remembering the incident from last year that took me to the basement and the secret elevator inside the building's hub. All the Thin Men and Ultra sympathizers were gone, and I should feel safe, but it still bothered the hell out of me to be here.

Terrence McCarthy smiled and held out his hand when I entered. He was a short, stubby man with deep black hair only on the sides of his head and nothing on top or the back. He looked to be in his seventies, so I figured the hair was dyed. I couldn't tell how much of that hair pattern was natural, and how much was a fashion statement. Envoys didn't tend to be showy and extravagant.

"My my, Dave Crowell," McCarthy said. He smiled so broadly I thought he was going to start bowing any moment. Wrinkles bunched up under his eyes. "A pleasure to meet you at long last."

"Good to meet you," I said, sitting in the chair he pointed to. "How long has it been?"

"Been?"

"Since you became director of Envoy services."

He beamed, then sat down in his own desk chair that looked a little like something he could drive around town. He activated the DataNet terminal on his desk, snapping keys. He glanced at it briefly before replying. I didn't think he was looking up his own employment record. "Seven months." He nodded. "Yes, yes, seven months. Time flies."

His office had a few framed photographs of the Seattle skyline in better days, including the old Space Needle no one could go inside of anymore. I was surprised to see them, and not holovid scenic windows or flashpaper posters. A bit of the old nostalgia, then? Or left over from the previous Director Amanda Hoban's belongings?

"How can I help you, Mr. Crowell?"

"I want to know more about your Envoy named Morgan."

McCarthy's cheery face drooped a little.

"Surely, you knew why I was here," I said. "It's not easy getting past Nick up front."

He recovered and regained his happy smile. "Of course, of course. It's just that your partner Mr. Forno already asked about him. Already did a check on him."

"Did he speak to *you*?"

"No, he—"

"Which is why I'm here talking to you." I took my comm card from my coat, pulled a flashpaper memo from the surface, and expanded it. "Morgan. Envoy for forty years. Retired last year. That's quite a career."

McCarthy nodded, still smiling.

"And quite a coincidence that he retired last year at the height of the Ultra scare and hired me now to look into something directly related to that entire mess."

"I have no knowledge of what Mr. Morgan asked of you—"

"Of course not. Right now, it's confidential. But I want to know how well you know him. If he was an Envoy for that long—you were an Envoy yourself before becoming director seven months ago— you likely worked with him."

"Mr. Crowell, there are many, many Envoys in the Emirates,

and most of them don't come here to check in. They're more likely to come to the major conferences scheduled throughout the Union. There's no way I can know every Envoy—"

"But you know Morgan. If not in person, then by reputation. And you know him now, Director McCarthy, with your finger on the case files of everything Envoy-related."

He dipped his head and looked down at his desk. Then he nodded. "Yes, yes. I know him."

"Did you work with him?"

"A few times."

"See? Not so hard to admit, right?"

"What do you want to know?"

"Have you ever known him by any other name than Morgan?"

He shook his head. "He's been Morgan as long as I've known him, and that's all I have in his records. I told your partner that."

"How was he as an Envoy? I mean, top of the line? Average? Ever in any trouble?"

"Top Envoy several years. Near the top, most years." McCarthy smiled. "He held court during some of the biggest agreements in the Union, participated in lucrative trade deals, mitigated inter-world squabbles, and mediated cases large and small."

"He was good."

"Very good. He reminds me of your dad," McCarthy said. "One of the best Envoys we ever had."

I'd been the last to know that about my dad, the information about his past hidden from me until I dug it up a year ago. He went missing when I was sixteen.

"It was a shame he passed on so early," McCarthy said.

"Disappeared."

"Yes, yes. I guarantee you, he would've had my job now if he hadn't . . . disappeared."

"Did you work with him?"

McCarthy nodded vigorously. "Oh yes, yes. I learned a lot from him. I asked to be assigned with him whenever I had a chance."

"What about Greist Sahl-kla? Did you work with him?"

"Yes, Greist, too. Another fine Envoy, until—"

"He went missing, too."

McCarthy spread his hands and laughed. "But found, thanks to you! And now he helps train our future Envoys."

"Did Morgan know my dad? Or Greist?"

"Oh, I'm certain of it. I could look that up—"

"I'll narrow that down for you," I said, scrolling through the flashpaper from my comm card. "Chicago Conference at the Knightley Building."

McCarthy paled. "The day the—I mean. Your father and Greist went missing. The day the—" He broke off.

"The day the Ultras first appeared," I finished for him. "Yes. Was Morgan there?"

Terrence McCarthy folded his hands in his lap and stared at me. It looked like he wasn't going to answer. His skin regained color, overly so, until it was obvious he was blushing. Whether from embarrassment or anger, or something else, I wasn't certain.

I raised my eyebrows as high as I could, waiting for an answer.

"He was."

"You're not telling me something. What is it?"

"Nothing, nothing. I—uh—just find it awkward talking about it due to the—*nature* of it. I mean, the importance of it. The—" He glanced up and to the right. "The tragedy of it."

"Did Morgan speak there? What was his schedule like?"

"That was a long time ago."

"The DataNet will have it, and you know it."

McCarthy used his feet to bring his desk chair closer to the DataNet terminal. I was pleased to see his terminal was as old and clunky as mine, and surprised his deluxe chair didn't run the damn thing itself. A few taps brought light to his face, and he scanned the information I couldn't see.

"Okay," he said. "He had a solo talk called 'The Best Mediation Practices in the 23rd Century,' a think tank table about Envoy recruiting—"

"Think tank table?"

"He'd sit at a table for the hour, and interested attendees could sit with him and ask questions about the topic. Very informal."

"Okay."

"Then a few joint panels. One called 'Persuasion for Politics,' and another called 'The Fallacies of DNA Models and Techniques on Shared Memory.'" After that, just a few—"

"Stop," I said. "Shared memory? DNA models?"

McCarthy nodded.

"Is there a description of the panel beyond the title?"

He looked. "No. Just the title and the participants."

"Who was on the panel with him?"

He scanned the screen, then his eyes narrowed. "Well."

"Well what? I mean *who* what?"

"Your dad," he said. "On the panel with Morgan. Your dad, and Greist Sahl-kla."

"Holy hell," I murmured.

"What does it mean? So they were scheduled together on a panel. So what?"

"The topic. The goddamned *topic*."

"Does it remind you of something? Mean something related to Morgan hiring you?"

"You could say that." My brain whirred a million miles a minute, recalling when Terree put me into the Memory for the first time. The Memor concept of shared memory. And DNA? Who was it who'd been the big DNA lock expert? Terl Plenko. Terl. Fucking. Plenko.

"But Mr. Crowell," McCarthy said, shaking his head. He pointed at the screen. "The conference was a sham. Almost all the talks were cancelled, or postponed, and none of those ever happened. Some, but—" He checked the screen again. "All of Morgan's talks were cancelled."

"Because of what happened when Greist made his deal with the Ultras. When he gave the Ultras some of the Envoys and the best physicists and structural engineers of the Consortium."

And my dad, who had something special the Ultras wanted. I didn't know what, but the Ultras took him and a few other Envoys to their own universe. Greist had been tasked with holding open the portal. It all made my brain hurt once again, and I thought I'd moved past all that.

"Very strange, very strange," McCarthy said.

"Morgan left, didn't he? Most of the Envoys, at least half of them, left the conference before all the Ultra stuff went down."

"Yes."

"But before that, he saw Greist. He saw my dad."

"I guess—"

"You were at the conference, too."

McCarthy nodded. "I didn't have any talks. I was pretty new. I actually planned on attending Morgan's think tank on recruiting."

"You saw Morgan leave, didn't you?"

He didn't say anything, but I saw his throat tighten. He was holding something back, and I needed to know.

"Tell me, Terrence, or I swear I'll throw this all up to the NIO and get them to do another clean sweep around here. I have a good friend higher up in the organization, and trust me, I owe her big time right now."

McCarthy reddened some more. "I was headed for his think tank, but then word came down about the cancellations. I saw Morgan just before he left, talking with Greist, very hush hush-like. Greist looked around somewhat guiltily. I don't think he saw me, but he slipped something to Morgan, said something I couldn't hear, and ran off."

This had to be near the time the Science Consortium had been meeting about the Transcontinental Conduit, arguing about its worth, waiting for Greist while my dad tried to calm things down. But Greist never showed. Baren Rieser—in league with the Ultras—and his lap dog Alex Richards gathered everyone the aliens wanted and started the whole mess. I'd been there with my dad but escaped.

"You have any idea what Greist gave Morgan?" I asked.

McCarthy shrugged. "No. Something about this big." He outlined a space with his hands. Smallish. Rectangular.

"Paper? A card?"

"Maybe?"

Could it have been a Tarot card? I hadn't asked Morgan where he'd found the card, or why he knew so much about them. *The Fool.* Yeah, got that right. I would get back to Morgan soon about Greist. Right now, I had to mull this new information over and see where it led me.

"Do you know where Greist Sahl-kla is now?"

"Oh yes. He's at the training station on Orgon. He just began a rigorous four-month workshop with new Envoy recruits. We're all quite excited about his new position within the Emirates. He's doing fine work for us, leading the new age of—"

"Good to hear," I interrupted.

It looked like I wouldn't be talking to Greist any time soon. I smiled calmly, stood, and put out my hand, trying to put him at ease. I wasn't sure I had everything I could get from Terrence Mc-

Carthy, but it was enough for now. It rang true. The other files of note about Morgan I already had, thanks to Forno. "I appreciate your time."

McCarthy stood and grasped my hand. "Sure, sure. Good luck with your case, Mr. Crowell. And let me know if there's anything else you need."

I might think of something. But for now, it was time to get to the port, find Forno, and head for Ribon. The next major step would depend on what Dorie had to say.

I pinged Forno and told him to meet me at my place. We had a journey ahead of us. I'd bring Plenko Death.

I'd bring every fucking Tarot card we had.

SENALL

5 DORIE LAY ON HER BED IN HER APARTMENT THE NEXT morning in New Venasaille and stared at the Tarot card so intently, she had a feeling it might come to life. It was Death, after all. Death on a white horse. Kings and paupers and kids lay dead at his feet. No one was immune to death. Even just bones, Death was protected by his shiny armor. She felt the power of this card, and it frightened her a little. She wasn't sure it was a good thing. When was Death a good thing? Terl's death? Her own death?

She'd come back from the Bubble and sent an encrypted note to Dave Crowell. He would figure out who it was from, and he would come. Maybe she should be going to him. It had crossed her mind, but then, there was the press conference in a few hours.

The card loomed large in her vision. She imagined the figure of Death shimmering on his white horse, moving slightly if she looked at it just right. Death, coming to life.

Could it be possible? Terl, *alive*? She couldn't fathom it; she couldn't wrap her mind around it. How could he have survived Coral? Survived the explosion that destroyed it and destroyed most of Ribon. They'd been on vacation. It was a chance to put some distance between his failed election and the RuBy she'd discovered. Not yet addicted but teetering on the edge.

In retrospect, Coral didn't seem the best choice for a vacation. The tour of the mined-out Rock Dome facility seemed an afterthought. She'd been mildly annoyed, but Terl had the idea he might gain insight into his art and sculpture and hoped that the tour could inform him about the minerals that had once been plentiful there.

And then there was the *moment*.

The moment he'd bent low to kiss her, told her *Union bright*, and left her. He'd be just a moment, answering the call of nature. He never returned. Ident card used to leave the Rock Dome. And that was it. Vanished. He didn't leave Coral—according to his Ident—

and after she returned to Ribon and fell victim to RuBy, Coral turned to fire, Dorie fled, and Terl Plenko the Movement terrorist, a copy of her own Terl—a *Thin Man*—came to life.

Dorie replayed the *moment* in the Rock Dome over and over in her mind, looking for clues. Had anyone spoken to him while they were there? Before or after he left her? She rewound and fast forwarded Terl's path, as she remembered it, from by her side, just after his kiss, to the visitor center. She had always assumed someone had got to him—an agent of the Ultras, most likely—and did what needed to be done to steal his pattern for the copy process. It had even occurred to her that he'd been secretly ferried off Coral for this. Nothing, however, had made her believe they kept him alive after the process.

She remembered the instant he died.

Or, more accurately, during the peak of her most RuBy-induced altered state, she believed she'd felt his passing. She'd wept and said goodbye to him then.

She fingered the Tarot card. Flipped it upside down, sideways, backward, and forward again. *It has everything to do with those you love*, Lorway had said. *With those you* loved. She said it was a gift for Dave Crowell, the ultimate collector of nostalgia. Dorie had to believe he knew something important about Terl. At the same time, she knew she had something just as important.

Perhaps her goodbye was premature.

Perhaps, because it was now absolutely necessary, her goodbye had just begun.

At ten o'clock, Dorie stood near the podium of the press room and gazed out over the modest crowd of reporters. Ribon officials were in attendance as well. Tom Sakson had not done anything to block the press conference, but he was in attendance in the first row, and that might be even worse. Aditya Thakur stood next to her, ramrod straight. She smiled at him, and he nodded.

Poor Adi, she thought. *He has no idea what's coming.*

Ross, who doubled as a press secretary, gained the podium and said good afternoon. Miniature drones hovered and hummed a good distance from him and projected his image to a window screen and to viewers across Ribon.

"Governor Senall has called this press conference to discuss tomorrow's joint assembly emergency vote on New Coral's separatist agenda," Ross said. "She will make a brief statement about this, but she's informed me that she will not be taking questions."

A murmur arose from the press room, then Dorie cringed as reporters yelled out in distinct voices to complain. "What? "We have a right to understand—" "Why not?" "Will the governor speak and answer questions today?"

Ross raised his hand and leaned into the microphone. "Please. Please quiet down. Thank you. The Governor of New Venasaille."

Dorie stepped up to the podium as Ross adjusted the microphone slightly. Then he left, and Dorie was alone at the podium. The teleprompter was invisible to most, just a blur of words on a wisp of transparent flashpaper directed within her peripheral vision. A simple movement of her head and a few blinks, and she could read the statement she had written for this moment. She'd written them yesterday, before her visit to the Bubble.

The press room settled, in the quiet all was ready to record what she had to say. She looked over at Adi again. Once again, he nodded his encouragement. With a flick of her finger, she minimized the teleprompter.

She would not be using it.

Although those sitting in the press room could not see the teleprompter, they understood what had just happened. They remained quiet but seemed ready to explode.

"I've lived on Ribon for a long time," she began. "Twice. There was—" She managed a half smile "—a period of mourning, reflection, and rebuilding that took place in between."

The press corps nodded knowingly. Tom Sakson, front row, smirked.

She continued. "As Ribon was reborn, I was reborn." She waved a hand dismissively. "Yes, most of you know of my past. The life before Coral. You know who I was with. I am not afraid to say his name. My Terl Plenko ran for political office on this very planet. He was a Helk, and he was a decent, loving person, and yet most of you still attach his name to terrorism, conspiracy, and invasion. You know he was not that person. You know the false Plenko who helped destroy our world. You also know of yet another Plenko who helped, in his own way, to rebuild it, when he sacrificed himself to the Ultras. Yes, I struggled with addiction. I know some of you are hearing that part of my past for the first time. My rivals would like to use that against me. Use the past against the present.

"But my fellow citizens, we are Ribon *now*. I came back to help this first reclamation dome become a reality. To become Ribon *now*. And even as we continue to expand and redefine ourselves, we face a political animal that wants to take a bite out of our common goals and our common vision. An animal that threatens the Ribon way of life."

So far, Dorie saw that she had them. And as far as Tom Sakson or Adi Thakur knew—even though she had turned off the teleprompter and she was saying all this from her heart and from no other memorized speech—it was going the way they expected it to go.

But no, it would *not* go there.

"I am a new Dorie Senall, and this is a new Ribon, and all of you are its life blood. I'm the governor of New Venasaille, but I stand for all our domes. For all of Ribon. We should love together, and, if it ever happens again, bleed together." She paused, looking down briefly at the empty lecturn on the podium. "My time here has been a blessing. Look at the progress we've made! New domes, new colonists arriving every day? My god, it's truly a miracle. This is a miracle we all need to embrace. A miracle we all need to sustain. I feel confident we can do that. There are so many capable people here. So many of you have brilliant futures ahead."

Once more, she paused. Looked out over the hushed room. They sensed it, she knew.

"'I will not rest from travel,' the great Earth poet Tennyson wrote about the hero Ulysses. 'I will live life to the lees.' In Ulysses' old age, he has a need to go back out and explore. He is bored *shitless*." The audience chuckled, nervously. "He thinks there are new things to discover out there. He tells his mariners that before the end there's got to be something they can do. Men! he says. We fought against Gods. Against *Gods*, for heaven's sake! Let's seek out a newer world and damn be the consequences. If we die, we die. 'That which we are, we *are*.' Ribon has been my newer world, but I have much more to do before I sail beyond the sunset."

Some whispers now, out in the audience. Reporters frantically checking their cards, their terminal connections. If they knew Tennyson—if they knew "Ulysses" at all—they knew where she was headed. In the poem, Ulysses lets his son Telemachus rule, then heads out with his aged mariners for more adventure.

"Because I love, because I cannot say goodbye to my will, I must say goodbye to all of you. As of this press conference I'm resigning the governorship of New Venasaille. In my stead, as per charter, Assistant Governor Aditya Thakur will serve." Dorie looked at Adi and his face was a mix of shock and dismay. "I understand Governor Tom Sakson will hold his vote tomorrow about New Coral becoming its own government. I urge all of you to consider the unwanted ramifications of that decision. United we are Ribon. Divided, we are simply a scattering of domes in constant need of repair, with you, the colonists, struggling to remain free from isolation. Do the right thing."

One more beat. A pause to let it sink in.

"There are more things to say about all this. I believe Acting Governor Thakur will do a good job now going over those points with you. He might answer questions, too. I don't know." Dorie looked over at him and the shock and dismay in his face had given way to sadness and resolve.

He nodded and mouthed *of course.*

Dorie turned the teleprompter back on for him, then leaned into the microphone. "Thank you, New Venasaille. Thank you, Ribon. I promise to do you proud out there in the dark, broad seas." She smiled. "Union bright."

The press room erupted as reporters tried to be heard, shouting, asking questions. Ross gained the podium, saying something back to them, but she didn't listen. She stopped in front of Adi, and after a pause, gave him a small hug. She'd opened the door for Sakson, really. Given him a chance against the inexperienced, yet rising star, Aditya Thakur, and perhaps control of the joint congress. She believed in Adi, but he had a fight on his hands.

"We'll talk later," she said. "I'm sorry I didn't tell you."

He simply nodded.

Ross was announcing the acting governor. Dorie clasped Adi's shoulder. "For now, go give Sakson hell."

"With pleasure."

She left the press room and didn't look back, the strong, confident voice of Acting Governor Thakur reciting her original speech as if it were his own. Adrenalin still coursed through her, but she felt relieved to be in the wings, and not on stage. Relieved, because she'd done it. Left on her own terms, to search for Terl. She hoped she wasn't making a mistake.

An aide she didn't know, a young man from one of the offices inside the Operations Building, reached out toward her as she passed.

"Governor—" He stopped and blushed. "Sorry. Miss Senall."

Dorie quickly glanced at his name badge and saw he was Shell personnel, part of Domelock security. "That's okay, Bryce."

"Miss Senall," he said, staring down at his comm card. "Notice from the Shell. A transport just entered New Venasaille. You have a couple of visitors who wish to speak with you."

She nodded. "Yes. I do, don't I?"

Bryce looked confused.

"Extend to them every courtesy, and send them to me in Adi Thakur's office, but start prepping right away for their departure. We'll be leaving before the end of the day."

"Leaving, Miss Senall?"

She paused long enough to extend her hand. He put his hand in hers and shook it. "For now."

To seek, to find, and not to yield.

CROWELL

6   I ENTERED THE BRINDOS BUILDING IN NEW VENASAILLE, following a man named Ross, and felt a wave of sadness. I recalled my previous visit to Ribon and the short time I had in the Brindos Building before Sakson, her assistant, whisked me out to the north dome of New Coral. I didn't get as emotional these days about Alan Brindos, or about his later avatar, Vanderberg Parr. Parr, who'd been lost on the planet Rook when he helped transport me to Greist Sahl-kla before the portal closed for good.

I rubbed my head, the thinning gray hair a side-effect of the quantum travel. I sometimes forgot about my hair, and sometimes the added wrinkles on my forehead, under my eyes, and around the corners of my mouth. That is, if I didn't look in the mirror too often.

Seeing Dorie, though. That was something I'd looked forward to for a long time. I'd seen her at her worst—which was not actually her but the copy—and at her best, as we battled the Terl Plenko copy. Moreso, everything she had done for Brindos had made me respect her even more. Then the decision to help with the reclamation domes, and look where she was now. I'd only seen her once after the second Ultra scare. There'd never been any romantic interests between us. She seemed more like family, but family I didn't visit enough.

The last time Tem Forno had seen Dorie had been even longer back, since he'd been on Helkuntannas tidying up his own life when I visited her the last time.

A thump and a curse made me look back at Forno. He'd been ducking through some of the doorways.

"They didn't think twice about these building specs," he grumbled. "Didn't they expect Helks to migrate back here or something?"

"This was one of the first buildings," I said. "They were in a rush. They changed specs for future buildings."

"So you say, Crowell."

"Dorie *does* write to me from time to time, you know. Keeps me posted about the reclamation project. Just relax."

"Yet, she sends one unregistered line of text in a message you have to decipher to know it's from her, and you come running."

"Not fair, Forno. You know what this is about, and we were coming anyway."

"Yeah." Forno rubbed his head, and the fur from his arm slid across my face.

I waved him away. "Jesus, Forno."

Ross escorted us to an office with the label *Assistant Governor Aditya Thakur* on a flashscreen embedded in the door. Our weapons left behind, per regulation. I didn't expect any trouble, of course.

"Miss Senall is inside," Ross said. He opened the door. "You can go on in."

I thought: *Miss* Senall? Not *Governor* Senall?

Then we were in. Ross closed the door, and Dorie rose from her seat behind a modest steel desk. The office was small, though bigger than my own space behind my plywood wall. A desk, a DataNet terminal on one corner of it, and that was it. Someone's long coat hung on a peg behind it. No windows.

Dorie's presence filled the room. She smiled and came toward us in a rush. She wrapped her arms around me, and I smelled a light fragrance at her neck as I drew her close. Her straight black hair was cut shorter since the last time I saw her, to her shoulders, giving her an almost regal look.

"Dorie," I said.

She squeezed a little harder before letting go. "Hello, Dave." Her eyes lingered a while on my face, and I self-consciously turned away. After we parted, Forno gathered her in for a Helk hug and enveloped her with his furry torso, lifting her off the floor.

"Dorie!" Forno said.

"So good to see you," she wheezed. "It's been a long time."

"Put the small human down before you break her, Forno," I said.

Forno set her down gently and grumbled. "To him, I'm like a cow in a china store."

Dorie laughed, but I just rolled my eyes.

"Why are you in the assistant governor's office?" I asked.

She lowered her head, as if embarrassed, but when she looked back at me, she spoke assuredly. "I shouldn't be in this office either."

"Either?"

"I resigned today. Assistant Governor Thakur is taking my place."

I didn't know what to say. Didn't know if this was good news or bad. She'd been so enamored with the Ribon project, and had come so far in her political journey, and suddenly she was letting it go? All I could do was ask. "Why?"

"I'm leaving Ribon."

"You are?"

"I'm leaving here with you."

I blinked. "You are?"

"You think I called you here just to talk? I need a damn ride."

"This is sudden," I said. "Do you know where you're going? Or why? I mean, do you have the visa? I mean—" I struggled with what to say. I had come here at her request, but I'd already decided to talk to her about what I'd learned from Morgan. About Plenko.

Forno chuckled low. "Oh, Jennifer is going to love you even *more* now, Crowell."

"Dorie," I said. I took a breath. "Please, sit down." I motioned toward the small couch in the room. "I have something to tell you."

She didn't move. She crossed her arms.

"It's important."

"I'll stand."

I said, "Fine, *I'll* sit."

"I'll take up space," Forno said. He shrugged. "It's what I do."

When seated, I rubbed my hands together and gathered up my nerve.

She noticed my nervousness and said, "Dave, tell me. There isn't anything you can say that will surprise me."

She was wrong, of course. I steeled myself and let it out. "Terl Plenko may be alive. *Your* Plenko may be alive."

She didn't even blink. Didn't grow pale. Didn't tremble.

Apparently *I* was wrong. "You already know something about this," I ventured.

"Yes," she said. She frowned. "You came all the way out here at my request. I had to see you."

"It's complicated. We were hoping to find out what you knew about him. See if maybe we could pinpoint where he might be."

"You don't know where he is?" She finally sat down on the couch next to me, hands clasped in her lap.

I gave her an apologetic look. "We have—a general location."

"And where's that?"

"Barnard's Star."

"You're right," she said. "That's pretty general."

Forno grinned. "But at least we know it's *Barnard's* star, and not someone else's," he said.

I stared at Forno.

"What? Helk snot. I can't bleed off some of the tension in here?"

"Jesus, you're always talking bodily fluids," I said. I turned back to Dorie. "How did you find out?"

She hadn't sat on the couch for long, and now she stood again. At her desk, she took the lid off a medium-sized container. I assumed it was some of her things from her own office. She'd already started packing.

"I have a gift for you," she said.

"A gift? From you?"

"It certainly isn't from me," Forno said.

"It's from Lorway," Dorie said. "She's at the Bubble facility nearby, for Thin Man study."

"Shit, I forgot she was there."

"She had this and said I should give it to you, and that I should go look for Terl."

"She told you that?"

"In an odd, roundabout way, yes."

"What is it?"

Dorie put her hand in the box, and when she took it out, before I could even discern what was on it, I knew what it was by its size. "She said you were collecting them."

"Holy *hell*." I stood abruptly. She handed me the Tarot card, and sure enough, it was Death, the card Morgan said we had to find. I'd expected a long drawn-out struggle to do that, but here it was, in Dorie's possession.

"Snot," Forno said. "The Morganism was right."

"Morganism?" Dorie asked.

"Ignore him," I said. "It's our client. Morgan."

"He told you I'd have it?"

"No, that's just it. He didn't say who would have it, only that we *had* to find it. And then we'd find Plenko."

She pointed at me. "Because of *that* card?"

I shrugged. "I don't know. Or all the cards that we have together. Including the one Morgan gave me, called The Fool."

"That doesn't sound like you," she said.

Forno said, "Well . . ."

"Shut up, Forno."

"Did Morgan know Lorway had the Death card?" she asked. "Or that I would get it from her?"

"I don't know." I held the card out as if it were a dangerous weapon about to go off.

"Jesus," Dorie said, and she sat on the couch again. "What does the card *mean*?"

"I've looked up more about this stuff than I care to ever remember," I said, "but it's not as frightening as you would think."

"It's not literally about death, is it?"

Forno shuddered. It was weird to see him shudder. He said, "The image of the bodies beneath his feet is pretty disturbing, though."

I shook my head. "Not all of them are dead. Some are begging. But they *are* all in his path. It just means everyone dies. King, poor man, old man, little kid. What the card means, I believe, is something you've already begun to realize. A major phase of your life is ending. Your governorship. You're starting a new phase. A search. The past left behind. Focus on what's ahead." I shook the card as an exclamation point. "Behind Death and his horse, there's a sailing ship in the background. A journey. And the card Morgan gave me, The Fool, suggests a journey as well."

"Or it's a change," Dorie added. "A transition?"

I thought about the change Brindos had gone through when he became Plenko. What Vanderberg Parr had gone through when he became Brindos.

The old Plenko had to die to allow the new Plenko to come to life.

"Something like that," I whispered, more to myself than any of them. "A change. A warning, perhaps. Move forward, no regrets, learn life's lessons. Look at the card. See? Death is looking forward, not as *us*. The sky is gray, not black. The sun's still not set. We have time to get things done. Put things right."

Forno said, "This symbol stuff is all well and good, but we're on a job for Morgan to find Plenko and give him this card. *Bring Death to Plenko.*"

Dorie drew in a breath at that.

"Again, not literally," I said. "Morgan wants him on Earth. Whether to keep him there or transport him elsewhere. Morgan made a promise to someone. We thought it might be you."

Dorie shook her head.

"So we don't know who that person is," Forno said. "We'd better find that out before we fulfill that part of the bargain."

"First things first," I said. "Dorie, you're going with us, and it all makes sense now. Can you get a visa to Barnard's?"

She smiled. "If only I knew someone at the head of the Ribon government." She grinned. "It would've been me, but I'll get it from Adi Thakur. I can scramble around and do a bunch of the legwork first. Then he can approve and sign. It won't take long."

"How long?"

"A few hours, maybe?"

"Then get started."

"When I have it, your ship will be ready. Since your ship wasn't a commercial TWT vessel, I had Shell personnel prep it for a quick departure through the domelock."

"What are we going to do in the meantime?" Forno asked.

"You could go scare Tom Sakson and his people," Dorie suggested. "He's not a nice person."

"I exist for the opportunity," Forno said.

"Actually," I said, "I have a better idea."

"Better than pestering politicians?" Forno looked at Dorie. "No offense."

"Every bit of it taken, my good Helk," she said with a smile.

"A short side trip," I said. "We have a few hours, right?" We were here. Why not go to the source of the Death card? It wasn't as if we could just punch through a jump slot to Ribon any time we wanted.

Dorie nodded. "You want to see Lorway?"

"Yeah. Can you get me into the Bubble?"

"Sure. I'll call Warden Rydell."

"You want me to come with you?" Forno asked.

"No, I have to do this alone."

"Then maybe I *will* pester politicians. Let me at 'em."

The question in my mind was: why could I never escape Lorway? From the very beginning of the Ultra scare, and at every turn, she had been there in front of me, some way or another. I had a hint of something in my head, a muffled question, but I couldn't be sure of it until I talked to her.

The Memor knew something important. Something she'd never told me. She would tell me now. She would because I knew who she really was.

It wasn't Lorway's rest period when I arrived at the Bubble, but between the outgoing governor's and new governor Adi Thakur's help, I was able to get Warden Rydell to pull the Memor away from the testing area and into a briefing room near his quarters.

When Jennifer Lisle confiscated my altered comm card after the showdown at Baren Rieser's House, it didn't take me long to find a new one that could "handle" some shadowy basement level progs. That included the freesource electromagnetic transblocker I'd used during the interrogation of Abby Graff a year ago. I didn't care if Rydell came flying in all red-faced when he discovered my blocker. I needed enough time to talk to Lorway without surveillance. I didn't want Rydell to deny anything.

My suspicions about her might be wrong, but I didn't care. If I was *right*, however . . .

Lorway was ushered into the briefing room. Nothing fancy about the room. No observation windows or fancy recording equipment—that I could *see*. Her orange ponytail looked even more faded than I remembered from those last minutes before she helped me with the quantum travel to Rook. White streaked her hair. Her lips were chapped, and I didn't know if that was a normal thing, or whether it was from whatever the Bubble people were doing to her during testing. Memor skin stayed unblemished until quite a bit into older age, but Lorway had new wrinkle lines and liver-like spots on her face. Captivity hadn't been terribly kind to her.

Unless there was another reason.

"Hello, Mr. Crowell," Lorway said as she sat in a chair behind a small folding table. Nothing fancy here inside the room.

"Surprised to see me?" I asked.

"I'm surprised and not surprised."

"You even *talk* with a quantum-forked tongue."

Lorway raised her eyebrows. She put her hands flat on the table. "I don't like your tone of voice, Mr. Crowell."

"Apologies, but I have some questions." I pulled my comm card from my coat, then sat down in a chair opposite her. "You don't mind if I record, do you?"

"The warden is recording this, I'm certain. You could get files from him afterward."

"I prefer my own."

She inclined her head. "As you wish."

I did turn on my recorder prog, but I also thumbed an installed node that initiated the transblocker. A quick squeal announced the prog had engaged, and then we were truly alone in the briefing room. *Let's see how long it takes Rydell to storm in.*

"You met with Dorie Senall yesterday."

"Yes."

"You gave her a card." He pulled out the gathered Tarot deck, found the Death card near the top. He showed it to her. "This one. You told her to give it to me."

"Yes."

"Where did you get it?"

"Like I told her, I can't say."

"You knew I had many of the other cards. You knew I was collecting them. How did you know?"

"Someone told me."

"*Who* told you?"

She leaned back and pulled at her ponytail. "Maybe, if you ask the right questions, I might be able to say a little, considering you're using an electromagnetic transblocker to keep Rydell out of range."

"So you recognize the prog. Good." I smiled and tapped the comm card dramatically. "And believe me, I have the right questions. I'm just getting warmed up."

She held out her hand. "Will you let me see the deck?"

I debated it for a few seconds, but I didn't see any point in denying her. I handed it over.

She thumbed through it. "You only need the Major Arcana," she said.

"You're not the first person to tell me that." He nodded at the deck. "Do you see the ones I'm missing?"

She didn't look up. Kept studying the cards, sliding through them easily, as if she were an experienced card dealer. *Or magician.* "I know which ones you're missing. And, like I said, which ones *you* don't need."

I made a shoving motion with my hand. "Shit, why don't you just take the ones you want, then?"

Now she did raise her eyes. "Really?"

I scoffed at her hopeful face and held out my hand. "God, no. Hand them back."

She fumbled with them, dropped them, but swept them up and, after some shuffling, returned them. "Mr. Crowell, you aren't going to discover anything you don't already know."

"But do I *know* I know it?"

"You're referring to the memory block."

"That's right. And it's pretty much gone, as far as I can tell. Regardless, I couldn't learn *every*thing from trips into the Memory. Only what people showed me through their interactions or told me in person."

"I believe in shared memory, Mr. Crowell," Lorway said, her eyes showing a tenderness I'd not seen before, "but I also believe in the human idea of the subconscious. So ask your questions. Make your statements. You came here knowing what you know, but your subconscious hasn't quite revealed it to you."

I paused and stared her down until her eyes flicked away a split second. "On the day we quantum traveled from Seattle, from the morgue, to Helkuntannas, you told us how it worked. Sort of. At least you gave us the gist."

"Okay."

"You lit up the letters U-L-T-R-A on Alex Richards' collarbone. There was a showdown with the last NIO agent, Jennifer Lisle. She shot Abby Graff."

"Correct."

It *wasn't* correct.

"But Graff was unhurt on the other side. *You* didn't travel with us. You stayed behind, incapacitated from the efforts. Then what happened?"

"I was taken in by the NIO."

"Or—" I paused. My subconscious was catching up. "You *did* travel. You traveled somewhere else."

"That is incorrect. I was captured."

Now I gave Lorway the twist. "Jennifer Lisle didn't shoot Graff. Director Aaron Bardsley did."

Lorway didn't say anything.

I pointed a finger at her. "You don't know that because you weren't there."

"I was—"

"No." I stood and circled the table, coming up behind her. She tensed but stared forward. "You weren't there. Your Thin Man copy was there. And your *copy* didn't make it. She died in that room in the morgue from injuries due to the stress of sending us on our way to Helkuntannas."

Now Lorway twisted her head back toward me. I saw the alarm in her eyes. "I know who you are," I said. "You're Lorway."

"But of course—"

"You're the *real* Lorway. You're older than your copy would be. You were there in Chicago at the meeting where you discussed the Transcontinental Conduit. When Baren Rieser took you all, and stole the Envoys, and kidnapped my dad. You worked with the Ultras, and you helped with the science to fucking build it!"

I came out in front of the table now, and she didn't meet my gaze. Head down, she stared at the tabletop.

I kept going. "Yes, you had your moment of doubt. You sabotaged the *Exeter* and caused it to run into the Conduit. DNA-locked telemetry signal embedded in the servo-robot's biomemory that would trigger upon your death. But you didn't die. Someone else triggered that signal."

She looked at me now. There were no tears in her eyes, only a cold resolve.

"Quit the act, Lorway," I said. "Who triggered that signal?"

She didn't answer.

"Who gave you that Tarot card?"

Silence.

"How long have you been here in the Bubble?"

This question she answered. "A long time."

"Let me rephrase that. How long have you been here in the Bubble by yourself?"

"You're saying I'm the only person locked up here?"

"How long?"

"Since the beginning," she said, her voice all breath. She suddenly sounded very old. "When they built this place. When the first reclamation dome was going up."

"They've released all the Thin Men, haven't they?"

"They were never here. It was a cover. The Thin Men are in other facilities around the Union, as was originally agreed upon."

"But not you, because you're not a Thin Man."

"They had to have a secure place for me."

"They?"

"The Memors. The MSA. It's my punishment. For my crime against the Union. Max Rydell has been part of the agreement since the beginning."

"When did they capture you? Where?"

"Right after the Conduit went down. They captured all of us."

"All of the Science Consortium? *All*?"

"The ones still alive the Ultras hadn't eliminated. Me, Bernice Talley, and the Helk, Cerm Knol. But I'm all that's left now."

"Who triggered the signal?"

I could tell she wanted to keep silent. She wished I hadn't pieced together so much of this. But she wavered. She opened her mouth to speak. Closed it. Started again.

"It was Terl Plenko, wasn't it?"

I didn't think she would confirm it, but she did. "It was."

"Not the leader of the Movement of Worlds. The real Terl Plenko. Dorie Senall's husband."

"Yes."

"You stole him away from the Rock Dome."

"He'd already been copied. His pattern in the buffer. I had help, but yes, I escaped Coral."

"And you took him to Bernard's."

She nodded.

"He's still there?"

"Yes."

"Can you tell me where?"

"I can get you close."

"And he wants to see Dorie. You gave her the card because he wants to see her."

"Yes, but he also wants to see you."

"I never knew him. Not the *real* him."

"He knows you."

"That's easy enough to say. A lot of people know me these days."

"He knows you from Chicago."

My eyes widened. "From the *conference*?"

"He was there. A special pass because he wasn't an Envoy. The Ultras targeted the young Plenko early on because of his early study of DNA-locks. They targeted Plenko and they targeted Joe Sando, Baren Rieser, Alex Richards . . ."

I made another circle of the room, knowing Max Rydell could come in at any moment. I sat down in the chair and put my arms on the table, palms down. "You got the card during the conference, didn't you?"

"Yes. I was told nothing about it. I was only told to keep it and never lose it, no matter what happened. He said some day it would be needed, and when it was needed I was to give it to you, any way I could."

I shook my head, confused. "Wait. Plenko knew I would some-day collect these? After I got the one from Terree? The one her father Greist gave her?"

She looked genuinely confused. "I'm sorry?"

"When Plenko gave you the card."

For a moment, she just stared at me, but then she smiled. She reached out her hands and took mine in hers. "Death isn't death when it's a new beginning, David," she said.

He thought she meant the Tarot card. "Yes, but—wait. *What?*"

"Terl Plenko might have given that card. But it came at the request of your dad."

SENALL

7 ON THE MODEST TRANSPORT SHIP *SINAI*, BOUND FOR BAR-
nard's Star, Dorie Senall gripped the sides of her seat as they
awaited passage through the jump slot. Dave Crowell was across the
aisle, and Forno sat in Helk-sized harness near the back. She craned
her neck and glanced at the two pilots up front. The lead pilot was
surrounded by the transparent film of the transport bubble. The slot
tracker readout blinked green.

Yes, she was nervous. She hadn't been through a slot since she'd
returned to Ribon several years earlier. She'd not, as a general practice, done much slot travel even during the days when Ribon was
a growing, thriving colony world. She never liked straying from
home. The Coral disaster displaced her, put her on a strange path
indeed, but once she returned—once the reclamation project started—she had never expected to leave again. She'd endured so much
hardship, had come through so much trauma during the first Ultra
scare, that it surprised her, this trepidation.

She pulled herself together. Gritted her teeth as the transport
hummed and trembled through the slot. She had changed clothes
when Dave visited the Bubble. The pants suit she'd worn during
her press conference had given way to comfortable gray slacks, a
black blouse, and a gray and blue button-down sweater. It kept her
warm enough in the chilly interior of the transport. On the seat
next to her was a hastily packed duffle bag of clothes and necessi-
ties; a heavier coat was on her lap. She didn't know how long she'd
be gone, but what she had with her would have to do.

Tom Sakson made some noise about her sudden resignation
and her nearly simultaneous decision to leave Ribon. He tried to
block her with a special citation aimed at Adi Thakur. Adi, to his
credit, tabled it long enough to get Dorie the visa to Barnard's Star
and get Sakson out of the Brindos Building without further incident. She worried about Adi, though. Sakson had pull. He would

make trouble. It was why she'd contacted Dave the way she had, with care, an unregistered ping, not knowing what Sakson might do if he found out. She hated leaving Adi in this position. But what could she do?

She had her calling. It matched Dave Crowell's own call. They'd had this unique connection between them that had always felt comfortable. Always felt safe. He'd visited only once after the strange events that first brought them together, but they kept up a dutiful correspondence.

Dave told her what Lorway said about what happened to Terl. That she had saved him at the Rock Dome. Got him off Coral. To Dorie, it seemed more like a kidnapping. Save him from what? They'd been there together. They should've left together. *Why did he need saving?*

More relaxed, she closed her eyes and thought about Terl. She had secretly dreamed he might return—an improbable hope—and announce himself in some typical invincible-Helk way.

Dorie lived several years with the artist and DNA expert Terl Plenko on Ribon in a modest apartment in the Tempest Tower in Venaisaille. She'd met him and discovered an almost unnatural admiration for the Helk, completely taken in by his charm, his intelligence, and his political activism. His passion for just causes and hatred for violence conjured a blistering whirlwind of activity; the rallies and movements he organized were the eye of a perfect storm of unity within a growing base of admirers.

It wasn't long before some of his followers began mumbling about Dorie's admiration of him as it changed into a controversial love between human and Helk. Dorie hadn't cared. She came to love him after they married, which they did to help legitimize his candidacy—or so they thought. They'd never consummated the marriage due to sexual incompatibility. While he worked in his field of expertise, offering services related to DNA coding, he made time for his sculpture, and the two of them also focused on Terl's political aspirations.

She'd never cared whether he won election or not. She'd have been happy if he did become Venasaille's provincial mayor, and *hoped* he would, but her naïve dreams of happiness gave way to the pressures of those who mocked him, and especially to those who mocked her love for him.

She withdrew from him at the peak of his political power, just before the election tore him down. At University, she discovered RuBy and fell down that hole.

Now, here he was again. A ghost between worlds, finding passage from the Rock Dome to the dome of New Venasaille, to give her a sign to rescue his corporal body from purgatory.

If you considered Barnard's Star purgatory.

It was a place shrouded in mystery, as far as she was concerned. She knew nothing about the world. Dave had told her it was a fast-growing colony, one of the largest. One of the most technological worlds. It had borrowed heavily from the Memors and Helks, infusing every scientific marvel it could into its culture. Dorie had become used to the slower pace of Ribon after the Coral disaster. Sure, technology created the massive domes, ensuring the safety of its citizens, but daily life kept pace with fewer demands, offering more simple pleasures. *Spontaneous joys.*

A particularly audible groan made her jump. It was simply the outer skin of the *Sinai*, the transport protesting its slippage through the slot, but it surprised her and brought her out of her reverie. She looked around the cabin again. Dave was looking at her with a bemused smile.

"Been a while," he said, meaning her, of course.

"A while," she agreed.

"Do you know the last time a ship didn't make it through the slot?"

She smiled knowingly. "You're going to tell me not to worry, that it's been years since anything like that happened."

"No, actually, a TWT single cabin passenger flight went missing last week on the way to Aryell."

She raised an eyebrow, not at all amused.

"They found the ship, eventually, all passengers safe."

She nodded, relieved.

"But it took an extra five days for a rescue vehicle to locate it, outfit a new slot tracker with the correct insertion codes to Aryell and do a cold jump from inside the slot."

"I'm now filled with the utmost confidence."

Dave waved it off. "Nah, we're good. Besides, you had your own people prep this thing, right? It'll be a dream."

"Unless one of Sakson's people found a way to sabotage—"

"No." He looked toward the pilots and nodded. "We're good."

She stared at his profile, not quite used to his aged appearance. Did it give him an even greater aura of confidence? She hoped she could be as confident as he was. Dave didn't know Sakson like she knew him. Didn't know his Separatist cronies and what they were capable of in a tenuous political climate, even if that climate was now a long way behind them. The transport breezed through the slot toward Barnard's Star, and she should forget about Sakson and New Venasaille.

"So," she said, straightening herself in the seat the best she could, "do you know where we're going? And don't just say—"

"Barnard's Star."

"—Barnard's Star. *Jesus*, Dave."

He smiled. "Morgan did that to me when he first hired me. Sort of. I assume you're familiar with the port of Bestus."

"Of course. After we arrive at the port, where do we go?"

"Bestus is completely metropolitan. Large. It'd be the best place to hide, you would think. Then again, it wouldn't take but a single sighting of the infamous Terl Plenko to have the entirety of the Union's resources coming down on him. A number of Union Arks already have their base in orbit around Osprey Station."

"So he's not in Bestus?"

Dave shook his head. "I don't think so."

Dorie grumbled inwardly. "Do you *know* where he is?"

"No." He reached into the bag next to him and pulled out the stack of Tarot cards. He fanned through the cards, taking them all in. "But I just might know someone who does."

"From the cards?" Her curiosity spiked. "Ah. Is it some kind of encoded message in the cards? Something that secretly spells out where?"

Dave shot her a bemused look. "No. Morgan scribbled the name on the back of one of the cards. I just can't remember which one."

She watched him fumble through them. A couple fell out and he had to pick them up. "Be careful. You're going to lose some."

"You should've seen Lorway handle the deck as if it were an extension of her own hands." He found the right card. "Here it is." He held it out so she could see the front. "The Hermit."

She thought that made sense, considering their search for Terl, who'd been missing, presumed dead, hidden all these years. "What's the name?"

"Heston Teska."

"That's a Helk name."

"Yep."

"And where's he?"

"In Bestus."

"Big city—"

"We'll search via the DataNet. NIO office there if necessary. We'll be arriving in the bright light of late morning. Morgan said he's in hiding, but not *technically* hiding. He'll be easy to find. Whatever that means."

Forno scoffed from the back of the transport, in his harness. "*Data*Net. How sweet. There are better ways to search—"

Another slippage groan echoed in the transport. It was followed by a disconcerting shimmy. Dorie reached for the armrest just as the shaking stopped.

"Of course, he may not *want* to be found, or be a part of this operation."

"There could be trouble?" She didn't like the sound of that at all. But when was there *not* trouble when she was around Dave Crowell?

"Yeah, there could be trouble."

Tem Forno chuckled. Dorie looked back at him.

"Now you know why *I'm* on this little expedition," he said.

It did make her feel a little better.

They were on final approach to Osprey Station fifteen hours later. Dorie awoke from a deep sleep when the proximity alarms pinged, and she unfolded herself from her prone position across two seats. The *Sinai* was about to exit the slot. Dave was talking to Forno in the back, but she couldn't hear what they were saying. When the alarm pinged a second time, he quickly regained his seat.

Barnard's Star. Long before the coming of the Memors and the Helks, long before the eight worlds of the Union and the jump slots, Barnard's Star was well known to humans: a red dwarf star with a storied history.

Dorie had learned some of that history in school on Ribon. The fourth closest star to Earth, Barnard's had fascinated scientists and stargazers for decades. At the time, no one knew whether Barnard's was a viable future habitat for humanity. Assuming anyone could ever get there—the most likely possibility had been to create generation ships to travel the extreme distance—would there be any livable planets that those future generations could colonize and survive on?

The answer had been *yes.* Then *no.* Yes. No. Then *maybe.* And then maybe yes. They bandied about ideas of possible exoplanets. About gas giant planets larger than Jupiter. Then Earth-sized planets. There was a time, less than a hundred years ago, that Barnard's Star was declared barren of any planets whatsoever.

The Memors gave the planet a name from their alphabet and number system. They might have called it Memory 2, or Memory 3. But when they gave Earth jump slots, Memors announced it *was* Earth-like. Although the Memors themselves had not colonized it, they thought it would be a good colony world for Earth.

Earth scientist Simon Daniels gave it the name Barnard's World. He'd been inspired by a science fiction novel published in the 20th century that used the same name for the *fictional* planet. There was a rival group who wanted to call it Hyperion, for the same reason, but Barnard's World won out. Now, if you mentioned Barnard's, or Barnard's Star—most humans used those names rather than the actual planet name—it meant Barnard's World.

The exit from the slot was smooth—more so than the actual slot travel, Dorie thought—and they docked at Osprey Station twenty minutes later. They waited for the umbilical, left the *Sinai,* and endured the Station's overly-long security protocols, which included declaring our weapons. They were allowed on a shuttle with seven other travelers to the surface port on Bestus, capital of Barnard's World. They had to do security all over again at the Bestus port, revealing their weapons once more, but finally received official permission to carry them for the duration of the trip.

She was ready for planet fall. Ready for a world that had natural air, real sky, no artificiality. Or so she thought. The port was stark. White, sterile, and underwhelming. The long, wide passageways from pad to exit were simply functional in getting visitors from point A to point B.

Bestus awaited beyond the port gates, which were also white

and featureless, and nothing could prepare her for the colony world's blatant blend of modern chic and alien technology. She paused a dozen steps from the gate, the brightness of Bestus already filtering through, daring her to go on.

Dave touched her elbow lightly. "You okay?"

She'd worried about this day for a long time. Not because of wild rumors about Terl alive somewhere, but because she had emerged from under the Ribon domes to walk on a planet's surface without breathing aids or environmental protections. She was scared, and she shouldn't be. She should have felt relief.

"Let's give Bestus our best," Forno said, urging them forward.

She nodded, smiled at Dave, and walked on. Most of the other passengers had already passed through the port gate. Forno crossed first, then she and Dave walked into the capital city side by side.

Bestus was bright and Bestus was flashy and Bestus was all chrome, silver, and burnished copper as far as Dorie could see. It was flashscreens taller than New Venasaille's dome. It was layered walkways that crossed avenues from angles not thought of before. It was massive structures, technological marvels that seemed to have no obvious purpose. It was quiet, for all its advanced grandeur. Everything moved through the city silently: people, machinery, and wildlife. Above all, Bestus was new. It *smelled* new. It was clean and sterile, like the finest dust-free mechanism, and she could imagine nothing that would rid her of that smell, other than leaving Barnard's World behind.

"Oh, Dave," she said.

"It's a bit overkill, isn't it?" he said to her.

Understatement.

Massive copper tubes larger than skyscrapers wrapped around the immediate city elegantly, connecting buildings, connecting the avenues to the buildings and stabilizing flashanalia powered by off-shoots that spiraled and shot out toward some unknown nexus in the distance, as if the city itself were one massive super computer or Memor sleep engine. The Helk influence was less obvious from here. She'd told Dave that Helk design reigned on the internal structure of Barnard's infrastructure, which included massive amounts of imported blackrock from Helkuntannas.

Forno was tapping the air with his heavy fingers, then drawing circles, then pinching the air as if he could pull it toward him.

"What are you doing?" she asked him.

Forno ignored her question.

"Dave, what is he doing?"

He shrugged. "A new dance routine?"

"It's good that *some*one knows how things work around here," Forno said, just as the air turned chrome and silver around his hands and morphed into a detailed interface outlined in white. It took less than a minute for the interface to expand, glowing with purpose and potentiality.

"How'd you know about this?" Dave asked. "Underworld secrets?"

"You learn about these things," Forno answered. "Maybe you just open your eyes. Maybe do a little research."

"I wasn't planning any off-world trips a few days ago."

"And look where that got us."

"Gentlemen," Dorie said, "can we figure out what we need to do and where we need to go?"

"*Working* on it," Forno said. "It's an information kiosk, half virtual, half physical, transparent 3D flashpaper lying in wait in hidden air receptacles."

"Memor magic," she said.

"Magic," the Helk said, "that should help us find our target, Heston Teska."

"How will that help?" Dave asked.

"The Morganism said he'd be easy to find. So I figure we just bring up the city's general information lookup and ask it."

Dorie doubted it. Everything in Bestus gleamed with promise, but you had to know the language. You had to understand what the interface was telling you. "It's silly, Forno. You can't expect that thing to just spit out—"

"Here he is," Forno said.

"*What?*" She squinted at the glowing interface, and she couldn't read a thing, but she saw a profile graphic of a Helk that looked huge. Hard to tell in a profile about actual size.

"That's Teska?" Dave said, coming closer to the interface.

"It's him. Second Clan. And his residence is listed on the grid. Actually not far from here. Like I said—" Forno stepped away from the air kiosk and it vanished, now tucked back into its air receptacle. "He'll be easy to find."

"But," Dorie said, "remember the part where he might not *want* to be found?"

"Then I guess we don't call ahead."

CROWELL

8 I FOLLOWED FORNO THROUGH THE STREETS OF BESTUS, DO-
rie beside me, and I was confident he knew where to go. I
was also confident because he was in front of us. He was a massive
walking shield. This was his thing.

The humans here seemed no different than on Earth in their
disregard for the Helk. Prejudice had no borders. They kept their
distance from him and cast sidelong glances at him; curiosity, dis-
like, and fear trailed in his wake. I glared back at them when I could.
I was shielded from their contempt in more ways than one.

The avenues twisted and turned, opposite of what I'd expected.
I'd expected an ordered, purposeful grid that mirrored the technological efficiency of several longstanding alien civilizations. Even
with the haphazard layout, we made general progress to the west.
We passed an open market that seemed more ordered than the surrounding streets. It was filled with tech sellers: dataheads, program-
mers, flash spammers, and the like. Dorie was intrigued by a booth
advertising portable, foldable transparent protection domes for in-
dividual use, but I steered her away from it. She'd just become free
of domes for a while, and she didn't need *that* distraction.

Forno had to duck under a low beam crossing the avenue as
we left the market behind. The avenue narrowed, becoming more
of an alley, the brightness dimming, the impossible buildings suddenly grayer. It was still early afternoon, but the sudden change in
light was alarming. The hair on the back of my neck stood up, and
I glanced behind me more often, worried about getting hemmed in.

Teska's location had been easy to pinpoint; he might not know
we were coming, but I didn't know what he'd do when he found
out. I scanned the buildings, craning my neck, searching windows,
doors, and nearly hidden nooks and crannies. With the buildings
closing in on us, the blaster in my coat pocket reassured me.

"This keeps narrowing," Dorie said. "Forno, are you sure we're going the right way? This seems like—"

"It's one way to get there."

"The best way?"

"I'm not sure at this point if there is a best way."

"Because?"

I answered. "Because they all lead to Teska."

Forno stopped. We all stopped. I watched Forno's shoulders, waiting. They rose slightly. He lifted his left arm and gave a signal only I would recognize. A curling of his fingers.

Shit.

In two seconds, I drew my blaster, powered it up, and raised it. I cradled it against my chest and waited. Dorie noticed, sidestepped closer to me, and froze. We were tucked in behind Forno, and anyone directly in front of him wouldn't see us. Our position behind him could be a good thing or a bad thing. I continued to watch his back. His left arm was still raised. I'd let Forno decide where he wanted us once he assessed the situation.

I chanced whispering. "What've we got?"

Three fingers.

"Where?"

Two fingers, forward. One finger up and left. At least no one was behind us. Yet. That was my job. I pivoted, still close to Forno, and scanned the avenue behind us.

Because the light had dimmed dramatically in the alley, it took a few seconds before I noticed a shadow near one of the nooks I'd taken note of earlier, twenty-five or thirty yards behind us. The shadow separated slightly from the wall, and I confirmed it was human. I saw no one else.

"One," I said. "Left. Thirty yards."

"Stay on him. Everyone needs to see each other, I think."

I agreed. "Dorie, slide right, move up to Forno, and keep facing the front."

She did, and I slid the other way, still looking back. I inched my blaster away from my chest a little.

"Now what?" Dorie whispered.

I asked, "Forno?"

"Could try that new dance number."

"We want something that won't get us killed," I reminded him.

"Oh. Right."

Dorie looked at him. "Seriously?"

"It worked to get us this far," Forno said.

"Not far enough, looks like," she said.

My guy stepped away from the wall enough to lean against it, his own weapon visible at his side. He wore a black leather coat that came to his waist, purple and green leggings, and a brown derby hat. So much for fashion sense.

I raised my voice and shouted, "We're looking for Heston Teska."

One of the men in front of Forno chuckled. "Keep looking. We've never heard of him."

"Maybe one of *you* is Teska," I said. I didn't actually believe that. What I did believe, early on in this encounter, was that they didn't expect us to reach Teska at all. I really believed they had orders to eliminate us. "You're the leader, aren't you?"

"Think so?" the voice said.

"Why don't you come out so we can see you? Have a civilized discussion?"

I heard footsteps. "Civilized?"

"Switch," I said softly.

Forno turned to face Bowler Hat, but Dorie stayed where she was. I turned to face the man who'd emerged into the narrow avenue. He wore a black longcoat that brushed the pavement, and the hood of his gray sweatshirt covered most of his face. He was taller than me, but certainly not taller than Forno. One other man was behind him, indistinct from this distance. They aimed their weapons. The man in the longcoat didn't have a weapon showing. I looked up and to the left and saw the man Forno had spotted earlier. His rifle tight against his shoulder, he looked through its scope, covering us.

Forno growled. "The guy in the back is closing." He raised his voice. "Stay back or I'll shoot your bottom."

That elicited a few laughs from Teska's men.

I held out my hands, trying to defuse the standoff. *We're all friends here.* Of course, I still had the blaster in my right hand. "See what I have to deal with?"

"What about the girl?" Longcoat asked.

I glanced at Dorie. "What about her?"

"Why's she with you?"

"Because she's with me. She's okay."

"Who says *you're* okay?" Longcoat asked. The man behind him raised his weapon higher. "I think my boys should just put you down now."

"Let me smack his lights out," Forno said.

"I *really* need to talk to Heston Teska," I said. "I've got a message for him. It's important." I put my blaster back in my right-hand coat pocket, kept my hand around it, then rummaged around with my left hand in my other pocket until I found the stack of Tarot cards Forno and I had collected. Earlier I'd put The Hermit on top, so I pulled it out and waved it at Longcoat. The light was dim enough that I didn't think Longcoat could see it very well.

"What is that?" the man said.

"Teska knows what this is, and why it's important. He knows how to find the one *I'm* looking for."

"But what *is* it?"

"See for yourself." I flicked the card at him.

It sailed right toward his head, until it somehow flipped and, its momentum lost, fell to the ground five feet in front of him. He bent down to pick it up.

"You've got *up*," I said, and pulled my blaster. To Dorie, I said "Down." The whine of my blaster powering back up prompted Forno, and he started shooting. Me too. A quick shot to the right of Longcoat, and his buddy fell. I heard a shot that might have come from the guy up above, but I was still standing without a hole burned through me.

I trained the blaster on Longcoat and held him there, mid-crouch. He gripped the Tarot card in his hand. "Stay right where you are, just like that," I said. "Forno?"

"Got both," he said.

"Dorie?"

"I'm okay."

A short gun battle was the best gun battle.

I took three steps forward, reached Longcoat, and put the blaster against his temple. Then I rummaged around in his coat until I found his weapon. A blaster similar to mine, though with considerably more firepower. You didn't find a weapon like that just anywhere on the street.

Longcoat still hadn't moved. He wasn't even cussing me out. I took The Hermit card from him, turned it so he could see the back, and said "Heston Teska. His name's right there. Your men are done. You're going to lead us the rest of the way."

He nodded, suddenly very compliant. The fight had gone out of him. I could tell it didn't make any sense to him to die here on this darkened Bestus alley.

"Any more of you?" I asked him.

"At the house, but you'll be okay with me."

"Take off that hood, for Christ's sake."

He did, but slowly. His hair was fiery red and cut short.

"What's your name?"

"Rob."

"How'd you know we were coming, Rob?"

Rob shrugged. "The kiosk. We have a lookup trace on it, and it alerted Teska when you looked him up."

Forno came up beside me. "Bloodshed. How fun was that?"

"Not too," I said. "You alerted them with your dance number."

"At least he was easy to find."

I turned to find Dorie had also come close. I handed her Rob's weapon. "Now you have one."

"Oh joy," she said, looking it over. She flicked a release, pulled the power cell out, snapped it back in, then gave it a half twirl until she had it snug in her grip and pointed at Rob, who backed up. He looked at Dorie with both surprise and worry. She closed one eye as if she were sighting down the barrel. "Do I *have* to have one?"

She knew her way around a blaster, that was for sure. "Nope," I said. "But then you aren't going any farther with us."

"Oh." She kept her aim steady at Rob's head and said, "Pew."

Rob flinched.

"And you *are* going with us," I said, "so it looks like you're stuck with it."

"You are one bad-bottom governor," Forno said to her.

"You mean bad-ass."

Forno grinned.

"Lead on," I said, waving Rob down the alley in the direction we'd been heading when we first entered it. "You saw what happened to the rest of your crew. If you fuck us over, send some kind of signal, or alert Teska in any way—"

"I won't," Rob said. "I mean, Jesus. You killed three of my men like *that*. And then you pinned me down. I *promise*." He said it to me, but he kept his eyes on Dorie the whole time. It was fear, I saw there. Maybe admiration.

Totally bad-bottom.

Turns out we'd been pretty close to Teska's compound when Rob and his men ambushed us. Five minutes after we started down the alley, we took a left turn and came to a tall but narrow doorway. Forno had a full two feet of head space when he passed through. We shuffled down a passage lit with old overhead fluorescents, then a similar doorway on the other end opened to a full, well-lit avenue again. The avenue led to a dead end, and there, surrounded by both marble pillars and green leafy trees, was the compound.

Compared to the rest of what we'd seen in Bestus—the tech-heavy glitz of the avenues and buildings and the disorienting structure—the compound was old-fashioned and reminded me of Earth during its better days. It was as if Teska had the same penchant for Earth nostalgia that I did. He was a Helk, though, not human, and that disconnect bothered me.

The largest structure was a white two-story plantation-style house with a red roof and a wraparound wooden porch and railing. A man and a woman stood on either end of the porch. The man was smoking a real cigarette, and a blaster sat on the railing in front of him. The woman had a rifle over her shoulder. I figured Teska had other security nearby. Probably some inside. My stomach churned, and I worried about being hemmed in again.

The size of the house surprised me, but the number of surrounding buildings—well, the size of the whole *compound*, actually—seemed over the top for someone like Heston Teska, a Helk I knew nothing about. Because Forno's access of the kiosk had led us right to him, we'd not taken any time to find a DataNet terminal to research him.

He'd been easy enough to find, but I bet I wouldn't dig up a lot about him on the DataNet; that is, if I could even locate and access a terminal.

We kept Rob in front of us and spread out behind him in a small V: Forno directly behind Rob with his Helk-sized blaster aimed at his head, and Dorie and I on the wings, blasters at our sides.

Rob raised his hands and waved them reassuringly, gesturing

that the two shooters on the porch should stand down.

The woman shrugged. A question.

"Here to see Teska," Rob said.

"So what?" she asked. "Why do they get to see him? They tripped the location trace. That's fishy. Why was nothing arranged?"

I took a chance and spoke up. "It's important. We have some—"

"Shut up," she said, "I'm not talking to you."

Huh. Okay. I shut up, but I was ready to enter overly-verbose mode at a moment's notice.

"Where are the others?" the man with the cigarette said.

"Dead," Rob said.

"Dead, how?"

"How the fuck do you think? Why do you think I'm standing here with these three and their blasters ready to take me out?"

"They're not getting in," she insisted. She stared at me with hard eyes and contempt. "If you manage to get past us, there are twice as many armed folks on the inside waiting to zip you up the moment you open fire. You won't have a chance, even with your sulky Helk here."

Forno snorted. "Sulky?"

Rob looked back at me. It seemed to be my cue to speak. "We don't want more bloodshed," I said. "It was unfortunate what happened earlier, but if we'd done nothing, we'd be dead."

She scoffed. "What's wrong with that?"

"We just need to talk to him."

"You're not talking to him."

Then Rob surprised me. He was still looking at me over his shoulder, but now he turned and held out his hand.

"Give it to me," he said.

I knew what he meant, and I didn't hesitate. I fished in my coat for the Tarot card and offered it to Rob. The Hermit. The card with Heston Teska's name on it.

Rob withdrew his hand without taking it and shook his head. "No. The other one."

I was taken aback. "The other one? *What* other one?"

Rob put out his hand again. "The other Tarot card. You know which one."

In the alley, Rob had held the Tarot card for just a few moments. He barely had time to glance at it. If he had enough time to see it was a Tarot card—if he even knew what one was—had he seen *which* Tarot card? Why would he know about any others, or assume we *had* any others?

I reached into my coat pocket again.

Dorie said, "Dave, no. You don't know what they'll do—"

"It's okay, Dorie," Rob interrupted. His eyes were soft and comforting as he looked at her.

What was going on? Every time Rob looked at her, I saw so many emotions crossing his face, it felt like someone else was controlling him.

"It's *not* okay," she said, frowning. "You've no idea what's going on, or why we must do this."

He *did* know something, though. That was the frustrating thing. I had no idea how he knew about the card, unless—

Morgan. Of course. *Morgan.* I'd bet anything he tipped Teska off somehow, told them I was coming. And if Teska knew, and Rob knew, then these two on the porch would know.

"Well, somebody say *some*thing," Forno said.

"Or do something," Rob added. His hand was still outstretched, waiting for the card.

Then I knew the real reason why he knew something.

Dorie.

Son of a bitch. He'd called her Dorie. No one had said her name since the moment we entered that alley. *He knew her.*

Or—he knew who she *was.*

I didn't hesitate any longer. I pulled out my partial deck of Tarot cards. I thumbed through them and found the right card.

"Dave. Please." Dorie's voice was distant.

I ignored it. "Here," I said, and handed the card to Rob.

Death.

"Ah," he said.

Bring Plenko Death.

Rob turned and walked to the porch.

"Be ready," I said to Forno. "I'm not exactly sure where this is going to lead us."

"You made a mistake, Dave," Dorie said.

"No, I don't think so." I gripped her shoulder but kept my eyes on the porch. "Just—just be ready."

The man on the porch had finished his cigarette. He threw it down and met Rob at the top of the stairs. The woman still had the rifle on her shoulder when she joined them. Rob held out the card so they could see.

The three of them looked back at us. The man and woman went back to their ends of the porch and Rob waved us up.

"Here we go," I said.

By the time we stepped onto the porch, Rob had the wide double doors open. "Wait," he said, and disappeared inside.

It happened so quickly, I didn't have time to object. We were now at the mercy of our weapon-toting bookends on the porch. We'd lost our "hostage"—if we could consider him a hostage at all. Our weapons were still drawn, but Bookend One and Bookend Two seemed in no hurry to zip us.

Rob reappeared without the Tarot card. "No weapons."

I shook my head. "We're keeping them."

"Put them away at least."

Dorie and Forno looked at me. In the silence, the porch seemed gigantic and the front door far away. It was disconcerting to stand there in that hushed tableau, everyone waiting on me to decide.

I nodded, and weapons disappeared into coat pockets or slipped into pants and under shirts, out of sight.

With a slight nod, Rob stepped aside, and that was our go-ahead to enter the house.

"Are you sure?" Forno asked. "You heard them. More firepower on the inside, our weapons hard to get to. A set up."

"No," Rob said. "It's safe. Teska's by himself. He's waiting for you. There's nothing to fear."

Famous last words. But I had a feeling.

"It's safe," I said. I was playing my hunch. Rob knew something about Dorie. He knew about the other card. Showing it to the Bookends seemed to pacify them. Heston Teska was ready to see us, and Rob had nearly guaranteed us safe passage. There really weren't too many other explanations as to why this was all so.

I took Dorie's hand and pulled her with me, ahead of Forno. She needed to be next to me when we talked to him. We crossed the threshold into the house. I heard Forno thump along behind me.

The front room was dim and dark, I thought, when I stopped and surveyed my surroundings. It was, but it wasn't so much because of the light. It was because the walls were dark. Almost matte black. I knew what I was looking at, having seen a lot of it last year.

Blackrock.

Thick slabs of it coated the walls. This wasn't that surprising. He'd told Dorie that Barnard's World incorporated internal Helk structures and design.

No, that wasn't surprising at all. What was surprising was the Helk standing in the middle of the room waiting for us. He held the Death card in his giant left hand. It wasn't *really* a surprise to me because I'd made a weak guess at it. But I imagined right now Forno, and most especially Dorie, were surprised as hell. Our entire mission on Barnard's had now changed, and maybe I should be happy about that. We'd been *looking* for a Second Clan named Heston Teska.

Except that he wasn't Heston Teska, and he wasn't Second Clan.

"Hello, Dorie," the Helk said.

It was Terl Plenko.

SENALL

9 THE THING ABOUT TERL PLENKO BACK ON RIBON, SHE RE-
membered, was that he never abandoned her. He drew her
back to him and tried to help her. No one else would have. This is
what she'd thought back then. This is what she thought after that
horrible day when he went missing on Coral. The day he disappeared from the Rock Dome.

But he *did* abandon me, Dorie thought.

It seemed a decade ago when she first told Alan Brindos her story. How she'd fallen victim to RuBy after Terl's disappearance. How
she'd lost time and became the pattern for a Thin Man. How Plenko
started his Movement of Worlds and became the most hated Helk
in the Union—the same Union he had sworn he loved passionately.

She learned the truth about Terl the Thin Man, head of the terrorist movement. He was a copy she'd gone to Temonus with, and he
was not *her* Plenko. She'd hoped beyond reason that her true husband would return to her. And if not, that he had died a brave death
and, right up to the end, fought against the violence that threatened
him. A fight in vain. The imposter, through his actions, cultivated
the now deep-seated distrust of those just like him.

But her Terl *had* abandoned her.

He hadn't died at the Rock Dome, or anywhere else, apparently,
whisked away by a Memor and deposited here. Instead of fighting
back, he'd withdrawn from the Union. He'd fled to Barnard's and
pulled the tech and chic around him like a blanket fort and hid.
From the Union, from the Ultras, from—

From *her*.

He stood in front of her now, in the gloom of a house coated
with blackrock. It pronounced his Helk heritage, but also sheltered
him from the Union. When Dave came to tell her about Terl being alive, she'd already known it. Lorway had told her. Lorway had
given up her Tarot card, then told Dorie that it was okay she'd never

had the chance to say goodbye to him. He was *not* dead. She needed to find him.

Death isn't death when it's a new beginning.

She wanted to find him. Wanted to with all her might, even though a slice of her heart had turned as black as these rock walls around her. She'd expected to feel this way. She'd *feared* she'd feel this way. She felt this disappointment, so she chose not to close the distance between them.

I'm frightened of what he's become.

She did not greet her husband with joy. Instead, she leaned a little closer to Dave Crowell.

Terl Plenko gave her some time. He didn't force this reunion on her too quickly, although he *had* done just that with this sudden appearance. But here, in this moment amidst the blackrock, she knew he held back, waiting. Waiting for her to say something.

Hello, Dorie.

Her reply should have been: *Where the fuck have you been?*

All she could manage was a half-whispered, "Terl."

He nodded slightly, still waiting for her to process this moment. He was Terl Plenko—*her* Plenko—and not the most infamous Helk ever known. She couldn't bring herself to rush and embrace him. Or slap him—if she could reach that high.

Dave broke the silence. "Well, *this* saves us some time."

Terl raised an eyebrow. "Dave Crowell, I presume."

Dave nodded, but said nothing.

If he knew who Dave Crowell was now, it was via reputation. Dave had never met the real Helk in person, only his copies. The Movement of Worlds Leader, for one, but also his *partner*.

She shivered. They *had*, however, been in the same building at the same conference on the very day the Ultras did their thing.

"Who's this?" Terl said, pointing at Forno.

"My partner," Dave said. "You don't look anything like your profile picture. Not that I'm good at telling Helks apart."

"Oh, sure," Plenko said. "I'm going to put *my* face on my profile picture."

Forno spoke up. "I'm Tem Forno,"

"I've heard of you." He waved his free hand at them. "Both of you made quite the name for yourselves."

"It hasn't helped pay the bills," Dave said.

"Things are a little old-fashioned on Earth these days, I hear."

"Also, things are a little sparse."

Terl nodded and glanced at Dorie. She had a feeling he would force the issue now, and he did. He'd waited long enough. He took a tentative step toward Dorie, and that was all it took. Dorie felt something let loose inside her, love taking over, and she came to him and wrapped her arms around his torso the best she could.

"Oh my God, Dorie," Terl said.

She asked her question now, but without anger, head still buried in Terl's fur. "Where have you *been*?"

"Complicated," he said. "You deserve to know. And you will. But not now, I think."

It felt electric, his presence. His scent, the texture of his fur, the looking up at his face—always the constant looking up!—and not caring one bit. Holding him after all this time. *After all this time*! She pulled back and frowned at him, not happy about waiting to hear where he'd been.

He had the Death card, small in his hand. "There are matters Mr. Crowell would like to discuss."

"Honestly," Dave said, "it could wait if you two need to catch up."

"I don't think it can," he said.

Dorie thought: *No, it can't*. But everything had led her and Dave to this moment. Morgan hired Dave to find Terl Plenko. Lorway handed her the Tarot card. Dave and Forno travelled to Ribon. She resigned the governorship of New Venasaille amidst a volatile political situation. They slotted to Barnard's World.

Now, here they were.

She shrugged. *Go ahead*, it meant.

Terl said to Dave, "Do you know what this is?" He held the Death card a little higher.

"Besides a Tarot card?"

"Besides a Tarot card."

"No, I really don't."

"Lorway gave it to me," Dorie said. The conversation with the Memor was still fresh in her memory. "I didn't understand at all why she had it, or why I should give it to Dave."

"But now you do," Terl said.

"To help find you."

"Well," he said. "I hoped so. But I didn't know Lorway had the card, or when you'd get it, if you even did, or if Crowell here found it, and figured out what it all meant. And he *did* figure it out, and it cost me a few of my men."

"And I still don't know what it all means," Dave said.

"You didn't know Lorway had it?" Dorie asked Terl, surprised. "But you gave it to her, didn't you?"

"But," Dave said, "she told me my dad set it up."

He hadn't told her that. "He did? But you—"

"Yeah, I kept that to myself." He looked at Terl. "Sorry about your crew out there. But they were ready to put us down."

Terl nodded. "I know. It happened. You're here now."

Dave spread his arms. "So. The card?

Terl paused. Dorie could barely see the card, almost invisible in her husband's meaty hand. Terl looked at Forno. He looked at Dorie. He looked down at the card.

"Can we talk in private?" Terl asked Dave.

Excluding her, Dorie thought. She was not important in this. She'd simply held onto the card for a short period of time. She was not in the inner circle. Not in the discussion about anything related to this.

She felt useless.

Abandoned. She couldn't quite get over that feeling.

Dave said, "Sure, let's talk."

Terl led Dave to the back of the blackrock room. Dorie watched them until they disappeared through a cut-away door in the in the ten-foot-high walls.

Forno found a spot on a Tem Forno-sized couch and ignored her. Dorie stared at the doorway where Terl disappeared, worried for a moment that she would lose him again, like she had on Coral, once again without a goodbye. Terl was with Dave though. He'd be okay. Dave would be okay.

She looked back and saw Rob; she wondered when he'd entered the house. He stood at the front door, leaning against the jamb. She had questions for him. Questions about Heston Teska, and how he'd come to be. How Teska—Terl Plenko—had escaped notice these last few years, when it had been as easy as a kiosk lookup to find him.

Yes, but three of his men died protecting his identity. Not an easy feat, then, for those unfortunates trying to find him. She wondered how many had tried and failed.

Rob stared back at her with amusement, as if he expected her questions. They were questions he probably wouldn't answer. But it was worth a try.

"How have you done it?" she asked him. "Protected him this long? In this house, of all places? It's anything but subtle."

Forno rolled his giant head toward her, curious, then saw Rob at the door. "That crossed my mind too," he said.

He'll grin, smirk, or frown, Dorie thought, and he'll say nothing. It wasn't as if he'd give away the secrets to this not-so-secret hideaway. But he surprised her.

Rob straightened. "Who said we have?"

*Some*one knew about Terl, that meant. Someone besides them. Then she remembered. "You mean Dave's client."

"Client?"

"A guy named Morgan. He hired Dave to find Terl."

Rob nodded. "Oh sure, Morgan. We know about him. He had a few Tarot cards. I thought you meant someone else."

"Who else would there be?"

Forno sat up. He looked alert, and more interested in the conversation now.

"Well," Rob said, "the *client*."

Now it was her turn. "Client? You just said—"

Rob interrupted her, shaking his his head. "The one who hired *Morgan*."

"Dorie," Forno said. "Listen . . ."

Rob continued. "The Client hired Morgan to find Terl and bring him to face justice. To execute him. For real, this time."

Dorie glared at Forno, appalled at what she'd just heard.

"Yeah," Forno said. "We kind of didn't tell you that part."

"Morgan hired Dave to bring Terl back?" Anger rose in her, and she fought to keep it under control. "To *kill* him?"

"The Morganism didn't say that," Forno said. "He said bring Death to Plenko."

"But bring him back."

"Yeah, but we didn't know what for."

"You agreed."

"We took Morgan's money," Forno said. "Look. We came and got *you*. You think we'd just roll over for Morgan? Give in to his goddamn boss, whoever he is?

"It doesn't matter," Rob said. "Whatever Plenko tells Crowell in that other room, that's more important. I don't know the details, but everything depends on it."

"Goddamn it!" Dorie shouted, her nerves all jangled, the pressure behind meeting Terl after all this time fluttering in her heart like a fledgling bird. "It *does* matter. I just found him. I may not understand why all this happened, but he's my husband, and I deserve to know why this is happening to him."

Rob's eyes were wide after her outburst, but he just said, "You will."

Dorie crossed her arms like a child waiting to get her way. "I'm not turning Terl in."

Rob said, "It's okay, Dorie. He *wants* to go back."

CROWELL

10 TO MY THINKING, IT WASN'T TERL PLENKO STANDING IN front of me. It was Alan Brindos. My partner, subjected to a torturous transformation from human to Helk in an Ultra-devised plan to create hybrid bodies so the aliens could live in our matter universe so opposite to their antimatter one. They were dying in their universe.

Brindos's death seemed a proper symbol of the finality of the Ultras and their universe. He had sacrificed himself for the good of the Union, just as the human copy of him, Vanderberg Parr, had sacrificed himself on Rook to save me and, ultimately, the Union yet again. I rubbed my gray hair, remembering the travel between universes and its effect on me.

Parr, who had essentially become the type of hybrid the Ultras had hoped for, cast us with his nearly pure RuBy essence to the abandoned jump slot station where Greist had long been imprisoned. With Greist's and Terree's help, I'd destroyed the tether that anchored their worlds, denying the Ultras and sending their universe, and my dad, hurtling away from us forever.

There'd been way too much death and confusion these last two years.

"Do you want to sit?" Plenko asked as he sat down in his own gigantic chair.

The room looked, in many ways, the same as the main room they'd just come from, but this one, which was smaller, seemed more hospitable to humans. More chairs my size, lower ceilings, and wooden planks peeking through the more decorative blackrock.

I sat across from Plenko in one of the smaller chairs and waited. The two chairs were uncomfortably close to one another, and Plenko's chair threatened to overwhelm me, like a giant wave about to crash. Plenko still held the Death card, which he passed neatly around and through his fingers, one by one, as if he were a magician.

"You and Dorie," I said. "Maybe you should—"

"I thought we came in here to talk about your problem," Plenko said.

"We did, but it seems strange considering the—circumstances. The history between you two. The whole 'oh-I'm-not-dead' thing."

"Let's talk about the card," he said, ignoring my efforts to understand his reluctance to talk about Dorie.

At the same time, I was having difficulty seeing Plenko other than the way I remembered him last: as my partner falling when my blaster put him out of his misery and cleared a path to get to the terrorist version of Plenko.

This Helk was Dorie's Plenko, and yet he wasn't reacting to Dorie's presence, and she'd come so far to see him. Why wouldn't he talk with her first? Why was he so standoffish with her? He was hiding something. Something he didn't want her to know.

Plenko was waiting for me to say something, so I broke my thoughts and talked about the death card. "That card isn't for Tarot, is it?" I asked.

He shrugged. "Well it *could* be. Functional. If you had a full deck, that is. A Tarot deck is a Tarot deck, whether it's simplistic or insanely, creatively funny, or, in this case, extremely complicated. But this is why you're here. You don't have the cards you need, do you?"

"I've been collecting them, and you probably know that. I've a lot of them now."

"An impressive feat, considering how they were scattered. You don't need them all, though. Just the Major Arcana—"

"I know. Both Morgan and Lorway told me." I pulled the deck from my coat pocket. My blaster was there too, and I felt secure knowing I could draw it quickly if needed. "I've a lot of the Minor Arcana, but Morgan said they weren't worth anything."

"Except for two."

"Let me guess. Two that I don't have."

Plenko nodded.

"But they're just cards," I said. "What's so special about them? I've tried to read significance into their historical meanings, symbols and fortunes and—"

"They're not just cards. They're more than you could dream up."

"I don't know. I could dream up a hell of a lot."

Plenko leaned forward a little, his head a mere foot away from mine. He held the card up. The image on it still made me shudder. *All those bodies under foot.* "Look at the border around it. Hard-wired into the partially plasticized card material along the border—though not all four sides, the cards open-ended at different edges—is a thin wire infused with nano ink and encoded with the energy of an Ultra."

I shuddered at the mention of the thin wire. And Ultra. Old associations died hard.

"Enclosed, controlled antimatter," he said.

"Shit," I said, thinking about Alex Richards and his Ultra tattoo. About Baren Rieser and his own inked numbers to quantum travel between worlds. About Vanderberg Parr, who'd become a hybrid, more Ultra than human in his ability to travel or send others traveling, powered by saturated, pure RuBy. Lost on Rook when the House and the portal disintegrated.

"You understand, I see," Plenko said.

"I'm starting to."

"Each card's wire includes DNA strands and profiles specific to the maker of the card, and the card itself has another unique quality. Have you really looked at one close?"

"I thought I had. I've studied these things for so damn long, I don't even know what I'm looking at anymore. We were going to have some of them analyzed but never got the chance."

I took the top card—it was still the Hermit, the card with Heston Teska's name scrawled on it—and squinted at it.

"No," Plenko said. "*Really* look at it. Deeply into it. Past the image. What do you see?"

I let my eyes relax, unfocused and gazed deeper at the card. At the background. At the material. Partially plasticized, he'd said. If only partially, then what else was it made of? I rubbed my fingers on it at the same time, concentrating on its feel for the first time. Somewhere in the card was the encoded wire. I doubted I could see it, but by zooming in and conceptualizing the texture, I believed I understood. I knew that texture. The unfocused visual of the surface, deconstructed into its colored pixels, or old-fashioned bitmapped colored dots, took on a dominant color.

Red.

On a whim, I put the card against my nose and took a long, deep sniff.

Plenko laughed.

I shook my head. "What?"

"Processing and manufacturing of the cards would've completely rendered the drug inert. No cinnamon smell."

RuBy. The sheer audacity of creating a seemingly simple Tarot card out of a partially illegal alien drug—one that also had roots in the Ultra universe—broke the rules of credibility.

It wasn't difficult to intuit where this Tarot thing was leading, and Plenko's expression meant he knew I was coming to an understanding.

"Somehow," I said, "this card will mimic the effect of quantum sleep. The ability to travel."

"So goes the theory."

"*Theory*?"

Plenko shrugged. "Not like it's been tested."

"You're kidding."

He waved a hand, a gesture that was part you-take-what-you-can-get and part maybe-I'm-not-kidding. "There might have been some single-card testing, Minor Aracana only, with DNA coded to a test subject or two."

"Who were all the Major Arcana cards made for?"

"That part should be pretty obvious, Mr. Crowell."

"You're going to say they were made for me."

He nodded.

For me. Why? Who would've taken the time to do such a thing? Greist? He'd been instrumental in the memory block, pushing me out of harm's way after the conference in Chicago. Was it another plan to trick the aliens he'd helped?

"The coding," I said. "In the wire. Whose DNA?"

"That should also be obvious."

It was, once he *said* it was obvious. "DNA of the creator. DNA of the artist. Jesus. *You* made them."

He nodded.

"*All* of them?"

"Except for three Greist made before the conference." A slight smile crossed his leathery face.

"For me. Why? I mean . . . *when*?"

Terl Plenko leaned back in his giant chair, eyes up and to the left, as if recalling everything from a far away, barely there memory. Probably a trick of the light, or maybe the angle of his massive body sitting in the chair that gave me that impression. He didn't need to access any memories. He knew.

"After the conference," he said.

"You were there in Chicago. You were young. Already on the path to DNA coding. Greist put you up to it. The same way he manipulated me and blocked my memory."

"Even then," Plenko said, his voice wistful, "Greist understood how the Ultras thought. He made so many back doors and Plan B's that no one could keep track of them. You know about most of them."

Forno and I had always joked about the next plan, Plan B, and how many Plan B's there could possibly be. "I didn't know about *this* one."

"Not much of a back door if everyone knows about it."

"You made the deck, altered the Major Arcana and parceled them out to keep them safe. Challenge me, with a little coaxing, to figure it out if things went awry with the Ultras."

"More or less."

"All while in hiding."

"Necessity."

I recalled my visit to the Emirates Building. "McCarthy at the Emirates said he saw Greist give Morgan a card. That was one that Greist made, then?"

"It was. Designed to be a signal card."

"To signal *me*."

The depth of Greist's manipulation of the scene and the people at the conference continued to amaze me.

"And so," I said, playing out the narrative, "you go through your life making these cards—or maybe you made all of them at once—your work in DNA locks proceeds, you meet Dorie, and soon she's a RuBy addict, and you're found out in some way by the Ultras, who copy you. You manage to escape them, elude them, and set up the trip to Coral with Dorie to tour the facility. Along the way, with the Science Consortium's help, you're snapped up and taken away."

"Pretty close."

"Lorway took you."

He nodded.

"Coral blew, you triggered the signal to initiate the *Exeter* incident, and while everyone chased the Movement of Worlds Plenko, you were whisked to safety. Here."

"Good work, detective."

"I still don't understand *why*," I said.

"Like I said. A back door. Greist's station that helped tether the universes? The second blackrock house on Rook? The whole fiasco from last year? It was a perfect backup. Except for the fact that we still did not get back everyone lost to the Ultras."

"Including my dad."

"Especially him."

"So this is your motivation with all this? To find my dad? To . . . to bring him *back*?"

"Him and others who went over there. But mostly him."

I didn't know if Plenko had any idea why, but I wasn't going to find a better time to ask. "What was it the Ultras wanted from him? Why did they find him so special?"

His response was immediate. "He was Lucky Lawrence."

"Yeah, I *know* that. He was called that long before the Ultra scare."

"No, I mean, that's why. He was the Ultra's good luck."

"C'mon," I scoffed. "This was an advanced race developing ways to hybridize Ultras and humans. Create portals and nano ink. You can't seriously tell me they decided they needed a good luck charm. What the hell for?"

"You know what I know," Plenko said. He stood now, towering over me before turning away and heading to the back of the room. He retrieved an ornate box from a hidden receptacle that revealed itself with the touch of his finger.

"And did he survive?" I asked. "Him or the others?" My breath caught a little, hoping for the right answer.

"No way to know. But if he did, we figured one person could get to him and find out what he knew. Understand, we didn't know much about the Ultras when all this started. But we knew a little about their universe."

Elbows on my knees, I buried my face in my hands. I rubbed my eyes with the heels of my palms and tried to lessen the tiredness and frustration buried there. The inevitable conclusion of this plan sucked, but it was the most hope I'd felt in a long time. It was a plan designed for me, and I knew what was coming next.

"You want me to find out, don't you?"

"Whether he's alive? Yes. This is what you want, isn't it? You searched and gathered most of a Tarot deck for this without any idea of how it would work. It was just a hunch."

Plenko sat again, and as soon as he was comfortable, he handed his box to me.

"What's this?" I asked.

"The next step."

"Which is what?"

"Travel."

The box contained a card, I was certain. A card like the others, partially constructed of RuBy with a coded wire running though it with Ultra stuff embedded within. That wasn't weird at all.

"You understand?" Plenko asked.

"If I'm going to find my dad, I have to quantum travel—sleep travel—to the antimatter universe of the Ultras."

He simply gestured, indicating the box with an upturned palm.

I opened it and found a new Tarot card.

The Tower.

Talk about a creepy, disconcerting card. A tower struck by lightning, fire coming from its windows, two figures falling, presumably to their deaths. I'd looked into it a little, but mostly, besides the references to the spiritual world and a physical place, I could not help but think of the six towers of the Transcontinental Conduit. Perhaps the eventual downfall of humankind, or maybe the Ultras, who'd strove to build a symbolic antimatter house in our world of matter.

"You kept this one for the end game," I said. "My reward for getting this far."

"It's not the end game, but it will, if all goes well, get you there."

"How can it? The sleep travel only worked because the universes were tethered. The Ultra universe has moved, theoretically, a great distance. How can that jump work?"

"You mention theory, and you're right. I can't guarantee anything, but it *should* work, with all the cards in combination. There's enough plasticized RuBy in all the cards, with the entirety of wire within, to do the trick, if it's the right person traveling."

"And how does that work? How am I the right person?"

"I made them for you. This one—" He indicated the Tower "—is coded with your own DNA taken in Chicago."

I felt the weight of all this pressing down like the G-forces from a transport rocketing out toward a jump slot station. Trusting some plastic cards to transport me between universes was an awful risk, and seemed wildly silly, but hell, Plenko was right. Wasn't this what I'd wanted? A chance to find my dad? Wasn't this the reason why I'd started the search for the Tarot cards?

"You think you can do it?" Plenko asked.

"If you think there's a chance, yes. But where will I go? Don't I need a target? If I'm thrown into the middle of their antimatter universe, I'll just cause a matter and antimatter explosion that'll destroy their universe."

"Or a nice chunk of it."

"They're already dying," I said. "They don't need me to force the issue because a few humans might be alive over there."

"You *do* have a place to go. You'll be able to visualize it."

"Where?"

"The Tower," he said.

Not the Conduit towers then. The only other reference I could think of—

"You mean Rook," I said, incredulous.

"Not Rook itself. The House."

"But that's all gone. Destroyed, by Cara's own death explosion. After Vanderberg Parr sent us on to Greist, he found some way to use Cara's impending destruction to torch the whole thing and sever the portal connection."

"He probably did. But not all of it."

He didn't offer more, and I searched my brain, scrambling for an answer. As I did, Plenko leaned back and smoothed the fur on his limbs.

"The one place both human and Ultra," he said. "The only place you could go and survive—theoretically—and the only place we know of that could withstand a serious antimatter explosion."

It made perfect sense. The same place I'd sleep traveled to before. "The Pool Room. It's the damned Pool Room."

"And from there you'll find a way to the heart of the Ultra's worlds."

That sent a chill up my spine. "And how will that happen?"

He just smiled.

"Another—" I laughed. "I have to find *another* card. Where now? Orgon? Memory? Because travel around the Union is totally my favorite thing."

He shook his head. The way he did it, with a look of sympathy and a tightening of his lips, revealed the truth.

"Fuck," I said. "Find a card in the *Ultra* universe? Really?"

"Find two of them." He stood again with a sense of finality. Our talk was nearly over. "Greist made two others besides the one he gave Morgan."

"What cards?"

"Unknown."

"So I should talk to him. Find out who he gave them to."

"No. I know who he gave them to. It was Baren Rieser."

Baren Rieser, killed by Abby Graff on Rook. I shook my head. "Nothing is ever easy."

"As you said, that part of Rook was seared by The Landry when her antimatter core blew."

"Those bodies would've vaporized."

"And the cards wouldn't have survived either, *unless* they were in the Pool Room for some reason."

I raised an eyebrow in question.

"Yes. You'll be stuck. Even if you figure out a path to your dad, assuming you can survive *that*, I don't know how you're going to get back."

I took the news fairly well. I had no other choice but to go. If I found my dad, if I couldn't get back, I'd still call it a success. I was ready for the consequences, just to see him.

"There's always a chance, of course," Plenko said.

"Can't get any worse."

"Actually?"

Plenko stared at me as if truly seeing me for the first time. No— he was *studying* me. Studying my face.

"Oh hell," I murmured.

"It's about the traveling. It works just like last time, except the distance is greater."

I saw it coming. I closed my eyes.

"The side effect of quantum travel," he said. "You'll be quite an old man when you arrive."

SENALL

11 WHEN DAVE AND TERL CAME OUT OF THE BACK ROOM, DORIE sighed in relief. She'd half expected them to have a disagreement, come to blows, or if not that, slip surreptitiously out the back on their own mission, leaving her here with Forno, Rob, and Terl's other cronies on the porch. Terl smiled at her, and she felt reassured.

Dave, on the other hand, looked like he'd just attended a funeral. His eyes searched the floor, he walked slightly stooped, and his complexion looked like he'd spent days in some dark room by himself. If I'd had to guess, he was having a silent conversation with himself.

Forno picked himself up off the couch and came to Dave, concerned. "You okay?" he said.

Dave looked up, seemed to notice the room for the first time, and shrugged. "Not really," he said. "But we need to talk."

"We *all* need to talk," Plenko added. "Rob?" He made a slight motion with his head and Rob left the house, joining the other two on the porch.

Dorie felt the tension take over the room as the four of them faced each other in a loose square. She made eye contact with Terl but didn't say anything.

"Mr. Crowell is going on a dangerous journey," Plenko said. "He's going to the Ultra universe."

Dorie should've jumped halfway out of her skin with this news. But no. She'd known this would happen, hadn't she? If Dave wanted to find his dad, he wasn't going to find him around here. Not around the Union, not around their universe.

"I'm going with Dorie," Plenko said. "Morgan is working with someone who wants me to pay for the crimes of the Movement of Worlds Plenko. I don't know who Morgan's client is, or why they think they have the power to make that stick, but I'll go and take care of that. I think it's more bluster than blunt force. I'm not worried."

"Terl," Dorie said, "you don't know what they've planned.

They've had all this time to prepare. You can't go. It's not *wise.*"

"It's time, Dorie." He looked at her tenderly and she lowered her eyes, unable to handle that sentiment. "I need to come clean. The Union *needs* Terl Plenko now. They all know the false Plenko is dead. They'll understand what happened."

"I'm not worried about the Union," she said. "I'm worried about this client and what he'll do. He and his followers will operate under a different set of rules for you. You *know* that."

"A risk I have to take." He put a hand to his broad chest. "I'm Terl Plenko. Not a terrorist. Not a Thin Man."

"I'll go along," Forno said. "I can help. In sheer brute strength, two Helks are better than one."

"No, go with Crowell."

Dave hadn't said a word since his meeting with Terl. Dorie wanted to know what the hell they'd talked about in there. What had Dave found out about the Tarot cards? About his dad? Whatever it was, it wasn't good. She knew that much just by looking at him.

"He can't go with me," Dave said.

Dorie shivered to hear his voice now, challenging Plenko's authority. This was the Dave she knew.

"This is *my* journey," he said. He directed the words at Terl. "I have to do this on my own. Those cards were made for me. No one else should have to risk their lives for me."

"Except for me, partner," Forno said.

Terl said, "He'll only go with you part way."

"But why at all?" Dave said.

"You can't initiate the travel here," Plenko said. "You don't have a person—like a Memor—to help you visualize and lend you power."

"What do we have then?"

"A noisy world."

"That's a bad thing?"

"You must get clear of the planet. Clear of the atmosphere. You attempt the journey utilizing these cards, so you'll need a way to slingshot from a normal relaxed state to the pure essence needed to travel."

Dave shrugged. "Tell me what that means in plain terms."

"You need zero interference, and you need a boost."

"*Still* not plain."

Dorie wondered what Dave would have to go through for this

trip. On the surface, it seemed he was ready and willing to go, seemed to be taking it all in stride, but she wondered if he was tapping down the part of him who didn't believe something good could come out of this. A trip to the *Ultra* universe, for god's sake. All this talk about interference and boosts confused her.

"It's simple," Plenko said. "Go off-world. You need to create a portal and use it to focus the cards, until Mr. Crowell's destination becomes clear. You need a jump slot."

Dave said, "I'm sorry, but what?"

"A jump slot. You need to illegally run a jump slot and take over a station to focus the energies of the sleep travel."

"Take over a station?" Dave said.

"Pretty much," Plenko said.

The four of them hashed out the early details of a plan, keeping Rob and the others out of it. Dorie thought it a wise precaution.

How did you take over a station? Dave's goal involved slotting to a station to travel somewhere other than where it normally sent passengers.

Another universe.

As they moved from the easy part of the plan—getting off Barnard's World—and on to the bigger questions—which jump slot and station would be the easiest to take over (if that distinction even existed)—Dorie found that she'd unconsciously inched closer to Terl.

Her pent-up anger at his choice to disappear and stay hidden from her, as well as her fear of what he had become, slowly dissipated, although she wasn't at all sure why. Perhaps, because they were all equals here, discussing an audacious plan—getting Dave to the Ultra universe in one piece—that outwardly had no real chance at succeeding. She believed Terl really *had* understood as far back as that encounter with Ultras in Chicago that what needed to be done now required him to vanish back then from the Rock Dome and leave her alone. Abandon her.

A widow, she'd thought.

She hadn't been alone for a while now. Not since the new domes went up and she became the governor of New Venasaille. Terl had been absent from her thoughts, but others had taken his place, such as Aditya Thakur, and Ross, her political backers, and new acquaintances she'd met outside the offices of the Brindos Building.

She'd learned to live without Terl.

He was here now, though. He was in earnest about helping Dave. He wanted to help her. He believed he could do some good by revealing himself now to the Union.

I'm not a Thin Man.

This was all okay. She could believe him, even though she held onto some doubts. She could work with him, and she *would* do whatever she could to return the favor and help *him*. Leaving Dave behind to do what he needed to do seemed wrong, but the plan seemed set. As a plan, it was insane. Suicidal, in fact. The question still remained: Could she go with Terl, let Dave do his thing, and find peace with it?

She glanced at Terl, then took a step toward him. This time it was a conscious effort.

There weren't *that* many jump slots in the Union. Each of the eight worlds had one, and depending on the insertion codes, you could get to any of them from any of the others. However, the Memors had also built long-range multi-use jump slots that were intermediate between some of the worlds. One of them was between Barnard's and Memory.

Not many people knew about these jump slots. Dorie did, having learned of them while governor of New Venasaille. Some ships, equipped with proprietary Memor technology, had the capability to make last minute decisions to veer from the existing slot between worlds to these intermediate slots and direct the ships to a different world altogether or, if needed, return to the planet of origination.

Dave had told her about the jump slot Greist built in the space between the human universe and the Ultra universe. That was where they *found* Greist, the Memor who took on the job of building the accompanying station in a forbidden place, out of the loop, with no berths for ships and no obvious use, except as a portal between worlds. It had balanced there dangerously close to the fluctuating slot. It had been an anchor to hold the spheres in place so that matter and antimatter did not cancel out the entirety of their universes.

That jump slot station might have been a good out-of-the-way slot to commandeer, but it had disintegrated when Vanderberg Parr brought the Cara Landry body, with a malfunctioning antimatter core, into the House to destroy the portal and untether the worlds at the cost of his own life.

"Seems to me we want one of the intermediate slots then," she said. "It has a skeleton crew, and although they have berths, very few ships use them."

"Why don't they?" Dave asked.

"Since the trick is to alter course and slide to another slot, and almost no traffic comes there to cause anyone to wait, there's no reason to sit and wait for a spot in the queue to open up."

"All makes sense," Forno said, "but there's a big problem that makes getting there near impossible."

Dorie knew what he meant. "The ships that access these slots have Memor slot drive tech that allows the shift."

"Certainly the *Sinai* is out," Dave said. "It's a basic transport that gets folks from slot A to slot B, nothing fancy, and it wouldn't have the infrastructure to even handle a Memor upgrade."

"Oh, well then, no problem," Forno said sarcastically. "We just hijack a Memor ship, right?"

Terl had said nothing during this exchange, and that made Dorie wonder. Was he searching his brain for answers or just passively listening to them debate whether they had a chance of getting to the intermediate jump slot or not?

Now he gazed pointedly at Forno and nodded. "Good plan."

Forno said, "No, no. I was *kidding*."

"Dorie's right. It's the only way to get there." He held up his hands, palms up. "Unless you want to take over one of the main jump slot stations."

"We did it before," Dave said.

Forno waggled his hand. "Well, *sort* of. With a little help from an NIO agent."

"*I* was an NIO agent," Dave said.

"Yeah, but Jennifer had more pull. And you'll remember we were on the run. You know—for treason and all that."

"Point taken."

"And we didn't take it over. We basically ran through it, working our way through Ultras and transformed Helks to get to a transport to take through the slot."

"You've had some experience then," Terl said. "That'll make things easier at the intermediate jump slot."

Dorie hoped something could make things easier to hijack a Memor transport to cross *over* to the slot. If anyone could find a way, it was probably Terl, but she didn't know how long he'd been out of the loop while in hiding. She wasn't sure he'd be able to help in this instance. Maybe Dave could contact Jennifer. Call in a favor.

As if in answer to her thoughts, Terl said, "I know a guy."

"A guy who knows about a Memor ship?" Dave asked.

Terl nodded.

"One equipped to get us to the intermediary station?" Forno asked.

He nodded again.

"I'm guessing he'll be hard to find," Dorie said. She was ready to believe him, but the voice inside her head kept doubting. "Hard to convince him."

"On the contrary," he said. "I know right where to find him, and he'll do what I say. Without argument."

So he *did* have some reach outside this compound, Dorie thought. A reach that showed his hand without revealing his face.

"We need him," Dave said, "so I say contact him. Who is he?"

"Someone you know a little about," Terl said.

"Yeah?"

"You've been looking for him."

Dave thought a second, but soon enough, a smile spread across his face. "Heston Teska."

Terl nodded and Dorie realized the truth. She said, "You took over Heston Teska's identity, took over his compound, remained anonymous. You have something on him."

"A little," Terl said. "You don't need to know what. We worked things out. He's ready to jump when I say jump. This way, that way. He's my arms and legs outside this compound."

The room fell silent as it sunk in. The hush extended longer than was comfortable for Dorie. Probably for everyone.

Forno broke the silence. "I *knew* something good would come out of my dance number."

CROWELL

12 I HEADED OUT WITH FORNO AN HOUR AFTER PLENKO TOLD us the news that Heston Teska was real. He was a First Clan Helk like Plenko, living in a city outside Bestus we *thought* we'd be led to so we could find *Plenko*.

Wanting to lay low until he left with Dorie for Earth, Plenko sent word ahead to Teska we were coming, then saddled us with one half of the bookends from the porch as an escort and guide. The woman with the rifle was named Emma, and she was none too happy about chaperoning us; she left the rifle at the compound in favor of a blaster, but I imagined a scenario that involved her sitting behind us in the transport so we couldn't see her, the ominous rifle never leaving her shoulder.

The transport was a four-seater hopter from Plenko's compound. It was probably Teska's, but it seemed that Plenko had the run of his place, and that included his transports. The hopter was good for short jaunts, city to city, and Teska lived in Gottelburg, a major city just two hundred miles west of Bestus. Emma piloted—there went the rifle scenario—and I took the back seat. Forno sat up front to her left. Although Emma was used to being around First Clan Helks, Forno could still knock her out the hopter window with one good pop on her jaw if needed. The hopter would crash, and we'd be dead, but Forno would think it worth it to get back at Emma's smugness and constant grumbling about chauffeuring us around Barnard's. I bet she really wished she could have shot us during that first confrontation.

The hopter, seemingly open air, was protected by a transparent bubble that in its rest state mimicked helicopters from 21st Century Earth. It was smaller, faster, and more maneuverable, and the bubble morphed in the same way transport bubbles on TWT flights locked in both pilot and course through the jump slots, but without lockouts, trackers, and insertion equations. The bubble left its rest state and transformed to a shape of optimum aerodynamic efficiency, matching the hopter's flight vectors, programmed to respond to changing atmospheric conditions.

Plenko sent us to Teska, he said, because Teska's contacts in Gottelburg had located a Memor transport and had it hidden away. Teska and his men could operate in secret and Plenko could stay off the grid. We didn't have to tell Rob, Emma, or anyone else in Plenko's camp about why we needed the Memor ship, or anything about my ultimate mission, and the same held true for Teska and his men. To all of them I was just a nuisance. I had Plenko's blessing, however, and that was all that mattered.

Teska would meet us on the outskirts of Gottelburg at an abandoned hangar that used to house surplus parts from damaged slot beams, wheels, and other discarded machinery from the jump slots. Those parts were huge, obviously, and they demanded a gigantic space. The hangar was empty now. Where all that shit had ended up, I didn't know, and neither did Emma, but the result was a place perfect to house something huge you didn't want seen, like a Memor transport capable of sliding sideways from an existing slot to an almost unguarded slot.

The hangar didn't show up on most ship's tracking systems, and was easily missed on visual, and that made it even more valuable for Teska's little secret. I was reminded of Plenko's House on Helkuntannas you could easily miss due to its clever integration into the blackrock cliffs outside Khrem. Of course, he'd also had a disorienting datascreen shooing off visitors. Teska had no desire to call attention to his hangar, and a datascreen was not subtle.

Emma maneuvered the hopter around the outer limits of Gottelburg and made her way knowingly to the hangar, the coordinates already locked in to her display. We were slowly losing light as the day wore on. By the time we'd left the city behind, only a scattering of homes and warehouses dotted the lush and green landscape that rolled and yawed beneath the hopter. I understood how a huge building like the hangar, in just the right place on one of the low points of a sloping hill, could go unnoticed.

As the hopter descended, Emma pointed out the hangar to the left of us. From my vantage point in the back, it took me a few extra seconds to parse what I was looking at as my eyes focused on the hangar, which was painted a forest green.

"Hold on," she said, and she banked hard left and dropped the hopter down at the same time.

I said goodbye to my stomach. I was certain Emma had done that little maneuver on purpose; a moment later, Forno cursed. His fist curled and I envisioned that punch to Emma's jaw again.

She made a deft roll right to flatten the hopter's path, and an instant later, we landed next to the hangar, which towered over us, as if we were at the bottom of an old river damn. I couldn't quite make out the top of it.

"Confirmed down," Emma muttered, palming controls, and rolling back physical and virtual throttles. "Secure. Hangar One, Gottelburg." She pointed out the front. "There's Heston's ride."

I craned my neck, looking for a line of sight between Emma and Forno. Another hopter sat there, exact same model as ours, and it looked empty. Had he already gone inside the hangar?

Emma diffused the bubble and stepped out of the hopter. We followed, albeit at a slower pace, uncertain of what we'd find. Emma, though, walked confidently, almost nonchalantly, past the other transport to find the south door of the hangar.

"He's inside?" I asked.

She shook her head, frustrated with us. "Jesus, where do you *think* he is?"

I didn't think anything.

Forno slipped past me, taking the lead as we approached the hangar. Emma let us go by her, then stopped and motioned us to go on.

"I've done my bit," she said. "That door's for you."

I reached into my coat and pulled my blaster. I heard Forno's weapon power up right after. "Then you won't mind if we remain cautious."

She shrugged. Motioned us toward the door again.

The hangar door, green like the rest of it, blended in so well that only the visible cracks around the door gave it any contrast. I pushed it firmly, let it swing open, and signaled my favorite walking shield to proceed.

Forno ducked a little and disappeared inside. I followed, blaster powered up.

The lights were low, but I took in the huge room and its contents in a quick glance. Taking up most of the room was the Memor ship. It seemed too small for a vessel with slot engine capability, but then again, it *was* from the planet Memory. It might even be an advantage to have a ship small enough to slip through the cracks of security on either end of the slot. The sleek, chrome and brass hull recalled our first walk in Bestus, when we marveled at the infusion of alien tech and design aesthetics. Its swept-back fins were tucked neatly into its torso, and I whistled in appreciation at the ship's preciseness, its simplicity, and understated beauty.

"You can whistle *that* again," Forno said.

"Only to get Teska out here," I said. I gripped my blaster tighter. It didn't make sense how nervous I was about him coming out. "If he's inside."

"He is," Forno said, pointing with his blaster at the cabin door. It was opening.

We raised our blasters as one when the door folded neatly in on itself and solidified into an access ramp with stairs up to the threshold. After a pause—a week's worth, it seemed—a massive First Clan Helk appeared and descended to the floor of the hangar building. He faced us and inclined his head.

I lowered the blaster when I saw him. "Oh for—"

"Fucking *Helk* snot," Forno said. "It's happening again."

"No," the Helk standing at the bottom of the ramp said. "It happened years ago. The pattern was in the buffer. You just didn't know about *all* the copies."

Again, it was not Teska. *Again*, it was Terl Plenko.

"How many?" I whispered.

"No more than you've now seen. There were three copies."

"That's not right. The Movement leader, Brindos when he was changed, and Teska Not-Teska. You'd be the fourth."

Plenko shook his head. "I'm not a copy. I'm the *real* Terl Plenko."

I had questions, of course.

Plenko didn't want to answer any.

Later, he said.

Now, I said, trying to be commanding.

No.

Instead, he insisted on showing us around the Memor ship: its controls, drive system—particularly the proprietary slot engine—and the overall layout. They'd stripped it down to the bare essentials, and the seating included just two command chairs at the controls, one more behind, and a Helk harness next to that. He wanted us to know the basics because we'd have little time to familiarize ourselves with the ship to successfully fly it through the slot (illegally, since there'd be no previous flight plan or schedule) and sideways to the target intermediary station (even *more* illegal), where we would put the Tarot cards to work, minus distractions from anyone or anything.

"You're going to have to convince me you're the real deal," I said, "and that you really *are* working to help me, and not leading us all astray. What proof do I have you are *you*? What proof do I have your counterpart back at the Bestus compound isn't the real you? Or that you're *both* not copies, and Plenko has been dead all this time, as we suspected?"

Plenko smiled and nodded. "You're right, you *do* have a lot of questions."

"He's good at questions," Forno said. "You should answer some of them."

Plenko inclined his head slightly, acknowledging the request. "I'm Dorie Senall's husband, the original Plenko, but you're going to have to trust me on that."

"I asked you to convince us," I said. "Trust is not proof."

"I agree. But that proof will have to come from Dorie. Only Dorie knows me well enough to prove it."

"She seemed convinced—or at least satisfied—that the copy at the compound was you."

"I'm not sure she was," Forno said. "She was struggling with it. She seemed uncertain. Maybe even a little frightened."

"There," Plenko said. "You see? You'll have to trust me until then."

I shook my head. "The plan we discussed—I mean the *other* Plenko and I discussed—means I'll travel to the Ultra universe before I hear that proof."

"That's right. So call it faith, not proof."

"What about your double at the compound?" I asked. "Seriously. Why are there two of you now, together, after all this time?"

"He was copied the same time the other copy—Plenko the Movement leader—was made. He came with us when Lorway took me from the Rock Dome. We were both hidden."

"And what will he be doing during all this?" I asked. I was afraid for Dorie, suddenly, knowing she'd been left behind with a Terl Plenko copy.

"He'll go with Dorie."

"You're sending the *copy*? That makes no sense."

"It makes perfect sense." We were all standing near the Memor ship's front screen, and now Plenko sat—or leaned—carefully on the control panel, avoiding the sensors. "Morgan's client wants Plenko to pay for his crimes. No one knows about any other copy. They've only heard that I, the original, exist."

"Tash," Forno swore. "The copy is going to take the fall for you?"

"He'll take the fall," Plenko said, "he'll pay for his sins, but he's going to get a chance to find out who's behind all this. See who the client is."

He was going to sacrifice himself. It seemed an almost noble gesture from a Thin Man with knowledge of Plenko and a love for Dorie. A copy often retained memories and feelings of the original. Dave knew that firsthand.

"It's not his first *choice* to give his life for me," Plenko said. "He'd like to come out of this alive if he can, but we don't understand the client's motivations. We don't know if my copy has a chance to survive or not."

"I don't like that this puts Dorie in harm's way," I said.

Plenko dropped his gaze, briefly hiding his face and, it seemed, his own worry. "I don't either." He regained his composure. "Morgan hired you, and he knows you, Forno, and Dorie left on this mission. One of you needs to come back with Plenko, and it must be Dorie. You'll be gone, and Forno will be waiting for you to return. *If* you return."

"I still don't like it that Forno isn't going with her," I said. "I'll be on my own after the jump slot. After he helps me, why can't he go back and join them?"

Plenko shook his head. "They'll already be gone."

"They won't wait?"

"Let me rephrase that, Mr. Crowell. They are *already* gone."

It took a moment for that to sink in, but when it did, the hairs on the back of my neck stood up. I stared at him, but he avoided eye contact.

"They left for Osprey Station right after you came to meet Teska," Plenko said. "To meet *me*. They're back on the *Sinai* by now and headed for Earth."

"Son of a bitch," I murmured.

"Can we get back to discussing the Memor ship?" Plenko asked. "I've a lot to show you."

Dorie and Plenko, alone at last. What would they talk about now? I wished I had a randomly placed, programmed marble camera in motion to record that conversation, but the last time I'd watched a holo-recording of Dorie, I witnessed her falling—the camera following her from above—one hundred floors to her death.

SENALL

13 DORIE SENALL WAS BACK ON THE *SINAI*, SITTING IN THE same seat she'd sat in on the trip out to Barnard's, but instead of flying with Dave and Forno, she now shared the ride with Terl.

After Dave and Forno left to find Heston Teska and the Memor ship, Terl had hustled her out of his compound with an urgency that surprised her. She didn't understand his impatience, or why Forno wasn't going along with her. She wanted to wait for him, but Terl insisted. They bickered about it, and the more heated it became, the more Terl looked to Rob, who added himself to the mix and helped Terl push her out the door.

Rob, as well as Charles—the man from the porch—took time to disguise Terl by wrapping him in heavy clothes and a dark coat with a wide hood that hid his eyes. They rushed out the door, and Rob kept a wary eye as they worked their way down the bright avenues toward the port. Citizens gave them plenty of room, keeping their distance because he was a Helk, their prejudices easy to see. They hadn't seemed to notice who the Helk actually *was*.

The entire time, Dorie felt confused and detached, as if she were just a nuisance to Terl. As if she had no say in the matter. As if she were a prisoner.

The pilot was up front, also a prisoner of sorts, stuck in his bubble, presumably in possession of the proper travel visa through the slot. After pre-check and warmup, they all strapped in, and the transport left Osprey Station and hit the jump slot. She wasn't going home to Ribon, however. She wasn't sure she'd ever be able to return, and it saddened her. She'd come so far there, found her place, and made herself into something. *Governor of New Venasaille.* She'd left it behind, and she still believed she'd made the right decision, although she worried about Adi Thakur and how he was getting on handling the mess she'd left for him.

She'd found Terl. That should've made the sacrifice worth it. She wondered how strongly she believed that. They'd only just reconnected, but she wondered why the gap between them felt so wide. Wondered why he'd been so eager to move her out of the compound. Wondered why she had this overriding distrust—or maybe *fear*—of him. She wondered—

How much she still loved him.

Almost an hour after entering the jump slot, they said their first words to each other on the *Sinai*. Leading up to that moment, Dorie silently fumed about Terl's treatment of her, still surprised at the suddenness of their departure.

"I want to understand," Dorie said. She wanted to say, *Why are you acting this way*? but she guessed he knew what she meant.

Terl stayed silent. The tightness around his mouth was obvious, the dark leathery complexion lightening, as if he were blushing.

"Why are you so driven to face Morgan?" she asked when he didn't answer. "Morgan and whoever his client is? Rob said you *wanted* to go. You're using me to turn yourself in. One of us—either myself, Dave, or Forno—had to be available to act as your captor, and it ended up being me, as if by default."

Dorie saw it clearly. Terl could tell Morgan that Dorie came back because the other two were convinced they weren't needed. It'd been Morgan himself who'd given Dave the card. Morgan helping him. Telling him he had a chance to find his dad; if Morgan knew what that meant—traveling to the Ultra universe—he wouldn't expect Dave to be the one to show up with the so-called fugitive Terl Plenko.

She couldn't figure Morgan out. He seemed both pro-Dave and anti-Terl.

"Using you?" Terl said. "What do you mean by that?"

"It's like I'm bait, or something."

He chuckled. "What else is going on, Dorie? Something else bothering you? Because this doesn't sound like you. You've been distant since I first saw you in the compound."

She laughed. "That's rich. You're the one who's kept distant. You think I'm distant? It's because I'm fucking confused about your motives. I distrust you."

"Distrust? Dorie, listen—"

"God*damn* it, Terl! I love you." She shook her head. "I—*have*—loved you. Don't you see? Am I important to you?" *Do you still love me?* "You've not said a word or asked a single question about our home since I found you. About Ribon."

"This mission is important. I'm sorry I've not been thinking about Ribon."

"You want to find out who the client is, and maybe that will be a success, but Terl, I found *you*. I may lose you again, and this time, it'll be forever. I don't want you hurt. I don't want you gone. I want to go home. With *you*."

"It's not my intention to die. But I must be part of the Union again. I can't do that hiding away like a frightened animal."

He looked so tired in that moment. She saw the weight of the Union pressing down on him, and he looked like an empty shell about to be crushed. "It'll be difficult," she said. "It'll be dangerous."

"Perhaps you'll protect me."

She didn't think she could, but she said, "Of course. You know I will."

The silence returned, and not much later, Terl fell asleep. She stayed awake for a while, her eyes toward the front, watching the back of the pilot bubble. Then she slept, too.

When the *Sinai* exited the jump slot and queued up for Egret Station, Dorie woke to find Terl already out of his harness, staring out the window at the shimmering upper arc of Earth. Its soft, moist atmosphere, like a membrane, protected the planet from the harshness of the sun, and it breathed in and out in concert with the life below it.

Dorie imagined both her and Terl under the membrane, as if tucked in bed, comfortable and very safe, rain pattering harmlessly on the roof above them.

"Union bright," Terl said, as he gazed at the Earth.

It was.

It was very, very bright, and maybe things would turn out okay here. She looked over his shoulder at the view, but as the pilot announced their final approach to Egret Station, she thought again of Ribon, and the dome of blue and gray that protected her home.

She longed to be under its protection.

CROWELL

14 "THIS SHIP HAVE A NAME?" I ASKED PLENKO, RUNNING MY hand over the control panel, as if checking for dust. We'd spent several hours going over the Memor ship's helm controls, including the pilot bubble, the slot drive, tracker, maneuvering thrusters—everything. The ship wasn't large. A two-seater, with barely enough space behind the harnesses, where Plenko stood now. The cabin was sealed from the back compartments: some supply lockers and the main engine hub and the proprietary Memor engine array.

"If I have the translation correct, the IDENT says it's called *Glass Spire*," Plenko said. "But it's ours now. At least for a little while. You can name it whatever you'd like."

"The *Tem Forno* has a nice ring to it," my partner suggested.

I ignored him. Instead, after a few seconds, the name came to me. "Call it the *Lucky Lawrence*."

"After your dad," Plenko said, nodding. "A fine choice."

"We'll need a hell of a lot of luck to pull this off," I said. "It doesn't hurt to pull from my dad's strength."

"The first hurdle is one of the hardest," Plenko said. "Piloting it from out here, ground to station, without clearance. It'll take some fancy flying to get past some of the Authority watchdogs."

"If we can maneuver well enough to avoid them, and we come in hot, it might not be so bad."

Plenko agreed, but he had a suggestion. "We chance discovery out here, but it's worth the risk to conduct some low-altitude flying tests. Get a feel for the atmospheric controls. You can't practice the next step—morphing the code and engaging the bubble for the jump slot—but you can verbalize the steps. Run through the preflight checklist. Mimic the procedure and the motions. You must be precise. Your movements from atmosphere to orbit to slot must flow."

"Is there a disadvantage to the special slot drive system?" Forno asked. "More time to engage? Increased runtime?"

"Maybe. That's why you need to be test pilots."

I felt confident enough. Plenko had a lot of the specs down. "What happens when we get to the slot? We won't have prior clearance. No flight plan."

I had some knowledge about this because Dorie and Brindos hijacked a press shuttle on Temonus, not a typical slot vessel at all. Hell, not even an off-planet vessel. They fled Temonus for the quarantined Ribon in a damn hurry. Of course, they'd had a trained pilot. He'd not been very willing, and complained about everything, including the fact that we were taking our lives—and his—into our own hands by taking the ship through the slot without a slot tracker, but we hadn't given him a choice.

"You'll have to run and jump," Forno said. "Slot speed will be overly high, but that's your only chance."

I remembered something. "Dorie told me that when they did the run to Ribon on that press shuttle, the pilot entered the insertion codes and morphed the trip to Ribon on the ground, before they even entered atmosphere."

Plenko was way ahead of me. "Can't do it in this case, due to the Memor slot drive. The calculations are too tight. Too sensitive."

I seemed to be out of questions, and Forno hadn't thought of any either. We were as ready as we could be to put some real time in behind the controls.

"Okay," I said. "Let's fly."

It didn't take long for Forno to master the low-altitude maneuvers, oddly enough, considering the size of the Memor controls. I didn't understand how Helks handled most Memor or human tools when forced to do so.

He'd learn the ship's controls because he needed to do the return flight solo. He had to prep the ship for the jump slot, followed by the sideways slip to the intermediary station. Once there, Forno would be my muscle and I'd do what I had to do to quantum travel. Forno would take the ship back to Barnard's.

Plenko barked out instructions from the row behind us as he practiced. The ship ran smooth and fast, and responded to every command, turning and accelerating effortlessly, no matter the speed. It was a hell of a ship.

We all kept a wary eye on the horizon, hopeful we wouldn't attract the attention of the planet's Port Authority. Forno worked the controls, and Plenko yelled at him to keep the speed steady and not overcorrect.

I *really* liked hearing someone else yell at Forno for a change.

When Plenko was certain Forno could run the *Lucky Lawrence* without serious flaws, it was time for the next step: play-acting the prep for slot travel. Forno practiced it now as the ship raced low along the lush landscape. Next, he practiced the insertion process, all pretend, step by step as I talked him through it from instructions given by Plenko. Forno didn't *do* the steps, just pantomimed them. I didn't ask how he knew all these piloting specs.

"You're in the control area," I said. "You're flying hot toward the jump slot. Probably chased by Authority. Access bubble controls to engage slot engines. When they fire, you reach down to disengage the slot tracker. Insertion codes ready. Morph the code to Memory, with alternative sideways slotting at the ready. Insertion codes entered, wait for codes to morph, nodes to emerge and construct holo-image of Memory."

Forno frowned, uncertain of a step. "Do I release the lockout?"

Plenko said, "No. You can skip the lockout."

"Okay," he said.

"Planet Memory image morphed and inserted," I continued. "Engage the bubble. In one minute or less, you're enveloped by the pilot's bubble. Preconfigured insertion code, run and jump speed. With proximity to slot, you should be automatically slotted. Station officials will be *extremely* pissed off. Wait for entrance into the jump slot, then reinject the slot tracker." I turned to Plenko. "And that's that."

Plenko said, "Do it again."

Over and over until Forno could verbalize the steps on his own, do all of it without errors, as he would have to on the way back. He wouldn't have me there to guide him or remind him of any of the specific steps.

Emma messaged from the ground and said she'd intercepted some chatter from Authority about a possible breach of flight protocol near Gottelburg.

"That's us," I said. "Better hurry."

We added the routine of slipping sideways to the new slot,

which would bring us to the intermediary station. Forno ran through the same routine as before but included the mimicked motions of firing the Memor proprietary slot engine. Luckily, there weren't many steps to this procedure. When the slot engine engaged, he'd initiate a simple 90-degree turn, but at a torque barely tolerable for humans.

Sideways.

We'd be in the intermediate slot and on our way to the intermediary station. Our biggest question mark was the station itself. Having never been to it—and having never *seen* it—no amount of prep would give us enough details about this one station. Small crew, no ships. That was all we knew.

We could guess though, so we played out as many scenarios as we could.

"Alert," Emma said from below. "Authority is on the way. I figure you have ten minutes, tops. If you're going to go, you better go."

Plenko acknowledged her, then told Forno to set the *Lucky Lawrence* down a hundred yards from the hangar. "You're on your own," he said, once they'd landed. "You have the Tarot cards you need for this step. The specs are on your com card."

"They are?"

"Pushed to you while you were practicing the slot routine."

"Encrypted?"

"Of course. Unauthorized ping. You have it, and you can read it."

Emma's voice again. "Hello? Going? Terl, you've got to get out of there, too. They might search the hangar now that they have coordinates."

"They're leaving now," Plenko said, patting me—as lightly as he could—on the back. "Me too."

There wasn't much else to say or do after that. We had to get gone, and fast. Plenko headed for the ship's exit. I worried about Dorie. I worried about Plenko's Thin Man being with her. I worried I wouldn't understand the Tarot cards well enough to get them to work for quantum travel once I arrived at the station.

I'd worry about Forno's return later on.

"Anything happens to Dorie," I told Plenko's retreating back, "I'll hold you responsible. There'll be hell to pay when I get back."

Plenko glanced over his shoulder. "*If* you get back."

I nodded.

"Fair enough," he said.

And then he was gone.

We fired hot, slagging the open field in our haste to depart, forgoing any low-altitude maneuvers. The acceleration couches and our harnesses took the brunt of the force. We might've done some damage to the hangar as well, but I knew Plenko and Emma had skipped out of there in time. We were ahead of Port Authority but left plenty of clues behind if they decided to pursue. The pressure on my chest lessened as the dampeners kicked in, and we reached higher altitudes.

"Pursuit?" Forno asked.

"Not that I can see."

We hit space. Forno already had the insertion codes ready. "Firing the primary slot engines." The ship whined as the drive engaged.

"Correction," I said.

"What?"

"Pursuit."

Forno throttled up, still burning against the last of Barnard's atmosphere. "Go faster," he said. "That's always best practice."

Then the *Lucky Lawrence* shivered.

I swore. "Something hit us."

"Slapper," Forno said. "Low yield. Getting our attention. They're not close enough yet."

"Keep flying."

"Slot tracker disengaged. I'm making a run for the jump slot."

The coms crackled over the ship's speakers soon after, a warning from the station.

<<THIS IS OSPREY STATION TO APPROACHING VESSEL GLASS SPIRE. YOU ARE NOT AUTHORIZED TO APPROACH THE SLOT. PLEASE RESPOND AND PREPARE TO BE BOARDED BY AUTHORITY VESSEL>>

I'd almost forgot the ship's registered IDENT, *Glass Spire*. Tracking showed the authority vessel gaining. Its IDENT was scrambled. They didn't want us knowing too much. "Keep going," I said.

"Like you have to convince me."

"Got the insertion codes?"

"Already entered. Code to Memory processing."

I saw the nodes popping out on the resin and the holo-image of Memory forming. "Cutting it close. You ready?"

"Ready as a Helk First Clan doing ballet."

"I can't even *begin* to picture that, let alone understand how—"

"On my toes."

The ship shimmied when the next slapper hit. We skewed wildly. I willed the engines to hang on. Not too much farther to go. I had a visual on the jump slot. Whether we made it depended on nailing the slot at the right time and the Authority vessel not tearing the ship apart. We needed some luck now.

Lucky Lawrence.

Forno engaged the bubble. The holo image to Memory appeared on the resin just as a transparent film surrounded Forno and the control area. Cutting it close, indeed.

The ship skewed again, but it was less intense. We were going to make it.

"Got vessels near the slot," Forno announced.

"It's the queue. Go right by them."

We did. Authority wouldn't chance firing now, but I didn't know if any other security could keep us from the slot. I didn't think so. We'd get there, then the bigger unknown would be the sideways jump.

But Authority *did* fire again, and this time we were pushed forward after a powerful thud. A wrenching noise. A warning light and a strident signal. *Lucky Lawrence* slowed, but kept on target, and the slot was *right there.*

"Ashtay!" Forno yelled.

I blinked. "Did you just use Pig Latin?"

He didn't answer. "What're they doing shooting—" He moved with purpose inside the bubble. "We've lost the slot engine."

"*What?*"

"Boosting primary with secondary power."

"That'll pull you—"

"I'll compensate."

The transparent bubble hazed my view of Forno, but I could still make out perspiration on the leathery skin of his forehead. I gripped the couch. Authority support ships were en route, but if we could just get to the slot, momentum would pull us in. We couldn't access extra power for boosting once in the slot, but we might have enough residual thrust to carry us through. Also, we weren't going the full distance to Memory, and if we could just get to the point of our sideways jump, the Memor engine could take us from there.

"Come *on*," I said.

<<THIS IS OSPREY STATION TO UNAUTHORIZED VESSEL GLASS SPIRE. YOU ARE NOT AUTHORIZED TO APPROACH THE SLOT>>

Earlier I'd said to myself, *we're going to make it*. Now? It didn't seem likely.

"Slow roller, coming in," Forno said. He glanced at me, his face a wash of emotions. "This'll do us in."

Fuck.

<<NO MORE WARNINGS GLASS SPIRE. WE ARE FORCED TO USE LETHAL FORCE. JETTISON IF ABLE BUT NOT LIKELY TO SURVIVE THIS CLOSE TO THE SLOT>>

"It doesn't make sense," I said. "They should just let us go. Why are they so protective of the slot? We're a Memor ship."

"Maybe they've seen through our IDENT. Maybe they know we're not who we say we are and they're protecting the intermediary station."

A number of people could profit from this mission failing. Morgan. His client. Or Sakson. Lorway. Even Plenko if we didn't know the whole story.

<<GLASS SPIRE RESPOND. RESPOND AND CONFESS AND WE'LL PUT IN A GOOD—>>

The ship lurched. Shot forward. Osprey Station silenced.

Silenced?

We were in the slot. Blackness and diamond points of light.

"The explosion gave us the final push we needed," Forno said. "We're slotted, but barely, and no slot engine. If we make the intermediary station, it'll be a miracle."

This also didn't make sense. "The explosion should've torn us to pieces."

The bubble had collapsed with the loss of the slot engine. Forno pulled away and shook his head. "Not our explosion."

"What do you mean, 'Not our explosion?'"

"Another ship in the queue. Not sure what kind, or how big. It was next in the queue, lining up for a better insertion point. Its destruction saved us. The blast pushed us into the slot."

I closed my eyes and felt the weight of the ship's sacrifice settle on me. How many had been on that ship? I took a deep breath. "Slot tracker?"

Forno shook his head. "Useless to reinject now that the engine is down. Maybe the Memor proprietary drive will let us if we can find the intermediary station. If we don't, we're adrift and likely lost in here, unless chance spits us out, or a rescue vessel bothers looking. The way Osprey was shooting at us, I'm going to guess we won't be on any priority rescue list."

It was strange seeing Forno this serious; no joking around now. "What about the main engines?" I asked.

"Useless in the slot. We'd burn up the ship trying to compensate. Even if the main engines worked. It'd just hasten the inevitable."

"What about turning the Memor drive on ahead of schedule?"

"Plenko said no. If we're not in sight of the sideways slot, he doesn't know what it'll do to the ship."

"If he doesn't know what it'll do, then maybe we chance it."

"You want to try, we'll try, but there's no urgency yet. We could just do nothing and end up drifting right to it."

He'd told Dorie about the TWT transport that had gone missing in the slot, that it had been found, all passengers safe. Five days for the rescue vehicle to find it. A cold jump from inside the slot with new codes. He wondered where Dorie was now. Gone with the Plenko copy, back to Earth, to Morgan. She was in as much danger as I was, maybe even more so.

Come on, *Lucky Lawrence*.

"Okay," I said, giving in. "Let her drift."

SENALL

15 DORIE AND TERL LEFT THE *SINAI* BEHIND AT THE STATION after paying the pilot the previously agreed upon rate. Apparently he had another booking and he was several days late. They thanked him and took the drop shuttle down to Seattle to meet Morgan. The place for the meet-up had been decided before Dave Crowell came to get her on Ribon.

She pinged Morgan to let him know they were back. Morgan didn't seem to care Dorie was bringing Plenko instead of Dave or Forno. He'd expected it, actually, figuring Dave would be on the quest for his dad.

"Why Zola II?" Terl asked her as they made their way downtown on a city transport.

"It's Dave's go-to. A hangout, a trusted place. He figured it was safer to meet in a crowded place, since Seattle proper is bare bones anyway. He said everyone calls it Zola's."

"We're going to be early," Terl said.

"Yep."

"Stake out the situation ahead of time. Be prepared as we can be for Morgan, in case he tries something."

"Yep."

"He'll try something."

"Probably." Dorie looked over at him. He wasn't too scrunched in the Helk-friendly transport. "Morgan wants you, after all."

"I'm bait."

"To find out about the client. Yes, but we'll bait and switch."

"How're we going to do that?"

She laughed. "We'll think of something."

"Not reassuring."

"I'm working on an idea."

"You were always good with ideas."

He'd said that in the past tense, she realized. It surprised her.

Was it because it'd been so long since they'd been together? Or something else? "Isn't that why you married me? For my scintillating ideas? It certainly wasn't for my body, considering the challenge we faced with that."

He nudged her. "We managed to get around it some."

That was true. Once she got past the novelty of a Helk's retractable penis, once she realized the size of it was quite proportional to a Helk's overall Clan size, the wonder and awe of it turned into practical *ideas* about their sexual options. It fit in other ways and places. She could never have vaginal sex with him, but even a Helk's finger was bigger than most human—

"If Seattle's any indication," Terl said, "Earth has seen better days."

She blinked away her thoughts, hoping she hadn't reddened with the specific memories of their long-ago intimacy.

"It has," she agreed, "and it's sad, but Dave seems to like it. He gets enough business to stay afloat. Downtown's at least affordable, and he's doubling up space for living and office. And he's got Forno, who keeps things light, and only complains about the cold."

Terl nodded, staring out at the city as it swept by.

"Nervous?" she asked.

"Can you blame me? I'm out in the open." He drew attention to how he was dressed with his giant hand. "No disguise. No bulky clothes and coats to hide behind. People are going to recognize me."

"It's Zola's. Patrons are eating, drinking, or they're plugged in."

Terl sneered. "Dataheads."

"If someone recognizes you, so what? What're they going to do to a First Clan Helk?"

"Zip me." He shrugged theatrically when she frowned at him. "Why not? Take out once and for all the loathed Movement leader Terl Plenko. The rumors true. Out of hiding, now fair game."

She understood his worry. More than once she'd felt the same misgivings about what his sudden appearance among humans would mean. Not that she'd ever expected it to happen. Nevertheless, she put on a good face. "You're overthinking it. You've more to worry about with what Morgan wants."

"I hope so," he said, and that's how they left it until five minutes later, when the transport dropped them off in front of Zola's.

They found a table conveniently flanked by other tables with customers. She preferred it to the quieter, more private table in the back. A waiter came to them—his nametag said **IAN**—and the young man gave them water and left after explaining the flash menus inset into the table. Dorie surveyed the place, taking notice of every customer. No one familiar. No one looked shady, no one seemed nervous, no one cast furtive glances in their direction. It bode well for both of them. It didn't seem like Morgan had been here ahead of them, and no one seemed to notice that Terl Plenko sat among them. Dave said patrons and staff were used to seeing Tem Forno, who was well liked here, so maybe that had worked to their advantage. She explained as much to Terl.

"We'll see how long that lasts."

"So far so good," she said. She looked at the menu. "Jesus, they have French fries here."

"What're those?"

She glowered at him. "Seriously?" He shrugged and she didn't hesitate, ordering a couple sides of them. "Also, we need to get you some coffee."

"Coffee I know," he said, "but I hate coffee. *Helks* hate coffee."

"Forno loves it. So you're having some. Keep up appearances."

They waited forty-five minutes without mishap. She saw a few younger men taking an interest in them, leaning in close to one another to whisper, probably having recognized Terl, who didn't notice. She didn't say anything, preferring to keep him as relaxed as possible. The young men didn't do anything stupid, luckily.

At the appointed time of the meeting, Morgan entered Zola's. She recognized him easily from Dave's description. He wore a three-piece suit, but no tie. He ran fingers through his hair, which was full, but cut short, sporting a hint of gray. He was alone, and Dorie breathed easier.

He smiled as he approached but kept his eyes firmly on Terl. Dorie saw a look in his eyes that immediately brought back her earlier concern. He was too eager. She had a thought of him wringing his hands in anticipation and it pissed her off. Dave and Morgan may have made a deal, but a lot had happened since then. She wasn't going to let her husband go without a fight. Morgan had some explaining to do, and if she wasn't satisfied, she wouldn't agree to the delivery of the falsely accused Terl Plenko.

Morgan finally looked her way and offered his hand. "Dorie?"

She stood and shook it. She wanted to say, *And you must be the Morganism*, but managed to avoid it. Still, thinking about it, she couldn't help giving him a knowing smile. Let him wonder.

Morgan sat down and turned his attention to Terl. "So it's true," he said, sizing up the Helk. "Terl Plenko in the flesh. Not dead."

"And not the Movement leader," Terl said, "as much as you wish it were true."

Morgan laughed. "Me? Hell, I don't give a shit, really. But I can imagine the reaction of humans everywhere when you're offered up."

"None of that makes any sense, Morgan," Dorie said. "The record is clear. The Terl Plenko who ran amok during the Ultra scare is dead. Taken out by Dave Crowell. Why do you—or, your *client*—think people need anything more? It's been two years since the false Plenko died. The Ultras are gone, and that's that. Earth is recovering, the Union is recovering. People are moving on. Sure, it's a long process, and there's still a lot of hate toward Helks, but it'll work itself out soon enough."

Morgan leaned back in his chair. "Oh, is *that* what you think?"

He didn't go on, so Dorie prompted him with a raised eyebrow.

Morgan looked at her but shook a finger in Terl's direction. "You think—no, wait. You *believe*, that this is just about Terl Plenko?"

Plenko laughed. "Isn't it? You want me dead."

"I don't want you dead. I wanted Crowell to bring you *Death*. The Tarot card. I wanted to *help* him. I just needed to have you brought back. I'm a mercenary, Forno. It pays a lot better than when I was an Envoy."

"At least Envoys weren't shady."

He laughed. "Let's say I straddle the line a little bit. There's nothing illegal about what I've done bringing you back. And you, my good Helk, came *willingly*."

"Your *client* wants me dead."

"He might, but it's more complicated than that."

"I'm waiting to hear about that," Dorie said. She was tiring of Morgan's elliptical responses. "If it's not just about humans' hate toward Helks, then what is it?"

Morgan leaned in again and redirected his finger, shaking it at her. "You should know better than anyone. He's your husband."

"*That* Terl Plenko was never my husband. My own copy had more of a relationship with that Plenko than I ever did. Even she understood it was better to take a high dive off a tall building than go on with the Movement leader."

"Well now we're getting somewhere," Morgan announced. "Congratulations. Dorie Senall takes one for the Movement, splatting on the pavement at the bottom of the Tempest Tower, and Ribon is destroyed, its people dead or displaced."

Dorie felt the heat on her face. Then the sinking feeling hit her when she realized what Morgan was getting at. "Fuck," she whispered.

"What's he talking about?" Terl asked.

She took a moment to gather her words. Her strength. "They not only think you indirectly caused the Ultra scare, but also believe you caused Ribon's destruction."

"Ribon?"

"You—gave *birth* to the Movement. Ribon was destroyed because of Coral, where Plenko had his base. You disappeared on Coral, at the Rock Dome. And then you ran."

Terl muttered something, but all Dorie heard was *Ribon*.

"It's not about Earth," she said. "Not about humans in general, but about those who lived on Ribon, and those who live there now, under the domes."

Morgan made a loud single click with his tongue. "And there it is." He leaned back.

Dorie stood suddenly, her breathing labored, anger rising so quickly she thought she might hyperventilate. "You son of a bitch," she said. It was loud enough, and her posture telling enough, that the customers at the other tables in Zola's took notice. The room grew silent, except for the occasional grunts and laughter of the dataheads, oblivious to anything outside their simulated reality.

"Just the messenger," Morgan said.

"A tashing *mercenary*!" Terl said. He stood now, his full height in play, and more customers pointed and whispered, realizing who he was.

"Well," Morgan said, "a job is a job. You don't fuck up the work, and you don't disappoint your client. I didn't *have* to listen to my old pal at the Emirates Building. Didn't *have* to keep the Tarot card Greist Sahl-kla gave me. I liked Crowell's dad, and it was only fair to help out his son a little, the eventual savior of the Union."

Some customers had lined up at the front register to pay and get out of there. Some had already left. A few of the more curious customers stayed put, including the two young men Dorie had spotted earlier. A few dataheads were just now thinking *whaaat?* and turning to see what all the fuss was about.

Dorie clenched her fists at her sides. "You're a deplorable little Morganism, you know that?"

Morgan's smile lessened, but he said nothing.

Dorie had figured it out. "Your client is on Ribon."

Morgan pursed his lips and inclined his head, then gave it a little shake. "Well, now, that's not a hundred percent true. He's *from* Ribon." It was a little awkward for him, but Morgan turned sideways in his chair and glanced out the window, at the street.

Dorie followed his gaze. "What?"

"He's from there, but right now, he's here." He pointed out the window, at the crowd that had gathered to watch from a safe distance. Morgan gave a little wave. "Right out there."

A man separated from the crowd and came through Zola's door. Then six more men and women fell in behind him with weapons drawn. The two young men from earlier now decided it was a good time to get out of there and crouched low around the soldiers and out the door.

Dorie took several steps around the table, and now the anger had reached such a high point that she found she was shaking. The man came within ten feet of their table and stopped, and the others fanned out to make a ring around him. He also wore a suit, but not as nice as Morgan's. No vest, but he had a blue tie.

Morgan finally stood. "Dorie, I believe you know Tom Sakson."

Sakson smiled the same agonizing false smile Morgan had. "Hello, Dorie."

Dorie waited a full five seconds, saying nothing, the tension between them so heavy it seemed like it would take them all down. Terl looked quite menacing sitting at the table, but he held back. It wouldn't do to get him killed now. He could do a lot of damage, but there were too many of them.

"You *fucker*," she said finally. "You set me up."

"Only a little," Sakson said. "You did most of it on your own. Nice speech, by the way."

"The New Venasaille government will not stand for your thuggery, Tom. The governor will not stand for this. The *Union* won't." She had worried about this happening. She'd hoped it wouldn't.

Tom Sakson laughed overly loud. It took him a bit to gain his composure. "Oh, you mean Adi? Aditya Thakur?"

"You know full well that's who—"

"Yes." Sakson frowned as quickly and as forcefully as he'd laughed. "Aditya Thakur is dead."

Dorie reached out and gripped the table, holding herself up. The chair was right there, but she wouldn't sit. She'd stand tall. Adi. *Oh, Adi!*

"Very unfortunate accident, I'm afraid," Sakson continued. "No, no, the government of New Venasaille *will* stand for this progressive policy from the Separatist Party. Reparations are due, Dorie. I have the cooperation of Seattle Authority to be here and take care of this now that I'm the acting governor of New Venasaille. And the Union?" He shook his head. "President Nguyen doesn't care a whit about Ribon. You yourself thought that. We're mostly on our own. We're small potatoes. A world making its way back, some new domes pimpling its surface, but—" He grabbed a French fry from Dorie's plate. "Small fries. It's to my benefit. To *Ribon's* benefit."

Terl flinched, and perhaps unconsciously took a step forward. The cordon of soldiers tightened and the weapons stayed trained on them. Plenko realized what he'd done and stopped.

"Plenko," Sakson said. "I've long wished to meet you. Now you're here, and justice can finally be served." He stared the Helk down, and his demeanor changed from polite politician to menacing Authority detective. "Terl Plenko, you're under arrest for murder and attempted genocide."

"Tom!" Dorie yelled. "It's been two years—"

"And you, Dorie Senall," he continued, "are also under arrest."

"That's preposterous," she said. "On what charge?"

Sakson motioned to his soldiers. "Detain them, with whatever means are necessary, including excessive force if it comes to that."

"On what charge, Sakson!" she yelled. "On what charge, you *fucker!*"

He didn't answer. He walked out.

Earth was now closed to her, and her own world was far away and dark and unrecognizable.

CROWELL

16 THE *LUCKY LAWRENCE* HAD DRIFTED A LONG WHILE. I wasn't sure how long, really. The concept of time in the slot was almost meaningless, particularly without engines, slot tracker, or a reachable destination. The onboard chronometer—which read three hours now—was one thing, but you'd never know how time had passed outside the slot in these dire circumstances until you broke free on the other side.

I didn't like our chances.

There was a slim possibility we'd picked up a trace. Usually that meant NIO, but I trusted Jennifer. She had no reason to do it. So it was deep basement stuff, someone unauthorized. Whether that person had a monitoring cobweb remained to be seen. The irony was that being in a jump slot was the only way to counteract a trace. So we were adrift, and lost, but no one could track us.

Small comfort.

As we drifted, Forno kept an eye on our position, even though he had no idea what to look for. In the meantime, I looked over Plenko's encrypted ping about the suggested use of the Tarot cards. The instructions were *suggested*, because Plenko didn't really know for sure. Only in theory. I had the cards I needed, but according to Plenko, two other cards, given to Baren Rieser, were in the Ultra universe at the site of the blackrock House that Vanderberg Parr had slagged. Destroyed the tether at the cost of his life. Had Rieser—on purpose or not—left the cards in the Pool Room?

My gut hurt. It was a slim chance at best, this mission, and a huge gamble on my part. If there were no cards, I'd be stuck there until my dying days, which, Plenko had mentioned, wouldn't be that long. I'd arrive quite the old man.

I set out the cards on the bulkhead, positioning them as Plenko instructed. This part, it seemed, rang true, for the fine nano ink-infused wires embedded in the cards lined up perfectly. *The energy of an Ultra.* Tuned to my DNA. Enclosed, controlled antimatter. I left out the Tower for now, considering that card could trigger the whole thing, and we were in no position, this deep in the slot, to do that kind of experiment. We needed quiet—which, ironically, we *had* here in the jump slot—and a specific position, which we *didn't* have. The intermediary station was the place. We'd commandeer it, ship off the small complement of personnel in whatever vessels had brought them there, or out the airlocks if we had to. At this point I didn't much care. We'd use the ensuing silence to focus the captured energies required for quantum sleep.

I loved a good theory.

Naturally, this theory could go bad even before we had the chance to try it. The diamond points in the slot flickered and gave absolutely no clue as to where we were or where the intermediate jump slot was. We'd recognize it if we came upon it, but it was a little like finding a single specific tooth on a small cog in a huge slot beam and wheel mechanism without any maps, blueprints, or training. Actually, we'd have a lot better odds finding the cog.

I loved the good theory a little less.

We'd not planned for a lengthy stay in the slot, or on the intermediary station, so food and water were running low, even with our attempts to ration everything. None of the food was very good.

An hour after eating something I couldn't even identify, Forno saw a blip on his monitor. "There's a ship, ahead, port."

I groaned, thinking they'd found us. But it was dead in the slot, dark—except for a faint warning beacon—and lifeless, according to the scans we could manage from our end.

"Scan again," I said. "Bodies?"

Forno shook his head. "No, it's deserted. I'm guessing even a rescue vessel couldn't get the ship out, so they had to save the crew. Left this behind."

"Hence the beacon. Wouldn't want a ship under power through the slot to run into it."

"How does that work, exactly?"

"The beacon warns the pilot and the tracker adjusts. Honestly, with as many jump slots as there are, there gotta be at least a *few* other abandoned vehicles in jump slots. We just never see them."

"Why didn't they just tow this one out? Or blow it up? It's not that far from the slot entrance."

I wasn't sure, but I suspected the rescue ship thought they'd come back and take care of it one way or another. I told him so, and he agreed.

"They could still be coming back," he said. "Particularly if something of value were still on that ship."

"What's the ship? It wouldn't be a Memor ship by any chance?"

"I don't think so, but so what? It's dead, even if it had the Memor proprietary engine. I mean, we already *have* one that works, if we ever get the chance to use it."

I nodded, then had an idea. "How close will we come?"

"You don't want to run into it. It's a lot bigger, a passenger ship of some sort. Not TWT. A cruiser, maybe, but if we hit it, we'd be goners."

"Can we grapple?"

"If we can get the grapple to work, and we're not out of range."

"Good. Let's try it. I want to see what's on that ship."

The grapple worked. It took forever to reel in close, but forever was meaningless now. The *Lucky Lawrence* had a spacesuit for me, but not Forno. Good thing Plenko had swapped out the *Glass Spire* Memor suits. Forno remained on our ship and monitored everything as I headed over with a high intensity flashlight and a blaster. It took another half-forever to cross to the dead ship's airlock and hand crank it open, and still more time working my way into the main compartment. Everything was dead and dark and cold. No air. I floated precariously around the compartment, getting a little nauseous, until I could get the magnetic boots to thunk down on the deck.

I clicked on the flashlight, and my suit's com crackled to life. Forno's timing was impeccable.

"What do you see?" he asked.

"Give me a minute, will you? I just got on board and I'm trying not to lose my lunch. Or whatever you call that stuff we ate an hour ago."

"Okay, be careful."

"Yeah. Not like this is a strong point for me, playing astronaut on an unknown creepy ship, in vacuum. I might have seen this flash vid once or twice."

"This would be the time the giant space blob consumes you," Forno said. "Then I'd be all alone."

"Helks don't get lonely. Shush, will you?"

But he didn't. "You have any ideas about what you'll find?"

"At the very least, some supplies. Food and water, I hope."

"And at most?"

I swept the light through the compartment and recognized nothing. The main cabin would be to the fore, engine room aft, and this space most likely for cargo.

"A miracle," I said.

"That'd work. You know whose ship it is yet?"

"Human for sure. Definitely a cruiser, capable off planet as well as on, maneuverable in a planet's atmosphere as needed. It's too dark to see much of anything, even with the flashlight. I'll know more once I get to the pilot area, but I'm guessing there's no Memor proprietary engine."

I spotted crates fastened to the bulkhead with straps. For sure, some of them would have food and water. They weren't going anywhere. Right now, I wanted to move on and see what I'd find in the main cabin.

"Scans still say no one alive, no one on board," Forno said. "Should be safe to explore."

I clanked over to the blast door. Since the ship had no power, I opened it manually. The main cabin was as dark as the back compartment. Passenger seating, twenty seats in two rows, a narrow aisle between. It was definitely not TWT; they never ran anything this small. This was a private cruiser slotted to either Memory or Barnard's before the breakdown occurred. Nothing fishy about it at all, except there were no passengers left behind. I focused the light on the seats as I proceeded up the aisle. There was no in-cabin storage on a carrier like this. All the seats were upright. No blankets or pillows left behind.

I came to the next door—already opened—which led to the pilot's bridge. My flashlight landed on the front pilot console. Residual emergency lightning still flickered near the controls. I moved up for a closer look and saw the green light of the warning beacon. The other light indicated a pilot log. It blipped red, which meant someone had already accessed and retrieved the information.

"Pilot's log is gone," I told Forno.

"More proof of a rescue ship."

"Maybe."

"Engines?"

I waved the flashlight over the controls until I found the readouts. "Telltales are dark, but it looks like the normal interface. Definitely not Memor. No signs of a proprietary engine."

"Anything else?"

"Not that I can see."

"IDENT?"

"No way to look it up. Let me check for a visual."

Circling the bridge, I checked the pilot's station, comm center, and seating area, until I found a metal rectangle welded onto the back wall of the bridge next to the doorway I'd come through.

"There's a manufacturer placard." I read it to myself, then aloud to Forno:

Union Transport, Inc. Aberdeen, British Isles. Class-1 Atmospheric Cruiser. "For the Union and its Enduring Stability." Christened This 1ˢᵗ Day of September. MMCXII

I stepped back, and the clank of the boot sounded overly loud in the room.

I bumped into a harness and realized I'd backed up some more. The ship description screamed in my brain, triggering a memory. An infamous ship. A ship that ought not to be.

"You'll have to toss me a skeleton about that number," Forno said. "Roman, isn't it?"

"It's 2112," I said.

A ship manufactured two years before everything went to shit during the first Ultra scare. A monumental, horrific disaster that occurred after Dorie's copy threw herself off the Tempest Tower, after the near destruction of Ribon: the sabotage of the Transcontinental Conduit on Temonus.

Why did it always come back to those damn towers?

As if fate planned that I circle the bridge counterclockwise, I saw the second placard, to the left of the door. The block letters were

legible before I came close enough to read the small print of the
IDENT number and registration information.

"Well, hell," I whispered.

"Well hell what?"

Crisp black block letters on gunmetal gray spelled out the ship
name.

E X E T E R

"It's the *Exeter*," I whispered.

Forno picked up my whisper on his end. "The *Exeter*. You're
joking, of course."

"Not a bit. The *Exeter*. UTI Class 1-A Carrier." My breathing
quickened and I immediately calmed myself, not wanting to screw
something up with my helmet's airflow. "The *Exeter* was destroyed
when it crashed into the Transcontinental Conduit on Temonus in
2114. It happened after I sent Brindos there to investigate a Plenko
sighting. After I asked him to see what he could find out about the
Conduit."

"Mirror's breath. That's not possible. That ship was sabotaged so
it would deliberately run into the wire."

"Sabotaged by Lorway. A signal was sent upon her death." God
damn it, why could I never escape Lorway? "But Lorway's alive. The
real Plenko sent that signal."

"Still doesn't explain how this ship exists. It's been two years
since the Conduit disaster."

"It has to be a different *Exeter*," I said.

"Likely true. The registry is the same?"

"It reads like it is."

"Then maybe it *wasn't* the *Exeter* that took out the Conduit."

Officials had gone over the wreckage. They'd found enough to
confirm the telemetry signal embedded into the servo robot and
the attempt to destroy the evidence. Enough to accuse Lorway.
There were logs and passenger manifests. The deceased captain and
crew members were known.

The static from the comm reminded me Forno waited for a response over on the *Lucky Lawrence*. "No, it was the *Exeter*."

"Then how do you explain this?"

It came to me quickly, almost as if it were the punchline of a
joke. "It's a copy."

More static as Forno mulled that over. "What—like a Thin Man is a copy?"

"Why not?"

"Well, because it's a *thing*. Not a *person*."

"How many Plenkos have we come across? How many Lorways? Hell, we found a Brindos copy even after Brindos became a Plenko, for that matter."

"Yeah, but it's not a *person*—"

"Didn't Baren Rieser have *two* blackrock Houses?"

"Whoa whoa whoa," Forno said, "hold up. One of those Houses was—Helk's breath, are you talking *Ultras*?"

"Did I say that?"

"Are you suggesting Ultras made this ship? Made an exact duplicate of the *Exeter*? Because that would be completely tashing crazy."

"And for what reason?" Forno didn't answer me, having a hard time wrapping his brain around this, I was sure, and so was I. "How long has this ship been adrift in the slot?"

"You'd need the pilot log for that," Forno stated.

"And someone took it."

"Someone took it and didn't rescue or blow up the ship."

"Because there was no rescue," I said.

"What're you talking about?"

"No passengers. It's a shell. Not a single thing out of place, but for the engine problem, whatever it is."

"It had no passengers? Are you *serious*?"

"As can be. No personal items, no pillows, blankets, garbage—things that you'd expect would be left behind if they were rescued in a hurry."

"Passenger manifest?"

"Gone."

"Attached to the pilot log," Forno guessed.

I nodded, then forgot he couldn't see me. "If there was even one to begin with."

"Which—manifest or pilot log?"

"Maybe both. If it's a shell, you wouldn't need either."

"That might mean there wasn't even a crew."

"Or a pilot. It's like a ghost ship. One deliberately left in here for two years, maybe more."

"Tash, you're making my skin crawl."

What would be the purpose of a famous ship—or a copy of one—left in a jump slot? I wanted to believe in the best of all possible reasons, that it was left here for me. Even back then, the Ultras knew who I was. My dad, Plenko, Greist, Joe Sando . . . all of us. I'd been hearing about so many Plan Bs, I now believed, whether right or wrong, that the Ultras had left this ship as a beacon so I could find it at this moment and be saved from certain death in the slot. Or perhaps I was to use it for something else. Or *some*one else. No one could explain the Ultras and what they thought or believed. Maybe they had harnessed the ultimate power of probability or the careful manipulation of time itself as a way to prolong the Ultra's existence. That might have worked until recently, separated from the confinement of flesh to an existence that defied understanding, until they could no longer sustain it. They were dying.

Perhaps, though, Lucky Lawrence had learned something.

There was nothing to it, though. This copy of the *Exeter* was in worse shape than our own. Not even a backup Memor proprietary drive—which we didn't need anyway—or a functioning slot engine, or a Tarot card designed to whisk us magically on to our intermediary jump slot, or an Ultra antimatter gadget prepared to put us out of our misery when the time was right.

"What do we do now?" Forno asked.

I didn't know. If I couldn't get us underway to the other slot, there wasn't much else we *could* do. Except— "I'm going back to the storage hold and check those crates."

"If it's a ghost ship with no passengers, why would there be crates of stuff?"

"That's what I'm wondering. To be honest, they might be like the rest of the ship. Empty. I'd been hoping for food and water at least."

"Don't let me keep you from your pessimism."

"I'll check back in a few."

The pilot cabin fell silent once Forno thumbed off the comm from his end. I clanked through the passenger cabin to the cargo area and shone my light on the containers strapped to the bulkhead.

Here goes, I thought. I wrenched open container after container, searching each one carefully, shining the light into each one.

"Forno."

After a pause, I heard him say, "Yeah? Find something?"

"No. Nothing."

"Shit."

"A couple more to look into but looks like we're out of luck." *Lucky Lawrence* indeed. The last two containers. I opened the first. Empty. Opened the second. Empty.

I slumped over the lip of the container, defeated.

"Anything?" came Forno's voice.

"No. But hold on a moment. I'm going back to the engine room."

"Going to crank up the Ultra squirrels?"

I didn't answer but continued to the engine room. I thought about Dorie as I picked my way through cargo toward the blast door. I wondered where she was, and if she and the other Plenko had found out anything about Morgan's client. I didn't trust the Plenko with Dorie, but I trusted Morgan even less.

If Forno and I got lucky, we might get out of this slot. It was, at least, a slim possibility now, when an hour ago it seemed like we were done for. Then what? Fucking quantum travel to another universe with some cosmic Tarot card reading? Arrive and demand the Ultras give me back my dad—if he was even alive—even though I would be damaged goods and be *older* than my dad?

It wasn't just Dorie I was worried about, though. I'd be leaving a lot behind. Forno. Jennifer Lisle. And—well—the entire Union of Worlds. A one-way trip that would leave little left of my life, all for an infinitesimally small chance to find my dad. Tell him hello, here I am. Or goodbye. Tell him about Mom . . .

It was a long shot at best.

I was through the blast doors and in the engine room. Although I wasn't a pilot, a jump-slot mechanic, or an engineer, I didn't have too much trouble recognizing the *Exeter's* main engines or the paired jump-slot engine behind the now inert shielding. It was boxed in on all sides—the hub—barely any room around it for techs who might need to service the engine.

Something caught my eye at the bottom of the hub. Something small and dark. The flashlight didn't help.

"Looks like there's a part down there," I said.

"Where? Junk? Debris? Or an actual engine part?"

"I don't know. It's small. I can't reach it."

"Jump the fuck in there."

"Shut up, for god's sake. I'm in a goddamn spacesuit. Give me a chance."

I lifted myself over and into the hub. I grunted as I let myself drop to the ground. I located the object, about the size of my hand, and picked it up in the glove of my suit. It looked smooth, and if I'd been able to touch it with my fingers, I imagined it would be cool to the touch. It could hardly be worth anything.

I shone the flashlight onto its surface. As I thought, it was nothing. A piece of debris.

"Just a chunk of something," I said. "Size of my glove."

"A chunk of *what*?" Forno asked. "This voice-only contact is starting to freak me."

"I don't know. A rock."

"What's a solitary rock doing—"

"Hold on." I brought it closer to my face and really looked at its smooth black surface. Then I recognized it without a doubt. For a moment, I believed it to be that bit of hope we'd been looking for. A way to gain back my earlier optimism. But I was just as sure that it meant nothing. Nothing, anyway, that could help us.

"It's a piece of blackrock," I said.

Pause. Static. Forno said, "What does blackrock have to do with anything?"

"Maybe nothing," I said, but the moment I said it, I didn't believe it. The scrap of blackrock might offer several solutions. "Maybe a lot."

"Damn it," Forno said. "I want to be over there and see it for myself."

"Come on over, if you want to die."

"Figure of speech."

"It's not a figure of speech. It's not even a broken idiom."

"If the blackrock means something, enlighten me. Is it Ultra?"

"No," I said. "Blackrock is found only on Helkuntannas."

"Not true. There's Bernard's. There's Rook."

He was right. The location of Rieser's second House was in the Ultra universe buffer zone.

"Isn't Rook where you're trying to get to?"

"I don't know *where* I'm going, Forno."

"So this blackrock is there by the engine. Why? Where did this ship that's not a ship come from?"

"The *Exeter* copy seems tied to the Ultras."

"And to Plenko, Rieser, and Vandenberg Parr."

My mind whirled as it sought out a logical explanation. For all I knew, it was just a stupid piece of blackrock mistakenly left behind. I stared hard at it, forcing myself to look deeper, remembering my experiences with it from last year. The surface, at first glance, was smooth, yes. Barely discernable, however, was a slight flaw in the material. Tiny, jagged discolorations marred the seemingly jet-black material.

"You there?" Forno asked.

I knew what I was looking at. "It's not blackrock."

"I thought you said it was—"

"It's *synthetic* blackrock."

"You mean the stuff the Helks use to make their thoroughfares and buildings?"

"That stuff. But not all the houses use the synthetic form. It's real blackrock in the Outcropping where we found Rieser's House."

"Also not made of synthetic blackrock."

"Right."

"So?"

"So, I'm going to look closer."

"Closer at the rock?"

"What did Rieser's blackrock have within it?"

I heard Forno's intake of breath. "Tashing Mother's mercy and Plenko's balls. It had *mortaline* in it."

I'd already found the faint line running straight and true through the blackrock. A line blacker than the rock's color. "So does this piece."

"Are you certain?"

"No. But maybe."

"Mortaline in a piece of synthetic blackrock? What the hell does *that* mean?"

"No clue."

"That's *my* line."

"Now that I look," I said, studying the bulkhead of the cargo room, "I think there might be blackrock embedded into the structure of the ship. The hull, even."

"Blackrock. In the skin of the *Exeter*."

"Seems like it might be. Mortaline helped the Ultras copy us with the wire of the Transcontinental Conduit. It helped anchor the two Houses through the portal between universes, like an antennae."

"How does that help us? It's just one piece of blackrock, synthetic or no."

"That's the mystery of the *Exeter*."

"Still unsolved."

"There's no reason for a single piece to be here."

"Right."

"Unless there is one."

Static.

"The *Exeter* is a copy of the original," I said. "It's possible the Ultras made it to replace the other."

"Or it existed first."

"Possibly. So—" I felt the weight of the blackrock in my gloved hand, and I shook it a little, as if trying to discover its true properties. "—I think it might *power* the *Exeter*."

More static. A long pause made it seem like Forno was a long way off, the long distance delaying his incredulous reply. "Don't be insane," he finally said. "It's a tashing *rock*."

"It's a key. Synthetic blackrock with a mortaline power source."

"And you know this . . . how?"

It was a good question. How *did* I know? The thought came into my head as if I'd had years of training on the subject. It made even more sense to me that this blackrock, within the entirety of the ship, was waiting in the strangest of places, in the very last crate. *Can't find your way home? Here, try this, your last Plan B.* Though, I didn't believe for a second that it was the last Plan B I'd encounter.

"I don't know for sure," I told Forno. "But I've heard of such a thing. In fact, I *saw* such a thing. And I can certainly test it."

"How?"

"The engine has to have an interface. An ignition panel. Give me a sec."

I walked slowly around the hub, dragging my hand along the surface of the engine, looking it over, up and down. I passed a service ladder at the second corner, which meant I'd be able to get out of this hole at some point.

Then I saw it.

I only recognized the interface because of its shape. The depression was the size and shape of my synthetic blackrock piece. I remembered the mortaline vault on Ribon, and the circular indentation that was the DNA lock, and how the key, Plenko's sculpture, had filled the space, spun, and opened the doors.

If I was right, the key would have a similar automatic sequence that would ignite the engines without me having to initiate any other preflight checks or having to guess what buttons to push or sensors to palm.

The blackrock piece fit perfectly.

It didn't spin or melt or otherwise gyrate dramatically. It just snicked into place, and the engine—with all its bells and whistles and hums and whispers—sprang to life. The blackrock key burned red, and the mortaline line within glowed white.

Forno must've noticed the *Exeter*'s return to life over on the *Lucky Lawrence*, for his voice came over the comm. "That looks like power to me."

"Up and running, main and jump slot engines."

"I'd celebrate, but it's a small victory."

I knew what he meant. "Yeah. We can pilot the ship out of the jump slot, but we can't find—or *use*—the sideways slot without the proprietary Memor engine in our *own* ship."

We'd come too far to just exit the slot and leave our plan behind. We needed to find that sideways slot. "We have power," I said, "and we can maneuver, and I think we might still be able to celebrate."

"How's that?"

"The *Exeter* is an Ultra ship. Do we agree on that?"

"An Ultra copy of the real *Exeter*."

"This mortaline is white-hot power. Mortaline powered the Conduit, back and forth through the wire. It powered the portal tethered to two universes."

"So?"

"So . . . what if the blackrock key is also a marker?"

"A marker of what?"

"Of *direction*."

There was a pause as Forno wrapped his big leathery head around that. "Like—a slot tracker?"

I left the engine room. As I ran through the ship, heading for the pilot's cabin, I spelled it out for Forno. "An Ultra slot tracker detects any deviation in the main slot. If there was an anchor on the other side, the mortaline could point to the sideways slot of the Memors, even without the proprietary engine. We find it, we can get to it. We're grappled together. I tow you there, and when close, I float over and we throw the *Lucky Lawrence* into the sideways slot and make our way to the intermediary station."

"Good theory."

"Are you ready to test it?" I entered the pilot room and engaged the pilot bubble. I didn't know how to morph the code to the station, but I didn't need to know. I only had to set the slot tracker and follow the resultant path to the sideways slot. On the *Lucky Lawrence*, we'd let the Memor engines do their thing.

It took only minutes to set the tracker and generate the lockouts. The tracker glowed white as it slaved faithfully to the keyed engines.

"Hang on, Forno," I said. "This could get a bit hairy."

"You mean furry."

That made me smile. Good thing he was on the *Lucky Lawrence* and didn't see me do it.

Minutes passed.

We inched forward. A half hour. A little more.

The shimmer of the sideways slot appeared a few seconds before the location trace pinged its proximity. What a welcome sight it was. I smiled, proud we'd figured this out. I disengaged the bubble, the engines rested, and the two ships floated. This time, though, we weren't lost. I stared at the slot, mesmerized, as the *Exeter*, on course to the slot, dragged our own ship behind it.

"Okay," Forno said. "You coming back over?"

I thought a moment and made a decision I'd not expected to make. "No."

"*No?*"

"I just decided. We're taking the *Exeter* with us."

Forno argued with me, but I didn't change my mind. I felt more at ease the closer we came to the slot.

"We run both slot engines, but we stay tethered," I said. "Match speed. We still need to travel to the intermediate station. The *Lucky Lawrence* has no main engine, but it does have the Memor slot engine."

"What about my return trip?"

"We'll be at the intermediary station, and the only way to get to it is with the Memor slot engine. Anyone on the station had to have a ship with that engine to get there. We'll grab a ship off the lot, so to speak."

Momentum kept us on a perfect line toward the slot to the intermediary station. Forno and I maintained a close eye on our respective pilot controls and kept up a constant chatter reading the navigation telltales.

The *Exeter* was a mystery indeed. If it *had* been meant for me, that was a very different mystery. How could the Ultras know I'd be in that slot, at that time, to find the ship? There was a reason I didn't know yet, but we might *never* know. Earlier, a pang of regret had washed through me, but I felt better deciding not to leave it behind.

"Ready." I engaged the pilot's bubble. We didn't need the *Lucky Lawrence's* engines. The Memor engine would take over and slot Forno automatically.

I settled into my bubble. Two years ago, I barely knew what a pilot bubble was. A good bit of experience dealing with Ultras had changed that. I did a preflight without too many nervous mistakes.

"Here goes nothing." Forno said over the comm. He fired the Memor proprietary slot engine. I fired the *Exeter's* slot engine. The engine engaged. On Barnard's, Forno had practiced the 90-degree turn we would've needed to break into the sideways slot, but since we'd been dead and drifting before this, we didn't have to deal with insane amounts of torque that maneuver would've forced upon us.

Our tethered positions barely changed on the margin of the slot until we engaged with it. The ships grabbed hold almost simultaneously, and finally, after long delays for both ships, the *Lucky Lawrence* and the *Exeter* slotted.

Sideways.

SENALL

17 DORIE AND PLENKO WERE TAKEN OFF PLANET WITHIN AN hour of their arrest. Dorie could hardly believe how efficient Tom Sakson had been taking them out of Morgan's hands. Morgan was gone, just like that, but she expected he'd show up again if Dave and Forno returned and found out about what had happened to her.

They were whisked out of the city, taken off Earth, and slotted to Ribon. She assumed Sakson had paid Morgan well, counteracting the money Morgan had paid—or *would* pay—Dave Crowell for his part in the scheme against Plenko.

Dave had been blinded by his need to search for his dad, and it had cost Plenko his freedom. His life, too, probably. She didn't fault Dave for that. He hadn't known until later how things would go down.

She couldn't imagine anything good coming out of Plenko's arrest and deportation to Ribon. Not while under the fist of Tom Sakson.

Reparations.

Tom Sakson was acting governor of New Venasaille. Her friend Adi was dead. Dorie had to deal with those things, even though she hated thinking about either of them.

They separated Plenko and her from the start. He was on the transport to Ribon, but not in the same compartment. It made sense, looking at it from Sakson's point of view. Why give them any chance to plan the things that might undermine the governor's power? Her compartment, a private room on the transport, was normally reserved for some important VIP, or some rich bastard who had extra money, so at least her incarceration was comfortable. She'd been told to stay in there and not leave her room. The door was unlocked. She wasn't handcuffed. Well—where was she going to go if she decided to make a break for it? She wondered if they'd given Plenko the same consideration. She doubted it.

A half hour into the slot, a knock sounded on her door. Again, she wondered about the treatment she received. No one banged on the door, no one barged in unannounced.

"Yes?" she said, mustering as much vitriol—or spite?—in her voice as she could. She stood in front of the single, narrow bed that came complete with down comforter and soft pillows.

Tom Sakson came through the door. He wore dress shirt and slacks, plus a tie left loose around his neck. His governor persona, she guessed. Dorie slumped her shoulders, feeling defeated, not wanting to talk or have anything to do with him.

"Are you comfortable?" Sakson asked. He closed the door softly.

"No," she said. "Are you going to answer my questions, Tom? Where's my husband? Why did you arrest me? On what charge?"

Tom pushed outward with his hands, palms toward her. "Slow down, Dorie."

"Don't tell me to slow down. What you're doing is illegal *and* uncalled for. I've done nothing to warrant an arrest by my own government."

"Many would disagree."

"You can't just say *many* disagree. Not unless you can back it up. I want to return to Earth with my husband. Bring me Terl Plenko. I want you to stop this nonsense."

"Ribon's citizens demand justice." He pulled at his tie. "Plenko is a criminal."

"He is *not*. Why do you continue to believe that? You're worse than the climate deniers from a hundred years ago."

Sakson's demeanor changed in an instant. He smiled, baring teeth, and took two menacing steps toward her. "You want the truth, Dorie? Here's the truth. I don't care what you believe. I care about what Ribon believes, because once Terl Plenko is dead, they will vote me in from acting governor to full governor, and not just of New Venasaille, but of all the domes."

"That's really it, then," she said. "It's just about your own personal power."

"The power of *Ribon*," he corrected her.

"With you in charge? That will only lessen our planet's power."

"I don't see it that way."

Dorie fumed. "You turned the people against me. They would've been content to see Ribon grow under my leadership. I'd already made great headway. You tipped the balance for the worst."

"You're delusional. No one liked you."

She was taken aback. There was no truth to that statement in her mind, but the way he said it made her doubt herself. It was true she had a difficult past, but she'd gone way past that. No one could hold any of that against her now. Not after all she'd done for Ribon.

Suddenly she realized what Sakson was doing. Where he was coming from.

"Tom. You know who I am. We were *friends*. You worked with me in those early days, and we set a strong course for our planet."

"I worked under you. Not with you. I was never your friend."

"You don't mean that."

"Dorie." He shook his head, and the look of pity in his eyes made her wince.

"Tom, don't—"

"You're a drug addict, Dorie. There's no way you should be running any part of this planet."

Hot tears threatened to spill down her face, but she held them back. Her lips quivered. "I'm not, and you know it. It's been years since—"

"A relapse."

"What?"

"I had to tell them the truth."

"Who?"

"New Venasaille. The other domes. They had to know what happened to you."

"*Nothing* happened to me!"

"I had to tell them about the RuBy, Dorie."

"I'm clean. Why would I—"

Tom slipped a finger across his palm. Dorie noticed the glint of a flash patch. An untrained eye wouldn't have noticed it, but she saw it and knew he'd signaled someone.

Not someone. Some*ones*. Her door opened and three men dressed in military garb she hadn't even seen before slipped inside. Dorie backed up, but the bed stopped her. She sat down just as two of the men reached the bed, grabbed her arms, and restrained her. The third man stopped and smiled.

Dorie saw the red squares of RuBy between his fingers and thumb a second before he pushed her back onto the bed, put his other hand over her mouth, and held her down by straddling her legs. She struggled, trying to scream, but it was no use. As hard as she fought, she wasn't a match for him, and although it took him a while, and he endured a couple of bites, he managed to pry open her mouth, slip in the RuBy squares, and clamp her jaw shut.

The squares dissolved quickly. Dorie felt them change from smooth surface to a film coating her tongue, the cinnamon taste gagging her.

"Once an addict, always an addict," Sakson said, "isn't that right, Dorie? Sometimes, the second time around is much more destructive. *Much* more." He leaned in between the men so he could see her eyes and shook his head. "You're far gone, Miss Senall."

The man holding her mouth let go, and she prepared to scream. Surely others on the transport would not stand for this treatment of her. But she couldn't do it. The cloying smell of cinnamon became a warmth in her throat, and she closed her eyes, not fighting the drug. She wanted to tilt her head back and let that warmth flow down, down, down, but she was already flat on her back. The guards let go of her, and she welcomed the pleasure of *inside*, without the distraction of *outside*.

"I'm sorry we found you this way," Sakson said. "It's a heavy dose, but you'll be okay for now. Later, the public will see you at your worst. And then—"

Dorie listened to his far-off words, trying to make sense of them. Who was that? What the hell was he saying, and why was he interrupting her dream?

Did he have more RuBy, or *not*?

"—RuBy will *do* its worst, and you will be out of our way forever—all well documented, I might add—and you will join your old friend Adi."

Is that you, Terl? What have you brought me? Is it—well, you know.

"Dorie, to you hear me? You understand?"

I am become a name. Sailing behind the sun, or something. Travel. Rest. Live life.

"Announce his capture, and his pending execution."

Execution? Terl? No!

"Tom, he—"

He's not a Thin Man. He's not a copy. He's not the bad guy. He's innocent.

"We've already done initial tests." *Someone else's voice. Test? What test?* "Tom, this Plenko is a *copy.*"

No no no no no no

"You're sure?"

Where is my own copy? Oh—there she is. Gross. You know, it's not the 100-floor fall that kills you, but the sudden stop at the bottom.

"Do you want some?" she murmured. "You want some of the action I'm offering you?"

"Ignore her."

The chance of a lifetime, girl of adventure.

"I'm not a copy," she insisted.

"Of course not."

"She died."

"Yes, but *you* are real, Dorie, and you are alive."

"Okay."

"For a while longer. But first: you have a speech to give."

That which I am, I am.

CROWELL

18 THE SIDEWAYS SLOT WAS LIKE ANY OTHER, NOW THAT WE were inside it. The way to enter it was different with the Memor engine, but we could still get into the slot normally due to our unique position.

We programmed the two ships to match velocity, proceeding slower than normal, trying to keep the grapple line from gathering too much slack, but occasionally we endured heavy jolts. Forno continued to grumble about us being separated and having to communicate ship to ship. Since the slot was uncharted, we had no idea how long it would take to get to the other end. We also didn't know how far we'd have to travel in regular space to the station. I was looking forward to getting off the *Exeter* and onto more solid ground, so to speak. We had no idea what to expect once we got there, so that tempered my enthusiasm.

Forno had been quiet about half an hour when his gruff voice came over the comm. "You still figure the *Exeter* was left for you?"

I still had a strong *feeling* about that possibility, but hell if I had an answer I believed in a hundred percent. "It seems unlikely. Two years in the slot?"

"You were the one who pointed out all the signs and portents. The little clues lining up just right."

"Coincidence."

"Or an intricate plan. How many we up to now?"

"Plan B. They're all Plan B."

"The idea of a larger scheme working because all the parts are set in motion by a single event should in itself tell you something."

"It tells me you should stop worrying about it. Let me do the worrying." But I couldn't let it go. "What single event?"

"The death of Brindos. Everything turned on that moment."

"I'm not sure that's the moment."

"And then the *next* moment," Forno continued, "was when you were able to travel back from Rook to our universe because of the sacrifice of Vanderberg Parr, another copy of Brindos."

I didn't say anything back right away. Was he right? The sacrifice of my friend. Twice. And what was the next moment? Another sacrifice? Whose? Mine? Or my dad's? Maybe my dad's capture all those years ago had triggered everything else, and I'd witnessed a long and intricate plan that synced together just right.

"Whatever it is," I said, the comm crackling a little due to slot interference, "I'd be quite happy for their intricate plan to be over. I'm tired of Ultras. I'm tired of Thin Men, and I'm tired of jump slots. I just want to say goodbye to *all* of it."

The comm line fuzzed, then Forno's voice came in crystal clear. "Not yet, partner. You've got a few more steps to take."

A few steps to take now, and eventually, a gigantic leap across the void between universes.

We came out of the slot an hour later. Life support for the *Exeter* had normalized during the previous hour and I was able to strip my space suit in favor of some freedom of movement.

Out of the bubble, I saw the station right away. Not so far away from the slot at all. We maintained a little slack between the two ships, and I inched us forward, keeping in constant communication with Forno.

The station was small. I wondered if it had a name. The main stations for the planets all had names associated with birds: Heron, Egret, Swan, Osprey, Crossbill. This one wasn't on any chart. A ghost station just like my ghost ship *Exeter*. I decided I'd call it Meadowlark Station, after the Montana state bird. When I was young, I learned to whistle the meadowlark's call and had conversations with the birds on my way home from school. They'd cock their heads and look at me quizzically, as if they couldn't believe the things I was saying in my broken meadowlark. Then they'd berate me with their own complicated calls.

The station called to me now; I hoped I could communicate with it. Understand it and reach beyond it into the void.

As we closed in, I saw two ships docked. One looked to be a small transport, and the other was a cruiser like the *Exeter*. What were the chances one of them had both a working drive engine and a Memor proprietary engine? If the ships were here, they *had* to have the Memor engine. There wasn't any way to use the sideways slot without one—unless someone wanted to go our route: get lost and hope against all hope that the ship drifted right to the entrance.

The next question was: who was here with those ships? Friend or foe? Civilian, Authority or military? I needed the space to attempt the quantum travel, and, according to Plenko, needed to be free of any distractions. I was reminded of my home in Montana, when I would lay on the lawn at night and gaze at the stars. Away from the lights of the city. Away from anything outside of the few lights burning in the house behind me. It took your breath away, that clarity.

Perhaps that same feeling would come to me here, in the middle of nowhere.

"No movement," Forno said through the comm. "No one's coming to check us out."

"Standard for most stations."

"Standard *if* you have a flight plan and a scheduled, authorized arrival."

"This isn't a normal station. A few sideways ships, no one sticks around long. We'll chance it. Can you get the *Lucky Lawrence* to a berth if I push you in the right direction and let you loose?"

"If I can get close, the automated docking system will take hold."

"If this backwater station *has* a docking system."

"There's that pessimism again."

"My favorite word."

"If it doesn't have one, I guess I go out in a blaze of glory."

"And take out Meadowlark Station in the process."

"Meadowlark?"

"You like it?"

"Works for me."

"How's it look on the actual station?" I waited while I assumed he checked his instruments.

"I've got life sign readings," he said.

"Number?"

"Impossible to be exact, but not many. Between three and five."

I gave a nod he couldn't see. "Not bad. We could handle that if we had to. If they're hostile."

Forno didn't think they'd *all* be hostile, and I agreed with him.

"Prepare to ungrapple," I said. I lined us up and headed straight for a berth, Forno in tow.

"Ready," he said.

I took a deep breath. "Disengaging . . . *now.*"

The grapple off, I maneuvered the *Exeter* out of the *Lucky Lawrence's* path. Forno let the ship coast in while I found another berth.

"Docking triggered," he said, obviously relieved. "Good news for me and the . . . Meadowlark."

"Good. Let me know when you're docked, and keep an eye on any activity. Weapons prepped?"

"Ready as can be. You too, I hope."

"Of course." I scanned the station with the *Exeter's* instruments. Now that they were powered up, I appreciated their sleek aesthetic. The outer hub seemed deserted. "I'm taking the next berth over. If all is well, I'll meet you in the middle."

We signed off and I commenced docking procedures. I hoped the station's automated system played nice with the *Lucky Lawrence.* Soon enough, the *Exeter* docked and powered down. When it was safe, I pulled the Tarot cards from the console, left the ship, and immediately lost the signal with Forno. I pocketed the cards and pulled my blaster.

It looked increasingly as if the station was deserted, but Forno's readouts had indicated life forms. Where *were* they? Whoever they were, they certainly weren't worried about two ships suddenly coming out of the slot and docking without authorization.

I saw Forno down the hub as we worked our way to each other. I shrugged, and he did a slow turn, checking our surroundings.

"A bit strange, huh?" he asked.

"We wanted quiet, but this is weird. *Too* quiet."

"You don't know how quiet you'll need it to be, so maybe it's just right."

"Maybe I should just hunker down here and get started."

Forno shook his head. "Need to check the place out. Ascertain whether either of those ships will get me out of here after you're in quantum flux."

"*Ascertain*?"

"I'm fancy." He grinned. "Split up and search?"

"No, we should stick together. Two against five sounds a hell of a lot better than one against five."

"Agreed."

We searched, working our way slowly around the hub. The other cruiser eventually came into view and we stopped to check it out. A simple flash panel granted us access. Unlocked, basically, and I thought: *too easy.*

Forno went to the pilot cabin and did a quick diagnostic. I did a quick search of the rest of the ship. When I finished and joined him, he beamed at me.

"Perfect order," he said. "Main engines, Memor proprietary engine, and a standard slot engine as well. It's fully equipped." He looked down at me. "Anyone on board?"

"Not a soul."

"Could you do it here?" he asked.

He'd read my mind. "Seems like I could. But then I wonder what it'll look like from your end. Also, could the process damage the ship? You have to travel back home in this. Makes me a little nervous."

"It might also be strange for me to see you . . . you know. Suddenly *disappear.*"

I nodded. "Let's check the rest of the station. If we're lucky and we're truly alone, we can breathe easier. If not, I want to know where everyone is, and where they stand."

"And if they won't . . . stand?"

"Send them out in the *Exeter.*"

"Set them adrift?"

"For a bit. Quick burn, then delayed burn and return. That is, if you can figure out how to do that."

"Probably."

"By then, I'm out of here, and you disappear before they realize you're gone."

"Then you should find your quiet spot and just let me search and take care of them."

"Not alone."

"Dave, please. I'm a Helk, and bigger than all of them together."

"What if one of them's a Helk?"

He frowned. "Good point."

"Also, how quiet can you be, scaring Meadowlark personnel?"

"Another good point."

I started toward the inner ring, eager to find our missing station personnel. "So we agree—"

"—to disagree." He side-stepped in front of me and put out his meaty arm.

"What're you doing?"

"Go back to the *Lucky Lawrence*."

I stared at him unbelievingly. "Not a good idea." I tried to push past him, but there wasn't a chance he was going to let me by.

"It's the best idea," he said. "The ship isn't going anywhere after this, so who cares if it's damaged from your trip? Besides, it's named after your dad."

"So?"

"It's lucky."

"You believe in luck all of a sudden?"

"No. But I believe in *you*. In *your* luck."

"Whatever that means."

He narrowed his eyes and looked up, as if accessing a memory. "Yeah, that does sound a bit squishy-feels, huh?"

"Touchy-feely—" I groaned. "God damn it, Forno. How much longer do I have to put up with that?"

He sobered. "Not much longer, it seems."

I said nothing. The weight of his statement held me back in the same way he'd kept me from leaving the hub with his massive arm. *Not much longer.*

God, I was really going to do it. I closed my eyes and saw all I knew passing in front of me like a parade. I would travel from here, leaving everything behind. But *why*? Why risk my life and strand myself in a hostile place for a chance to see my dad? Reunite with the dad I'd barely known and who could not possibly still be alive in an antimatter universe?

Shit, wasn't that it? To know him? To know more about who *I* was? And everyone who put this plan into place wanted to know more about the Ultras and who *they* were.

As if reading my thoughts, Forno said, "Are you sure about this?"

I ran my hand across my brow, then let my fingers massage my temples. I shrugged. "Yes?" I heard myself say. I nodded. "Yes. *Yes*, damn it. I have to do it."

"Then go back and do it. Don't wait." He inclined his head toward the station's center. "I'll take care of whatever I find in there."

I had no reason to disagree with him anymore. "So I guess this is goodbye."

He shuffled his big club feet, then poked at something invisible with a stubby toe. "I guess so."

In that moment, I realized I'd never said anything to him to indicate his importance to me, never called him friend to his face, never embraced him. Of course, I wasn't sure how to hug a Helk. I'd probably just get a close-up of his retractable penis or something.

I extended my arm and he enveloped my hand long enough for a semi-human handshake. With my other arm I reached up and patted his shoulder. I understood that much about Helks and friendship, so I knew that counted.

"Take care of Dorie for me," I said.

He nodded.

"And Jennifer."

He smiled. "Of course."

"Be *careful*."

"I will," he said. "Sleep well."

He turned and bounded away. I watched him go, tracking him until he disappeared inside the inner station.

Oodgay eyebay.

I headed back toward the berth where I'd docked the *Lucky Lawrence*.

It was time for a Tarot reading.

SENALL

19 DORIE WOKE IN A RED HAZE.

She recognized the feeling. She understood the *need*.

Oh god oh god oh god

How much RuBy had they given her? Too much. Yes, it was *way* too much to give someone who hadn't touched the drug in over two years. A drug much more damaging and much more addictive than anything humans should ever touch or taste. Its pull on you, once you'd experienced it, was massive.

Oh god oh god

The moment of panic passed, and she reined in her fear. Her mouth was full of dust and her head filled with pins and needles, but she calmed down and scanned the room. The same one as before. She wondered if someone had left some RuBy squares somewhere. Probably not. Make her suffer and beg for it.

Oh god

She painfully sat up on the bed, grasping the rumpled comforter. She waited for the spinning to stop. Her gaze fell on the door.

It was a different door. She felt no vibrations from the transport, so she knew now they were somewhere on Ribon. But where?

She looked at the door longingly. Was it locked? It most certainly must be.

Closing her eyes, she forced herself to think, but it was more difficult than she'd expected. There was an ache in her throat, and the *need* would not go away.

Sakson.

He'd done this to her. Sakson and his goons. To discredit her. He'd ratchet up the dosage and parade her in front of all of New Venasaille. Show that she was worthless. An addict. He'd say she was a quitter who'd given up on Ribon just like Aditya Thakur had.

How could the citizens of New Venasaille believe *any* of that? After all she'd *done* for them? She couldn't wrap her head around it.

She couldn't think straight. She inched to the edge of the bed and reached for a side table. Sweat coated her forehead and threatened to drip into her eyes, but she shook her head and kept reaching. There was a ceramic red and white bowl on it. She wondered what might be inside.

Maybe RuBy. Just a little. A single square. It certainly would help her concentrate.

It was empty. She stared inside, anger rising, before picking it up and throwing it against the door. It shattered into red and white shards, as if it were some dangerous, RuBy prototype. It would've been better than nothing.

No, it wouldn't. *Don't take anything, Dorie. No more of it.* She almost believed someone else was telling her this.

With a concerted effort, she stood, wobbling a little. Tiny steps. Shuffling toward the door. She fell to her knees. For ten seconds she didn't move. Closed her eyes. Concentrated. Crawled the rest of the way to the door. Leaned into it and pushed herself up. Hand trembling, she reached for the access panel.

Locked.

Or was it? She found a second sensor and opened the door. As if in a nightmare, she stepped out onto a gigantic stage lit with too-bright flood lights. She looked out on the audience, and every seat was occupied, filled with copies of Adi Thakur. He looked up at her with hundreds of wide eyes, patiently waiting for her to say something. Say something? They chanted *Do-rie, Do-rie, Do-rie,* and then one of the Adi Thakurs asked *What do you want?*

She would say, *RuBy? Anyone? Just a square. It's all I need. Just a little to concentrate, and then I'll be fine.*

She blinked, and the door remain closed. Locked.

This wasn't good. She was Rubed out and she still wanted more. Where was Terl? What had Sakson said? Something about testing.

We've already initiated some tests. He's a copy.

That couldn't be true. She was imagining it in the same way she'd imagined a theater full of Adi Thakurs. How could Terl be a copy? He was the original, and all the other copies were dead.

"Come sit down, Dorie," came a voice behind her.

She wasn't going to look. It was another RuBy dream, she was certain. She was alone in the room. *You're not going to talk me into it. You're not going to make me believe it.*

The compulsion was too strong. She turned, and Tom Sakson sat on the edge of the bed in the same spot she'd been sitting earlier. In his hand, red squares of dyed paper glistened and looked like red diamonds.

"Have some," he said, holding them out toward her. "It'll help you concentrate."

Dorie drew closer to him. "Are you real?"

He seemed puzzled by the question. "I'm not a copy of anything, if that's what you're asking."

She wiped her forehead, then reached out shakily and took two squares, and just like that, with barely a thought, she rolled them, dye coming off on her fingers, and laid them on her tongue. Soon enough, she felt the peace overtake the need, her skin tightening like a tuned drum. Slowly, she closed her eyes, leaned her head back, and waited.

The RuBy dissolved and she basked in the glow, wondering why she'd ever given it up in the first place. Somehow, she found a seat on the bed next to him.

"There's more," Sakson said.

Magically, there were other red squares in his hand.

She shook her head violently. "Shouldn't . . . take that much of it . . . at once."

"Oh come on, Dorie." He put it unceremoniously into her palm. "I need you to concentrate."

"You need me to lose myself."

"Lose yourself?"

"You think I'm a copy. You want to drown me in the Red so you can discredit me."

Sakson shook his head. "You're wrong, Dorie." He smiled, then softened his gaze, looking at her with pity, like a disappointed father. "You're not a copy. But you're already discredited. The news is out. Number one story. There *might* be a few pictures out there by now. You know, illegal pushes to comm cards, flashreels, and so on."

"Then why give me more?"

He shrugged. "You have some last-minute work to do convincing the other domes that your lack of responsibility makes you a terrible choice for president."

She scoffed. "Oh, and you're so much better."

"Not better. Just determined."

"To do what?"

"Get the truth."

She sneered. "What truth?"

Sakson leaned in and wiped the beads of sweat from her lip. "About Plenko."

"Terl," she whispered. "Where is he?"

"Dorie," Sakson said, his voice tinged with regret. "Plenko is dead."

"A long time ago. The bad copies. The ones who threatened the Union—"

"No, not those." He pointed toward the door. The ceramic pieces from the red and white bowl littered the entryway. "The one out there. The one we captured."

"No," Dorie said. She felt the ache in her chest that could've been grief, could've been the *need*. She rolled and popped the other squares quickly before Sakson changed his mind and took them back. "You wouldn't do that. You need him."

"Need him?"

The new RuBy squares hit her hard, and she struggled to stay focused. "As a spectacle. To have him pay for the sins you incorrectly say he committed against Ribon."

Sakson patted Dorie's knee. "Oh, but we do, Dorie, we do. But we need the right one."

"He is *not* a copy—"

"Yes. He *was* a copy, and he's gone. Plenko's dead."

Dorie's lower lip quivered. "Then what do you want?"

Sakson turned awkwardly on the bed to face her, grabbed her shoulders, and stared into her eyes. "Plenko's dead, but we want *Plenko*."

She blinked. *The King is dead. Long live the King.*

"Dorie," Tom Sakson said. His grip on her shoulders increased. He was red with anger. "Where is the real Terl Plenko?"

CROWELL

20 ON THE BULKHEAD OF THE *LUCKY LAWRENCE* LAY THE Tarot cards in the correct position from Plenko's instructions. Once again, I marveled at the intricacy of the wires in the cards and how the cards synched up like a schematic. Each card, in essence, held a bit of an Ultra's antimatter in check in that nano ink, and the energy of it all tied to my DNA.

Everything was as I had it before, including the space where I would slide in the Tower to complete the "circuit."

I hoped Forno would be all right. I couldn't imagine what he'd run into in there. Life sign readings, but no life forms. There *had* to be people on the station, and Forno would run into them at some point. He'd either subdue them or get himself into a whole lot of trouble.

I couldn't worry about Forno now. I had to get on with it, while I had the chance. I was leaving for good anyway, we'd said our good-byes, and I had nothing left to do but make that long, complicated trip to the Ultra universe.

Good God, listen to me. How *insane* was this?

The Tower waited. I studied it. Lightning. Fire. Bodies falling. But the symbols and purpose of the card mattered not at all. All that mattered were those RuBy lines and the resultant pattern.

I reviewed the encrypted instructions. When the circuit was complete the nano-infused ink would link up across the cards and create the portal and tether to Rook, and to the Pool Room. There wasn't anything else I needed to do except stay in contact with The Tower and use it to visualize the Pool Room. The skin of the card needed the DNA of my own skin, and that energy would help power it.

From then on, it was all theory.

I took a deep breath. I lay The Tower down on the bulkhead below the other cards, then carefully, with three fingers, pushed it up into the empty spot.

Nothing happened.

I gave it some time. Could've been on some kind of delay. But a few minutes later, the cards lay there as inert as before. A dead circuit. Why wasn't it working? I had a quiet space, without interference. Plenko outlined the plan to me point by point and said we didn't need anything else. I'd know when the place was right. This station had to be the right place. What other out-of-the-way place would be more appropriate than a station almost no one could get to?

The answer came to me: Inside a *jump slot* almost no one could get to. My spirits fell. Did we need to return to the jump slot? *That* would be annoying. It didn't make sense to me. It shouldn't make a difference whether I was here on the station or back in the slot.

Unless it wasn't the place that was important. What if it wasn't the station keeping the cards from activating, but the *ship*? It became obvious to me. Matter. Antimatter. Traveling. I gathered up the Tarot cards, and I was as certain about the thought in my head than anything I'd felt in a long time.

I needed the *Exeter*.

I made my way quickly to the *Exeter*, wondering how Forno was holding up on his end. I didn't want to think of him running into a situation he couldn't handle, but I liked the idea of that trouble coming to *me* even less.

On board the *Exeter*, I quickly accessed the pilot cabin and found a spot on the bulkhead where I could lay out the cards once more. I had no idea if I was right about shifting my ground to a different ship, but the procedure hadn't worked in the *Lucky Lawrence*, and this ship seemed the best option.

Once again, I lay down The Tower and slid it up into its spot, my fingers firmly on the card. Like an intricate line of dominos falling, The Tower lit up white along the edges, and I nearly whooped with excitement. But I needed to concentrate. Remain quiet. A mind and space free from interference.

The Tower's pattern completed, then the light of the wire made the jump to The Fool. The passage was slow enough that I tracked its progress easily. I kept pressure on The Tower as The Fool lit. Then the light jumped to The Devil, then cycled through the Major Arcana cards one by one in what seemed like a random pattern. Just before the jump to Death, the line of white stopped and paused, like an old-fashioned sparkler that seems to fizzle out, then starts up again.

Death lit up in the most intricate pattern of all the cards, whispering through the card in hot white lines that outlined much of the image before reaching the point where it would cross over to the next card. The *last* card.

After another pause, the fire of saturated ink jumped to The Chariot. It was the first card I'd collected, given to me by Terree. The outline of white shimmered brighter on this card, and the passage of the signal through the wire slowed down considerably. It seemed appropriate.

The Chariot was my ride.

I kept pressure on The Tower, its energy increasing as the white light of the wire snaked through the card. I felt a keen sense of both dread and excitement. I'd be an old man, yes, but I'd be in Ultra territory. And maybe, *some*how, as unlikely as it seemed, I'd find the way to my dad.

I had no further instructions from Plenko on what would happen next. All I knew was that if whatever happened actually happened, I'd be back on Rook, terribly aged, and that maybe I'd find the Tarot card Baren Rieser was rumored to have owned. Long shot at best.

What I did know was what I'd learned from Lorway when we'd first traveled, thanks to the Ultra tattoo on Alex Richards. The Tower burned under my fingers, and I felt a throbbing fuzziness behind my eyes. I concentrated on the Tower's image, and then the image of the Pool Room. Immediately a wave of nausea passed through me. It was a signal. I was close to translating to wherever the cards were going to send me.

It was at that instant I realized I'd left my comm card on the *Lucky Lawrence*. I wouldn't be needing it where I was going—useless in that world—but it would've been good to have it for any return to the Union . . . as unlikely as that seemed.

Here goes nothing. And everything.

The Tower solidified around me. Then a bright flash knocked out all my senses, and I slept. Slept for a little while; slept for a long, long time.

*

Flash.
Nausea.
Light.

Awake. I opened my eyes, and I was filled with both fear and excitement arriving for the second time in my life on Rook—if that was indeed where I'd ended up—the buffer world placed on the margin of the Ultra universe where things made of matter could exist safely. Had I actually crossed the brane and survived? That prompted my memory about the one side-effect of the sleep travel. Had I truly aged as much as Plenko said I would?

Before I could gather my senses and get an idea about how I felt—whether my body ached, my eyesight had deteriorated, or my brain lost its operant functions—I noticed my immediate surroundings and realized, to my horror, that I'd failed.

I was still in the *Exeter*. The Tarot cards were dark and, in fact, singed along the edges and patterns where the wire had conducted the white-hot energy designed to transport me out of there. I couldn't see out the front viewscreen of the *Exeter* so I must've blown the station's power. I wondered what had happened to Forno.

I slumped forward and pressed my head against the closest card—The Fool—and thought: *no kidding.*

My back hurt in that position, though, so I straightened carefully. Sharp pains stabbed my lower back. I felt tired and drained, my joints hurt, my ears were ringing, and nausea threatened to overwhelm me. Nausea was a byproduct of sleep travel, but the other symptoms were just indicative of old age.

Old age?

I took another look at the viewscreen and realized it wasn't just dark out there. It was desolate. I gazed down at my hands, and they were wrinkled, and my fingers knobby from swelling.

I *was* old! The viewscreen prompted another look outside. That was not Meadowlark Station out there. I pulled myself out of the chair, pain rippling down my back when I stood straight. Slowly, I hobbled to the airlock. I was old, but my brain didn't fail me as I cycled through the exit procedure. I didn't have time to process what I felt about old age.

No alarms warned about unbreathable air. When I stepped off

the *Exeter*, I nearly slipped on the slagged rock of Rook.

I'd traveled, but so had the goddamn *Exeter*. I'd pulled myself *and* a Class II Cruiser through the Tarot card portal into another universe.

Damn, I was good.

It must've had something to do with the *Exeter's* unique structure, which we'd decided was Ultra in origin. That shiver of antimatter embedded into the blackrock key and in the outer skin of the hull. It had to be that. There'd been very little reason otherwise for a copy of the *Exeter* to be waiting adrift in that jump slot. Son of a bitch, it *had* been intended for me. Left behind by *some*one so I'd find it for this very purpose, as unbelievable as it sounded. There were unanswered questions, of course. It was too much of a coincidence. The ship there, in that slot, at that time, needed for this purpose.

Unless it wasn't a coincidence. I was missing *some*thing about it all.

I was standing outside the Pool Room, and I'd expected to appear *inside*. If I had any chance of acquiring a Tarot card here—one I didn't even know the name of—it would be because it had had been inside the Pool Room during the blast.

The obsidian plain of Rook reflected only a little of the weak light of its far-off sun, but as I gazed out past the ship's resting site, I saw what was left of Baren Rieser's second House: A few ragged pieces of wall, some blackrock rubble, and—yes, there it was.

The Pool Room. A perfect rectangular enclosure jutted out from the rubble. As Plenko had guessed, it had survived the Landry's antimatter detonation. I worked my way toward it, careful not to lose my footing or my balance on the blackrock. I'd never given much thought to the difficulties old age would someday bring just getting around. Now, I had to learn how to be old without experience. I'd missed a lot of workouts.

As I hobbled closer, I noticed the Pool Room hadn't completely escaped the damage. The blast had compromised the Pool Room's steel door. Probably disengaged its sophisticated DNA lock. The massive door was open, detached at the top, and it leaned precariously inward toward the entrance. At least I wouldn't have to figure out how to get inside. Of course, if I'd arrived inside with the door intact, I would've had to figure out how to get *outside*.

I approached the remains of the House and took a wide arc to my right to come upon the Pool Room's door from the front. Scanning the slag at my feet, I wondered—somewhat morbidly—about the final resting spots of Abby Graf, Baren Rieser, the Landry, and Vanderberg Parr, for of course nothing physical remained of any of them. I might be walking over their DNA essence and not know it.

The ground around the broken walls was uneven with rubble and littered with jagged, melted blackrock, and it made footing difficult. Once in front of the Pool Room door I stopped and peered into the darkness. I gasped, and shivers went up and down my back. I retreated a couple steps. Within the darkness was a darker shadow. I thought: oh, it's a piece of blackrock wall or rubble rising up from the middle of the room.

But it wasn't.

It moved. It was alive, and it stepped forward toward the door and the weak light of Rook. That's when I knew it was a person. Human.

He reached the opening, saw me, and stopped.

"Hey," he said. "Who the hell are you?"

SENALL

21 DORIE COULD HARDLY KEEP HER EYES OPEN AND FELT LIKE shit. She needed more RuBy and she needed it *hours* ago. No. No, she didn't. The drug was talking. Damn it, her attention wavered. She saw herself on the wall of the room—her prison—sitting ramrod straight, gesturing occasionally, and she wondered: how do I *do* that? She waved her arm at the wall, but her image didn't mimic the movement. Oh good. It wasn't her copy.

"I'm not a Thin Man," she murmured.

What she did know is what Tom Sakson had told her: she'd been filmed a few hours earlier. She didn't remember saying anything to anyone until now, staring at herself on the room's vid screen because of a U-ONE broadcast. She felt relieved it wasn't a copy of her, but she was also appalled at the things she heard herself saying.

"*I am a RuBy addict, and Terl Plenko is a terrorist who turned against Ribon and caused the deaths of thousands. He turned me into the person I am today and used me for his . . . his. . . diabolical plans.*"

She fumed, fists clenched at her sides, and she wondered how they got her to say that. It wasn't true. It was a lie. All of it.

She silently cursed Sakson and wished he was there in the room with her now, so she could spit in his face. Her spittle would be red and smell of cinnamon as it oozed down his cheek.

"*Terl Plenko is alive and living on Barnard's World.*"

The copy of her—no, it was really her, Dorie Senall—trembled as she said that. Her movements, her speech, it was all fed to her from Sakson, certainly. Couldn't the public tell this was rigged? Fake?

"*We found another copy of Plenko, but we'll be ready for the real Plenko when he arrives. I've seen him. I'll lure him here, and we—Ribon—will have our justice. Please support Acting Governor Tom Sakson in this and know that you are in good hands.*"

The broadcast flipped to commentators around a circular desk. Its surface swirled with images of the smiling newscasters, then alternated with statistics and polls. A poll on Plenko and the public's preferred punishment showed capital punishment leading all other possibilities at 60% Union-wide, and 91% on Ribon. Of course, the only vote that counted was that of Ribon. All other Union worlds and their up-to-the-minute polls meant nothing. The commentators discussed the implications of her speech, but she couldn't bear to listen, let alone watch.

The sound flicked off a second later. "I imagine you don't want to hear any more of that," said a voice behind her.

How did he *do* that? He was always in the room with her when she thought she was alone. RuBy usually accompanied his sudden appearances though, so there was that to look forward to.

"It's all lies, Tom," she said. She walked away from him—and probably a number of RuBy squares he had to offer—and stared up at the vid screen. LIVE FROM NEW VENASAILLE flashed in the bottom right corner, and she laughed at the falsehood. It should've said RECORDED EARLIER, but of course, U-ONE didn't care about anything but ratings, and Sakson only cared about the word getting out the way he *wanted* it to get out.

"Well, you're the Plenko expert, aren't you?" Sakson said. "You may be shit at being governor, but you've got that magic touch rallying citizens to a cause."

She still wouldn't look at him. "What happens to me now?"

"You're still the lure that will bring us the real Plenko."

Now she looked at him. He held the RuBy squares very deliberately, in plain view; she could easily take a few steps and snatch them. She licked her lips deliberately. They were chapped; in the corner of her mouth a sore nagged her.

"And after that?" she asked.

Sakson held up his hands. "We'll see. I'm not sure New Venasaille will be a good place for you anymore."

Dorie almost agreed with him. What would she do without Adi? Without Plenko? The Plenko from the *Sinai*. She'd talked to him and only half-believed he was real. If he'd been a copy, he was dead now. Her husband—*her* Plenko—if he came to Ribon, would be dead soon enough.

She took two steps and found the RuBy in his hand. She slipped the squares into her palm. There was something she really wanted to do, but she couldn't quite remember.

"It's all lies," she whispered.

"Of course."

Her body didn't do what she wanted it to do. God, this stuff was *insidious*. She rolled the RuBy squares, studied them carefully, then popped them, one by one. *Oh. That was better. Much better.*

Sakson lifted her chin and kept looking at her until her eyes focused and she could make out his ugly face. "You're the biggest lie of all, Dorie," Sakson said. He kissed her on the cheek, and she pulled back, disgusted. She almost fell. He smiled, and that, too, disgusted her.

Then she remembered what she'd wished for earlier. She staggered forward and spit in his face.

CROWELL

22 I WAS A UNIVERSE AWAY FROM HOME. I STUMBLED BACK at the sight of the man in front of me, but my eyes stayed locked on him. An impossibility. How in the world—?

"I said who the hell *are* you?" the man asked.

Standing in front of me was Vanderberg Parr.

Actually? Alan Brindos. A copy of Alan.

The Brindos.

He had more lives than fucking Terl Plenko. How could he be alive? Parr had sacrificed himself—I thought—to destroy the portal between universes. Caught in the antimatter detonation caused by the Landry.

"Hey," Parr said. "Rook to old man. Who *are* you?"

Of *course* he didn't recognize me. I'd aged so much, even though I'd only been away from here a year. How could he have been here by himself a whole year? I stood as tall as I could—or as tall as my back allowed me to stand. "You're Vanderberg," I said.

"That's not the topic of discussion here," he said. "*Your* name is."

He didn't seemed surprised I knew his name. "I'm Dave Crowell. I left here a year ago. You—"

"Crowell!" He squinted at me, checking me out. "Jesus, you aren't kidding. It *is* you." He shook his head. "It wasn't a year ago. It was just a few days back, and holy Ultra, you crossed the brane, back into this universe!" He shook his head, disbelief in his eyes. "It sure did a serious number on your good looks."

I self-consciously put a hand to my face. "Not much choice, I'm afraid."

"Some type of time dilation."

"What?"

"You said it's been a year for you, but it's only been a few days for me. So, you know: *Time* dilation. Ultras explained some of it to me." He pointed to his head. "But good thing you did. There's nothing to eat here, and I'm fucking *hungry*."

I looked behind him at the damaged door of the Pool Room and put it all together. "You made it into the Pool Room. It saved you from the blast."

"Well yeah. You didn't think I was going to let myself die when there was a perfectly good place to hide, did you?"

"It didn't occur to me."

"I almost didn't make it. There was Cara, her glow so bright I could barely stand to look at her, and I had this moment of crisis." He frowned, and he struggled with something deep inside him; it took him a while to continue. "Here I finally knew who I was—or close to it—and there was my One about to send the House and me to Kingdom Come. To the Dead Lands. You know? And I thought about what you said, about Alan. About—*me*. Your friend. And all of a sudden, as the Ultras were feeding what they could squeeze into my brain, I understood I still had a part to play in *your* journey. I chose life. I ran to the Pool Room and forced the door closed just in time. It wasn't completely secure, so the blast knocked it loose. But hell, I was alive."

Parr smiled at me, and I couldn't help but smile back. I'd never expected to see him ever again, but damn if I wasn't glad he was here. Glad to see Alan. I didn't have the code card anymore with the image blender prog, so it really *was* Alan Brindos standing in front of me, not the artificially altered visual of him.

"So you're still a hybrid." I asked him. "Part Ultra."

He nodded. "I've been fine here so far. I've had time to process everything. Time to download the Ultra's knowledge."

"Useful for parties, I guess." I was getting achy standing for so long. I found an outcropping of blackrock, shuffled over to it, and sat before my knees gave out. "No RuBy though."

"The withdrawal was difficult, but at the same time, I was gathering more and more of my Ultra self and felt less of a need for it."

"And what does your Ultra self tell you about me now?"

Parr remained standing. "You're old. Did you know?"

"Know it would happen? Yes."

"But you did it anyway."

"Yeah. Plenko told me."

"Ah, you found Plenko."

I shot him a look. "You knew about him?"

"Sure." He pointed to his head. "Well, *now* I know."

"I've come to look for my dad."

"I know."

"As impossible as that seems to be—wait. You know?"

He pointed to his head again.

"Christ, what *don't* you know?"

He came within a few feet of me. "Look, let's get to the point, shall we?"

"All right."

He reached into the pocket of his coat—the same coat he'd worn a year ago. "I found these in the Pool Room. As soon as I did, the Ultra brain did the rest and I realized what they were for. The whole backup thing set up for you."

Plan B the next.

The Tarot cards he held out to me were barely visible in the low light. The sky had darkened. God, I had no sense of time here. I took one of the cards from him with a shaking hand. I didn't know if it was shaking because I had developed some kind of tremor in my old age, or I was just nervous about it.

The Ten of Swords.

I'd read up about it, as I had most of the cards, and this one was scary, no matter how you looked at it. Consider the image on the card: a man face down with ten swords in his back. Beyond that, though, it was symbolic of some unwelcome surprise in the future. It could also mean something bad had already happened: that you'd been backstabbed by someone you cared about.

Those scenarios did not instill in me much hope.

"I figure you might be looking for that," Parr said.

I felt a shiver run up my back. Or maybe I was cold. "I've been collecting the set for a while. But I didn't know what I'd find here. And the other one?"

He gave it to me. There were three swords on the card, two up, one pointing down. "The *Three* of Swords."

"Minor Arcana," Parr said, "like the Ten of Swords."

In my mind, I was already reviewing the card's purpose in the deck. Like this turn of events, the card represented the unexpected.

"The Ten of Swords is the one you need now."

"For what?"

"For travel to an Ultra world."

"And the other card?"

Parr's eyes ticked up, and he pursed his lips in thought. Or whatever it was the Ultra brain was doing.

"Not quite clear. Downloading the information and seeing the through lines could take some time. Hang on to both of them."

I pocketed them, then gulped hard. This time, my shiver was a visceral reaction to the renewed hope inside me. *An Ultra world.* A world—an *anti*matter world, not this buffer world—where I might find my dad. I didn't know how it could be remotely possible for him to be alive, or for me to get there alive.

"You're lucky," Parr said.

"How's that?"

"You have *me.*"

"Because you're an Ultra/human hybrid. A—what was it? 'A special creature.' You can exist in both universes."

"Pretty much."

The thing I really needed to do, I thought just then, was apologize to Parr. Even though it had happened a year ago, on my timetable, it hadn't been that long for Parr. "I'm sorry I punched you in the nose."

He smiled. "And stepped on my hand."

"Could you blame me?"

"No. And in the end? It worked, didn't it?"

It did. Parr changed his mind about the Ultras' designs for our universe and helped us escape Rook. Blew the portal. And yet, here he was, still alive.

"We were all very lucky," I said. "So—speaking of lucky—what downloaded knowledge did the Ultras give you about why they took my dad?"

"He's Lucky Lawrence."

"That's just it. Plenko said he was the Ultra's good luck charm, but he didn't elaborate. Maybe he didn't even know."

"Your dad," he said, "was a failed Ultra experiment."

"How so?"

"They were going to turn him into a hybrid."

My breath caught, stunned by this news. Parr waited for me to say something. "A hybrid," I mumbled. "Like you?"

"Well." He shrugged. "In a way. But a *reverse* prototype. The Ultras thought—well, *if* they could find a way for your dad to survive long-term in an *anti*matter world, they could figure out a way for the Ultras to survive in a world made of matter."

"And did he survive . . . *not* being a hybrid?"

Parr looked away, blinking. Processing his Ultra brain probably. "It seems so. You wouldn't think so, considering the problems the Ultras had over in our universe, but he did."

My dad—alive. Could it really be true? Everything from last year rushed up to remind me of this quest to find him. Everything Terree had helped me discover through the Memory, about the life I'd lived before with him up until I was sixteen, when he disappeared. The past projected into my consciousness like family home flashvids, Mom and Dad together, and me, happy most of the time, but slipping past my escorts when I could; you know, just being a *kid*, but at the same time learning what my dad did as an Envoy.

"So." I took a deep breath. I needed to slow my breathing, the pounding in my chest. I hated feeling so helpless. "How do you help me get to an Ultra world and find my dad?"

Parr spread his arms wide. "My dear Crowell," he said, grinning ear to ear. "You solved that problem on your own. You found what the Ultras left behind and brought it with you."

He pointed behind me, and I craned my neck. The *Exeter*.

I'd been right. "Jesus, the Ultras *did* leave the ship for me."

"Sort of."

I had a hard time believing it, even though the *Exeter* had fallen almost magically into my path. "How could they possibly have known I'd come along, in that jump slot, at that time?"

Parr scoffed. "Please. No *way* they could've known."

"So how—" In an instant, I knew. The truth bled out of me. "It wasn't the only ship."

"The Ultras are a little obsessed with copies." He grinned.

"So you just seeded jump slots with copies of the *Exeter*. The one ship that fucked up the whole Ultra Transcontinental Conduit plan, and that's the ship they copied?"

"If you can't beat 'em, join 'em." He walked past me, abruptly, toward the *Exeter*.

I stood, and my knees creaked. Halfway to the ship, Parr stopped and waited for me to catch up. I drew alongside him, and the two of us stared at the *Exeter* until my back started to ache. I fidgeted, and Parr noticed.

"Won't keep you waiting," he said. "You discovered that the *Exeter* has special properties, including that Ultra skin."

"It's unique, to say the least."

"Your ship is what gets us off this buffer world and safely through antimatter space." He patted my shoulder lightly, as if afraid he might break me. "The *Exeter* will take us to the Ultra world where your dad lives."

Dad. I kept trying to catch up to that idea. Dad was *alive*.

Something occurred to me. I fumbled around until I found the Ten of Swords Tarot. "Then, if we have the *Exeter*, we don't need this."

"Not to get there, but we'll need it on that end."

"We'll power it up there?"

Parr almost laughed. His eyes crinkled enough to show his amusement. "It's a calling card. Without it, the Ultras will throw you into the antimatter and consider it good riddance."

This didn't ease any tension. I closed my eyes. I concentrated on the positive, and in a few moments—Parr stood there waiting me out—the tension actually did drain from me. The prospect of seeing Dad again did a lot to make me forget my dread. It was as if I'd been reborn, my aches and pains gone. *I'm coming, Dad.*

How lucky was *that*?

SENALL

23 HOW MANY DAYS HAD IT BEEN?
    Here, in her room, mired in the perpetual high of RuBy,
Dorie couldn't tell day from night. She floated on a cloud of contentment half the time and sank into waves of despair the other half.
Any time she felt like she couldn't go on, she miraculously found
RuBy in her room. On some occasions, she'd pop it and manage to
quiet some of the strange voices that haunted her: voices unintelligible, strident, mocking, and unforgiving. She had no recollection
of others sharing her room and wondered if she'd been transferred
to a different facility. Maybe the voices were the ghosts of Ribon.
Her RuBy-induced fears revealed stranded colonists unable to flee
the hammer of Coral Moon, its shattered bulk pounding the planet
and its people into submission. She wept for them, the poor, poor
things. Then came the low pathetic whimpers she didn't want to
hear. When she tried to tune them out, she realized they were her
own whimpers. Exhausted, she'd curl into a hard ball and whisper
herself to an uneasy sleep.

For a while, she counted the days—or what she assumed might
be complete days—by keeping track of the squares of RuBy brought
to her. Before long, she couldn't tell one square from another or
distinguish the time between them.

She had it bad. She had it *so good.*

How many days had it been?

Waking one morning-day-night, she felt the cobwebs give way,
and she regained enough clarity to take a measured look at her
room. Her head throbbed and her throat was raw, coated with partial blisters from RuBy squares that hadn't dissolved properly. She
bought a hand up to her mouth to rub at the sore on her lip and
noticed her fingers were stained red from the RuBy dye.

The room was bare except for the narrow, lumpy bed she sat on. The light was dim, as if in a room with only a couple of night lights. Four gray walls, and a door in the front. It was wide open. She leaned forward and stood, careful not to pitch forward. Waiting a few seconds, she weighed the risk of taking a step ahead. She extended her arms like a tightrope walker, then risked a step, and another, pausing only to maintain her balance. When she felt confident enough, she walked ahead to the open door and through. Now outside the room—she knew it was actually a *cell*—she glanced at the stenciled label on the upper half of the door: *Room 12.*

She fought her muddied brain, forced it to think, and realized where she was. The Bubble. She'd come here to talk to that Memor, what's-her-name. Dave visited too, a little later. The Memor could come and go from her room—Room 15, she remembered—and she had a rest period somewhere else. For tests?

Yes. The Bubble was for Thin Men. A place to study copies. But this Memor was not a Thin Man.

She remembered now. *Lorway* was here. The only prisoner in the Bubble. There were no Thin Men here. Just Lorway.

And now Dorie. An original, like Lorway. Not a copy. Not the Dorie who fell from the Tempest Tower who was one of the poor, poor ghosts of Ribon.

Was Lorway still here? Room 15 should be just down the wide hallway. What advice would the Memor give her now? Perhaps something more practical than *Death isn't death when it's a new beginning.*

She inched toward Room 15, her shoulder brushing across the wall for support. Her head was foggy, and she was thirsty. Her muscles ached, and she wanted more RuBy. She had come to a new place, but RuBy didn't wait for her. She could think, and she wasn't sure she wanted to think. *Sakson, you fucker.* Had he extracted what he wanted from her, then thrown her in the Bubble to suffer through withdrawal?

When she reached the door, she leaned in and peered through the doorway. She would've been disappointed. The room was nearly empty. Not only was Lorway gone, but so was her multi-colored dresser and framed mirror. The only evidence the Memor—or it could've been anyone, really—had ever been in this room was scattered debris: discarded fabric, bits of scrap paper and metal, and other garbage.

She knew she hadn't dreamed her encounter with Lorway. That was a different time. That had been Dorie the governor, not Dorie the RuBy addict.

She was about to turn away when she spotted something that glittered on the floor amidst some of the debris in one corner of the room. First, she thought: RuBy. But no, it was larger, and it wasn't red. She crossed the room and looked down, and with her foot, pushed aside some wrappers, wood scraps and burnt paper.

There. She bent over and picked up a Tarot card. It was not the one Lorway had given her of course—she'd given that one to Dave—but an unfamiliar one. She remembered Lorway telling her to give the Death card to him, and that she had a few others—some minor ones—she kept for sentimental reasons.

This card was singed along the edges, as well as throughout the card, outlining the stained-glass window with five coins, and in front of the window, two figures: a cripple and, maybe, a beggar.

Her head was clearer, and she found herself able to think cogently instead of wondering about when she'd find more RuBy. She still ached and felt horrible. Crowell and Plenko had discussed using these for Dave's trip to the Ultra universe. If Dave had successfully crossed because of his Tarot cards, then what was this card doing here, seemingly damaged? She moved the scraps around some more and found another card.

It had no burn marks. The card showed a Devil and what she believed were Adam and Eve. The difference between this card and the first one was that this card's edges weren't singed.

She had a thought, and she looked up into the corners of the room, wondering where the cameras might be. Lorway was a Memor. Had she known about this card, kept it, and discovered how to use it . . . to travel? A minor card, so maybe she wouldn't go far. Enough to escape the Bubble? Triggered by Dave Crowell's use of the other cards?

If so, where had she gone?

If so, Dorie was alone in the Bubble; except, she supposed, for Warden Max Rydell and other Bubble personnel.

She explored the rest of the "cells." The doors were all open, and they were all empty. She remembered Max saying Lorway and others had "rest" time somewhere outside the cell area, but no other door led to any rest area. Finally, when she'd finished her search and found nothing, she backtracked to the main security door she'd come through during her visit with Lorway. It was shut tight and she had no access to the inset panel that housed the DNA lock mechanism.

She was stuck. Pounding on the door got her nothing but sore hands and a raging headache. If anyone was on the other side, they were not interested in the crazy RuBy addict.

She slid down the door and sat on the floor, riding out a wave of nausea. She was sweaty, and her throat burned. There was nothing she could do. She was trapped inside the Bubble, cut off from everything and everyone, and she was tired of feeling helpless. She wanted Terl here. She wanted Dave here. One was probably dead, the other far, far away. How long had Dave been gone, journeying to his quiet spot and to the Ultras? How long until she knew for sure what had happened to her Plenko?

How many days had it been?

Dorie woke with a start and realized she'd fallen asleep against the security door. Her body ached more than before, but was it due to withdrawal symptoms or because she'd slept in an awkward position against the steel door? As usual, she had no idea how much time had passed. Nothing had changed in the hallway. Although not confined to a cell, she had no other freedom than the hallway, from security door to the end wall.

Dorie pushed her back against the door and slid up until she could stand, wobbling only a little. For now, it seemed the best thing she could do was go back to a cell and lay down on one of the beds. Get more rest. She felt better, but she wasn't a hundred percent, and she still craved the Red. If Sakson appeared and offered it to her, she might take it.

Halfway down the hall, she thought she heard a thumping noise. She stopped. Had she imagined it? Staying as still as possible, she listened so intently she heard the heartbeat in her ears.

thump, thump, thump

There was no denying the sound, which came from the far end of the hall. She swallowed her fear, which was considerable since she'd checked the place earlier and found nothing. Was this due to the RuBy? But no, she was coming down from it. The sound was real, but where was it *coming* from?

She pinpointed it: last cell on the left. Room 1.

thump, thump

She'd *checked* that room, damn it. There'd been nothing in there but the small bed. Was the door in the same position? She couldn't remember. Now, her hands shaking, she grasped the handle and pulled the door wider.

Still empty. But—

thump, thump, thump

The thumps were louder now that she'd come to this room. Her pulse beat faster as she took two brave steps past the threshold, fighting back her fear.

"Hello?" Barely more than a whisper, no one within ten feet of her would've heard it. She said it again, projecting into the room. "Anyone there?"

thump thump thump thump thump thump thump

She cried out in surprise. The thumping was beneath her. Mercy, there was someone—or some *thing*—under this room. She scanned the floor, looking for signs of an opening, but she saw nothing.

Monsters under the bed.

The idea came to her quickly, and she tottered to the bed, grabbed hold of the end of the frame, and, with relative ease, pulled it away from the wall. The casters screeched as she pulled, and in the space under the bed was a circular trap door of a highly glossy metal. She would've expected something more ostentatious, the metal decked out with a high-tech control panel, or a DNA lock, but in the middle of the circle, a heavy bronze ring rested snug in a slight indentation the same shape as the ring. She knew it would lift and open the door. Did she *want* to open it?

thumpthumpthumpthumpthumpthumpthump

The pounding grew more urgent. The "monster" knew Dorie was up here, but the renewed, more frantic pounding was something a reasoning human would do, not some kind of beast. There weren't *really* monsters, were there?

The thumping started again and didn't stop. She made a decision. Before she changed her mind, she bent over, grabbed the ring, and pulled. The thumping stopped.

She forced herself to kneel. The lower deep was dark, but she saw the shape that separated itself from the shadows and edged closer to the opening. Something clattered to the floor near the shape—probably the thing that had done the pounding—and quiet fell on Room 1 all over again.

Dorie held her breath, waiting for the thing to leap out at her suddenly, finally freed from its trap. Instead, she heard an indistinct mumbling. Ever so slowly, something reached for the opening. She made out the hand and fingers first, then the arm, and yes, it was human, and whoever it was wanted out of there very badly. The fingers couldn't quite latch onto the edge of the opening, just out of reach.

Dorie took a chance, a big breath, and extended her arm into the hole. The hand grabbed hers, and deep inside she wanted to scream, afraid she'd made the wrong decision.

She pulled. Then she grabbed the arm with both hands, leaned back, and tried to hold on. The person on the other end finally gained enough leverage to snag the edge, then swing another arm up. When both hands were firm and gripping tightly, she let go and sat back. After that, the person pulled up, working his way through the opening.

Dorie cried out once his face was visible. A nearly transparent strip of sprayable polymer effectively gagged him, but she knew right away it was Aditya Thakur.

"Adi!" she yelled.

She leaned forward again and stretched her arms under his, helping the best she could, until he'd clambered out onto the floor of Room 1. When he rolled enough so he could get to his knees, she wrapped him up and squeezed tight.

"Adi," she said. "Oh, Adi, they said you were dead!"

He didn't answer. She'd forgotten about the polymer gag; she worked it off his face, the surface responsive to her own skin and DNA so she could break the seal. He still didn't say anything, but this time, he took a long, deep breath, as if the gag had kept him from breathing normally for a long time. They helped each other stand, and Adi breathed deep once more.

"Hello, Governor Senall," he finally said.

Dorie smiled, but inside she was ecstatic for the return of Adi Thakur. Her friend. He'd been appointed acting governor after she'd stepped down and left Ribon, but he still considered Dorie the right person for the job. Tom Sakson had pulled off his little coup, but Dorie wished it were otherwise.

"I'm so happy to see you," Dorie said. She couldn't get over the shock of Adi appearing almost literally out of nowhere. "How in the *world* did you end up here?"

Adi brushed himself off. "It's a long story."

Dorie swept her hand to include the room and, effectively, the entirety of the Bubble. "We're locked up tight in a maximum security facility, maybe being watched, and we're not going anywhere any time soon. We've got time. I want to know what happened."

"It was Tom Sakson," he said. "You were right to worry about him."

"Adi, I know about Tom. He arrested me as soon as I returned from Barnard's."

Adi nodded. "I can believe it."

"He gave me RuBy. He forced it on me. Discredited my reputation." She held out her hands so he could see her stained fingertips. "I lost so much time. I didn't know what I did during those times, or what *he* might have done."

Aditya Thakur sighed so pitifully that it frightened Dorie. What did Adi know? As if the whole thing with Plenko, Dave, and his father wasn't enough to scare her to death, she dreaded what Adi was going to say. She frowned, trying to anticipate Adi's news. "Why are were here in the Bubble? Why did he say you were dead, and why did he Rube me out against my will?"

Adi reached out and put a hand on her neck. She felt a chill when he did it, even though she knew it was meant to calm her. "I'm sorry."

"Why's he done this to us?"

"He doesn't care about me," Adi said. "He wants Plenko. He hates Plenko more than anyone else in the Union for what he did to him—and to Ribon."

"That was not *my* Plenko!" Dorie shouted. "And it was the Ultras who dreamed all that up."

"I know. Of *course* I know that. The thing is, he's determined to keep going until he knows that *all* the Plenkos are dead. He arrested me, kept me in confinement in New Venasaille. He killed the Plenko you came here with. He used you as bait, and now he has what he wants."

Dorie thought she'd misheard him. She narrowed her eyes quizzically. "He *has* what he wants?"

"Almost. He sent a coded ping through the slot to Barnard's World, wideband. You're here in the Bubble for ransom. Sakson told me all of this, then threw me in solitary while you were passed out." His eyes misted, and he had a hard time looking at her. "He'll kill you, Dorie. Sakson will kill you if Plenko isn't delivered to him."

Dorie said nothing, waiting for the other foot to fall.

"Morgan was the go-between. Plenko screwed up, I guess. Morgan found out where he was. Morgan's task is to bring him to New Venasaille and he'll be given to Sakson in exchange for you."

What Crowell and Forno had been hired to do. *Bring Death to Plenko*. The Tarot card, sure, but literally too.

"I'll bet on Terl," she said. "He won't let Morgan take him."

"Morgan doesn't have to take him. Plenko is giving himself up."

CROWELL

24 FOR ALL THE TALK THESE PAST TWO YEARS ABOUT MATTER and antimatter, I had no way of knowing what it would be like to be in a universe that would gladly cancel out your entire existence. No human who had ever lived, or who was alive today, knew anything about it either. Except my dad, of course, who had lived much of his life within it.

Humans had lived their existence on a single world, in a galaxy that was an infinitesimal speck within an infinite expanse. Only recently had jump slots connected us to more—space.

Although many theories suggested the idea, the Ultras introduced us to more *universe*. Ultras had tried—and failed—to prove that matter and antimatter could coexist in our universe. They'd succeeded—at least for one person—in their own universe, even though the Ultras had no need for bodies on their turf.

So. The Ultras were dying. Our universe proved unsuitable for them, and the threat ended. It was my turn to be scared, now that the *Exeter* had left behind the buffer world of Rook and slipped past the complicated, Ultra-manipulated and physics-defying demarcation line. The ship sliced through antimatter space without difficulty, as if it were an ice breaker cutting through polar ice.

Vanderberg Parr gave a short lesson—as he understood it—on the science behind the *Exeter*'s special antimatter skin, going way beyond my ability to follow it. As for the journey itself through antimatter space, I saw no noticeable difference as I stared obsessively out the viewscreen. I'd secretly hoped for color spectrum shifts, psychedelic whorls, or other oddities, but antimatter and matter were identical in all ways, except for electrical charge, and I found space travel as boring here as in my own universe. I was surprised Parr looked so comfortable in his harness next to me, considering he was part Alan Brindos, who had despised space travel more than me.

I'd become used to Vanderberg Parr looking like Brindos. I guess distance, time, and old age made it a little easier to see him as someone else and not my long-lost friend. While Parr had most of Brindos's memories and mannerisms, the Ultra part of him sometimes scared the hell out of me. Parr boasted a constant connection to his Ultra database, accessing at will with his special hybrid status. Sometimes Parr tuned out in the middle of a conversation, as if he'd turned himself off to recharge. It was . . . disconcerting.

A lot of shit had happened since I'd investigated the fall of Dorie's copy off the Tempest Tower. I could even go back to when I solved TWT Vice President Brenden Thorne's murder, helped by Brindos and my old Authority partner Shirley McCoy, when we first discovered the highly dangerous prototype of the drug RuBy. It seemed it would all end one way or another when this wild, insane search for my dad ended.

Old age meant having to recharge as often as Parr did. I grew tired quickly. Being bored took a lot of energy, I guess. Even after a good nap, I'd find myself nodding off while staring at the viewscreen or making conversation with Parr.

After one such cat nap, Parr laughed at me and asked if I was part Ultra, accessing my own database.

"I wish," I grumbled. "If the Memors could give us jump slots to get from colony to colony, why don't the Ultras have special alien powers or super science to get us from one spot to the other quickly?"

Parr flicked his eyes up and left, then right, pausing several seconds to consult his Ultrafied data. "They do, but nothing we can use."

"Because of this ship?"

Parr frowned at me as if I were an imbecile child. "Because we have *bodies*."

"Oh. Right."

"It's okay. They didn't take your dad too far from Rook, in case their hybridizing experiments didn't take. This trip may seem long traveling through regular space, but if you compare the relative short distance to the entirety of the Ultra universe, it's more like a long walk."

Boring, but also physically difficult for the elderly. I shifted uncomfortably in my harness. My back felt like the vertebrae had separated, and I kept hearing little pops and snaps when I stretched.

If we didn't get there soon, I might become a human accordion.

Living on the edge. I wondered if the thin skin of the *Exeter's* antimatter hull would protect us the whole way. I wondered what the Ultra world would look like when we arrived. I wondered how the hell I was going to leave the ship and search for my dad, or if I would be quarantined on the *Exeter* and have to wait for him to come to me.

All that *wondering* used up what energy I had left, and I closed my eyes. Better to spend these boring hours asleep anyway. I held off a while, hoping Parr might announce the appearance of the Ultra world on the viewscreen, but he didn't, and I, plenty tired of waiting, succumbed to sleep.

It might've been my second nap of the day, or my sixth. Hard to tell, really. All I knew was that I woke up, and I was not dead. Parr was awake, but unmoving, staring at the viewscreen. Was he aware I was awake? Would he be happy or disappointed that I was still alive?

"I'm happy you're still alive," Parr said.

"Damn it, are you a mind reader, too?"

"Pardon?"

I waved him off. "Never mind." I looked more intently at the viewscreen. "Where are we?"

"Sensors and—" He pointed to his head "—my Ultra brain, indicate we're approaching the Ultra world. Visual in a few minutes."

Anticipation welled up inside (or it was the start of a heart attack), and I almost forgot to breathe (or a lung was collapsing). It wasn't right of me, treating my old age as something I resented. No wonder old people became crochety in their later years and yelled at kids to get off their lawns.

We were nearly there, the place I'd long searched for. The low odds of ever finding my dad had suddenly turned in my favor. *A universe away!* I took a deep breath. What would I say to him? What would I *ask* of him? Perhaps he was happy here. Happy in the knowledge that his universe was intact, his son alive. Then I wondered how much he knew. Perhaps he was blind and ignorant of all that had happened on our end. I crossed my arms and stared at the viewscreen, waiting with anticipation.

And then I saw it. Tinged green, hazy clouds and fog obscuring most of its features. As it grew in the viewscreen, the immensity of it took my breath away. It hung in space like a picture, waiting for us to close in and click it on, as if it were a paused vid on flashpaper.

I took it all in, my eyes sweeping from pole to pole, and there didn't seem to be any ice caps. I thought I detected the glittering of water, and the occasional flash in the clouds that could've been lightning. I saw the edge of a large moon orbiting, and I wondered if I was experiencing some type of moon illusion.

The *Exeter* crept closer. Next to me, Parr said something I couldn't hear, but it sounded reverent.

"Does this world have a name?" I asked.

Parr shook his head, and he had that remote accessing-the-database look again. "What comes closest is a translation of a long, complex number. The Ultra worlds are numbered, and the number of worlds are near infinite."

"The numbers for most worlds are literally too high to count."

"Correct. Unless this happened to be world number one."

"But it's not."

"No. I believe I can detect twenty-six numbers for this world."

"*Rook* had a name."

"Reiser named Rook because it was convenient for humans. And it's in the buffer zone, so it's not technically an Ultra world."

"Well, regardless, *this* world needs a name."

Parr extended his hand to me, palm up, indicating I should decide. "Anything besides Dad's World."

I gave a low chuckle. The name came to me quickly, and it felt immediately appropriate. A name that spoke about the world's relative placement close to the buffer zone, and my dad's ordeal as an Ultra guinea pig. "We'll call it Pawn."

Parr nodded knowingly. "That works." He cocked his head toward the viewscreen. "Welcome to Pawn."

Closer now, some of the green clouds gave way to some wispy greenish yellow features that might've been land masses.

"What happens now?" I asked.

Parr accessed for a moment, cross referencing something. His sudden scowl was so Brindos-like I had to look away. I couldn't tell if Parr was more Brindos or the pre-hybridized Vanderberg. At least his potty mouth had cleaned up a little.

"We find out where to go. It's a big place."

"How do you know where?" As soon as I said it, I knew how stupid that was. Even now, Parr was accessing his Ultra parts.

"I have the coordinates," he said. He leaned over the console and his fingers flew over the console. "I'm not sure you'll like what happens next," Parr said, "although it's the simplest solution to getting—" He indicated the viewscreen again with a nod. "—down *there*."

"Because if I leave the ship—"

"Not pretty. So we rely on an Ultra trick."

I groaned. "Aw shit, don't tell me. Not that. Not the glow thing."

"Time for the Ten of Swords."

I found the card in my pocket, but I left the Three of Swords alone. "You said this was a calling card. So the Ultras would know—"

"They'll know, because it's the only way you'll get to them from here."

"And glow."

Parr nodded. "Hold it up, facing you."

I did, and then Parr's hand brightened. In a few seconds the fingers were wrapped in a white light.

I stared at him and fought back a feeling of despair. "Damn, I really hate glow. Do I have to?"

Parr reached his hand toward me. "Sleep," he said.

And I did.

SENALL

25 DORIE STEADIED ADI THAKUR AS THEY LEFT ROOM 1 AND walked into the hallway. Adi, still weak from the solitary confinement, had lost track of the days he'd been in the Bubble, as she had.

She wondered if cameras were tracking them. No one had come in to stop her from freeing Adi, and no one entered the detention area now to throw him back in. Were the guards and Max Rydell even in the Bubble anymore? Before Adi and herself, Lorway had been the only prisoner—or, as Max liked to put it: subject. Had Rydell, under Sakson's orders, freed Lorway as part of the protest against her? She couldn't figure out how that would help him.

"There's no one here," Adi said as he swept his eyes back and forth, spotting the empty rooms.

"That's right. You were dumped down there without knowing who was in the Bubble."

"It's a facility for studying Thin Men." He looked questioningly at her. "It's *not* Thin Men?"

She told him about Lorway, the only Thin Man in here, and how Dave Crowell had found out it was the real Lorway. Now she was gone.

"That's quite a story," Adi said.

"I found two of these in her old room. This is the first."

She held out the singed Tarot card. Adi took it, and he didn't know much more about Tarot than she did. She outlined Crowell's quest to gather them all, and explained they had a role to play in helping him find his father.

"Lorway had the Death card and she had me take it to Dave. I gave it to him in your office after I stepped down as governor. Lorway never mentioned having any other cards."

Adi rubbed his fingers on it. "It's charred."

"But why? That's what I want to know."

Adi held it closer to his face. "Burned within, and around edges. That's a strange pattern."

Dorie remembered something. "Dave did come here to see Lorway after I did before we left for Barnard's. Do you think he gave her this card?"

"Why would he do that if he was collecting them?"

"Apparently only some of them were important for what they were designed for."

"Which was what again?"

"Jumping to the Ultra universe."

"Oh, is *that* all." He grinned, but then he held up the card and added, "Could this be one that was used for that purpose?"

"To cross universes? No, no, there were a lot of cards involved, and a number of conditions needed." She took the card back. "Do you know what card this is?"

"No. Stained glass window, five gold coins. There are cards named by their numbers, aren't there?"

Dorie scratched her head.

"Do you think Lorway used it somehow?" Adi asked.

She'd thought about that earlier, before finding Adi. Where would one card take someone? What would trigger it? "Dave and Plenko talked about DNA coding. From the artist, but also for Dave, who would be the one to use them. So maybe. This is obviously a minor card he didn't need, so could it have been tuned to her?"

Adi looked thoughtful. "And when they discovered she was gone?"

"They removed the bed and larger items, like her dresser. No one else was in the Bubble, so they didn't concern themselves with a lot of the small bits."

"And you found two cards?"

"Yes, I did." She pulled out The Devil card and handed it to him.

"Fire and brimstone," Adi said. "Probably a bad card. Things hellish? Bad stuff coming.

"Like death."

"Or something leading up to it."

"Like—an addiction."

"RuBy?"

"Maybe."

They walked back to Room 15 and Dorie steadied herself against the cell opening, feeling a little nausea. She still had plenty of moments when she fought the side effects of RuBy withdrawal. She felt certain if she'd found some, she'd roll a square and pop it. The uncertainty passed, and she spread her hands to indicate the refuse scattered on the floor. "I found them in that corner," she said, pointing.

Dorie thought of herself and Terl. The Devil card could easily symbolize their own dramatic history of love and loss. She turned the card over. "What? I never noticed. There's *handwriting*." She turned the other one over, too, but only The Devil had something written on the back.

Adi came closer. "What does it say?"

She put a hand to her mouth, and it trembled against her lips. Through her fingers, she said, "Tempest Tower."

Over the years, Adi had heard her talk plenty about the days of the first Ultra scare; Dave Crowell's introduction to it all started when he viewed the holovid of her copy deliberately killing herself by throwing herself off the Tempest Tower in Venasaille.

Tempest Tower.

Dorie Senall plummeted one hundred floors to her gruesome death. What did it mean, written on the back of this card? Was it a reminder or a warning for Dave since most of this Tarot deck had been meant for him? Dave had all the cards he needed to make his dark passage to the Ultra universe. She wondered if he'd ever seen it and pondered its meaning—if he'd seen the message at all. If Lorway used the singed one—if it had been fixed to her own DNA—then why couldn't a different minor card tether to someone else? Had Lorway written the note for *her*?

The temporary home of Dorie Senall and Terl Plenko, both Thin Men. Plenko the artist, leaving behind the mortaline sculpture of a twisted planet and its mass of tiny writing bodies struggling to be free. A sculpture that revealed the DNA of the artist and Dorie Senall.

"It's for me," she said. "I think it has to be for me."

"How's that possible?" Adi asked.

"Because Terl Plenko—the real one, my Plenko—made these Tarot cards."

"I don't think I'm seeing the connections."

"Lorway escaped, and now it's time for me. The Tempest Tower.

A lost relationship. The sorrow behind that. And then there's my copy's suicide."

Adi flinched. "Dorie, you're not thinking—"

"No, of course not. It's symbolic, right? *That* Dorie was trapped in her addiction in a different way. She had no choice but to jump. Have you ever read *The Tempest*?"

"Shakespeare."

"Miranda has never seen any other person other than her father Prospero on her island. And then people come, and she's amazed."

"O brave new world, that has such people in it," Adi said.

"Right." Dorie clenched her teeth, feeling a resolve she hadn't experienced in a long while. "New Venasaille is our new world, and goddamn it, I need to get back to it."

Adi nodded in agreement and gave a proud smile. "But how?"

Dorie thought. They would need quiet, and it wasn't going to get any quieter than it was here, with no one else around. She turned the card back to the picture side and stared at the image of Eve carrying a basket of red apples. A red-orange fire blazed behind Adam.

Red.

Abruptly, she sat down, cross-legged, and put the card on the floor in front of her. Adi sat down across from her.

"You have an idea?" he asked.

"It's my DNA." She held out both hands to Adi. "Look."

He shook his head. "What am I looking at?"

She wiggled her fingers. "The sign of a true addict."

RuBy.

Her fingers were stained red from the recent quantities of the drug forced on her. Even in the years between her last use of it and the time of her capture in Zola's, the red on her fingertips had not gone away completely, only faded. The fresh abuse had painted them a dark red now. She could still smell the cinnamon on her fingers, even though she had not had any new squares in a while, and she'd fought through the withdrawal in the Bubble.

Still, she fought the craving for the alien drug almost every minute.

"If this works," Adi said, "where will you go? Where did Lorway go? Will you end up in the same place? Will you end up free or back in Sakson's hands?"

She shrugged. "I believe it might be the Tower. There's a good reason why it might be where I travel, connected to it as I am. I tried to get it preserved as a memorial, remember? A small remaining portion of it anyway, which was just as well, because it wouldn't have fit under the dome otherwise. Work started on the project, but never finished. And, well—" She paused, self-consciously rubbing her fingertips. "There's something there I might need."

"Need? Need what?"

You want some? Some of the action I'm offering you?

A leap of faith. She wondered what her copy had felt when she took her own leap off the Tempest Tower. *Chance of a lifetime. Girl of adventure.*

She shook her head to clear the echoes of her copy, reached out, and placed her fingers lightly on the card. What else could she do? It seemed as good an attempt as any. "You'll have to remain completely quiet," she said.

He nodded and waited.

"And Adi," she said, "the card's for me, so if it works—"

He waved her off. "I understand. You'll come back and get me. Right, *Governor* Senall?"

She smiled. How she loved him and his confidence in her. She nodded vigorously. Closed her eyes. Concentrated.

Nothing happened.

Except *maybe* she noticed a slight tingle in her fingertips. Or she could've imagined it. Maybe it was because she had no RuBy and still felt the need for it. She peeked through her eyelids and moved her fingers to either side of the card. Then all the fingers, minus the thumbs, centered. Then along the borders of the images, since the first card had shown its burn marks around the outlines of the card.

There *was* a tingle. She opened her eyes fully. Adi gave her an encouraging look. Glancing at the card, she saw a sputter of light. Silverish, subdued, and fleeting. The tingle became a definite sensation of movement.

Surprised, she lifted her hands, her heart beating faster.

Adi frowned a little and mimicked the motion, his hands down on the floor, fingers splayed, but he put extra effort into it and grimaced in a way to show he meant he was pushing down harder.

More weight. A firmer touch.

She swallowed, then nodded. Fingers back on the card in the same position as before, she pushed down.

Light returned.

She felt the heat of the card under her fingers as the light became a white line that spread through the outlines of the card. It was working. It was *working*!

Lightheaded, Dorie ignored the strange vibrations that made her want to break contact. She concentrated on the fire. The chains uniting Adam and Eve lighting up now. Her head ached with pulsing throbs that seemed to match the sputters of the white light as it traced the card.

Then nausea.

Then it seemed Adi was frozen in place.

A blinding light assailed her, and she closed her eyes against it.

She didn't open them. Couldn't feel the card. Instead, she gave in to a peaceful calmness, as if reveling in a RuBy high. As if she were floating. Floating, but descending, as if from up on high, released from an ivory tower. There were burn marks on the tower in jagged shapes.

She slept.

CROWELL

2 6   I WOKE.
    The smell of something burning. The air heavy with the feeling of *wrongness*. There was light. But only a little, tinted sky blue, and ghostly, with no visible source. I lay flat on my back, and the surface pressed hard against me. My hands were at my sides, and through them I felt the coolness of the surface. It reminded me of concrete. Like I didn't have enough back problems without having to put up with unforgiving concrete.

Where was I? Where was Parr? And was Dad . . . here? Were the Ultras—or the essence of them—here too, wherever this was? Parr had glowed me out of the *Exeter*, I assumed, initiating quantum sleep, and drawing on the power of the last Tarot card. At the same time, he'd managed to keep my matter away from antimatter.

The Ten of Swords. An unwelcome surprise. Something bad has already happened.

The burnt smell from the singed edges of the card had stayed with me through whatever dark passage had deposited me here to—well, wherever I was now. I couldn't comprehend how I could be in a place inhabited by Ultras—in an antimatter universe—and still be in one piece.

But here I was.

Either that, or the process had failed, and I was dead. I convinced myself that wasn't true, although it seemed likely I hadn't ended up where Parr assumed I would. I still couldn't see a thing, save for the blue tinted light that revealed—

Well . . . *some*thing.

For a second I was back with Terree, when he'd first explained to me the idea of the Memory—back before morphing male—and how I accessed, through the memories of Greist Sahlkla, all that transpired at the Chicago conference a long time ago. Then I'd remerged from the Memory and realized I was still in my office. Terree had sent me back through these layers of sleep to learn the truth.

I had awoken now, and what I saw emerged from the blue light as if I were returning from the Memory. A figure, long and lanky, like a Memor, stood rigidly in front of me.

Terree?

No. The figure coalesced, swam in my vision, and solidified as awareness caught up to me. The room came into focus too. Empty of everything but a few crude pieces of furniture, cobbled together inexpertly with wood and metal, and the persistent blue light emanated from the walls themselves.

The figure slumped, as if he'd suddenly became aware of something terrible and unexpected.

The Ten of Swords.

It was human. He was male. He was middle-aged—but how could I not recognize him? How many years had passed? Many. How well did I know him? Not at all.

But it was him. *I remembered.*

Though younger than me, I recognized him because I recognized myself in his gentle face. Recognized the kindness my memory of him dredged up. As my eyes continued to adjust to the low light, I saw the subtle characteristics of a man who'd lived the recent years of life in the worst of conditions, in a place utterly foreign to him.

He was lucky to be here. Lucky to be alive. But then again, wasn't that who he was?

Lucky Lawrence.

"Dad?" The word barely audible, as if the light itself absorbed sound.

Lawrence Crowell regained his composure and stood tall. Tears were in his eyes the same moment I felt my own tears well up. "David," he said. "Is . . . is it you? Really you?"

I nodded, and we continued to stare at each other, as if waiting for someone to make the first move. How did I explain this moment? Explain the years of loneliness I'd felt—sometimes without really knowing I was lonely—that now lifted and escaped from me like a prayer. I couldn't. It was all too surreal, too difficult to grasp.

I'd aged far past him, grandfather-like, but he was still my dad.

Finally, the moment of sheer astonishment broke, and we closed the distance and wrapped our arms around each other. I held on a long time, and didn't want to let go. Maybe because I was afraid I might fall when he released me. I was an old man whose aches and pains of the past day had been debilitating and frustrating, and now I held on for dear life. The strong arms of my dad's embrace comforted me.

I didn't know what to say. After all this time, what to say?

I missed you. I love you. I wish Mom could've—

I was saved from the decision, for my dad spoke, and his voice was his voice. The voice I remembered from my slumbers in the Memory last year. The same calmness, the same timbre, the same—peace.

"I was told you'd be coming," he said. "I didn't know when, but—I've been waiting."

We finally parted from one another. I had to look up at him, just like I did when I was a young boy. Seemed I'd developed a hunch and shrunk a little because of the aging process.

"The Ultras told you?" I asked.

"Yes."

I shuddered at the thought that the strange, bodiless, dying, antimatter Ultras had known about my journey and that they let my dad in on it. Did they tell him recently, when I came into their universe, or did they tell him back when they first stole him from my mom and me? Was he, or was he not, their prisoner?

Prisoner or not, he's here, and that's what you wanted.

I wanted to know what happened, but I didn't want to just blurt it out. Sure, it was one of the biggest questions of my life. I needed to know how it all went down, that day at the conference in Chicago. The one I witnessed in the Memory.

Get away from here! Stay away from us.

He saved my life. Saved my existence in our own universe.

Run!

"They took me," my dad said, filling the silence, "but you know that now. They had no reason to, at first, other than the fact someone referred to me as being lucky, and the Ultras love the idea of luck. It's a concept new to them. They stole me, at first, because they wanted to understand what luck was. It wasn't for insurance. It wasn't so they could glean whatever scientific knowledge I might have that would help them. They wanted to understand luck. They wanted *my* luck."

Hearing my dad explain the Ultras like they were newfound, ignorant friends was chilling. "I assume you explained to them the irony of your luck running out when they took you."

"I did, but they didn't see it that way. I was alive. I missed both Ultra scares. I arrived here in one piece—not a small feat considering this universe's antimatter existence—and I learned what I could of them. I learned they were dying, and because they had secured luck for themselves, they might have a chance to survive."

"But they were wrong," I said. My voice rose, and heat rose to my face. "The answer to their problems was to invade our universe, and it didn't work."

"No, it didn't."

"And they used you, their lucky charm, to create a human who could live in an antimatter world. Dad, you were an *experiment*."

He shook his head. "No."

"They did it because they wanted to find a way to exist as hybrids in *our* world. It was the only way they could live."

"*No.*"

My dad strode away from me until he came to one of the crude pieces of furniture. He sat down and the chair creaked noisily.

"Don't you see, David? What luck really means? To you and me, to your mom, to humans? What it means to the Ultras?"

I just stared. My knees were shaking, and my dad noticed.

"Come sit down," he said. "Before you fall over."

In that moment, I didn't trust what he said. I *wanted* to. He was my *dad*. Stubbornly, I held firm. "Your leaving wasn't lucky for me. For Mom. For the Union. The Ultras tried to wipe us out so they could live."

"They didn't succeed."

"No. But they caused a lot of pain. And death. Destruction."

"Bad luck."

I started. "What?"

"Why do you assume when I talk about luck that it's a good thing?" He motioned to the other chair again. "Please, sit."

This time I relented and gingerly folded myself into the chair closest to him.

"The Ultras found out about luck." He leaned toward me, eagerly. "They found out about *bad* luck, too. There were a few others the Ultras took that day to bring here—Envoys, mostly—but none of them made the passage successfully. I was the only one. I was lucky. And that got them wondering."

"Their invasion was a failure because of bad luck?"

"Their attempt to use me in their plan failed, and that was lucky for *you*."

"For the Union."

"Yes, of course."

"So what are you saying? You were *not* lucky for them, because they couldn't engineer you into an Ultra hybrid to help them learn how to do it in our own universe?"

He nodded.

"Vanderberg Parr. *He's* a hybrid. He was my partner. My friend. A copy of him, anyway. You know him, right? Know about him? He lived on Earth, and then he ended up on Rook."

He nodded again.

"A special creature, he calls himself." My partner. My *friend*. A copy of him anyway. An Ultra.

"He brought you here in the *Exeter*. One of the ships put in the jump slots for you."

"You *know* about that?"

"Sure. And about the card that brought you here. The Ten of Swords. Plenko told me."

"He told you—" I paused, confused, as if I'd just been sucker punched. A strong left uppercut. "How could he have done that? The Ultras stole you. You were gone long before the Ultras made copies of him. Before the real Plenko did his thing. Before they used him to—"

"You know this. Parr. He's able to survive in both worlds and access eons' worth of knowledge of the Ultra group consciousness. But also human consciousness. Helk and Memor consciousness."

"Then that's how Plenko told you. Through Parr. He's a copy of Plenko *and* Brindos."

He smiled. "Talk about your special hybrids."

"The Ultras were successful." I stated it with a mixture of awe and revulsion. "They had their prototype. They could—" I broke off, not knowing how to finish, not wanting to say it out loud.

"They could've won." Lucky Lawrence nodded wisely, acknowledging my conclusion.

"But they didn't because Parr betrayed them," I said. "He let us go, and the tether to our universe was destroyed."

"*That* was lucky."

"But how are you involved? You say you taught the Ultras bad luck instead of good."

He nodded. "I wasn't needed. They had Parr. I'm certainly no hybrid, and I can't survive in an antimatter universe any better than you could."

"And yet here we are, on Pawn."

"On what?"

"This Ultra world. I named it Pawn."

"Because you thought I was a Pawn."

"Parr too."

"Parr's the only non-Ultra who can survive in either universe." My dad swept his hand to indicate the room. He pointed to the walls that shimmered with blue. "This is just a buffer. A construct allowing my survival the same way Rook guaranteed your own. The same way the *Exeter* kept you alive on your way here."

"That's how you helped them. You figured out the science to create Rook. To create a place for you to exist here on their world."

"I already *knew* the science surrounding matter and antimatter, and I'd taken it further than anyone before. I'd done talks on it around the Union as part of my Envoy work. I was going to speak at the Chicago conference about it. This is the luck the Ultras thought I had. What I could give them."

"But all you could do was create those bubbles. You couldn't make it work on people like you and me. So you've been here all this time, a failed experiment?"

"Well, it's been a long time, but not as long as you might think."

I nodded knowingly. "Very little time had passed for Parr, stranded on Rook, while I was gone."

"I'm guessing it's been a handful of years for me, subjectively. Time dilation. And some tricks the Ultras have up their sleeves."

I shivered at the thought. I'd been without my dad for—*how* long? And it'd only been a short time for him. It explained how, though he looked middle-aged, I had recognized him for who he was in this room. *He's almost exactly the way I remember him from my youth, before he disappeared.*

"It's obvious the Ultras let me come here to see you," I said. "And although Parr betrayed them, the Ultras don't seem to care that he's alive and helping me. Why? What can the Ultras do now?"

"Nothing."

"It's true then? They will really die out?"

He nodded. "There's something eternal in the idea of light and energy and a relativistic existence without physical form, but consciousness can't handle that kind of phenomena for long. They had no foresight of that, and now, only hindsight about the neural basis of immortality."

"Neural basis—"

"They're dark matter and antimatter and light and kinetic energy and—well. For a long time they were physical beings like us. Wait until you see the kind of civilization they built! Many of the structures on their worlds seem as fresh and new as they did when the Ultras entered their advanced, ultra-evolved state of being."

"You've seen them?"

"I've not even been outside this building. But I've been shown some digital representations."

"Do they still talk to you?"

"Sometimes. They use the nodes built into the buffer patterns in here to communicate digitally, even though they aren't digital themselves."

"So what do they say to you?"

He shrugged nonchalantly. "They don't say much or ask much these days. They've accepted their fate. They still study me, but mostly I'm a curiosity. I'm stuck here, so what can I do?"

"And now *I'm* stuck here." I slumped in the chair and felt the heaviness of age weigh me down.

Lucky Lawrence turned his hands over, palms up, and spread his arms wide, a gesture that communicated something other than agreement.

"I'm not?"

He brought his hands together into a faint clap. "So. Let's wait for Parr."

"He's coming? But the card only transported me."

"Yeah, well, *he* doesn't need it to move around the Ultra world, does he? He just needed to dock the ship and make his way here."

*

Over the next hour, my dad and I talked. We ignored the world of the Ultras—and the reality of the buffer prison—and reminisced about those early years when he was still a part of the family. I told him about Mom passing away peacefully, about all the memories and good times from years at the lake. About her long-time guardian Tilson Hammond that Greist had put in place.

It was clear he missed Mom dreadfully, his eyes misting up when I told him about her death. He talked a long time about her. He filled in the gaps about the reality of our lives when we were all together, about his career as an Envoy, and everything that the removal of the memory block had not quite answered.

We eventually came back to the Ultras. Like all of us, he'd never "seen" an Ultra. There was no way to describe them other than how he'd experienced them. What did he do all day, in this buffer zone? Listening and learning about the Ultra culture. Devouring books and entertainment—flash or otherwise—that the aliens had "downloaded" during their time in the Union of Worlds. Exercise on a matter-bubble that paired to his own steps to give the illusion of motion, the boundaries of which bloomed with images of this alien world—Pawn—as well as others where the Ultras had lived their physical lives. Eating processed food he didn't know the name of, where it came from, or—if it was safe enough for him to eat—how it made its way through antimatter space. And sleep. Lots of sleep, though he was never allowed quantum sleep.

We always came back to the Union. Earth. The lake, the marina. The places he visited as an Envoy. We laughed and cried, we celebrated and consoled one another, and I felt certain, even though I'd grown tired and my lower back had begun to rebel sitting so long in the Ultra furniture, we could've talked for hours more. At some point however—and I don't know how long he'd stood there—Vanderberg Parr caught our attention.

"Glad to see you made it here okay," he said to me. He nodded at my father. "A pleasure, sir."

My dad nodded in return.

"Your trip here was a safe way to travel actually," Parr said to me, "if you have the means. You're more likely to have a fatal accident crossing a busy Helk thoroughfare. Those blackrock roads soak up so much heat and play tricks on the eyes."

The Helk part of Parr related that bit of knowledge. He didn't even have to do his little eye movement and pause for data retrieval to put that out there.

"It looks like you have a ship now," I said to Parr.

"Excuse me?"

"The *Exeter*. It's yours. Explore the Ultra universe. Meet new people."

"What people are you referring to? I'm alone no matter what universe I'm in."

"You have us," I said.

"Comforting," he said. "Not quite true, though."

A tremor ran up my back when he said it, and I anticipated some strange interpretation of our predicament. *Not true*? I squinted, trying to guess the intent of his message. My dad spoke, making me jump a little, and I thought I might've tweaked a muscle.

"Did you bring it?" my dad asked.

"Of course," Parr said. He looked at me as if I'd missed the punchline of the best joke ever told.

But I understood. "You mean the other Tarot card." I found it in my pocket and held it up.

The unexpected. I knew it meant more than that. Much, much more.

"You can travel home with that," my dad said. "To our universe."

The news gripped me like hands around my waist holding me back from doing something stupid. The feeling of helplessness dug deep. It was just too much to deal with. Things had dug so hard and for so long that I thought it might weigh me down more than this newly decrepit body. "Look," I said. "To get to Rook I needed an entire set of cards with an intricate pattern that lined up perfectly. How is one card going to get me home?"

"I've learned the details now, from the Ultra mind," Par said. "The card's charged with extra nano ink and three times the power of RuBy."

I balanced the card in my hand as if it were a comm card. "That's *enough*?"

"How did Baren Reiser go back and forth?" Parr asked.

"His tattoos. The infused ink."

"And RuBy, don't forget."

I rubbed the card carefully, tracing the swords: Down the first sword, up the second, then down again. The smoothness reminded me of my dad's nearly unlined face, and was a reminder of my own marked, wrinkled one.

"No," I said.

"No?" Parr asked.

"I can't."

"You can," my dad said.

"I *won't*."

I knew the truth. The Three of Swords. Three men stuck in a universe not meant for any of them. But only one sword pointed in a different direction.

"The card's only good for one trip, and for one person," I said finally. "You would both be left behind."

SENALL

27 DORIE SENALL WOKE, AND AFTER A QUICK GLANCE, SHE knew where she was. The muted light of morning made the dome of New Venasaille seem translucent. In its way, it was a beautiful image, one she'd always loved, knowing there were few other views like it in the Union.

She was in a cold room she recognized at once. A famous Ribon landmark from before the Coral Moon disaster.

The Tempest Tower.

Well. Not *exactly* the Tempest Tower. A section of it had survived after the disaster, then engineers preserved it, and it was due to her efforts as president of New Venasaille that the council approved her idea to commemorate the loss of the original Venasaille. A visual reminder—a memorial—of what had come before the first dome and the new city.

But it never came to fruition. Funding dried up, excitement waned, and it was abandoned.

"Room" was an understatement. Tempest Tower boasted luxurious suites during its heyday. Now, under the dome, it was just a neglected eyesore. The Tower had once been over a hundred floors high. The disaster had damaged it badly, particularly the lower floors and foundation, so because dome construction required removal of most of it, the mostly undamaged upper section underwent a delicate removal process—nearly fifteen floors' worth. The rest of the Tempest Tower was scrapped, a foundation rebuilt, and the intact floors set down, the process itself a marvelous technological achievement.

By the time work stopped on the project, most of the remaining suites remained uninhabitable and the building, and particularly the most damaged suites, were designated off-limits, surrounded by yellow flashpaper that scrolled *Do Not Enter* across its surface.

Dorie knew this suite due to its layout. After all, she had personally spearheaded the project and diligently inspected each suite.

She had lived here. Before the Ultras. Before Terl was copied, before he was lost at the Rock Dome, before Terl Plenko the Movement leader moved in to the suite with her own copy.

This suite was *not* safe. At least not enough for anyone to spend significant time inside. Flashpaper warning tape across the door most assuredly. It had no furniture. Dust coated most of the surfaces. The walls were gray with grime that was never cleaned up after the Coral Moon disaster. Too far down the project's "to-do" list. She recognized the white couch—now gray—where her copy had proposed the idea of Plenko's terrorist Movement to Jennifer Lisle. Blood spots lost in the neglect. There'd been a wall vid, but it was gone. Paintings and wall hangings gone. A few overturned chairs. A table still upright in a corner.

The entrance to the most sought-after amenity of the original Tempest Tower suites—a spacious balcony with state-of-the-art electromagnetic shielding—was marred by ruined French doors off its hinges, debris littering the floor. Beyond the doors was the damaged balcony; all that remained of it was a half-moon section just beyond the door for anyone crazy enough to test its limits.

She knew this suite.

The uppermost floor of Tempest Tower. The 100th floor. The suite of one Dorie Senall, the copy who fell to her death rather than give up the whereabouts of her lover, the interstellar terrorist known as Terl Plenko.

Not my Plenko.

She stood and stared at the broken French doors. The missing balcony. She knew why the card had brought her here. She was connected to this suite. Through Terl Plenko. A place of beginnings and endings.

The end of her old life—a life of RuBy addiction—and the start of the new: leader of a new Venasaille. She'd had a taste of the old life recently, succumbing to the machinations of Tom Sakson, falling prey once again to the old drug. Back when she'd decided to get clean, however, she'd chosen this suite as a symbol of her new life.

She ditched the RuBy here.

Ditched it and, although she had never pretended to have forgotten where it was, hid the RuBy in the suite, on the remaining section of the balcony.

Dorie took several tentative steps toward the balcony. The RuBy would be out there. She doubted it had been disturbed all this time. She believed this was why her Tarot card had brought her to this spot. It was as if the card could sense the RuBy that still connected her to Ribon's past, like a chain. Like RuBy-infused Tarot cards, silvery lines of force embedded in the card tuned to the DNA of its owner, as if it were a niche-holo tracker. Like the echoes of her copy's voice from the infamous holo-recording captured by the NIO's marble camera.

A few more steps and she was at the threshold, looking out at the remaining balcony. No electromagnetic shield would protect her if she walked out there.

I'm going to lower the shield.

She stepped outside. The good news was that the suite was no longer a hundred floors up. Fifteen floors now. It was still a long way down, and she inched closer to the edge of the half-moon platform, conscious of that fact. The balcony wall that used to give occupants a little protection had disappeared, except for a section about the width of a U-ONE vista screen. Dorie aimed for it, knowing her secret stash was there, crammed into the inset panel that used to house the sensor for the electromagnetic shield.

Jesus, be careful.

Finally, having reached the wall, she put her hand into the panel housing. Back, left, and up. Behind the touch plate itself, in a space she'd hollowed out herself by gutting the sensor's dead and useless control mechanisms, she found the package. It was slippery to the touch, but it was just the covering she'd use to wrap the RuBy. She had only needed to keep the squares bundled together, not protect them from the elements. Not here under the dome, where the so-called weather conditions were programmed for comfort.

There you are. She withdrew the package, removed the protective layer, and the cinnamon smell was as strong as ever.

Okay, Dorie, you're home.

Sort of. Take a moment and relax.

She left the partial balcony and reentered the suite. She took one square of Ruby—just one—and rolled it. The temptation was too strong. It'd gnawed at her the moment she woke in the suite. You never got the goddamn drug out of your system. You could only hope to dry up and stay away from it. She should stay *away* from it.

Getting Rubed out, she believed, might feed her need, but it might also give her fleeting clarity—amidst the pure rush of the high—suggesting a path forward from here. She believed she might experience an instant of foresight and a flashpaper-thin wisdom to guide her through the problems she faced ahead. With her eyes closed, she thought about the choice she couldn't make, knowing Adi and others would be disappointed in her, but as much as she dwelled on the ramifications, the more she lost control of her will power.

She deserved this time.

This inevitable, insightful moment.

The release.

The *high*.

She placed the RuBy on her tongue, almost reverently, taking her time, letting it linger there. Clarity. Insight.

Spit it out.

Then she closed her mouth and waited. She felt the kick. Shudders rippled through her. She tensed, realized she shouldn't be standing right now. The floor was still carpeted in places, and she lay down on a good-sized patch.

The echoes were strong and loud here in her suite. They *weren't* insightful solutions.

You don't know who I am, do you?

"Get out of my head, Dorie," she mumbled.

This room wasn't safe, but it didn't matter. Here, the echoes intensified, as if the RuBy itself acted as a conduit to the past. She thought she might hear the gruff voice of Terl himself, *her* Plenko, wherever or whenever he was. She thought she might even hear the whispers of Dave, far away in the Ultra universe—if he'd even managed to cross over.

I want to share something with you.

"I don't want it."

I'm talking about the fucking Movement!

"That's in the past. Plenko's Movement fizzled. It didn't hold."

How would you like to be someone? Someone with a hand in shaping the future of sentient life?

They didn't win. The Ultras didn't *win*. We are who we are. We're not copies. We're not hybrids.

That's some good shit.

Tell me about it.

CROWELL

28   "YOU WOULD BOTH BE LEFT BEHIND," I SAID. "THERE'S NO way I'm doing that. Seriously. Dad, I just *found* you."

"Go back, David," he said. "There's nothing for you here in the Ultra universe."

"Uh, hello, there's *you*."

"You've seen me, you know I'm okay—if a little bored—and so that's that. You should go."

Parr cleared his throat. "There's a significant chance the trip would kill Dave," he said.

"He's right," I said. "Look at me. Physically, I'm now more than several times your age. What will the return trip do to me?"

Dad looked away. He knew the answer, but he couldn't say it. Well, of course he couldn't.

"More theory," I said. "Another Plan B, more of a working concept than anything."

"Our Plan Bs have worked pretty well so far," Dad said.

He was right. I could hardly keep them straight: mortaline wire, The Memory, Baren Rieser's blackrock House, Lorway's sleep travel, Rook and the duplicate House in the Ultra universe, the tethered portal, the Tarot cards, the *Exeter*—and what else? There was a limit. I'd come to the end. There just wasn't any way to move forward from here.

Where was here? I'd gone looking for Dad. I'd found him, hadn't I? I'd decided to risk everything to cross over, and I'd accepted long ago it was a one-way trip. I'd said goodbye to Dorie. To Forno. Nothing anyone could say now would change that. Nothing.

It was over.

"What's the use of leaving you behind and returning as a 90-year-old man? If I even survive? At least here I spend them with you."

"He has a point," Parr mumbled.

"You have a partner who'd miss you. Friends."

"Hell, I don't even know if my partner survived after I left him behind. Also, he's a Helk, and they don't get lonely."

"Your partner's a *Helk*?"

"His name's Forno." I looked over at Parr and smiled sadly. "Actually, my last two partners were Helks."

"One of us got better," Parr said.

I had to smile at that. I'd grown so used to him *looking* like my old partner that when he channeled the *personality* of Alan Brindos it took me by surprise.

My dad knew enough about Parr to know what we meant. "I never understood why humans were so distrustful of Helks. I mean, even before Plenko and the Movement."

"Perhaps it's their tendency to be three times our size," I said.

"Oh, that," my dad said. "I'd forgotten."

I looked at Parr intently. His eyes narrowed, expecting something. I thought maybe he'd anticipated the question I was about to ask him. "Tell me I'm wrong, Parr. Is there any way I return to the Union of Worlds alive, or as someone other than an old and feeble invalid?"

He looked to say something right away, but he paused. His eyes flicked up as he plumbed his Ultra database, his body stock still, almost rigid. When he started doing that on Rook, I'd found it annoying, but now I waited patiently. He must have understood the weight of this question. His eyes flicked back and forth, up and left, down, up and left, jittering haphazardly, and now they flipped, up and down. It looked as if he were in REM sleep with his eyes open. I'd never seen him take this long accessing his Ultra know-how. It felt oddly comforting that he was taking extra time to search.

The eyes returned front and center. The pause that followed was also unlike Parr. His reply was direct. "No."

"No?" I saw my dad lower his head, but I tried to stay focused on Parr. "That's it? Just . . . no?"

"Analysis shows that returning as an old and feeble invalid is the least likely of the two options."

"Shit," I said. "I hate it when you're right."

"There's very little reason for me to be wrong these days," he said. "One of the perks of being a hybrid."

Dad raised his head and searched Parr's face for the truth, as if he doubted the hybrid's sincerity. As Parr stared back, Dad's acceptance became obvious. His lips tightened, and his eyes settled on me. They glazed with tears.

"I'm sorry," he said.

I shook my head. "Don't be. We'll be here with each other. There are worse ways for me to live out my life. Maybe the Ultras can help with the back pain."

He didn't even smile. "Now we can all be bored together," he said. "You know. Since living in an antimatter universe doesn't give us a lot of options. We'll have to take turns on the Ultra treadmill."

I laughed at that. "Do you realize the shit I've gone through the last three years? Nothing wrong with sweet boredom."

Parr cleared his throat.

I turned to look at him, and so did Dad.

"So," Parr said, "about that."

SENALL

29 DORIE SENALL TOOK AT LEAST TWO MORE SQUARES OF RuBy as she lay there on the floor of the suite, maybe more. She kept the buzz steady, not dipping into sudden lows, avoiding the initial fist-clenching highs, wanting only to luxuriate in steady, mind-numbing euphoria.

What should've been on her mind were her next steps. The RuBy hadn't given her any hints after all, damn it. It couldn't be that she'd taken the RuBy out of *need*, now could it? She should be debating whether to flee Ribon altogether or plan her revenge against Tom Sakson, instead of trading one Bubble for an alternate drug-induced bubble.

It would take her a longer time to break RuBy's hold on her than when she'd sworn off it after the first Ultra scare. Her determination to do right by Dave and the remaining population of Ribon, as well as her desires to public office had helped, of course. Didn't she want the same things now? Need the same people in her life? Need to protect the citizens of Ribon?

"Help me, Dorie," she mumbled.

The echoes of her long-dead other self had quieted to an unintelligible murmur. Instead, she imagined conversations in this suite between ghost-Dorie and Movement leader Plenko:

What do you want me to do, Terl?

Bring her here to Ribon. Get her to trust you. Offer her a ticket to Coral Moon.

But Coral will soon be gone.

We are all struggling to be free, Dorie. Do you hear me? *Free.* We show the way to humanity's future. You and I have already experienced a grand part of that future.

You are a Thin Man now.

As are you. Here, this is for you.

How beautiful, Terl.

And how horrible. This is what happens to Ribon, and the Union, if we don't break free.

Is this sculpture—

Yes, made of mortaline. I may not survive to see the new sentient life we've promised. You know that, don't you?

Yes. But you won't die.

I will. But there are copies. The pattern's in the buffer.

The Movement's near and Plenko's near, his revolution made.

There's comfort in that.

Here. Roll and pop one of these. They'll help ease your way.

Wake up, Dorie. I've told you I don't like that shit.

But you need it.

The Ultras need it, not me. Wake up.

What?

Wake up. Wake up, Dorie.

No.

"Wake *up*, Dorie!"

Someone was shaking her. She opened her eyes and the image hovering over her wavered, blurry and indistinct. Focus returned slowly and details sharpened around a wrinkled face, tired eyes, and thin dry lips. Orange hair with white streaks, disheveled and wispy.

Dorie looked on in surprise. "Lorway?"

The Memor nodded. "You gave me quite a fright."

Sitting up on her own, Dorie blinked away the last of the fuzziness around her eyes. Lorway reached out, took Dorie's arms, and pulled gently so she could sit up. Lorway still wore the blue gown she'd worn in the Bubble.

"You *did* make it here," Dorie said, rubbing at her temples. A headache had started.

Lorway smiled broadly. "Lucky, so I could save you from yourself, it looks like."

My self, or my copy's self? "You left the card for me. You knew I'd—" She stopped, her mouth too dry to speak.

"Take your time. I have some water just over here." She pointed in the direction of the main door of the suite. "Stay upright. I'll be back."

"Don't go."

"I'm not. I'm just going to get the water. Stay with me."

Dorie nodded. Closed her eyes. Coming down now, head still

pounding, senses returning. She leaned back, wanting to lay flat on the floor again.

"Stay upright."

Lorway's voice. Lorway? Oh, right. The Memor had known where to find her. At the Tower, at least. Maybe she'd searched all fifteen floors until she found this suite. Jesus, *that* wasn't dangerous, going through all those damaged rooms. But she'd found Dorie's body on the floor. What must she have thought? That she was dead? After all the planning, the twists and turns, all the subterfuge needed to thwart Tom Sakson and the whole Union government, all those who'd put her in the Bubble in the first place, she'd just decided to give up and end things?

"Here."

Water moistened her lips. Dorie drank, slow at first, then more deeply. Lorway made her slow down.

Lorway said, "I was right here."

Dorie didn't understand, and she frowned.

"Not in this very room, but in the Tempest Tower. I visualized it as you did. I ended up on the sixth floor."

"The 91st floor."

"What?"

"It was the 91st floor before the salvage. Before the reclamation attempt."

She nodded. "I understand. I knew you were involved with that project. I left the Bubble, left that Tarot card. I'd kept *both* cards well hidden, believe me. I was told to. I didn't know if you'd find it, but if anyone needed to find me, I bet it would be you, that you'd be imprisoned, and if you knew what the card was, you might be able to escape."

"You were told to? *Who* told you?"

"And I was right," she said, ignoring the question. "Now tell me what's been happening."

Dorie, feeling a little better, told Lorway everything since her first visit to the Bubble, when she was still governor of New Venasaille.

Lorway turned solemn. "Dorie, how'd you get the RuBy? If Sakson threw you in there and cut you off from it—"

"I found it here." Dorie pulled her knees to her chest. "I hid a stash several years ago when I kicked RuBy after Coral Moon. This was my suite."

Lorway's eyes widened. "*Your* suite?"

"Mine and Terl's. And then my *copy's* suite. She was here with Movement leader Plenko after my Plenko disappeared, and after I lost time and ended up on Temonus."

"Memory's mercy," she said. "But why?"

Dorie shrugged. "A test, maybe? I figured if I could resist RuBy, cut myself off from it, even if I knew where to find some, I could tell myself I was no longer beholden to it. I'd forgotten about it until—" She placed her forehead on her knees, not wanting to look at Lorway. She fought back tears. "Until Sakson fucked me up. Fucked up everything for me."

"I'm sorry," Lorway said. She reached out and grasped Dorie's upper arm. "Don't despair. Fight it and you'll be back to being yourself in no time."

"Maybe. But what do I do now? I'm out of the Bubble and I'm no closer to finding myself than I was two years ago. All I hear is the ghost of the Dorie who lived here. Who died here."

"Then it's even more important you live."

"To do what? Run away? My Plenko is—" She stopped, suddenly remembering something.

"What?"

"My god. Sakson had me so high I didn't—well, he said they'd done tests. The Helk I thought was my Plenko was a copy. I sensed something wasn't right about him from the start. Then on the trip to Ribon. He was *helping* Dave, though. He might've been a copy, but he was good, and not the same as the Plenko Dave killed."

And Brindos. God, poor Alan.

"Then you can still look for him," Lorway stated.

"There's no guarantee he's still alive."

"No. Do you want to look for him? Or do you want to be governor of New Venasaille again?"

Dorie thought about it. These were things she could do well enough. Which appealed to her more? Which was the most logical?

She felt like she could stand and not fall over, so with Lorway's help, she got to her feet. Nothing would ever be the same between her and Plenko, even if she found him, which didn't seem likely. Maybe, though. Over time. She owed her life and her service to Ribon, and particularly to New Venasaille. She'd left for a reason, but she'd not known the full truth about Sakson.

She took a deep breath as Lorway steadied her. "I want Tom Sakson gone. I want him and his cronies out of my fucking dome."

Lorway smiled. "Governor then."

"Damn right."

"And how will you go about doing that?"

Dorie slipped away from Lorway and walked gingerly to the ruined French doors leading to the damaged balcony. She looked past it, taking in all of New Venasaille she could see, from foreground to the far curve of the city's dome. The diffused light had dimmed. Had she been there on the floor that long? She took a half dozen steps onto the balcony. Night crawled in, shadows inching across the dome.

"Jesus," Lorway said, "be *careful*. That doesn't look very safe."

Lower the shield.

She realized the remaining squares of RuBy were clenched in her hand, held tight while she Rubed out on the floor. Relaxing her fingers seemed a great effort, but she did, and she found the red papers crushed and torn. Perspiration had activated the dye and her palms were coated in red; tiny rivulets traveled along her lifelines. A few fragments of paper floated in the simulated early evening air flow, like glowing ashes rising from a fire. She watched them float out past the balcony wall, then she shook her hand and set the other squares and fragments free.

Finally, she turned back to the suite and faced Lorway. She raised her hand to show the blood-red palm, a symbol of both her failure and her new determination. She was out for blood. "We're going back to the Bubble," she said.

"We are?" the Memor said. "*We?*

"I need your help, and I need a trusted friend." She brushed the last remnants of RuBy from her hands and re-entered the suite. "I need Aditya Thakur. There's no one else left in the Bubble. We're busting him out."

CROWELL

30 MY DAD AND I STARED AT VANDERBERG PARR AND WAITed for him to go on. He'd gone absolutely still; he was accessing his Ultra database.

"About 'that,'" I said. "About *what*?"

Parr came back to us, eyes front and center. "About travel within the Ultra universe. Now that we're here, and the Ultras have access to this matter-bubble, we can initiate a process by which you could literally leave here with me and walk straight to the *Exeter*."

I blinked. "Meaning?"

"Less boredom. See the sights. Didn't you tell me earlier I'd be able to explore the universe? And I'd have friends."

"So how would that work?" I asked. "Become a hybrid? Wear a protective antimatter suit?" *Those inflatable Halloween costumes are real lifelike, and I've got one just your size.*

"Easy. We set you up like they did Baren Rieser," Parr said.

"Excuse me?"

"You'd look good bald."

"You mean get the nano-ink head tattoos?"

"There's a limit to the number of inked sections we can fit, safely, but yes. If you're willing."

"Hold on. Didn't Rieser use the tattoos to move between universes to avoid the aging process? Can't I use them in that way to go home?"

Parr shook his head. "Not without the tether. The distance is far too great now. For smaller jumps from here to the *Exeter*, however, the tattoos will work fine for you."

"My dad too?"

"I believe the Ultras might not let him go, considering their fascination with him. Always learning, the Ultras, even on the brink of their own extinction."

I looked at my dad, and he smiled warmly. "You could always

come visit, I suppose," he said, "or finish up here when you're down to your last tattoo."

The irony wasn't lost on me. Dad, the much younger man now, had his life ahead of him, and I was the one who might live just a few years more. My dad wouldn't want to spend the rest of his life doing nothing, but to keep moving, and use every moment of his life to gain knowledge and wisdom.

"I'm barely the same man I was two years ago," I said, "changed in more ways than one."

Parr was his own good example of that. Brindos, too, when he became a Helk. We are who we are, but identity is never in stone, always in flux, and there exists an ultra-thin line between our original mold and the next copy.

"You're the same on the inside, Dave," my dad said.

"I don't think that's entirely true anymore."

"Do you *want* to do this?" he asked.

I came to a decision. "Yes. What's another alteration cost me except whatever hair I have left?"

Through Parr's hybrid connection and my dad's own communicative setup—in digital shill mode—the Ultras confirmed Lucky Lawrence would stay put, and I had the go ahead to travel with Parr aboard the *Exeter*.

It made me sad to hear Dad would have to stay.

Parr left the matter-bubble to gather the nano-ink and tools needed to transform my head into an antimatter travel map. Meanwhile, Dad and I had more time to talk about all the things our last discussion hadn't covered. This time, I talked more about the Ultras from the Union's perspective, as well as my own, outlining much of what had happened to my friends and me: on Earth, Temonus, Aryell, Helkuntannas, and Barnard's World.

He was particularly interested in my relationships with Forno, Dorie, and Jennifer Lisle, none of whom had ever played into the complex plans of the Ultras, but he also asked about Plenko, the Science Consortium, and the Envoys. I told him as much as I could about them. He seemed to take in everything quite thoughtfully, as if knowing them vicariously through me might help him understand me more. I felt myself tiring, and I really wanted a good nap.

I'd never taken a nap in my entire life, and I couldn't deprive myself of this time with my dad.

He understood. We found ourselves more than once coming to each other for long hugs. The last time, just before Parr returned, my dad wept openly, his tears wetting my own cheeks. I cried inside, but it might've been because my tear ducts were for shit.

"It's not even fair," I said to him.

"They never are."

"They?"

He smiled. "Goodbyes."

Parr came back into the room, and I noticed immediately that he had none of the things he'd gone to retrieve.

"We've been here another hour—not that I haven't relished the time with my dad—and you come back with nothing?"

"Not exactly nothing," Parr said.

"Is it invisible?" my dad asked.

Parr smirked. "No. I've made inquiries to the Ultras and acquired new knowledge that has opened an alternate path that might amend our present plans."

"I don't think you could say that any more generically," I said. "What the hell does that mean?"

Parr gave me a serious look. He did the Parr thing, a quick eye flick, a moment's silence. "A solution to the problem of traveling between universes."

"What?" I asked, completely taken aback. "You mean—*me*?"

"Remember when you and Forno found the *Exeter*? Well, you also figured out that there were more copies of it. This is true. Several others are in the same jump slot you traveled through before making your way to the sideways station. Using the Three of Swords to cross the gigantic gap between universes now means there'd be a solid anchor point: one of these other *Exeters*."

I scratched my head, confused. "You're saying I can go back without harm? Without aging?"

Parr shook his head. "No. I'm saying you'll have an anchor point, which makes the prospect of surviving the trip much more likely. That is, if you start the process back on Rook, where you entered the Ultra universe. If you look at it with an evolutionary, DNA-lensed perspective, a change will happen, most certainly."

"I feel a 'but' coming on," I said.

Parr said, "*But*. It would be in the opposite direction. But not by much."

The opposite direction. My brain caught on. Younger. I'd be goddamned *younger*.

"You're kidding," I said.

He put out his hand, palm down, and wiggled it. "Not quite."

I groaned.

"The Ultras can also get you back close to the day and time you left the Union. This I didn't know about, other than they have some sort of effect on time and relativity, and most of that science is still funneling into my consciousness." He looked puzzled.

"I feel another 'but'—"

"But—"

I waited for the next revelation.

He told me.

My dad hesitated, but I didn't. I said, "What about the Ultras?"

"They agree."

I nodded, looked at my dad, then back at Parr. "So when do we start?"

Parr said, "Right now."

We did.

SENALL

31 THE THING ABOUT MAX RYDELL WAS, HE HATED HIS JOB.
Dorie knew this to be true because he'd told her as much the few times she'd spoken with him while she had the governorship. Granted, she'd never had the need—or opportunity—to speak with him much at all. What went on in the Bubble hadn't concerned her, and to be honest, Rydell had kept silent on almost everything related to the workings of the facility.

He'd told her, however, how much he disliked working there. He agreed to the post after the Memors of the MSA recruited him. They respected his time with the NIO during the first Ultra scare when he spearheaded the initial operation to hunt down Thin Men at large in the Union. What better person to oversee the Bubble and its unusual test subjects?

Or, as Lorway had revealed to her after they left Tempest Tower, its *one* unusual test subject. Lorway, the only prisoner of the Bubble—that is, until Sakson dumped Adi Thakur in there. *And then me.*

So the warden didn't like his job. And honestly, what kept him there now, if Lorway was gone? Did he really care about Adi Thakur being there? She believed he hadn't even been there when Dorie woke up inside. Skeleton staff dismissed, perhaps. And Rydell, sick of his job, preferring to go home to New Venasaille each day when off duty, instead of taking advantage of the complete living quarters assigned to him in the Bubble. It was a lot of trouble—and maybe expense, if the MSA wasn't covering it—to pass through the Shell and stomach the mind-numbing delays and security concerns of the domelock.

How many hooks did Tom Sakson have in Max Rydell? Would Max even listen to her if she showed up on his doorstep?

Time to find out.

"Are you sure about this?" Lorway asked her.

Dorie sprawled out on the old couch and Lorway knelt on the floor beside her. "Of course. We need the information, and Dave told me how Terree did the trick on him."

"It's not a trick."

"Fine. When she put him into the Memory. And you can do it, too?"

"Any Memor who's studied the principals of it can, yes."

"There's no danger to me or you, right?"

"Mostly right."

Dorie frowned but let that go.

"I'm not taking you in as deeply," Lorway said. "You'll be aware of yourself, more so than Crowell was, but you'll be seeing through someone else's eyes. My understanding is that Crowell sank a lot deeper into the Memory, through many layers. Even then, he would tell you it all just seemed as real as anything, except seeing it from someone else's perspective."

"So let's do it."

It didn't take long. She didn't spend time explaining things, since Dorie had a basic handle on the process, matching consciousness before searching for others in New Venasaille. Someone Dorie had talked to. Someone who'd unconsciously communicated with her own brain. Someone with the correct mindset she could lock onto so she could view information from that person's point of view.

Lorway, seemingly with little effort, channeled the Memory and, even though Dorie knew it was coming, Lorway managed to surprise her. She reached out and touched Dorie on the forehead.

As it turned out, she was Tom Sakson. When had *this* moment taken place? It wasn't that long ago; Sakson had taken control of the domes by then. The Memory had taken her to this moment, and Sakson had obviously gained enough clearance to access New Venasaille's grid and was discussing dome protocols with Rydell.

She was disgusted at the idea of looking through Sakson's eyes, but thrilled at the idea of eavesdropping on this slice of the immediate past, Sakson none the wiser as he discussed Bubble security with Rydell. The warden brought up a flashscreen, accessing New Venasaille's directory of Bubble personnel, as well as the lock codes to the facility's entry access points, and Sakson studied the data.

Dorie could see it, too. The information scrolled slowly, and the list was not long: fewer than a dozen names, all okayed and installed at the Bubble by the MSA. At this point in time, only Rydell knew the identities of the subjects within, supposedly all Thin Men, but he must've known from the very beginning that Lorway was the only occupant, and not a Thin Man at all.

Dorie cursed him under her breath, angry that he'd kept that information from her. Even now, if interrogated, he would say he answered to a higher power: the MSA.

Sakson then asked for the Bubble's lock codes.

"It's highly irregular," Rydell said. "They are not to be shared—"

"You will with me," Sakson said. "Or you will never return to the Bubble."

"Are you threatening me? Do you know who I work for?"

"C'mon, Max. You've never liked working in the Bubble. Admit it, you'd just as soon be on Memory working directly with the MSA."

"I don't, and I do, but the choice isn't up to me."

"You're right. The MSA probably wouldn't take you back. So walk away and enjoy your retirement. The MSA would understand."

"And someone else would be put in my place, and you'd be right back where you started. You would never gain access."

"I already have access." He flashed his comm card at the warden. "Frilse Halskla, MSA Under-Director approved it yesterday."

Max Rydell seemed stunned. He stepped back from Sakson's comm card, as if it were a weapon, and frowned. "But how—?"

Sakson didn't miss a beat. "I used to occupy one of Memory's Thin Man facilities. I was a subject."

"*What?*"

"Well, not *me*, per se. I was copied. I woke up in an alley in Venasaille, pre-Coral disaster, having lost a couple of days. Only later did I realize what it all meant, after the truth became known and the search for Thin Men began. The MSA informed me of my copy's capture, and I went out to see it. Strange indeed, seeing a perfect copy of yourself. The Memors had already conducted an entire battery of tests on it."

"So you received special privileges there."

"And spent enough time on the premises to warrant some visits with top MSA officials. The conclusion is, I have clearance."

Max Rydell nodded.

"But I still need the access codes."

"Why do you need them?"

"I have new—*subjects*—to put in there."

Rydell sputtered, then shook his head. "That's not allowed. All subjects must be approved prior to—"

"You're out, Max."

The warden looked like he'd just been stabbed in the heart. He put a hand over his chest as if he were trying to keep blood from flowing. "What do you mean I'm out?"

"We just talked about it, remember? Retirement."

"Forced retirement."

Sakson shrugged apologetically.

"And my staff?"

"Gone too. No one needs to watch the inside. Let Lorway rot in there. Let my new detainees rot in there." He shrugged again, slowly, methodically, letting the warden see this was the way it was. No choice. "The codes, Max."

Rydell stared hard at Sakson, almost daring the new governor to force the issue somehow, but his resolve wavered. He flicked the flashscreen and a new report appeared.

And that was how Dorie found out where Max Rydell lived in New Venasaille and learned the access codes to the Bubble. She hoped Rydell would allow them access—even willingly—through domelock, out of New Venasaille, and over to the facility. It was possible Sakson had revoked his privileges completely, but she also thought the MSA might still have some pull regarding his passage through the Shell. Then, with the access codes, Max Rydell would simply be a passenger—willing or not—as they rescued Adi. She was quite certain now that the Bubble was otherwise deserted.

Adi was alone.

Dorie woke on the couch and instantly felt sick to her stomach. Her lips burned and her mouth tasted of sand. Her left eye twitched. This wasn't a side effect of the Memory but was typical of RuBy withdrawal. Lorway hovered over her, concerned, but Dorie waved her off. She wished she'd saved at least one square of RuBy. She looked at her red-stained hands and wondered if she might get some from there. The image of her licking her palms and Lorway's appalled expression kept her from doing it.

"Well?" the Memor asked.

"I got it all." Dorie put out a hand and Lorway helped her sit up. Her head pounded like a jammed jump slot cog, but she sat still long enough for the cranking in her skull to die down.

"What now?" Lorway swung her orange hair behind her shoulders. "It's getting late. Should we rest here?"

Dorie looked back toward the balcony, but stayed where she was. Night had fallen. She could just make out some of the upper arc of the dome. Stars shone as muted chips of light, the Shell distorting and diffusing their brilliance.

"Fuck no," she said. "Let's go wake up Max."

CROWELL

32 VANDERBERG PARR HAD BEEN RIGHT. *I COULD GO HOME.* I said my goodbyes amid tears and laughter, knowing I'd soon be alone on my journey. So fleeting was our small Crowell family reunion that it didn't seem at all fair to be hurried along. Parr had to step in and physically part us because of the Ultras' impatience. Now that they'd decided, they wanted me out of their way. In evolutionary terms, their race was on its last legs—their final crawl toward death—and they didn't need other distractions around them.

It was time to go.

But first, the Ultras digitalized a kind of bubble suit after all—an anti-antimatter one (just my size)—and I made my way to the *Exeter*. Oh, the Ultra's buildings and artifacts were magnificent. Even the buildings were artifacts now, irrelevant considering the Ultras had no use for them. I followed Parr, emerging onto a giant terrace that overlooked four other layers of terrace below me, and each one staggered outward, as if they were stairs for giants. Pillars reached even higher. In front of me, a gigantic wall of mountains seemed to cut us off from the rest of the world. The fading sun came from behind me and turned the mountains into a wall of deep color, the surface crawling with dark blues and light-streaked greens. Above them, up toward the large impossible moon, the sky darkened into startling shades of green, then dark blue, until almost black. It took me a few seconds to catch my breath.

Parr led me to a wide plaza, and on one end was a spacious elevator. We stepped inside and some mechanism released it; the elevator followed the contours of the mammoth building, and we descended.

The doors opened to a giant walkway, suspended in the air without any visible means of support other than where it tied off a good distance away to a giant ring that I took to be a staging area for space transport. Other walkways were attached to the circle, spaced evenly from other buildings, and inside the circle, more walkways like spokes of a great wheel. Far in the distance I saw more buildings like the one I'd come from. The sheer *immensity* of the construction awed me. I stopped and took in the spectacle, and Parr had to remind me to keep moving.

Where each spoke ended was a node or bubble. Attached to our walkway was a ship. The *Exeter*. There were no protective walls or railings along the walkway, so I kept to the middle, keeping pace behind Parr, trying not to stare at the spectacle before me for fear of veering off the path.

Before long we were on board. The *Exeter* blasted away from the ring, and I would've been afraid for anyone on the ring surface when it did, but of course there would be no one. At one time there must have been, when Ultras had a physical existence. Maybe proper safety measures existed back then.

We left the Ultra world and its moon behind and made our way to Rook. I'd forgotten how boring the trip had been. It seemed like an eternity since I'd crossed the first leg of antimatter space, but eventually we stood on Rook, gazing in at the ruined Pool Room.

Parr left me with the Tarot card—the Three of Swords—then gave explicit instructions how to activate it. I wouldn't have the *Exeter* to travel in; Parr needed it to return to the Ultra world, so the Ultras pinpointed a spot in the jump slot where another copy of the *Exeter* would be. I didn't ask how they figured that out.

Parr stood nearby as I made myself comfortable in the Pool Room. He would return to the Ultras after I'd left.

Everything else seemed anticlimactic.

Flash. Nausea. Light.

I was soon awake, and it seemed I'd made it through; I was back on the *Exeter*. It was disconcerting at first seeing the ship that had brought me to Rook, but I knew this was a copy. I'd quantum traveled across the brane, from antimatter universe to matter universe and into the jump slot.

But how old was I? I felt fine. No aches, no pains. I'd not aged. I *had* to be younger, as Parr had promised. Not by much, he'd said.

I was alone.

Tem Forno was not there. Either he didn't make it off Meadowlark Station, or he found a ship and headed back to Barnard's World. Contacted Plenko, let him know what had happened. Maybe he'd decided enough was enough and headed home. To Helkuntannas, that is. He hadn't expected anyone to return from the Ultraverse, so why go back to Earth when he could stay warm on his home world?

I was suddenly depressed at the thought of being back on Earth without him—or anyone else, really. There was nothing else I could do except re-orient myself to my new surroundings. I fired up the new *Exeter's* main drive—I knew how to reconnect the key in the engine hub—and made my way through the jump slot.

SENALL

33   MAX RYDELL CAME OUT HIS FRONT DOOR SQUINTING, a robe wrapped hastily around him. When he saw Dorie on his doorstep he raised an eyebrow, then gave a knowing nod. When he saw Lorway he even chuckled, impressed that the Bubble's original subject had escaped from a high security holding facility. He not only hated his job, but he was also ready to get back at Tom Sakson any way he could, and he told them so.

The fog of RuBy still swirled in Dorie's brain, and the withdrawal symptoms persisted, but she pushed through, explaining their objective.

"I no longer have the Bubble's access codes though," Rydell said. "Those were wiped from my comm card. They were complex enough that I never memorized them, just entered them as needed. Typically, my people were there to admit me with only a cursory glance at the codes. No direct input needed."

"Don't worry about that," Dorie said. "I have the codes."

Max stared blankly at her.

"It's complicated."

"They change monthly."

"Then the ones I have should be good, if Sakson hasn't changed them."

"He has no authority to change them. He may have secured special permissions from the Under-Director, but those particulars are off limits. Although—" He shook his head. "Now that he *has* those codes—"

"We don't need to worry about him right now. He'll stay away from the Bubble for the time being. He told you to let Lorway and me rot in there."

Rydell scratched the back of his head. "I'm not even going to ask how you know he said that."

Dorie smiled but said nothing. Instead, she urged him to get dressed. "We're going to need something to protect us if we run across any trouble. You have any weapons?"

Rydell groaned. "Do you know what time it is? You want to do this *now*?"

"Yes. Weapons?"

He thought, pursing his lips. "A few unlocked blasters and an old rifle."

"Flashlights, too. I assume you have some good ones. And we're going to need your shuttle to pass through the domelock."

"You know," Max went on, as if he hadn't heard her, "if they log me out of the dome with the Bubble as my destination, that could get back to Sakson."

"We won't be there long enough for him to do anything."

"Unless he's asked to be notified right away. Then—"

"For fuck's sake, Max. Quit worrying and hurry up. Your forced retirement hasn't started yet."

"How do you know about—"

"I'm a mind reader." She looked over at Lorway, who gave her a bemused look. "Also, I've got a good memory."

"Shit, Dorie, that doesn't explain *any*thing."

Dorie gave him a hard look and he looked visibly shaken. "That's Governor Senall to you, Max Rydell. I left Adi in charge. Sakson made himself acting governor, and there wasn't any election. I'm taking back my city."

An hour later, after expected delays getting out of the dome—including time-intensive security checks at the Shell, questions about why they were leaving the dome this time of night and where they were going, with Max Rydell explaining that he was escorting ex-Governor Senall back to the Bubble—Dorie spotted the smaller dome of the Bubble, lit by spotlights surrounding its perimeter. Otherwise, as they approached the facility, the pitch black of night covered everything for miles.

This would be the third time in recent memory she'd been inside the Bubble. She was trying to forget the second time inside, but her recent RuBy trip reminded her of it. Licking her dry lips, she swallowed, and an old cinnamon-flavored residue caught in her throat.

She coughed harshly but recovered, and Rydell headed toward the access point. They landed the shuttle nearby and used flashlights to light their way as they hurried to the outer door.

"No one here," Lorway said, scanning the outer door. "Unless they're waiting inside for us."

Rydell shook his head. "They won't be. Tom sent all of them away. Let you two rot in here and shut it down. He gestured to the access point interface. "I'm locked out, as I said. Codes need to be entered manually."

"I've got them," Dorie said. "Show me the interface."

Rydell guided her to the panel, then palmed a sensor that opened it, silver panels disconnecting and sliding back seamlessly into the building. "That's as much as I can do. The codes are entered here." He pointed to twelve dark evenly spaced protuberances that looked like old-fashioned punch keys.

Dorie brushed him aside. "Give me some light."

She paused only a few seconds after three flashlights lit up the panel. She searched her memory for the first codes. She pushed the raised keys quickly in an order that matched the first code numbers. When the panel clicked, she lifted her hands and waited for the panel to invert. The punch keys melted back into the plate, the plate flipped, and a digital display of glowing numbers turned on.

Four more sets of coded numbers. Each time she entered the next batch of numbers, the plate flipped, and the new display glowed in a new color with a unique set of numbers. The last plate's numbers shone white on black.

"Stand ready," she said, and Lorway and Rydell took up a position on either side of the access door, weapons ready. She input the last memorized numbers and there was a loud *thunk* as the door's inner locking mechanisms disengaged. The door cracked in the middle and the two halves slid back enough to allow access before grinding to a stop.

No one waited on the other side. Lights blazed in the entry way and the reception area was quiet and sterile. Rydell slid past Dorie to open the security doors, which didn't need a code but a set of complicated keys he had on him.

"Sakson's people took my keys, but I've had a set stashed at my place for a long time. You never know, I guess."

Dorie nodded absent-mindedly. "Keep moving. Let's find Adi."

The Memor nodded and they entered the next vestibule.

The Bubble truly had been abandoned. Dorie saw the door to the subject area and swallowed hard, pushing back her nervousness. Not too long ago she'd come to this door and Max Rydell had given her access to see Lorway. The next time, captured and Rubed out, she'd passed out against this door on the other side, trapped.

The security door's DNA lock had not yet been reset to eliminate Max Rydell's entry. He cycled through it, and the door opened.

Dorie thought, *the hell with caution*, and pushed Rydell aside and entered the subject block.

"Adi!" she yelled.

They split up and ran through the facility, calling his name. She'd only been gone a day, maybe two. She tried to remember. Adi should be okay. Dehydrated a little, perhaps.

Dorie went straight to Room 15, the last place she'd seen him before using the Tarot card and leaving him behind, and he was there on the floor, face down, unmoving.

Was he okay? Was he alive? Maybe someone had received orders before fleeing the Bubble to get rid of any subject left. Sakson, ridding himself of his enemies. She whispered now. "Adi?"

Lorway came to the door, followed by Rydell.

Adi Thakur stirred, a small groan coming from him as he turned himself over. *Alive.* He'd just been asleep.

"Oh thank God," Dorie said.

"Dorie," Adi said, smiling up at her. "I knew you'd come back. I knew you'd win."

She grinned wide. "I'm back. We've not won yet, though. Things aren't going to be much better out there until we stop Sakson."

He noticed Lorway, then Rydell next to her. He frowned.

"He's okay," Dorie said. "Mostly." She reached out to him, and he grabbed her hand. "So, can we get the hell out of here?"

He nodded, smiled, and she helped him to his feet. Rydell handed him water he'd grabbed from the now-empty living quarters.

"What now?" Adi asked.

Dorie thought about that. What now indeed? Even with Adi, the four of them could do little against Sakson, especially if he was holed up in the Brindos Building with his people around him. She hadn't thought much about how to approach that problem, having focused only on getting Adi out of the Bubble.

Now, though, she had to think things through. It was four o'clock in the morning. It'd still be dark when they returned to New Venasaille but inching toward sunrise. She wished Terl was here to help her. Or Dave Crowell, and Forno. That would've been quite the team to challenge Sakson. She had to face the truth, though. Dave was stuck in the Ultra universe—if he made it there—or he died trying. Forno had left with Dave, and who *knew* where Terl was.

Certainly by now, the means of entering New Venasaille's dome had been blocked. She couldn't imagine Sakson hadn't heard about all this.

"We have a plan?" Max Rydell asked. "That was the easy part."

Dorie shrugged. "I'm open to suggestions."

They all stared at her; they were quite silent.

CROWELL

34 "YOU'RE YOUNGER," PLENKO SAID. HE LOOMED OVER ME, and I felt the need to shrink back a few steps. I kept forgetting. This was the *original* Plenko. The original. *He's on your side.*

"Parr figured out a bizarre workaround that the Ultras agreed on," I said.

Plenko seemed to take this as logical. He didn't press me on it. "Quite fortunate you found Parr there again." Plenko studied my face. "It really is quite remarkable. Just like the images I saw of you on U-ONE after the first Ultra incident." He continued to stare.

I'd arrived on Barnard's after coming out of the slot at Osprey Station. There was the expected confusion with the *Exeter*'s IDENT, since it was a ship that *had* existed in our universe. This one was different, of course. I had a solid script of what to say to smooth everything over.

Parr had been true to his word. The Ultras had put me back in our universe at the correct day, the correct year. I stood in Terl Plenko's main room, marveling at my good fortune, and at the same time waiting impatiently while the Helk checked me out. Before that, Plenko's two pals, Rob and Emma, searched me.

I said, "No word from Tem Forno? Did he make it back?"

"He's okay. Got away from the sideways station—"

"Meadowlark."

"Yes, he said that's what you named it. Anyway, he did a 180 and ended up on Petrel Station."

"He went to planet Memory?"

"No, he took the slot from there to Crossbill."

"Helkuntannas." I was trying to keep up. "He went home?"

"In my ship, I might add. I'm afraid after all he did to help you get to the Ultra universe, he decided to cut his losses."

"He went *home*?"

"That means *you* get to turn me in to Morgan."

"Turn you in?" The Helk finally gave me some distance, then sat down. I now could look at him at eye level.

"I've already given myself up," Plenko said. "I figured Forno would help with the exchange. Keep things on the level. Sorry, but just like Forno, I didn't expect to see you back in our universe."

"Trust me. I didn't figure I *would* be back. But surrender to Morgan . . . Why would you *do* that?"

"Because they have Dorie. She's being held and is to be exchanged for me."

I couldn't speak right away, surprised. This certainly didn't seem like a thing Plenko would do, but it was most assuredly a thing *Plenko* would do, for Dorie. Then I thought: *Would Dave Crowell?*

Well, of course.

"I'll do it. I'll help make the exchange. I'm going with you. Where's Morgan?"

Plenko lowered his head, chin on his chest, arms flat on the arms of the gigantic chair. When he looked up again, it was with a sad, knowing smile. He looked past me, toward the door of the room.

Morgan stood there, blaster at his side.

SENALL

35 EVEN WITHOUT A PLAN, THE FOUR OF THEM HAD TO GET inside New Venasaille's dome. Getting out of the dome had been easier, with Rydell simply playing his warden role and convincing the somewhat lackadaisical security team at the Shell that he was transporting Dorie and the Memor to the Bubble.

How to explain Dorie's return, though? Add to that the appearance of Adi Thankur and Lorway and it seemed near impossible to get through. As she'd already figured, Sakson would be wise to them by now.

They'd all been silent on the ride to New Venasaille, but Dorie kept thinking through her options. Desperation threatened any logical plan, so she came around on her thinking and considered something more drastic.

"We'll crack the Shell," she said simply, as if it were the most straightforward decision she'd ever made.

"You're joking," Adi said.

"You have any other ideas?" she asked.

Adi shook his head, but he didn't seem pleased. "You passed legislation and spent time and resources increasing dome entrance security so vessels couldn't *do* that. And Max's ship—"

"Don't worry about that," Rydell said. "I'm out of a job, and that shuttle's going to lose access anyway. No great loss if we fuck it up."

"This ship have a name?" Dorie asked.

"*Guardian.*"

Cracking the Shell was a term for a maneuver designed to subvert dome security by accelerating through the domelock and avoiding deterrents in the transparent ring beneath the skin of the dome known as the Shell. No one wanted unauthorized vessels in New Venasaille's airspace, so stringent entry protocols were in place. To "crack" it, pilots would gun vessels through the domelock when it opened and did not stop in the Shell's holding area for inspection, as required. The ship powered through unchecked, its speed too fast, entry angle all wrong, its guidance system ineffectual. Over the years, the Shell had seen expensive repairs when ships that attempted this maneuver failed to avoid the ring itself, damaging it, or shearing off docking berths and platforms, or even causing deaths—to both Shell employees and other vessels docked there, as well as passengers on the offending ships.

Dorie's legislative-backed improvements—faster domelock openings and closings to make it more difficult to shoot the gap, added slow zones with more obstacles just inside the dome's skin, construction of strategic grapples and nets, and stiffer fines and penalties—had worked well, and she knew she'd made it harder for them to pull off the maneuver now. Doing the maneuver had never made sense to her. Few who attempted it succeeded—particularly after the security upgrades—and those who succeeded had almost nowhere to run and hide inside the dome. Dorie could count on one hand the number of ships that had made it through and escaped detection afterwards.

"The positive side to this is that I'm familiar with the entry area due to the numerous trips I've made over the years—even the early days when Tom Sakson was an assistant—and I know the particulars behind all the security upgrades. Also, more importantly, Adi knows them even better, having overseen the improvement modifications."

"Our chances improve a few percent then," Adi said in a joking tone, though Dorie believed he would jump on the plan if she made the decision.

"They do improve," she said. "*Now* I know why I needed you out of the Bubble. Prepare for the maneuver, Max." The ex-warden had the shuttle on a direct course to the domelock. She knew *he* had never tried to crack the Shell.

"Speed?" he asked.

"Steady for now. When they contact us, comply with everything they ask of you. It's no use trying to do this if they don't open the domelock. When I say, increase speed to maximum. The window is slim and the timing tight."

"And the deterrents in the Shell?"

"Guess and by gosh."

"What?"

"Something my granddad used to say. I can get us around them, I think. The bigger problem will be any pursuit."

"Or shooting," Adi said.

"Or that." She'd weighed the consequences. She understood security's mentality. Save lives and avoid conflict. "I don't think they'll target us. The likelihood of possible casualties—"

"Tom Sakson doesn't care about casualties," Lorway said from the seat behind Dorie. "If he realizes he's lost you as a hostage, he could very well risk everything. Look at the great lengths he went through to discredit you and dump you in the Bubble. Don't underestimate him."

"I'm not," Dorie said, "I'm *anticipating* him." She believed Sakson would pick a more opportune moment—assuming they made it through the Shell—to make his move.

"If we make it somehow," Rydell said, "where do we go? It's hard to hide in a dome, even one as large as New Venasaille."

Dorie had just been thinking about that. She frowned, momentarily at a loss for words. She felt a twinge in her throat and a sudden wave of nausea. RuBy still held onto her and she didn't like the feeling.

"I've got some ideas," she said, although she had trouble prioritizing them. "Let's get through this first."

Ten minutes later, the first ping came through the shuttle's comm searching for its IDENT. Dorie didn't know if Rydell's shuttle had an official IDENT, or if he'd just named it *Guardian* himself. Rydell answered the ping and read a transcript of an alert from security: they were to decelerate and approach the domelock for entry and immediate inspection. Dorie knew what that meant: they would be boarded. Held for the duration. While the inspection process was not unusual, the command to decelerate was. The *Guardian* was already at an acceptable entry speed before the request, and the slower speed toward the domelock meant the security team had heightened concerns about passengers and cargo. The order gave Shell personnel more time to assess any irregularities.

Or, more likely, security knew exactly who was on board, and Sakson had initiated seldom-used procedures designed to secure and impound their shuttle.

"Slow, or keep steady?" Rydell asked.

"Slow just enough to let them see we're complying." She kept her

eyes locked on the horizon and the approaching curve of New Venasaille; she'd soon have a visual of the domelock. "Be ready to crack it."

Rydell tensed, but he nodded. "Any hints on the timing?"

"Watch the simulation profile the dome broadcasts to your terminal," Adi said. "The moment I see venting, the pressure's equal-
izing and we make our run."

"Will you be able to see that in this light?" Rydell asked.

"I hope so," Adi said. "We're getting a little now."

Dorie saw some faint light on the horizon. "We should be close
enough to spot it with what little light we have. The light of the
city from inside the dome will help. By the time the lock cycles and
cranks, we'll already be screaming for the gap."

<<TWO MINUTES TO DOMELOCK, GUARDIAN PILOT>>

The voice came over the comm as expected, but the following
instructions were not according to procedure.

<<GUARDIAN WE NEED YOU TO SLOW A QUARTER.
APPROACH CAUTIOUSLY. EXPECT LOCK TURBULENCE>>

"Bullshit," Adi muttered. "We fixed that problem years ago.
They don't think we know that?"

"Of course they do," Lorway said. "Sakson's trying to keep everything calm and orderly. He wants a record of this to show he was
justified in doing—well, whatever he plans on doing."

"Yeah, for the good of New Venasaille, right?" Rydell said.

<<ONE MINUTE TO DOMELOCK. GUARDIAN YOU ARE
RESTRICTED FROM NORMAL ENTRY PROCEDURES. PRE-
PARE FOR ALTERNATE LANDING>>

Damn it, they knew.

"Ignore it," Dorie said, eyes on the dome ahead and below.
The domelock was visible, and yes, the light was pushing back the
darkness now, revealing the massive panels and access structures
that flared outward from the top of the arc like a sea bird with outstretched wings. A minute passed, and she told Rydell to ignore any
requests from the Shell. The dome was close. A mile or two.

The shuttle stayed on course, dropping slightly toward the
dome. She had to wait. The burst of speed and improper entry angle
from above would clue in security to the attempted crack. "Steady,"
she said, to Rydell, to all of them.

Adi was the first to see the release of particulates and swirls of
dust. "Venting!" he said.

"Go!" Dorie yelled.

The *Guardian* simultaneously jumped forward and sank. The dome rushed at them, and right away voices from Shell security popped over the comm. Dorie didn't know if the others were listening, but she paid little attention to whatever was being said. She heard them shout Rydell's name. Something about aborting. Cursing. *Was that Sakson on the comm?*

The lock had opened. The automated process started, and the panels slid quickly. They could not close again until fully open, but when reversed, the lock could close just as quickly.

One of the improvements to Shell security had come about because most pilots who tried the crack entered at a forty-five-degree angle. Speed being what it was, there was too little room from the skin of the dome to the ground to land safely. So architects positioned the obstacles, grapples, and nets closer to the top of the arch to catch vessels shooting in sideways. Normal landing maneuvers required ships to slow enough so they could land horizontal after a slow descent.

Adi, knowing intimately the positions of the deterrents, had the final move in the attempted crack, one that security would not expect. "Nose down into the lock," he shouted. "Vertical. Nose down!"

Dori expected Rydell to balk, but he didn't. Her stomach dropped as Rydell performed the course correction perfectly. Lorway groaned behind her. Adi actually *whooped*.

"We'll avoid some of the security measures, but not the normal docking berths!" Rydell yelled as the *Guardian* dove.

"I know. And hit the ground before we can course correct," Dorie said.

"Then what—?"

Dorie swallowed hard as they hurtled toward the gap. She fought back nausea. "When this is over, we'll rebuild the berths."

Rydell chanced a glance at her, bewildered.

They were almost to the gap and the doors had fully opened. Now, though, they started to close. She didn't hesitate. "Clip the berths. It'll slow us down. Avoid HQ, walkways, and ships the best you can. Level out before impact if possible."

There were no guarantees this would work. Or if it did, work without casualties, including their own. But this was war. War that Tom Sakson had started. She had to finish it.

"Then what?" Lorway said.

It was hard to hear her amid the constant chatter of the comm, the whine of the *Guardian's* protesting engines, and the now audible cranking of the rapidly closing domelock.

"If we're alive when we land, we run like hell."

The *Guardian* shot the gap as the doors squeezed in and the rumbling of the lock machinery deafened them. It was going to be close.

"Brace!" Rydell yelled. "We're going to feel this one."

Dorie gripped the seat as the *Guardian* twisted and skewed. The lock had closed, but the heavy doors had nipped the shuttle's tail. Navigation lights flashed on the console, and warning alarms added to the cacophony of their nightmarish descent.

"Thruster failure," Rydell said. He seemed as calm as he could be, considering the ship had started to drift and spin. "I'm compensating manually and doing the best I can to redirect toward the Shell berths."

Despite the injury to the ship, Dorie saw a positive. They'd slowed a little. "Any empty ones?"

No time to think. The berths were upon them. They gripped whatever they could hang on to as the *Guardian* sideswiped the first berth, still nose down, out of control. The ship shook and Dorie thought Lorway might've been thrown from her chair. The Memor yelled something, then she heard Adi say "I got you." Dorie kept her attention on the viewscreen. Once the ship crashed through the bottom of the transparent ring, they'd have just seconds before impact somewhere on the streets of New Venasaille.

Rydell grunted as he tried to flatten the *Guardian's* trajectory and find reverse thrusters. A second level of berths rose to meet them. The second collision clipped a personal cruiser docked there. *Please be empty*, she thought.

The *Guardian* groaned as it skidded sideways after the impact, speed noticeably lessened. They crashed through the bottom of the Shell, sending shards of transparent metals flying like broken glass. Rydell managed to get the nose of the ship pointed upward.

A few seconds later the *Guardian* hit the ground. The jolt was intense, the ship's nose slamming into a building as the belly of the ship settled. Dorie's whole body shivered with the impact and she felt muscles protest. At her side, Rydell was slumped forward, blood running from a cut on his forehead. He was out cold; he must've hit his head on the console.

"Max!" she yelled, and she shook him awake. He'd passed out for only a few seconds. He touched his forehead, grimaced, then unbuckled from his seat. She turned and Adi and Lorway were okay; they nodded at her.

"*Move*," she said.

The door had sprung partially open, and they each slipped through the opening and onto the street. Miraculously, Rydell had landed them upright and had avoided collisions with structures and pedestrians. The few residents up early and out on the streets backed away and stared in shock at the *Guardian* and its survivors. Whether any of them recognized her or Adi, Dorie didn't know, but there wasn't time to worry about it. Any of these people could be witnesses and point out which way they'd gone. They had a bit of an advantage because of the early hour, with fewer potential witnesses, but it would only take a couple bewildered bystanders to point security in the right direction.

She looked up toward the top of the dome and saw Shell hopters screaming, heading their way. Sirens cut through the noise from a distance. Someone had ordered both air and ground pursuit almost immediately.

"Run!" She pointed down a side street.

"Where to?" Adi asked as they sprinted away from the ruined shuttle. "We need to get inside somewhere."

"Need to get distance first. But I know a place."

They needed to lie low. Avoid capture. Rest.

It was time to go back to the old, neglected ruin that no one ever took note of anymore.

Except me.

The Tempest Tower.

CROWELL

36 ALL IN ALL, I FELT GOOD. NO ACHES OR PAINS OTHER than what might be expected for someone my age. Plenko kept glancing over at me. *Like images on U-ONE, after the first Ultra scare.*

As far as travel through the jump slot to Ribon went, it was as boring as ever. Morgan had pulled whatever strings needed to get us back to Ribon, and we'd decided to fly the *Exeter*, since Plenko's *Glass Spire* was long gone. They didn't seem to care—or notice—the significance of the name *Exeter*. It had the proprietary Memor drive, but it wouldn't come into play during regular slot travel. Morgan took the helm. He didn't seem too worried that Plenko—Helk's breath, he was *First Clan*, many times his size—was not restrained in the ship's main cabin. I was also unbound. Then again, what could either of us do at this point? We waited, barely spoke to one another, and the *Exeter* flew on.

Did I mention how boring space travel was?

I fell asleep.

We were out of the jump slot and near Swan Station above Ribon when I woke.

"We'll be heading straight to the Bubble," Morgan said as we maneuvered past the station and headed for the planet's surface. "No delays," he said, referring to the fact we wouldn't be queuing at Swan Station for rest or resupply.

The *Exeter* navigated Ribon's atmosphere and had just ducked into the troposphere when a priority message came through from New Venasaille.

Morgan took the call, silencing the speakers and answering on his own. He listened for a while, then said, "This complicates things." He listened some more. "Okay, we'll be careful."

He flipped off the comm. "Dorie's escaped from the Bubble," he told us without taking his eyes off the main screen. "She's apparently had help from Max Rydell and Adi Thakur."

The Ultras' time dilation know-how was flawless. I smiled knowing Dorie was free.

I glanced at Plenko and a barely discernable, proud smile spread across his face. To Morgan, I said, "So we're going straight to New Venasaille?"

"Eventually," Morgan said. "Once we can pass through the domelock."

"What's the hold up?" Plenko asked.

Morgan turned to us, and I could tell he was not pleased. "Dorie cracked the Shell."

I didn't understand. "She what?"

"She flew in without proper entry protocols and caused a lot of damage before their ship crashed. The lock is secure, but the docking berths are a mess, and the Shell itself is compromised. It's out of commission, and we'll have to wait a little before it's safe to enter."

"Crashed," Plenko muttered. His smile had disappeared and now he looked angry. "This is all Sakson's fault. If she's dead I'll—"

"You'll do nothing," Morgan snapped. "We're still trading you for her."

"She's alive?"

"Witnesses saw four passengers emerge from the damaged shuttle and run off. She's alive, but nowhere to be found. Sakson's security detail is searching for her. For all of them." He flicked something on the console and leaned back, hands behind his head. He'd hit the *Exeter*'s auto pilot. "We wait. It's only a matter of time."

I felt relieved, though the earlier optimism about the timing nudged me toward impatience. I didn't want to *wait*.

Morgan had told me earlier about Dorie and what Sakson had done to discredit her. About the death of the Plenko copy. Morgan was a mercenary, he had a job to do, and he didn't care if we knew the truth. Dorie had escaped and it seemed like she had a detailed plan to retaliate against Sakson and his mistreatment of her. Certainly, this cracking of the Shell, as Morgan put it, seemed part of a larger strategy. It was impressive.

"Sakson's just reacting now," I said. "He no longer has the upper hand."

"I'd call you two his upper hand," Morgan said, "and he'll lay you out on the table to get what he wants, and that's *you*, Plenko."

"We'll see what Dorie has to say about that," the Helk said. "You think what she's done *here* is bold, you should see her when she's had a little RuBy."

Morgan laughed. "If she's off it now—and I don't know if she is—she'll have to deal with the aftereffects. Eventually, that could be much more damaging. She'll make a mistake. How are four people going to hold off Sakson's security squad, hmm? How can Dorie win? Can't say I wouldn't mind seeing it, but it's very unlikely."

I didn't believe Dorie would ever do anything to jeopardize the city of New Venasaille. Morgan had suggested the best thing for the city was for Plenko to turn himself in and exile Dorie from Ribon, so the city could move on. I couldn't agree.

Morgan didn't know the real Dorie Senall.

SENALL

37 IN THE TEMPEST TOWER, IN THE ORIGINAL SUITE OF Dorie Senall and Terl Plenko and, later, their copies, the four fugitives huddled quietly, afraid to move because it was unsafe. Structurally unsafe, yes, but also because any sound or movement might bring Sakson and his security squad down on them.

To be honest, they all lived in a domed city. There weren't that many places to go and hide. She'd never told Sakson about living in this tower. All he knew was she'd tried to save the remains of the tower as a way to remember what happened to Ribon. They couldn't hide at Max's place. Not at Adi's, or Ross's, or her own residence.

They stayed off the balcony. The sun was up outside the dome, and the gauzy light turned New Venasaille golden.

Dorie had led them here through the side streets of the city, varying their speed, even cutting through open buildings, and out exits she knew well whenever they heard the whine of pursuit hopters. They twisted through the grid of the city, mindful of pedestrians and the citizens beginning their normal morning routines, smiling, nodding, speeding up again, crossing over *here*, sliding over *there*, never going in one direction for long, until finally they came to the Tempest Tower.

Now, she lay on her back in almost the exact spot where she'd taken the RuBy from the stash she'd hid long ago on the ruined balcony. Lorway rested against one wall, Max Rydell another, and Adi was splayed out next to her; he had fallen asleep.

She decided this suite would be a better place to hide, protected behind the *Do Not Enter* flashpaper and its designation as a structurally unsound room.

They were doing what they needed to do for now: rest. It also allowed Dorie time to puzzle out what to do next. She had no immediate answers. Four of them with three weapons. What could they possibly hope to accomplish? What had she been thinking when she'd pulled them all into this fool's errand? No, it was wrong to think that way. Hadn't she told Lorway she wanted her city back? Yes, she did. The stakes were high, and the odds stacked against her even more than she'd realized.

When she'd been governor, she hadn't had but a few loyal assistants and some bodyguards at her disposal if she needed them. Already, it seemed, Sakson had built up his little squad of security beyond what she'd expected. He'd gained control of the Bubble and he'd intervened to subvert Shell personnel.

She hadn't thought of Ross in a long time and wondered where her secretary was now. She'd have to ask Adi about that. If he even knew.

Okay then.

Take the fight to Sakson. She'd be stupid to engage in a *fight*, but if they showed up at the Brindos Building without running into Sakson's goons before then, she might come across those who'd been loyal to her, but who'd had to bow down to him to keep their jobs. Maybe. Maybe with a little extra backup, she could turn the situation to her advantage. For all she knew, Sakson himself was out there with his squad searching for her. However, he also could've chosen to remain in the building, directing them from there. How many bodyguards would he have around him in there?

She should wake Adi. Tell him her idea. Tell them all she'd decided on the best plan of action. But—

She was tired. God, she was *exhausted*. She—

The sky whined.

The dream was deep and clear and altogether confusing. In her dream, she met the Ultras. She'd been chosen as an ambassador to cross the brane between the universes via the rebuilt tether, passing easily and without any severe aging, a creature made of almost pure RuBy, her skin red like a lobster's, nostrils plugged with cotton to give her a respite from the constant cinnamon smell, and rebuilt fingertips from a nano slurry, and those too were already on their way to turning permanently red. And here were the Ultras, reconstituted and reformed from their sub-personas—it must be an antimatter thing, she thought—and *they* were utterly crimson. In fact, they were the direct source of the drug, and they willingly scraped the dead cells from the skin of their elongated, half-formed limbs and offered it in super-convenient papers to their new subjects, those infuriating Matter People. Pop as many as you want! Sure, now that they had lucked into the secret *after all this time*, after the Ultra scare this and Ultra scare that, and realized what we all needed was more RuBy—*you want some?*—and literally fed the waiting, desperate humans from their own bodies. Ultras were alive and well, they were back, thank you, and they didn't really need hybrids anymore, and they didn't need to invade our universe to survive, but then they saw how fun it was to enslave us and make us do their shit jobs. After all, they'd lived a long time without bodies and frankly had gotten used to the idea of not having limbs to do shit jobs, so why start now? And there was Dorie, ambassador to another universe, once Governor Dorie from some fucked-up planet, now 100% drug-protected—no need for any antimatter suit here—passing along wisdom to the Union about the best way to cross over to this *new* place, because after all, humans were dying, weren't they? Dying and sluffing off new bodies, skin and tissue making the multitudinous seas incarnadine, turning the white moon Coral, and it wasn't so bad, because hey, the Ultras knew all about digital shills, and wouldn't that be a nice way to live for a while? Scratch away kids, it comes off easy. Keep scratching . . .

The sky whined.

Again.

And then she was awake, crying out, her hands scratching at her clothes, and suddenly Adi Thakur was there, whispering, saying *Dorie, stop. Dorie, they've found us.*

She came to her senses. The whine came from outside, past the balcony, and hovering there, facing them, were several solo-hopters, looking and sounding like giant insects in the morning light.

"They're here," Adi said.

Lorway and Max Rydell stood nearby, and Dorie's first thought was to wonder how that could be possible. Then she wondered if they should be grouped so close together like this.

From the hallway came the thump of boots, and voices barked down corridors and up stairwells. They weren't even trying to be stealthy. Sakson's squad had them surrounded.

"Drop the weapons!"

The voice snapped loudly from one of the hopters, momentarily blocking out the whines of the engines. The damaged balcony doors swung on their hinges, pushed by displaced air.

Dorie nodded timidly. "Do it."

It was her fault. All the steps she'd taken had come to nothing. A lot of bad decisions had caught up to her and she wondered why anyone should have ever trusted her. Trusted a RuBy addict.

She bit back her self-pity and grit her teeth as Adi laid down his blaster. Lorway followed. They stepped away from them. Max Rydell held firmly onto his rifle, and he exuded such a grim resignation that she was taken aback. He was not going to let go of his weapon.

"Max," she whispered. He didn't move. She didn't know why she was whispering now. "Max," she implored, raising her voice.

This time Max looked over at her, but he didn't budge from his stance or lower his weapon.

"*Drop. Your. Weapon.*" The pilot on the hopter must have increased the volume on the loudspeaker. All it did was turn Rydell's attention away from Dorie and back to the hopters hovering there.

Voices in the hallway. Dorie heard one ask if they were clear.

"Max, put it down," Dorie said. She held out her hands palms down and patted the air, hopefully giving the hopter pilots a signal that she was trying to get him to comply. "Put it down and listen to me. You can't do anything. You'll only endanger the rest of us."

That made Max turn to her again. She saw his eyes soften. The rifle lowered a little. "What do I have now, Dorie? The Bubble's done. I'm out of a job. What else is there? I'm fucking tired of this, and I'm scared, Dorie."

She nodded. Then she smiled. "Max?" She pointed at herself. "That's Governor Senall to you. Put down the gun. That's an *order.*"

Slowly, he returned her smile and nodded. He turned to the window, intent on raising his hands to show compliance before he put down the rifle.

"Max!"

Both hopter pilots opened fire.

Max Rydell was pushed backwards with the impact of the concentrated beams of the hopter guns. They drilled perfect holes in his chest, and after a stunned look of surprise, he fell and hit the floor hard. He didn't move.

"*Max!*" She started toward him, but Adi grabbed hold of her wrist and held her back.

"Clear now," the loudspeaker announced.

The doors to the suite opened and half a dozen squad members in helmets and protective vests crashed through the warning tape, the scrolling words disappearing as the flashpaper snapped. They entered the room, weapons raised, and took positions around the four of them: three who were alive, and one dead on the carpet.

Another squad member came through behind them and gathered the weapons from the floor. She left the suite with them, and an instant later, Tom Sakson walked in.

"Hello, Dorie," he said. "Welcome back to New Venasaille."

CROWELL

38 WE LANDED THE *EXETER* A FEW MILES AWAY FROM NEW Venasaille's dome, unable to enter during repairs of the domelock and the Shell. I fidgeted in my seat. We'd sat there almost two hours now. What good was perfect timing coming from a completely different universe and have to sit and do *nothing*. This was more boring than travel in the jump slot.

I glanced over at Plenko. Well, I glanced over and *up* at him. First Clan. I *still* couldn't get used to that. He saw me staring and shrugged before turning his attention to the back of Morgan's head, which he'd been looking at for the past hour.

So, Dorie was alive. Probably. Escaped, maybe. If that was the case, how easy would it be to have Plenko reach out with one hand, cuff Morgan across his temple, and take him out? Wait first for the all-clear signal, maybe, get authorization, *then* smack him. Fly the *Exeter* into New Venasaille ourselves.

Dorie was the unknown factor. If there was a chance Dorie could get clear of everything related to Ribon when Plenko turned himself in, then maybe I should just let him do it. How often did Helks sacrifice themselves for a *human*?

I debated with myself for another five minutes, then Morgan suddenly cycled up the *Exeter*. Sitting up straighter, I spent one last second playing out the perfect counterstrike scenario in my head until Morgan spoke.

"We've been given the go-ahead," he said. "The domelock is still not a hundred per cent operational, but they've rolled back the doors enough to allow ships to enter—or leave—for vital reasons."

"I guess Sakson considers us vital," I said.

Morgan nodded. "He wants us there immediately."

"And Dorie?" Plenko asked, sounding hopeful.

"They found her," Morgan answered. "She and her friends. All of them found and neutralized. Max Rydell, the warden of the

Bubble, is dead. They'll all be in custody soon."

The *Exeter* lifted off and made for the top of the dome.

Plenko swore under his breath, something I couldn't understand, and I figured he'd just insulted Morgan because the mercenary turned his head slightly, as if acknowledging the Helk.

"I hope you're ready to see Sakson," Morgan said.

"I'm ready to see Dorie," Plenko countered.

"Yeah, *maybe*. I'm not sure Sakson will allow it. If I were him, I'd put Dorie on a cruiser and shoot her through the slot so fast and so far away that she'd have to start her own colony somewhere."

"I will *demand* to see her."

"That's not for you to say. Give her up. You don't owe her anything, but you owe a lot to Ribon, it seems. Me, I don't care one way or the other, but from where I sit, that woman is trouble."

Plenko tensed, his massive fists on his lap clenched so tight I thought he might find some superpower within them. Something other than brute strength, that is.

Morgan concentrated on the approaching domelock of New Venasaille. "Big trouble," he repeated. "I've never trusted anyone who rolled the RuBy has much as she did, no matter what you say."

I wished Morgan would shut up. Even Plenko, who seemed to have the best claim to knowing her, had found himself separated from her, taken away by Lorway at the Rock Dome. That's what I'd been told, anyway. Just part of a bizarre, intricate plan surrounding an unlikely Ultra invasion from an antimatter universe. I'd played my part, but at what cost? I'd traveled from place to place, from Montana to Chicago to Aryell to Helkuntannas, to Barnard's World, to Rook, to the Ultra universe. Hell, what did I know?

Now, as Morgan put the *Exeter* in position over the domelock, guiding it through the gap, and down to the damaged berths, I thought about loved ones left behind. A worker on a walkway signaled, leading the *Exeter* away from a damaged section and over to an intact berth. Morgan complied.

I'd left people behind, I'd left heartache behind, and here I was, back on this side of the galaxy. This side of the Ultraverse.

Your lucky day is coming.

I hoped so. Because I never expected to be back here, with renewed energy, still trying to learn what made people tick. Who they *were*. Originals. Copies. Helks. Memors. Ultras.

It was hard to identify yourself when you couldn't even keep track of the different versions of you.

Me in the past or future—was it the me now? If someone pointed at me and said they remembered me *then*, or remembered me *later*, would they refer to me twice as one thing, or once to each of two things? Did I remain the same person? Would I still exist?

Yes. If I was a different person, I would still exist, just as if I had remained the same person. I'd seen that effect in Vanderberg Parr, himself a copy of Alan Brindos. The same person becoming one. Becoming a hybrid.

Who am I? What am I?

Maybe all I wanted was to get past this. All the subterfuge, all the trickery, all the copies, all the quantum entanglement and quantum sleep, genetic blueprints, all the universes, matter and antimatter.

Maybe I just wanted to be a normal citizen with an interesting job, sip a fine glass of Temonus whiskey and fall in love with the blue poison. Let Dorie have her RuBy, and Forno his warm jacket.

But you don't even know. It's my lucky day. I am not the same person I was when this all started. You thought you knew, but that was before.

You never saw this coming.

SENALL

39   DORIE SENALL STARED AT TOM SAKSON WITH A LOOK
of hatred so intense that the man, for an instant, looked
away from her. He covered his discomfort by pretending to take in
the details of the suite, Max Rydell's lifeless body, and his squad,
which had complete control of the situation.

"This is the last time, Dorie," Sakson said. "No more chances,
no more reprieves. This ends here. Your life is forfeit."

Dorie laughed. "Really? So you're going to go completely rogue
and bypass the council, the laws of Ribon, and become judge, jury,
and executioner now?"

Sakson said nothing in return. Instead, he nodded at one of
his squad members, a large beast of a man who closed in on Dorie and put her roughly on her knees. He held her there, one hand
pushing her down with strong pressure on her shoulder, his other
hand wrapped around his blaster. Right after, Sakson—looking a
little nervous as he crossed the floor of the suite—came up to her,
crouched low, and shook his head.

The silence afterward, compared to the noise of the raid on the
building and the suite, stretched on forever. Now it was Dorie who
looked down at the floor, not wanting to see Sakson gloating in
front of her.

Finally, Sakson reached down and grabbed her chin, wrapping
his hand around it. He pulled her face upward. "I believe I owe you
something in return," he said.

He spat in her face.

Dorie cringed as the spittle ran down her cheek, but she didn't
look away. She didn't show weakness, and damn if she was going to
let him think he had humiliated her. She felt it, for sure, but Dorie
grit her teeth and didn't react.

"I'm guessing Max didn't tell you that anyone incarcerated into
the Bubble is tracked? A simple procedure, a surveillance stud em-

bedded in the skin behind the ear. I didn't have time when I put you and Adi in there, due to the urgency of the moment, and by that time Max was mostly—" He looked over at the warden's ruined body. "—well, *fired*. But *Lorway* had the tracker stud."

Dorie couldn't help it. She glanced at Lorway, her eyes searching the Memor's face. Lorway shook her head.

"Don't blame her," Sakson said. "She didn't know about it. Well, *blame* her, since she's the one who brought us to you. In the end, after searching way too long for you in the city, I remembered the tracker. Max gave me what I needed to take local control of the Bubble facility." He bent down and studied her face.

Dorie returned his gaze, hardening her eyes. She felt herself swallow hard. Sakson surprised her when he wiped the spittle roughly from her face.

"Demeaning, isn't it?" He straightened. "Nothing to say? Very well." From his hip he extracted his own personal blaster and he pointed it at her forehead. "It'll be easier this way."

Now Dorie struggled against the nameless squad member holding her down. The situation, she knew, had not only become dire, it had rushed forward with a sobering inevitability she could not ignore. She was going to die. Sakson was right. It would be too easy for him to do this, in front of witnesses, his own people, and still, somehow, he would be able to explain it all away. She wondered about Adi and Lorway, and whether they would escape Sakson's revenge. Probably not. That twisted her gut even more, knowing she had led them to their deaths.

"Let them go," she said finally. "They had nothing to do with this."

"They did, Dorie."

"I pulled them into it. They followed out of friendship, but I planned everything."

"You can't expect me to believe Lorway was a friend," Sakson said. "It doesn't matter, though. They know what happened here. What *will* happen. I can't allow them to controvert the way things went down."

Dorie struggled to think of something. Could she delay the inevitable? No. She didn't believe a delay would amount to anything.

She was truly alone in all this. She'd be dead, Adi, would be dead. Lorway dead.

Terl dead.

She wondered how Sakson would handle the squad members involved with this raid. Were they that trusted that Sakson didn't have to worry about their silence?

Sakson's blaster hummed.

He aimed. He wasn't even going to say anything more. Just pull the trigger and be done with it.

A crack snapped the air.

One of Sakson's crew surrounding the three of them crumpled without warning. When the man struggled back to his feet, another blast put him down for good.

Sakson, startled, raised his weapon, then swept it around the room, confused. "What the fuck!" he said.

"Sniper!" the squad member holding onto Dorie said. He ducked low, taking Dorie down until her face kissed the floor of the suite.

In the next few seconds, three or four more shots echoed through the room and two more squad members went down, including the one who'd held her to the floor. Dorie covered her ears, wondering how this could be.

"Away from the balcony door!" Sakson yelled, and the remaining members of his squad pulled back, hugging the wall of the suite.

Lorway and Adi had dropped to the floor. They seemed okay, and when Dorie managed to glance over at Adi, he nodded at her. He was fine. Lorway was alive too, also on the ground, behind Adi. She raised her head slightly, trying to get her bearings.

Who was shooting into the suite? she wondered.

Sakson had moved against the wall. He kept an eye on his three captives and said, "Perimeter?"

"Jennings has it," one of the squad said. She was a tall heavily armed woman in bulky gear, pinned against the opposite wall. Her long blonde hair had come loose from whatever had held it underneath her squad cap. "He has two others out in the hall and two at the tower entrance."

"Well, fuck, find *out!*" Sakson yelled.

Dorie waited. For what, she didn't know, but she couldn't do anything right now. If a moment presented itself, she would act. She kept her gaze on Sakson, who kept looking back and forth between the suite door and the balcony.

A distinct snap echoed in the room, and it was all wrong. Too loud, and completely out of place. Dorie felt the floor tremble, and then it seemed to roll like an ultra-real thrill ride.

The three other squad members cried out when the floor tilted slightly, and a snap became a crack and a loud groan. The room was not *safe*. Dorie's heart twisted with renewed hope. The suite's fragility might well kill them all, or it might lead to their getting out of this mess.

The suite's door groaned, then snapped shut. Dorie remembered that even without power, the entry mechanism had a mechanical failsafe of sorts.

Sakson cried out when the wall behind him separated from the floor and he had to move toward the middle of the room.

Into the line of fire, Dorie thought.

"Where's Jennings!" he yelled. He didn't wait for an answer but raised his blaster and fired it through the opening to the balcony, as if he'd spotted the sniper firing into the suite. "He must be in a building across the way," he announced. "Shelby, reconnoiter."

Dorie looked up and watched Shelby, the tall blonde woman on the other side of the room, inch along the wall to the main entrance, stepping over Lorway's feet, hugging the wall the best she could, keeping her blaster aimed at Dorie and her friends, the balcony, and the door, as if she couldn't make up her mind.

"Got you," Shelby said.

Dorie knew, and Sakson must also know, that no building across from them was high enough for a sniper to have a clear line of sight. The Tempest Tower, even at its reduced size, dwarfed most buildings in New Venasaille. Where were the blasts coming from?

Shelby—was it a first or last name?—made it to the door just as sniper fire erupted again, jagged lines crackling the wall and drawing a line that reached for her. "Shit!" she yelled, ducking lower. The blasts went over her head. At the door finally, she sat back on her heels and reached for the door's sensor. It didn't work as a sensor, the DNA mechanism compromised long ago, but the simple act of touching it would unhook the mechanical latch.

Dorie scrambled forward on her knees toward Adi, but the floor of the suite buckled just then. Dorie's stomach lurched, the floor tilting and falling. She yelled out, expecting the worst, but something below the suite must have stopped its fall. The pops and groans in the suite were constant now, and she knew it was a matter of time before everything gave way and collapsed.

Shelby reached high enough to hit the sensor. If there was a click, Dorie couldn't hear it amid the noise. Sakson kept to the wall, looking like a cornered animal. He couldn't keep his blaster steady, and he'd stopped firing out at the balcony. Instead, he stared at Shelby prying the door open. He did his best to aim that way, as did the other two squad members, who were flat on the floor.

The door opened.

Shelby had a split second to look up, yell out "Fuck!", and then she was thrown back into the room as if she'd been pulled back by an invisible force. Before Sakson or any of his squad could react, the suite became a maelstrom of blaster fire as giant shadows swarmed the room.

Dorie's mouth dropped in surprise. *No fucking way.*

Shelby groaned and regained her feet painfully, but when she finally stood tall, her long legs still wobbly after being cast aside like a rag doll, blaster fire from a half dozen weapons erupted from the doorway and lit her up like a firework, black lines of energy carving through her torso, singing her hair, and severing her neck. There was a look of surprise on her face, but she was already dead. She sank to the rickety floor as if readying herself to pray, then fell sideways. Singed blonde hair, set free by several of the particle beams, floated like gossamer before coming to rest near her body.

Dorie stared now at half a dozen Helks—mostly Second Clan by the size of them—who ringed the door. One of them was Tem Forno, Dave Crowell's partner, dressed in that shoddy old coat that had once belonged to Terl, and later to Brindos.

"Drop the weapons," Forno said, and Dorie glanced behind her in time to see the two remaining squad members comply. They tossed them toward the line of Helks.

Sakson was pinned against the wall, unarmed, his blaster at his feet. A support beam from the suite's ceiling had wrenched loose, and one end of it had crashed to the floor near him. It held him tight, diagonally, ceiling to floor. He pushed against it, but it didn't budge.

Dorie rose, carefully, slowly, and walked to him. She bent down and reached for his blaster. He tried to kick at her, but the beam blocked any serious attempt. She knew that given time and effort, Sakson could pry the beam away to get loose. But Dorie and Forno's group of Helks wouldn't let that happen. She looked over at them.

They all wore long heavy coats, their leathery heads looking like caps in the dim light and dust of the suite.

"Forno," she said quietly.

Forno smiled, his sharp teeth gleaming. "Sorry I'm late."

Five minutes later, after three of Forno's crew secured Sakson's last two squad members and took them out of the suite— "Hold them in the shuttle for now," Forno said. "Someone's coming for them." —Dorie Senall was still standing as close to Sakson as she could stomach. He would not look at her. A cut on his forehead bled freely, but she didn't think it was life threatening.

"You had to know this would end badly," she said to him.

"I knew no such thing," Sakson said. "Everything was in control. If it hadn't been for these fucking Hulks, you'd be dead already and I'd be explaining away how a RuBy addict tried to undermine a peaceful succession of power."

Forno frowned. "You *tashing* asshole—"

"Believe what you want," Dorie said. "I've got a completely different story to tell."

"Ribon deserves healing," Sakson said, as if not listening. "Plenko must pay, and you've done nothing but aid his cause during all this."

Voices rose in the corridor, and Forno and his team went on alert.

"You're delusional," Dorie said. "I've not seen him for two years. He doesn't deserve your hatred. How many times do I have to *tell* you?"

"As many times as you want. It doesn't make a difference."

"Fuck you," Dorie said, quietly but with so much animosity, it surprised her.

"Dorie," Forno said. "Morgan's here. He's clean." He glanced out the suite door. "Let him in."

Morgan came through into the ruined suite. He looked grim, as if he hadn't expected the scene in front of him. How could he have?

Morgan's hands were in front of him, bound with polymer. Dorie squinted, looking behind him. Where was *Plenko*? It wasn't Plenko behind Morgan, obviously, or she'd have seen him towering over the mercenary.

Dorie recognized her in an instant. Jennifer Lisle, assistant director of the Network Intelligence Organization. Lisle and a few of her agents followed closely behind Morgan.

"His instructions count for nothing," Lisle said. She flashed a badge. "Jennifer Lisle, NIO. Thanks to Forno, we were able to knock this thing down." She nodded at Forno.

Forno nodded back. "Thanks for the travel visas."

"Don't mention it."

"Where's Crowell?" he asked.

"Right here," came a voice. Crowell appeared behind Lisle, looking a little perplexed.

"Always late to the grouping," Forno said.

Crowell looked at him quizzically. "The what?"

"The *party*," Forno said. "Helk's breath, you didn't even correct or ignore me."

Dorie took another look at Crowell and her eyes widened in surprise. Somehow, the process of travelling to the Ultra universe—or maybe it was the process of coming back to their own—had reversed some of the aging. He seemed even younger than a year ago when he'd visited New Venasaille after the last Ultra scare. He was more like himself after the first go-round with the Ultras. It was exceedingly odd, since she'd become accustomed to his new look, and because Dave had been told he would be an old man when he got to the Ultra universe.

She glanced again at Sakson, who was looking at the floor again. She had never seen someone look so defeated. Except maybe Alan Brindos, in his Helk state as Plenko, just before the end when Crowell had shot him.

Crowell came into the suite and glanced around, frowning, figuring out who everyone was, taking in all he could. The other bodies were long gone, but Sakson was still pinned against the wall by the fallen beam.

"We should get out of here," Dorie said. "This suite—it isn't safe."

Lisle nodded. She signaled Forno, and he lumbered over to Sakson. She and her team raised their weapons, and Dorie backed up a few steps. With barely an effort, Forno wrenched the beam away from the wall and freed the man.

The wall shuddered and everyone braced themselves. Sakson was quick. Quicker than anyone could've expected. In the moment, without hesitation, he ducked under Forno's massive arm and went right at Dorie. He put his arm around her neck and twirled, putting himself behind her.

He had a weapon.

Dorie gasped as the point of the blaster pushed against her neck. How had that happened so quickly? How'd he get the weapon? In a moment of embarrassment, she realized it was his own. He had smoothly wrenched it from her grip as he situated himself behind her.

"Stand back," Sakson said.

Not a single weapon lowered. They were all trained on Sakson. Or, more accurately, at Dorie, aimed as closely as they could to where Sakson hid behind her.

"Drop your weapons or she dies," Sakson said.

"Don't do it!" Dorie yelled. Sakson tightened his grip on her and slid the blaster to her temple. She couldn't see any part of him and could only stare helplessly at everyone in front of her. "Tom," she said as firmly as she could, "there's no way out of here. No one's going to let you leave. You kill me, they'll kill you."

"They don't want to see you die, do they? *They* don't want to die, do they?" He yelled loudly in her ear now, and she realized it was because he was addressing Jennifer Lisle and the others. "Give me a path. I'm leaving, and I'm taking her with me."

"Yeah?" Lisle's aim didn't waver at all. "Anything else you want? You might as well ask."

"Morgan comes with me, and we take his shuttle. We'll let Dorie go before we leave New Venasaille. I want safe passage."

Jennifer Lisle seemed to be thinking it over, but Dorie could tell it was all for show. Her blaster remained steady. Dorie studied everyone else: Adi and Lorway hugging the floor, Forno to her right, a few steps away from Lisle, Morgan on the other side of her. Dave Crowell was slightly behind her. The rest of Lisle's team had spread themselves out along the wall, left and right, and behind them, towering well above, were Forno's Helks.

Once again, she wondered where her Plenko was.

Lisle didn't seem too concerned about Morgan, and Dorie thought she knew why. Morgan had come in ahead of the NIO director, and that said something. Lisle and Morgan had already made a deal. Lisle confirmed it.

"Not going to happen," Lisle said. "Morgan's clear of this. Technically, he's done nothing illegitimate, except, perhaps, zipping through jump slots without proper visas and maybe being too mercenary. He's also ex-Envoy. He was hired to do a job, and he did the job of finding Plenko and bringing him back, even if some of his intentions were less than honorable."

"I want to see him," Sakson said. "I want Plenko in this room right *now*." He jammed the blaster into Dorie's temple so hard she winced with pain.

"We know why you want him," Lisle said, "and that's why he's being held in a secure location. Look around you. It's fifteen to one, and half of us are nearly three times your size."

No one spoke, but the cracks and pops and groans of the suite continued, a reminder of the increasing danger.

"Well," Sakson said. "I could just wait for this room to come down around us."

"You're not going to do that," Crowell said.

Dorie saw him take two steps toward her. He also had a blaster. Sakson backed up the same two steps, pulling her with him.

"I'm also not going to *kill* her, is that right?" Sakson scoffed.

Now Dorie revisited her earlier flashback of Dave Crowell facing his partner Alan Brindos, fully morphed into a Helk, but in constant pain, with no relief possible, his inevitable death at hand. After a signal from Brindos, Crowell shot his partner, and when he fell, Crowell was able to shoot the false Plenko, the Movement leader, who'd been hiding behind Brindos.

Sakson was hiding behind her. Would Crowell do it again if she gave him a signal? Maybe. But why would she do that? She wasn't in the kind of pain Brindos had been. She might still be a RuBy addict, technically, but she was a *recovering* addict, and she still wanted to be governor of New Venasaille again.

Fuck, she didn't *want* to die.

"You might," Crowell said. "I can't stop you if you do." He took another step forward. Sakson took them both back a step. "Let her go. Your disagreement isn't really with Dorie, now, is it? Politically, maybe, but that's not what this is about."

Dorie kept her eyes on Crowell, trying to figure out what he was up to. Lisle wasn't telling him to get back, but then again, she and Crowell had been through a lot together. Maybe they had planned something in advance. She gave him a quizzical look, but he ignored her.

"What's this about then?" Sakson said. His breath was hot against Dorie's neck.

"It's about Plenko. You want to kill Plenko and—"

"I want to humiliate him. A spectacle for all of Ribon to see."

Crowell shrugged. "Okay. But eventually kill him. Let me ask you something."

Crowell, what are you doing? She felt herself falling into the rhythm of his words, even as the floor rumbled, and something else—some structure or beam or wall—fell inside the suite. Another groan, and the floor skewed again, and there was a definite tilt now. Sakson, surprised, stumbled backwards, losing ground, but kept his grip on Dorie.

Crowell seemed not to worry. "Do you know how many times Dorie has seen or heard about Plenko being killed?"

The question surprised her. It had an effect on Sakson too. She felt the pressure on her neck lessen.

She knew the answer. "Four times," she said.

"That's right," Crowell said. "Four. Times. That includes the Plenko she believed she lost years ago."

"So?" Sakson said.

She'd expected his voice to be uncaring, as if he were sneering as he said it, but it seemed to be a simple, legitimate question.

Dave Crowell then did something else that surprised her. He bent down and placed his blaster on the floor. He kicked it to his left, and it slid toward the wall until one of Lisle's agents put his foot on it. She expected Crowell to make a gesture that would reinforce the fact he was no longer armed. Raise his hands, for example, palms toward Sakson. But he didn't. He kept his hands at his sides, and he looked thoughtful.

"Think a moment, Tom," Crowell said. He moved again, but this time he angled left. He turned and came back, past his first position, until he reached a spot on the other side before stopping. He was pacing. He was lulling Sakson a little. "Think what that must be like for her. I understand how you feel, too, but that's the problem. You're convinced there's a Plenko to kill, when a good number of them—including one who was an incredibly good friend of mine—have died already."

Crowell's voice was mesmerizing. Dorie couldn't take her eyes off him. His pacing continued, but she realized he was closer to them now.

Sakson noticed too, and he backed up again, but not very much. He was quiet, as if considering a possible counterargument.

Finally, Crowell stopped pacing. He stood in front of her, and he was definitely closer. With a little more freedom of movement, she could've reached out and touched him.

"Dorie doesn't need to see it happen again."

"Why would she?" Sakson asked.

"Because you're going to let her go and take me as your hostage."

Sakson tensed behind her. "What?"

Dorie said, "Dave, no—"

"I'm unarmed. And Plenko is here. He's in the hallway."

"Crowell!" Jennifer Lisle said in a harsh whisper. "*No.* What are you thinking?"

Crowell ignored her. He reached out a hand. "Let Dorie go, then grab my hand. Grab it and pull me right to you. I'll take her place."

Dorie searched Crowell's face, younger, and yet in some ways older, as if the years had been piled on to him, then taken away too quickly. Was there a signal in those eyes of his? Did he need her to do something? He was unarmed. Sakson had the blaster, and what Crowell was offering was doable, if Sakson took him up on it.

She'd known Dave Crowell for a few years now, and she thought he was the kind of man to shoot his way out of trouble—or to turn Forno loose on someone—and not the kind of man who talked quietly and offered himself up as a—hostage? Crowell was the kind of person who had the guts to shoot his friend and partner for the greater good.

What are you doing, *Crowell?*

"He's really out there?" Sakson asked. "In the hall?"

Crowell's voice matched the smile that came across his face, calm and worthy of trust. "Sure he is."

Jennifer Lisle was frowning, but she kept quiet, possibly realizing he was up to something.

"He's come this far," Crowell said. "He *agreed* to come here with Morgan, remember? Turned himself in. He only cares about one thing, and that's to see Dorie. Give him that. Let her go to him. After that, we'll work things out."

Sakson hesitated, and Dorie heard the indecision in his breathing. The way the blaster shook a little against her neck. "They have to lower their weapons as we switch."

"Of course," Crowell said. He smiled serenely, then kept smiling as if it were the most natural thing in the world, turning slowly, moving his hand to each person in the room, a signal to lower weapons, but she realized the gesture also told them to remain vigilant. It was impressive to see each blaster and rifle dip down as Crowell made his full circle.

He faced Dorie and Sakson again. He extended his hand.

The pressure on Dorie's neck was gone, and she felt distance between her back and Sakson's hip and shoulder.

"That's it," Crowell said. "I'm coming to you. Here's my hand."

Finally, suddenly, Sakson shoved her in the back, aiming her body left. She stumbled a little but stayed upright. She turned enough to see Sakson snag Crowell's hand and pull him in.

She should've run toward Jennifer Lisle. To her, and past her. To Plenko. *Was he really out in the hallway?* But she didn't. She faced Sakson and Crowell, and it happened so fast, so suddenly, that it took her a second to realize something was wrong.

There was a flash. A sound that sizzled, and kept on sizzling, and Sakson yelled out, screamed, and he was shaking violently, his grip around Crowell's lower arm loosening. The air smelled of ozone. Something green glowed on Crowell's fingernails, she saw now.

Finger capacitors!

Sakson let go of Crowell and stumbled backwards, his body gyrating, his blaster discharging white beams into the floor. His momentum took him through the broken French doors and onto the balcony.

Dorie didn't wait. She ran. Even now, she visualized every weapon in the room coming up, even as Sakson's blaster spit fire into the floor. His weapon was inching upward, most likely involuntarily, his hand clenched around the trigger, but she followed onto the balcony. She thought she heard Lisle cry Hold! Hold your fire! and someone else say Dorie, no, stop! and movement all around her that might be those fifteen against one moving in, or it could be the suite itself coming apart.

She caught up to Sakson.

Even as his blaster snapped upward in a last violent gesture, she ran into him, throwing her shoulder and all her body weight into his chest. He pinwheeled, the blaster beam circling dangerously, then he slammed against the wall of the balcony. His torso folded backwards, and he pitched over the unshielded edge like a rag doll.

It wasn't a hundred floors, but it was enough. Dorie didn't see him fall, only heard the blaster going, and going, until it stopped.

CROWELL

40   I PULLED DORIE BACK INTO THE SUITE AS QUICKLY AS possible, and afterward, Jennifer Lisle ordered everyone out of there, the hazard more real than ever. We gained some distance from that hallway, rounding several bends until we reached a safe zone. It was the last time anyone would be allowed inside the Tempest Tower.

Dorie kept looking for Plenko, but he wasn't in the hallway. I'd lied about that. I had to. I'd been the one to tell Lisle to keep Plenko away from the Tower for the very reason I'd outlined to Sakson. If things had gone sideways in that suite, Dorie might have watched yet another Plenko die in front of her.

Jennifer Lisle took Morgan in, supposedly for further questioning. Adi Thakur was sent to the Brindos Building to smooth things over in the governors' office and prepare the way for Dorie's return to office. Lisle apologized to Dorie again, saying the NIO had more to discuss with Terl Plenko, and to be patient, she would see him soon.

"I don't even know if I can trust he's my Plenko," she said. "After all this time, after all those copies . . ."

No one said anything to that.

Eventually, Lisle cleared us, let Forno's Helks prepare for a return to Helkuntannas, and Dorie, Forno, and I were dropped off at the Brindos Building. She was willing to take me straight to the domelock for a shuttle to Swan Station, but Forno wanted to stop somewhere for much-needed coffee.

"Where to?" Lisle asked.

"There's the Tempest," Dorie said.

"The what?" I asked. "We just came from there, it's off limits, and I don't think—"

"Tempest *Bar*," she said. "Remember, when you visited a year ago? It was the only place in town at that point."

"Right. The Tempest." I pointed to Forno. "You're buying. I seem to have come back to our universe without anything, including my comm card and money."

"Figures," Forno said.

We were shuttled to the bar, which was huddled close to the outer wall of the dome, and we found a table in the back.

"Same one we sat at before," Dorie said with a smile. "Do you remember *that*?"

I said, "Of course."

We settled in. Forno had to snag a Helk-sized chair from a nearby alcove while Dorie and I slid around to the far end of a bench behind the table. Forno studied the flashpaper menu inset into the table and ordered coffee. I asked for coffee, too.

"You hate coffee," Forno said.

"Not today."

"What, no French fries?" Forno asked.

"French fries?" I asked. "Really?"

Forno shrugged, but he looked at me strangely. No, wait. He was looking at me *knowingly*. I turned to Dorie, and she was giving me the same look.

"I mean—*yum*, French fries," I said. "Do they actually have them here?"

Dorie shook her head, but she had a smile on her face now.

Okay.

Shit.

I didn't have them fooled.

"Looks like I have some catching up to do," I said. I leaned back in the chair and studied them as if seeing them for the very first time. I mean, second time. The Tempest Tower suite being the first time.

"You do," Forno said.

"When did you know?"

"When you didn't correct my mangled Earth idiom. And because of how much younger you looked."

"It took me a little longer," Dorie said. "When you started talking to Sakson. When you put down your blaster and gave yourself up as a hostage. When you had everyone in that suite hanging on your every word. When you juiced Sakson with your finger capacitors."

"Which you had taken out six months ago," Forno said.

"Envoys have an option to install them," I said. "The Ultras charged mine for me."

"It takes a special talent to talk like an Envoy," Dorie said. She raised an eyebrow. "Unless you already are one."

I nodded.

"Welcome back to our universe," Forno said. "And welcome to Ribon, Lucky Lawrence Crowell."

I grinned, mildly embarrassed, but happy to stop the charade with these two.

"Now," Forno said, "tell me what went on in the Ultra universe, and what the hell happened to my partner."

SENALL

41 LAWRENCE CROWELL TOLD THEM EVERYTHING.
Dorie listened with Forno as he explained how Dave found Vanderberg Parr still alive on Rook, how they traveled to the Ultra planet, and how the two Crowells reunited.

Once Vanderberg Parr told Lawrence he could go back instead, and the Ultras could limit how much he aged (Parr hadn't exactly told the whole truth when he'd claimed he could move Dave to our universe and make him younger), Dave made the choice to stay and let his dad go. Lawrence needed to know as much as possible about the people in Dave's life, including Forno and herself. Jennifer Lisle, too, and Terl Plenko. They spent hours talking, apparently, before the time came for Lawrence to walk out in his Ultra suit to board the *Exeter* and come home.

There was more Lawrence said about the return trip and Dave's plans to live out his life in the Ultra universe, but Dorie tuned him out. She didn't want to come across as rude, but she was distracted.

When would she get to see Terl?

Not soon enough.

Adi Thakur didn't call her until after they'd left the Tempest Bar. She hurriedly said her goodbyes to Forno and Lawrence; Forno was taking Lawrence Crowell with him to Earth. When they returned to the Brindos Building, Jennifer Lisle told Lawrence someone would brief him about the Ultras, and then he could go home. When they released them, Forno would pilot a skiff to the domelock, where Lawrence Crowell and the Helk could hop a shuttle to Swan Station and the jump slot back to Earth.

Adi informed her Terl Plenko was in a holding area in the Operations building across the thoroughfare. The NIO was still processing him, and they had more questions to ask about what had happened on Coral, his escape from the Rock Dome, and his operation in the city of Bestus on Barnard's Star. The room was not barred, locked, or guarded. Only Jennifer Lisle was there, and once Dorie opened the door, the assistant director left the room to give Dorie time with him.

Plenko sat on the only table in the room, using it as a chair, and he stood when he saw her. He towered over her, the leathery skin of his head marked with small bumps. Goosebumps. It was too cold in here for him. He had a plain green tunic on that covered him from shoulders to knees.

"Hello, Dorie," he said.

It was almost too much to bear, hearing Terl Plenko say hello to her. The last one to do so had not survived Sakson's rage. Even before that, she'd had doubts about that Plenko being her Plenko. Would she be able to tell the difference now?

"Hello," she said back. She didn't hesitate, wanting to get something straight right away. She didn't move from her spot just inside the door. "I need to know the truth. I need to know you are my Plenko. I can't have someone else just *tell* me you are. I want to believe it's you, but you must allow me this moment of uncertainty."

"I understand."

Dorie came forward, covering half the distance to him. "Tell me something. Something only you would know."

He didn't answer right away, taking time to think of something, staring at her so forcefully, she had to look away. "You know," he finally said, "most Thin Men retain the memories—or most of them— of the original. So will anything I tell you actually convince you?"

"I don't know. I just need to hear . . . *some*thing that seems right. That *feels* right."

He cleared his throat. "Well—"

"C'mon, Big Guy. Something good."

Terl Plenko's face softened. It was as if someone had flipped a switch, the change was so stark. "Dorie, I never stopped thinking about you."

Dorie felt a fluttering in her heart, but she simply gave him a look that told him: *And?*

"I couldn't come back for you. Once I knew you were still alive? I knew you were hiding out with the Movement in the Helk quarter on Temonus."

"Information you could've gleaned from any number of people."

He nodded. "Okay." He sat on the table; it creaked ominously under his weight. "Okay, you're right."

She waited some more, and she so wanted him to give her a reason to believe, that she ached all over. She folded her arms over her chest, not wanting him to see her trembling.

"I gave Lorway that last card."

"What last card?"

"The one she left for you in the Bubble. It was designed for you."

"What do you mean for me? I just thought it was—"

"I designed it. It was infused with your DNA. Your DNA, cross-engineered with RuBy. And—" He shrugged and looked sheepish. "It had a trigger."

"I don't understand. What kind of trigger?"

Plenko waved a hand dismissively. "Complicated."

"Tell me."

"It worked similarly to the other Tarot cards. If you used it, the quantum travel could be directed more accurately. It could pinpoint an exact location."

After a brief silence, Dorie said, "The Tempest Tower."

"More specifically, to the suite."

"You're not the only Plenko who knew that suite."

"No, but I'm the one who made the cards—including the Minor Arcana—and the only one who knew the suite's *new* location."

"You mean when it was no longer on the 100th floor."

"The trigger needed RuBy on the other end to make it work. To get you there. RuBy with your DNA on it to give the card something to hunt for. Not just on its surface, but in the drug itself."

"But I'd long ago given up RuBy, and—"

She stopped cold. Not long after transporting to the suite, she braved the balcony to find the RuBy she'd hidden there after she'd stopped using. Behind the old electromagnetic shield panel. The panel no one ever knew about except—

Terl.

She said, "Behind the panel."

Terl Plenko nodded. "I knew about that hiding place. No other Plenko could have known about it."

"Somehow, you worked with Lorway."

"We . . . kept in touch. Even while she was in the Bubble."

"How'd you manage that?"

"There were a lot of Minor Arcana Tarot cards for quantum travel. Dave Crowell never needed those to get to the Ultra universe. I had a few trusted friends on Barnard's I could send. I didn't dare go anywhere near there myself. I especially didn't dare trying to contact you. In your new position as governor, it was too difficult to try and get to you."

Dorie considered this and found it believable. "She swapped the package, didn't she?"

"When she traveled to the Tempest Tower before you did. She knew where *I* had hidden the RuBy in the suite."

"And where was that?"

"In the cubby. The same one where Alan Brindos found the mortaline sculpture. The key that you yourself carried to help Crowell and Brindos open and destroy the vault of mortaline."

A planet twisting out of shape . . . a sea of bodies struggling to break out.

"They were so intent on that sculpture," Plenko continued, "they never searched much farther back in that cubby. It was well hidden."

"You had that planted there that far back?" she asked incredulously. "Even before the start of the first Ultra scare?"

"Lots of Plan B scenarios."

"Why didn't you just leave it there then? Wouldn't the trigger still have worked?"

"It would have. But you needed to find it. You needed to touch it, either the covering or the RuBy itself. That was the location tracer. That's how we found you."

"You and Dave. I mean, *Lawrence.*"

"Well, and Forno. He called it in to Jennifer Lisle." He gave Dorie a look of sympathy. "I'm sorry. I didn't expect you to roll and use it."

Dorie lowered her head, but she nodded. She couldn't blame him for what happened. She'd even thought it had helped her in that situation. Really, Sakson had already caused her relapse. Even now, she would need time and distance away from the drug—and a good therapist—to get back to where she'd once been.

More importantly, she knew. *Terl.* She knew this was truly her Terl Plenko. A wave of sadness washed over her—the last of the years without him whispering away—followed by a fresh wave of happiness. She broke into a wide smile and crossed the room to him.

He was ready for her. He slid off the table and fell to his knees so he could wrap his arms around her waist, and she could put her own arms around his neck. Barely.

"Oh God, Terl," she said, her eyes misting. "I've missed you so much."

"And I've missed you. I should've contacted you somehow."

"It's okay. It's fine. You're here now, and everything's going to change. I love you. I love you, and I'm clearing your name once and for all. I'm bringing you back—"

"From the dead?"

"No," she said, shaking her head. "It isn't death when it's a new beginning."

EPILOGUE

DAVE

I STARED AT THE SHINY BULKHEAD OF THE *EXETER* AND BAR-
en Reiser looked right back at me. Well, not really Reiser. It
was *me*. The reflection showed my bald head covered in purplish-
black tattoos, each one a number. One through nine, different sizes,
spaced somewhat evenly. Nine opportunities to travel safely within
the Ultra universe, getting from Pawn's matter-bubble to the *Exeter*.
The first passage had been via the matter antimatter suit, which was
cumbersome and not terribly practical. I supposed if I used up all
my numbers and I still had some life left in me, I could try the suit
again.

That was it, though. By then, I might not be able to walk around
very well. I already felt a great deal of aches and pains, even when I
was just standing. Sometimes just *sitting*. How long would I have?
How long could I zip through Ultra space with Parr until death took
me? We could travel a long time on the *Exeter* until forced back to
Pawn for resupply. I was already old, but I couldn't rest now. I had
Parr as a guide. He had all the knowledge of the Ultras and he had
all the knowledge of Parr's life and he had all the knowledge of my
friend Alan Brindos's life.

Now, in my own twilight years, I *wanted* space travel.

Dad was gone. Back to our universe, back to my old life, and he
was welcome to it. For me, I wanted to do something of note. Get
a glimpse of the end of the Ultras before my own came. I had nine
free passes.

"You look just like him," Parr said suddenly, interrupting my
thoughts. "Reiser, my old boss. Older of course."

I didn't say anything. The full impact of my choice hadn't hit
me yet. I knew it would later. All I was leaving behind. The people,

especially. Dorie. Forno. Jennifer. Plenko. And of course, my dad. It might not seem fair to most people that I'd spent so much time and effort to find him, then let him go; on the contrary, it wouldn't have been fair to *him* if I'd denied him the opportunity to go back. Let the younger man live out his life in familiar—and at the same time *un*familiar—circumstances.

He'd figure it out. I'd found him. I got to say my goodbye, even though I'd had to travel a long way to do so. My other friends would go on with their lives, and they'd have each other. They wouldn't be lonely. Not even Forno. Hulks didn't get lonely.

And I had Vanderberg Parr. He was the closest I had to a real friend now.

"You look just like *him*," I said, turning from my reflection.

"So you've said."

"I'm going to ask something of you that's important. Important to me."

Parr stayed quiet, waiting for me to go on.

"Your name's nifty and all, but I'm going to call you Brindos from here on out. I don't know if I can call you *Alan*—I've rarely even called you Vanderberg—but I'd like to reunite with my friend."

Parr waited some more, knowing I wasn't finished.

"You're him," I said. "Enough so that I can still believe it, and enough so that I can take this time to get reacquainted with the Brindos part of you."

"The Brindos."

"Right. Will that work for you? Will that be okay?"

Parr seemed to mull this over. He didn't even do his eye flick thing. He didn't have to access Ultra databases to decide on this. He only had to check with the Brindos part of him.

"It would be okay," Parr finally said. "I mean, if you feel like you have enough time to do that."

I rubbed my hand over my tattoos. "My days are numbered, right?"

"Reiser used to say that."

"It's true for everyone."

I wasn't worried about it. I'd have the time I had, and that would be fine. I hadn't forgotten what I'd decided after I'd left the Ultra universe the first time, when Parr had helped me escape. I'd thought he'd sacrificed his life to do it. I never said anything to officials at the NIO, or the Kenn, about Parr being Brindos because Brindos deserved to rest in peace.

That is, in *our* universe.

All bets were off here.

I clapped my hands loudly and rubbed them swiftly together. "So. Where to first?"

"We have options," he said. "I've got the nine nearest habitable star systems plotted and on the console for you."

Of course he did. I smiled at his decision, then pointed to my bald head. "Pick a number between one and nine, Brindos."

LAWRENCE

W HEN I ENTERED THE OFFICE OF THE CROWELL AND FOR-
no agency in downtown Seattle, the Helk was already in
there waiting for me. I'd taken some time to walk around the neigh-
borhood, familiarizing myself with the area. It had surprised me
how rundown and neglected it looked.

Forno sat in a huge chair that seemed cobbled together from
mattresses and wood and metal pipes. He was wearing a large
trench coat. Dave had said his partner hated our cold planet, but he
kept coming back to it.

"You get a chance to look around?" Forno said, his voice gruff.

"Yeah. Shouldn't you move that chair behind the desk? You're
the senior detective now, right?"

Forno shook his head. "Not the way the name reads on the
business license."

"I'm starting fresh."

"But you're going to have to remain at the top. It was your decision, remember, to work here and be Dave. Just be *Crowell*. You've
got Dorie and Jennifer both working to that end so you can make
your identity stick. I think I can get used to only calling you Crowell."

"Like the Morganism. Just Morgan."

"Like that."

"Just don't call me Lucky."

Forno raised his hands. "I will not."

I moved around the desk. After I'd sat down, I spread my hands
over the empty desktop. "It's going to take me a while to get comfortable with all this. I'm an Envoy, not a detective."

"If the showdown on Ribon showed me anything, it proved
your Envoy training could come in handy. Plus, you *like* using the

electric handshake. I've already ordered you a portable charger."

I smiled. "Nice."

"I'll help you rise to velocity."

"What?"

"Get up to speed. Well, Helk snot, *this* is a nice change."

"Right. Idioms."

Forno stood and fished inside his trench coat pocket. He withdrew his hand and without warning threw something at me.

"What's this?" I asked as I caught it.

"Dave's Tudor watch. He'd want you to have it. Doesn't fit me."

"People still wear these things?"

"Not many. But Dave liked old things."

I knew that from my last conversations with Dave on the Ultra side of reality. Before coming into his old office, I'd stood on the old Seattle pier with a flask of brandy Forno had given me—another old thing of Dave's—and it reminded me of the blue poison from Temonus I tried once on a trip for the Envoys. I'd not finished it, as it was way too strong for me. Although the brandy was new to me, it was easier to get down the gullet, and I liked the burn of it.

Sometimes older was better.

Sometimes you had to teach an old dog new tricks, Dave said before I left.

"I'm trusting you to teach me everything I need to know," I said to Forno.

"Sure. That mean you're in?"

"I'm still getting used to being back in the matter universe and not worrying about being obliterated."

"Hey, I've had to get used to the cold. I'm *still* working on that."

I nodded. "Then I'm in. On one condition."

"What's that?"

I pointed behind Forno. "You help me take down that hideous plywood wall."

Forno smiled. "It's about damn time."

ACKNOWLEDGMENTS

I T'S BEEN SIX YEARS SINCE THE SECOND BOOK OF THE UNION of Worlds debuted, and that one came out only two years after my debut novel, *The Ultra Thin Man*. When I decided to put all three books, including this brand new one, back out with a uniform look, art, and design, I thought I might wait until 2024, which would be the 10th anniversary of the first novel's publication. But everything seemed to align for this year.

First and foremost, I have to thank my pride and joy, Artemis, the artist behind all three of the covers. Am I lucky or what, to have that kind of talent in the family working for me? I always knew the day would come when they would do so. Of course, I'm now on the hook for a number of their school loan payments coming up soon!

I'd like to thank Brenda Cooper and Risa Scranton, who gave valuable feedback on this third book. I could also list all my writing and publishing buddies scattered here and there, but this acknowledgments would go on way too long. A special thanks to Tor Books, too, for putting that first book out into the world.

This trilogy has been a long labor of love (particularly if you know how much the first novel gestated, and how long it took to get it into the hands of the reading public), but now that it's done, what's next? Well, I've written a short story set in the Union of Worlds ("The Silent Passage" appeared in *Crooked V.2*, edited by Jessie Kwak, and takes place between the second book and this one), and a prequel novelette, *Slightly Ruby*. I am not adverse to writing more stories, or more novels in this universe, but not that *other* universe. We close the book on the Ultras! But Crowell (just Crowell) and Forno have some work to do, I'm sure. The Union is big and there could be other colony worlds to visit in the course of a good mystery. Other ideas are rattling around in my brain that are *not* part of the Union, so I'll be working on those, too.

Lastly, my deep love and thanks to my entire family, who've supported my writing dreams all these years.

ABOUT THE AUTHOR

Patrick is the author of *Rain Music*, a dark fantasy with ghosts, music, and magic set on the Olympic Peninsula at the site where he runs the yearly Rainforest Writers Village writing retreat. His first novel, *The Ultra Thin Man*, appeared from Tor Books. The sequel, *The Ultra Big Sleep*, debuted soon after, and the final book in the trilogy, *The Ultra Long Goodbye*, debuted in 2023. He was the editor and publisher of *Talebones* magazine, which began in 1995 and ended with its 39th issue in 2009. In 2000, he began Fairwood Press (fairwoodpress.com), which has published over 120 book titles to date. He's a graduate of the Clarion West Writer's Workshop. He has sold short fiction to *Unfettered III*, *Unbound II*, *Gunfight on Europa Station*, *Seasons Between Us*, *Crooked V.2*, *Like Water for Quarks*, *Madam President*, and others. He has been a high school teacher for 38 years, and is the proud poppa of Artemis, a budding designer and artist who does some art now and then for Fairwood Press. You can find out more about Patrick at patrickswenson.net.

Patrick Swenson's
THE UNION OF WORLDS

SLIGHTLY RUBY
small paperback
$8.99
ISBNs: 978-1-933846-64-4

"A richly realized near-future noir tale . . . a potent cocktail of genre homage."
—Stephen Susco

"Aliens, detectives, murder, political intrigue, grand space opera, and unforgettable characters. It's great fun."
—Jack Skillingstead

Book 1
THE ULTRA THIN MAN
HC & trade paper reprint
$19.99 / $31
ISBNs: 978-1-958880-04-3
978-1-958880-05-0

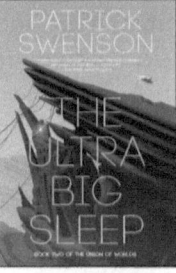

Book 2
THE ULTRA BIG SLEEP
HC & trade paper reprint
$19.99 / $31
ISBNs: 978-1-958880-08-1
978-1-958880-07-4

"Swenson's deft touch with complex themes of interstellar noir resonate . . . A great ride!"
—Fran Wilde

"Swenson's innovative blend of classic noir and science fiction rises to a perfect, twisty-turny crescendo."
—Beth Cato

Book 3
THE ULTRA LONG GOODBYE
HC & trade paper
$19.99 / $31
ISBNs: 978-1-958880-10-4
978-1-958880-09-8

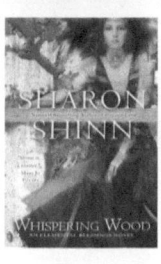
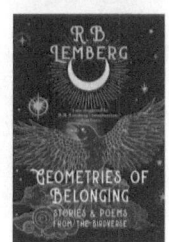

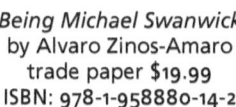